CHRISTOPHER FORD

STICKMAN ODYSSEY

AN EPIC DOODLE

BOOK ONE

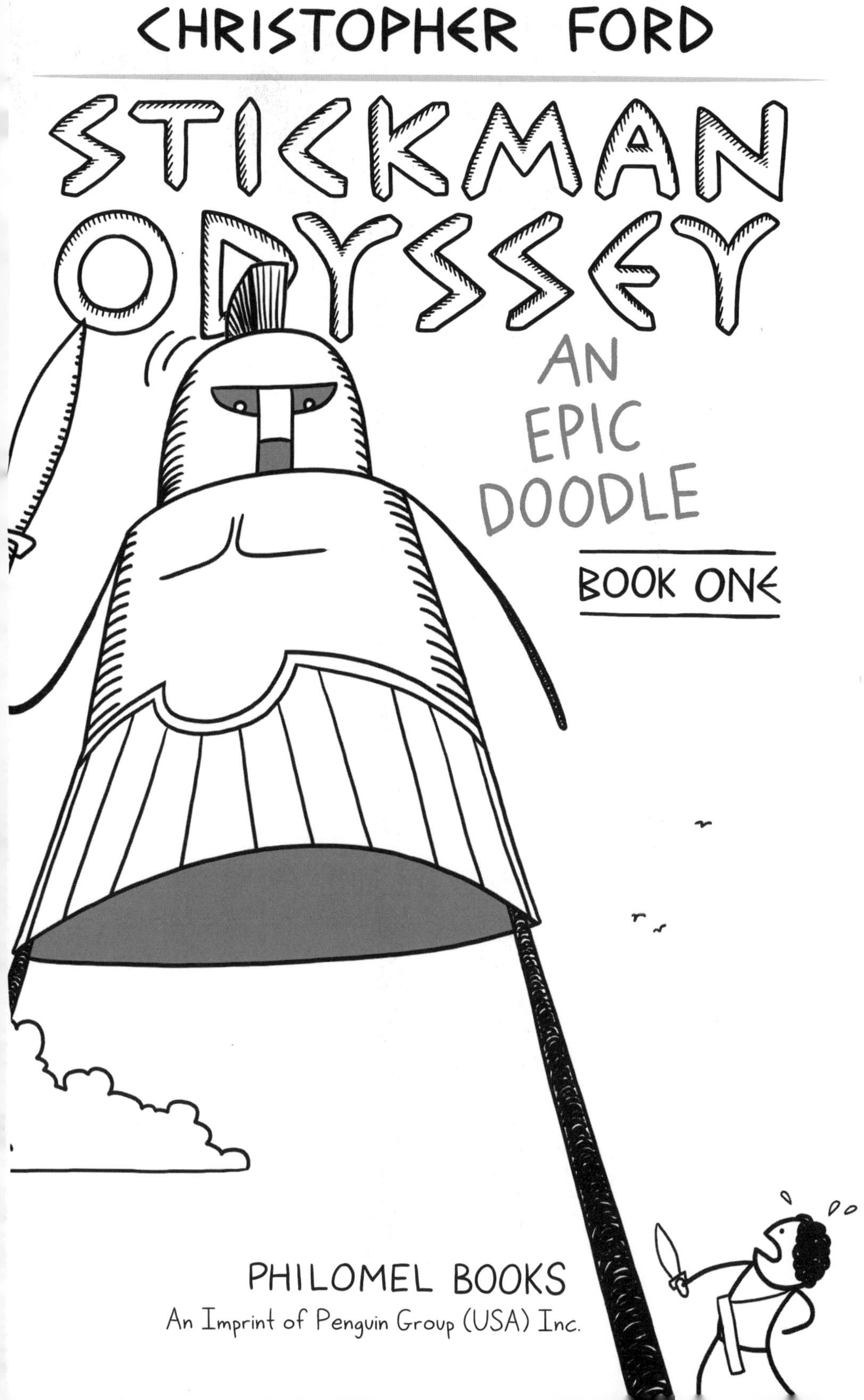

PHILOMEL BOOKS
An Imprint of Penguin Group (USA) Inc.

PHILOMEL BOOKS

A division of Penguin Young Readers Group.

Published by The Penguin Group. Penguin Group (USA) Inc., 375 Hudson Street, New York, NY 10014, U.S.A. Penguin Group (Canada), 90 Eglinton Avenue East, Suite 700, Toronto, Ontario M4P 2Y3, Canada (a division of Pearson Penguin Canada Inc.). Penguin Books Ltd, 80 Strand, London WC2R 0RL, England. Penguin Ireland, 25 St. Stephen's Green, Dublin 2, Ireland (a division of Penguin Books Ltd). Penguin Group (Australia), 250 Camberwell Road, Camberwell, Victoria 3124, Australia (a division of Pearson Australia Group Pty Ltd). Penguin Books India Pvt Ltd, 11 Community Centre, Panchsheel Park, New Delhi – 110 017, India. Penguin Group (NZ), 67 Apollo Drive, Rosedale, North Shore 0632, New Zealand (a division of Pearson New Zealand Ltd). Penguin Books (South Africa) (Pty) Ltd, 24 Sturdee Avenue, Rosebank, Johannesburg 2196, South Africa. Penguin Books Ltd, Registered Offices: 80 Strand, London WC2R 0RL, England.

Published simultaneously in Canada.
Printed in the United States of America.

Edited by Michael Green.
Designed by Richard Amari.

The doodles and stick figures in this book
were rendered with a Wacom Cintiq 21UX.

Library of Congress Cataloging-in-Publication Data Ford, Christopher, 1981– Stickman Odyssey : an epic doodle / Christopher Ford. p. cm. Summary: In this humorous take on the Odyssey, Zozimos, banished from his country by his evil stepmother, has many adventures as he prepares to return home to reclaim the throne that is rightfully his. 1. Graphic novels. [1. Graphic novels. 2. Adventure and adventurers—Fiction. 3. Mythology, Greek—Fiction. 4. Humorous stories.] I. Title. PZ7.7.F67St 2011 [Fic]—dc22 2010036900

ISBN 978-0-399-25426-0
7 9 10 8

To
the Ancient Greeks
and my parents for introducing us.

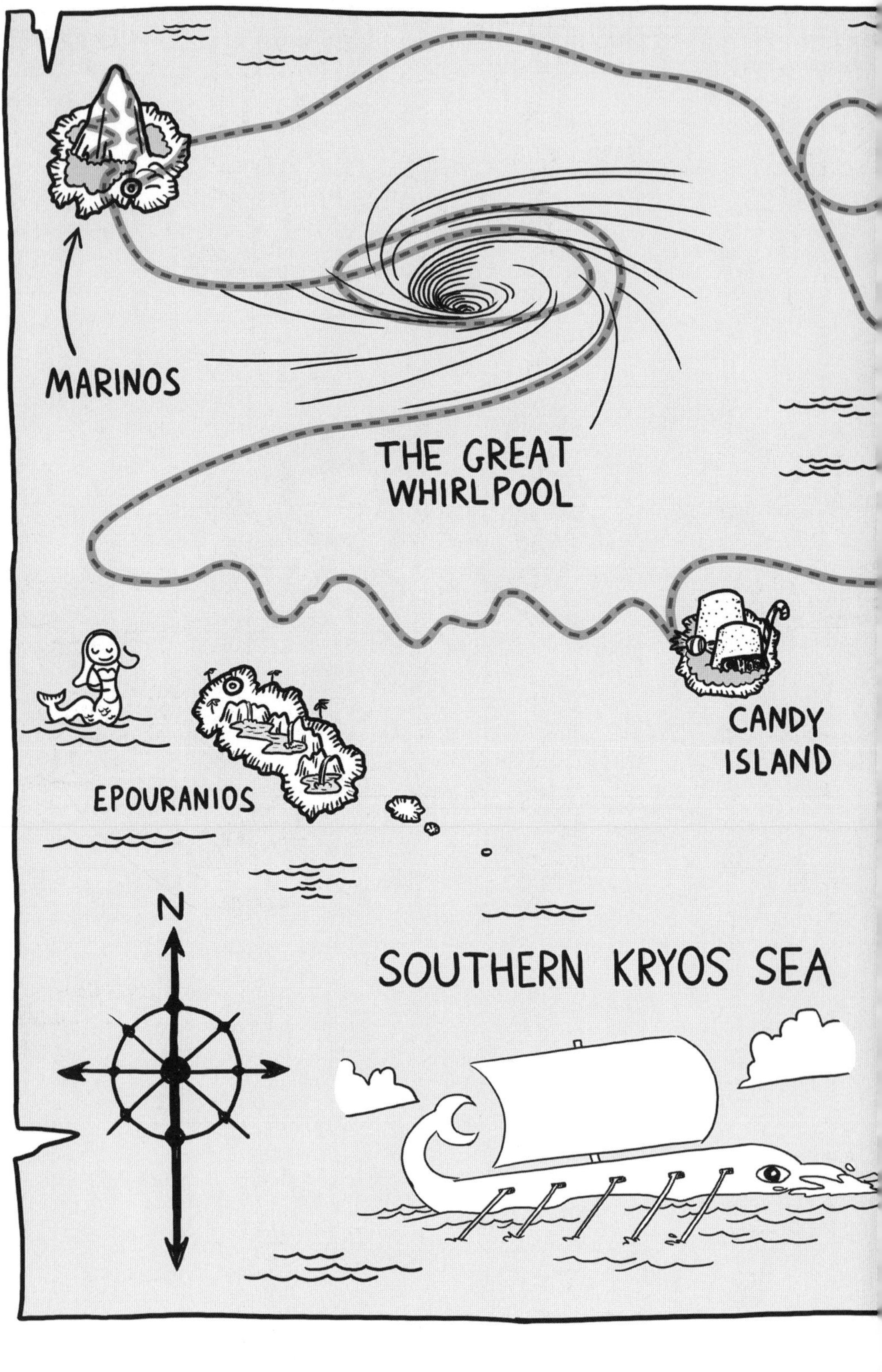
MARINOS
THE GREAT WHIRLPOOL
CANDY ISLAND
EPOURANIOS
N
SOUTHERN KRYOS SEA

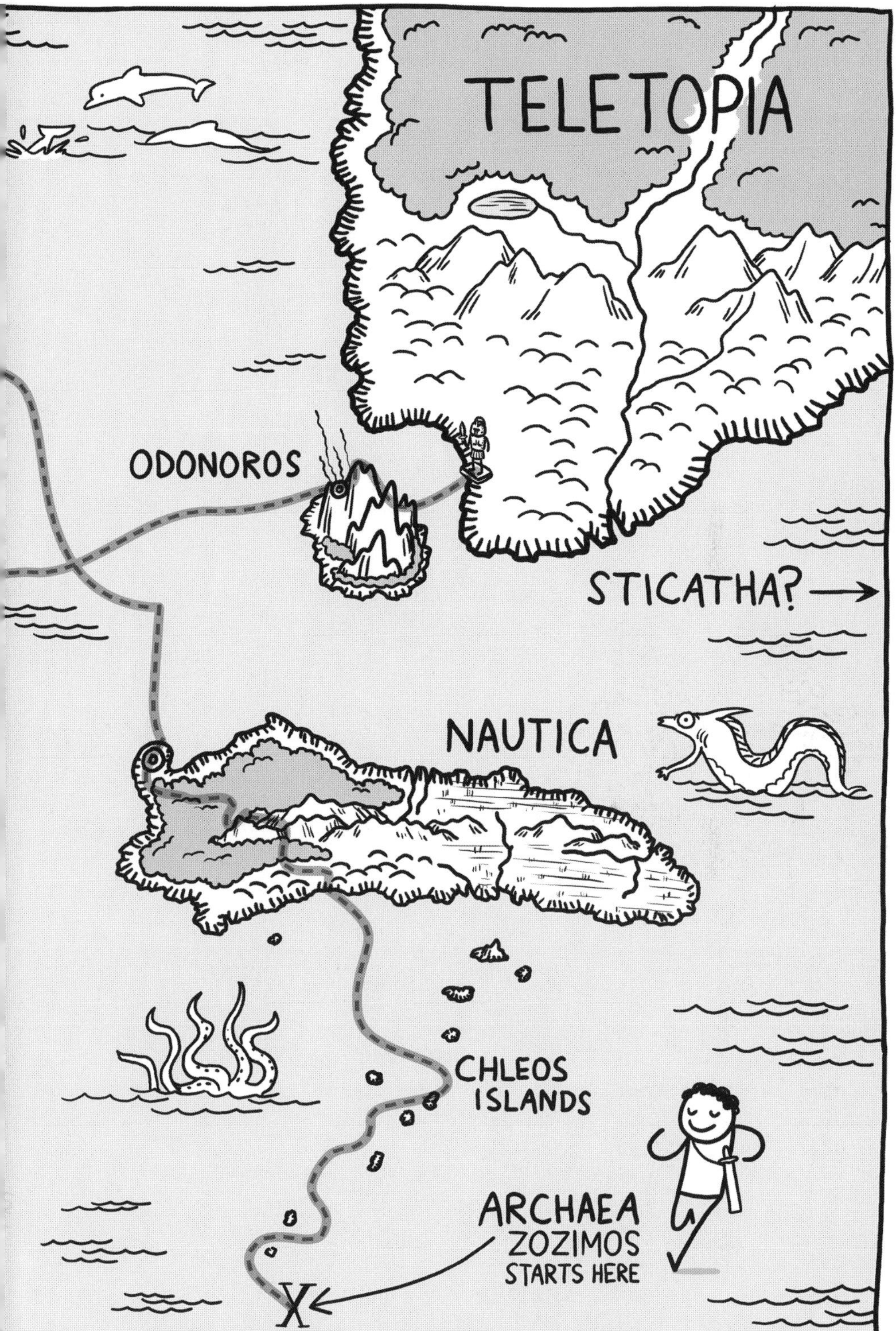
TELETOPIA
ODONOROS
STICATHA?
NAUTICA
CHLEOS
ISLANDS
ARCHAEA
ZOZIMOS
STARTS HERE
X

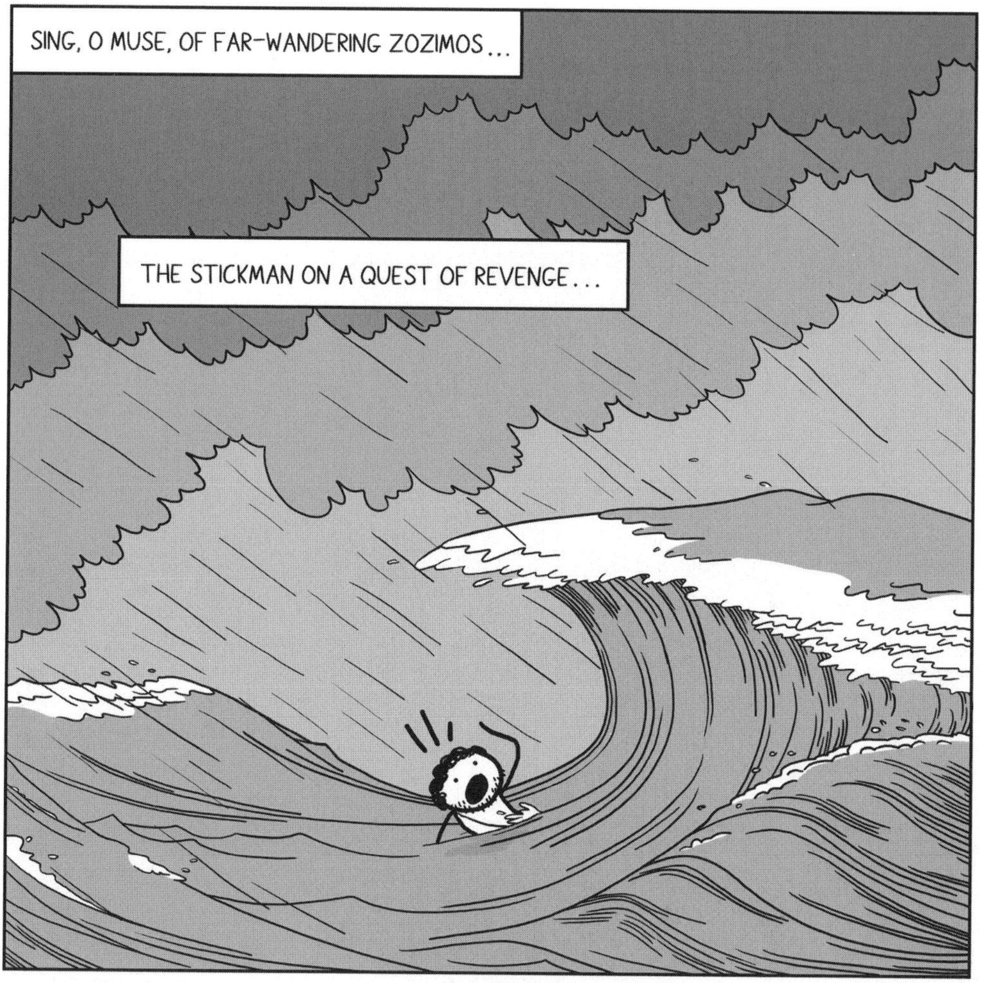
SING, O MUSE, OF FAR-WANDERING ZOZIMOS...
THE STICKMAN ON A QUEST OF REVENGE...

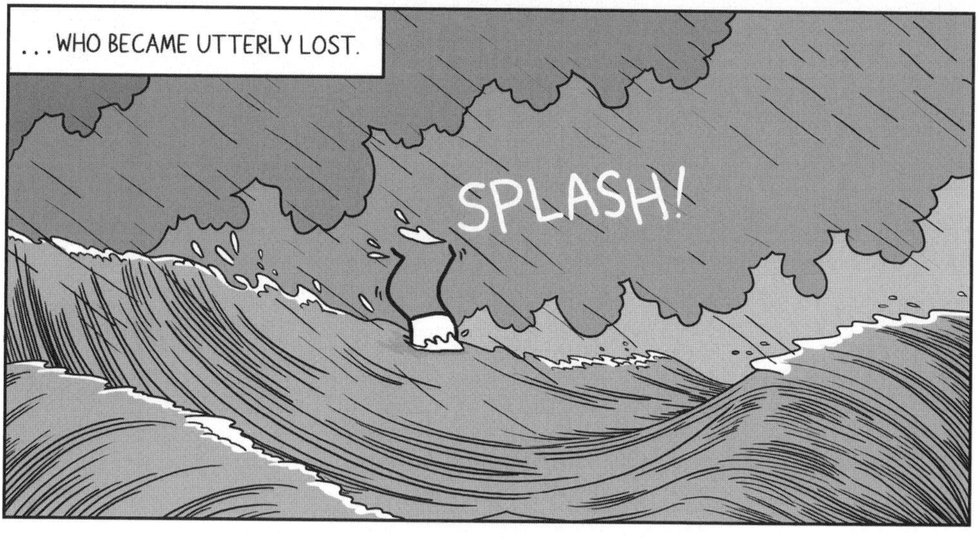
...WHO BECAME UTTERLY LOST.
SPLASH!

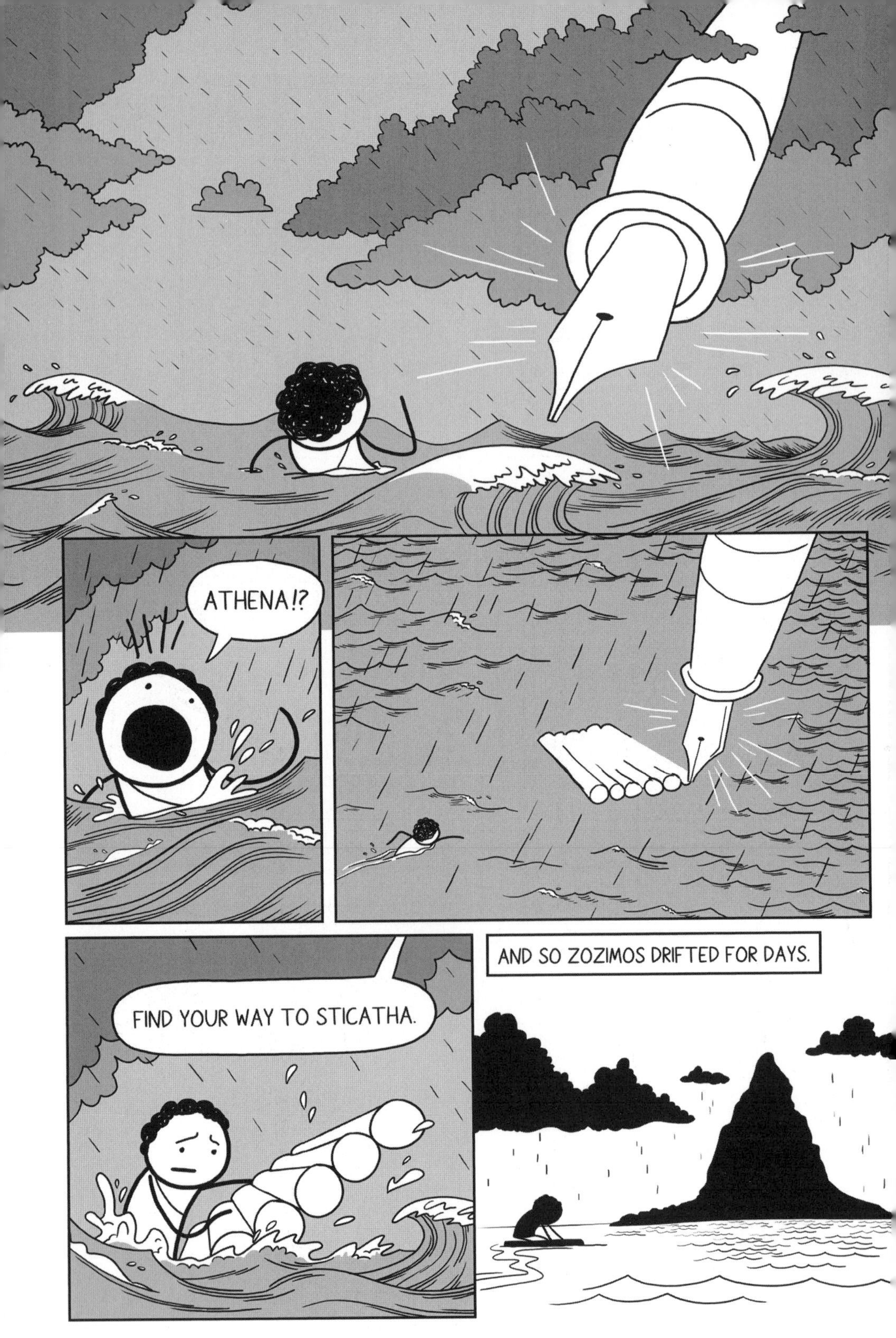
ATHENA!?
FIND YOUR WAY TO STICATHA.
AND SO ZOZIMOS DRIFTED FOR DAYS.

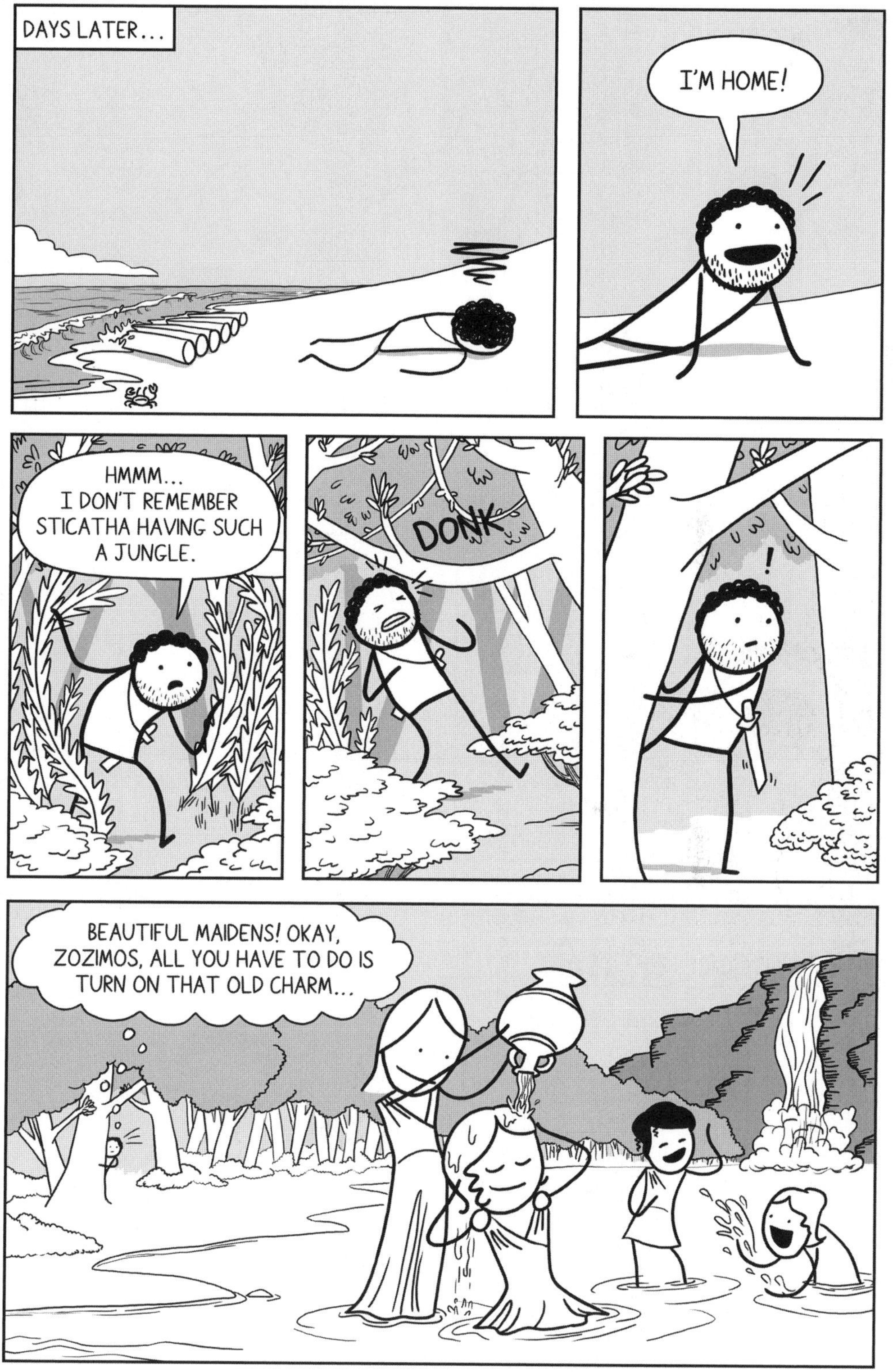

DAYS LATER...
I'M HOME!
HMMM... I DON'T REMEMBER STICATHA HAVING SUCH A JUNGLE.
DONK
!
BEAUTIFUL MAIDENS! OKAY, ZOZIMOS, ALL YOU HAVE TO DO IS TURN ON THAT OLD CHARM...

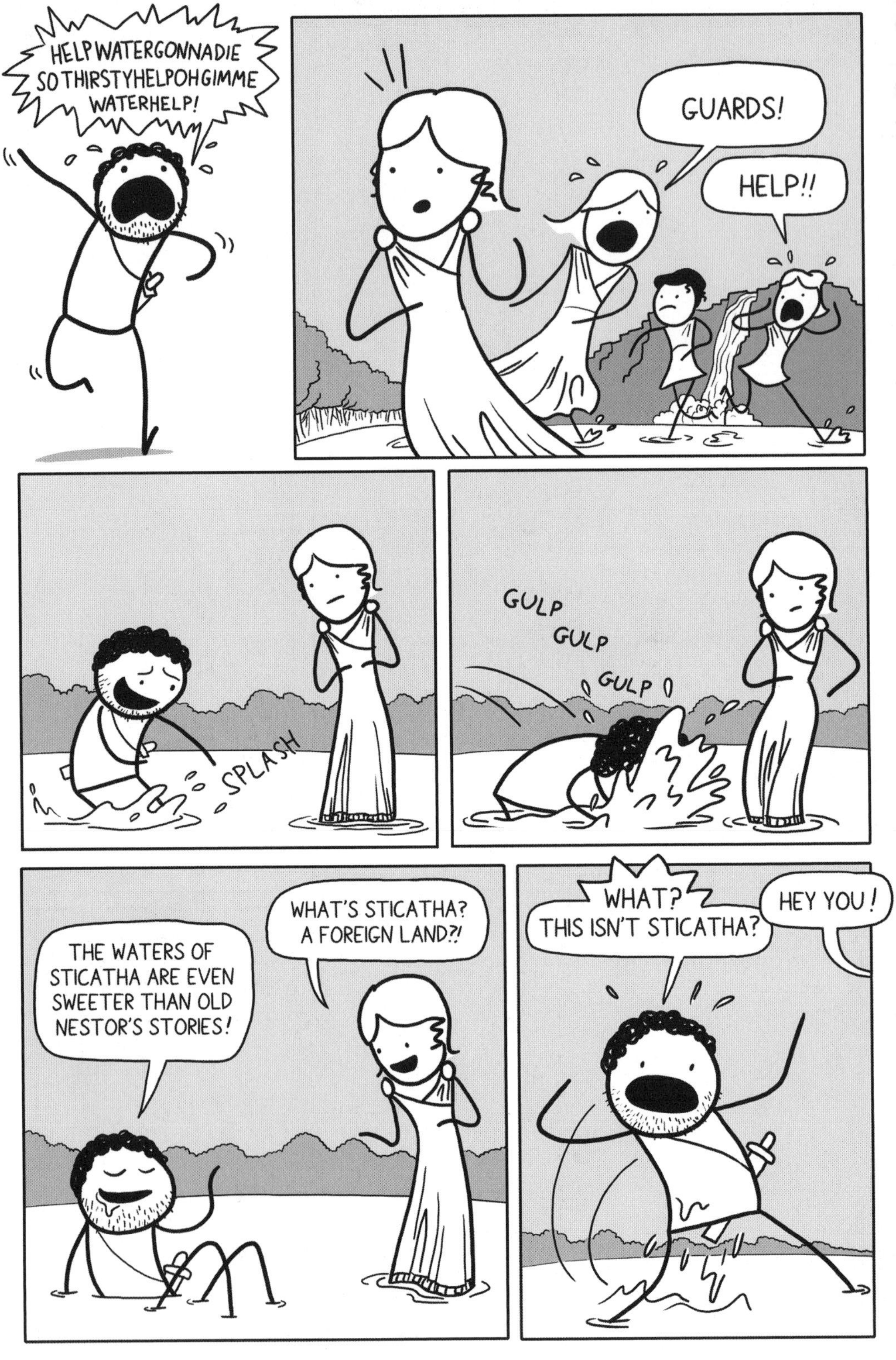
HELPWATERGONNADIE SOTHIRSTYHELPOHGIMME WATERHELP!
GUARDS!
HELP!!
SPLASH
GULP
GULP
GULP
THE WATERS OF STICATHA ARE EVEN SWEETER THAN OLD NESTOR'S STORIES!
WHAT'S STICATHA? A FOREIGN LAND?!
WHAT? THIS ISN'T STICATHA?
HEY YOU!

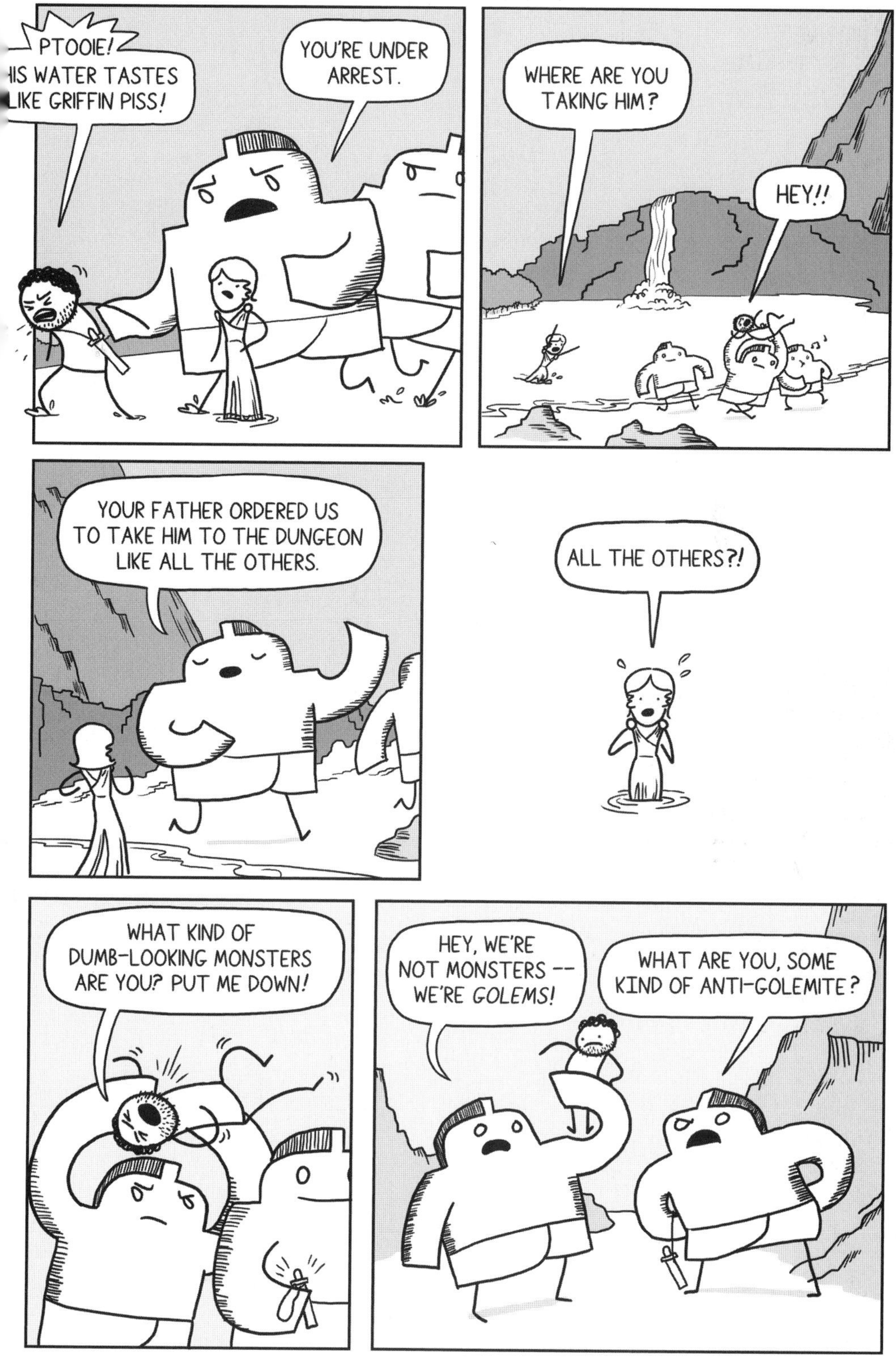
PTOOIE!
HIS WATER TASTES LIKE GRIFFIN PISS!
YOU'RE UNDER ARREST.
WHERE ARE YOU TAKING HIM?
HEY!!
YOUR FATHER ORDERED US TO TAKE HIM TO THE DUNGEON LIKE ALL THE OTHERS.
ALL THE OTHERS?!
WHAT KIND OF DUMB-LOOKING MONSTERS ARE YOU? PUT ME DOWN!
HEY, WE'RE NOT MONSTERS -- WE'RE *GOLEMS*!
WHAT ARE YOU, SOME KIND OF ANTI-GOLEMITE?

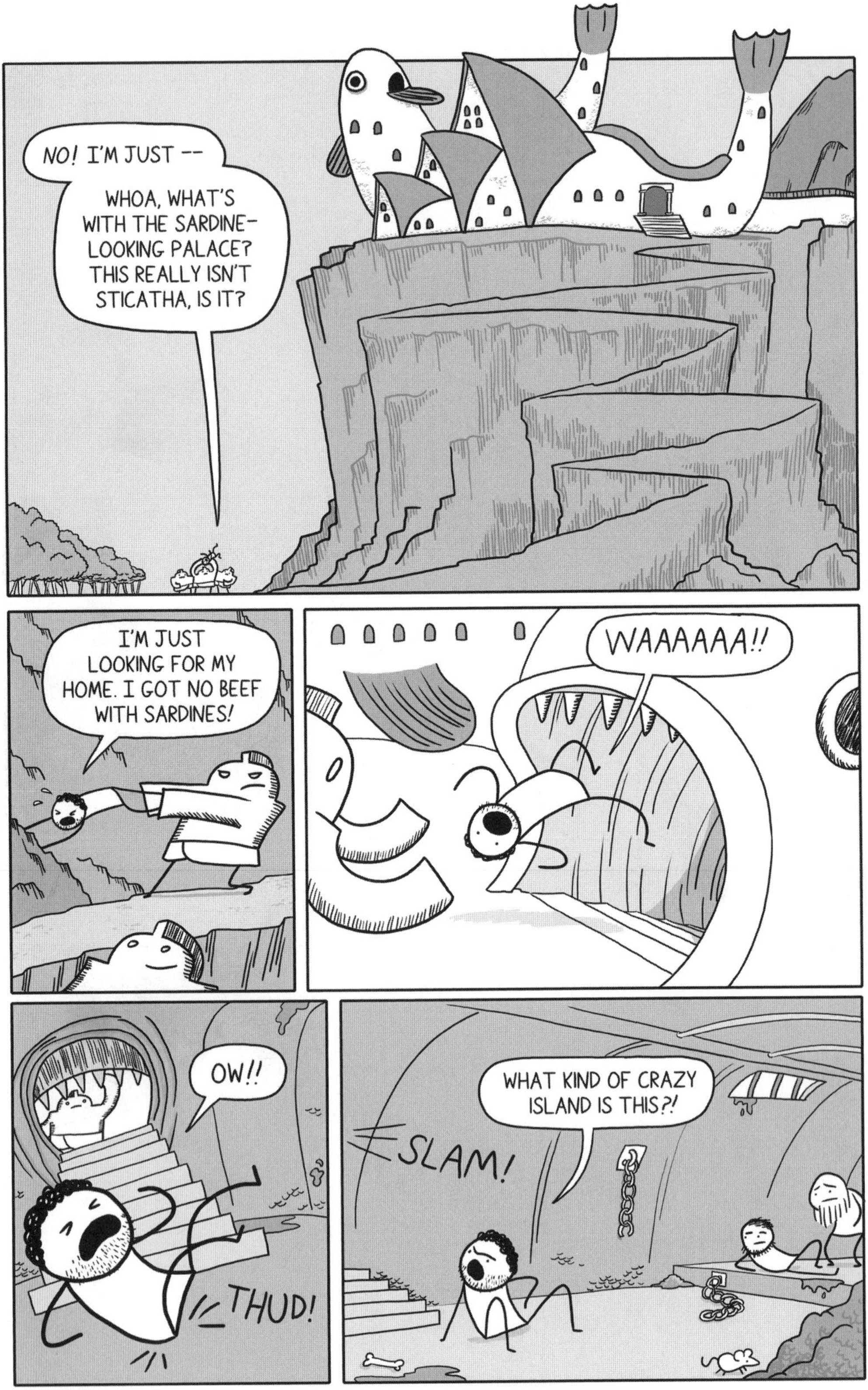
NO! I'M JUST --
WHOA, WHAT'S WITH THE SARDINE-LOOKING PALACE? THIS REALLY ISN'T STICATHA, IS IT?
I'M JUST LOOKING FOR MY HOME. I GOT NO BEEF WITH SARDINES!
WAAAAAA!!
OW!!
THUD!
SLAM!
WHAT KIND OF CRAZY ISLAND IS THIS?!

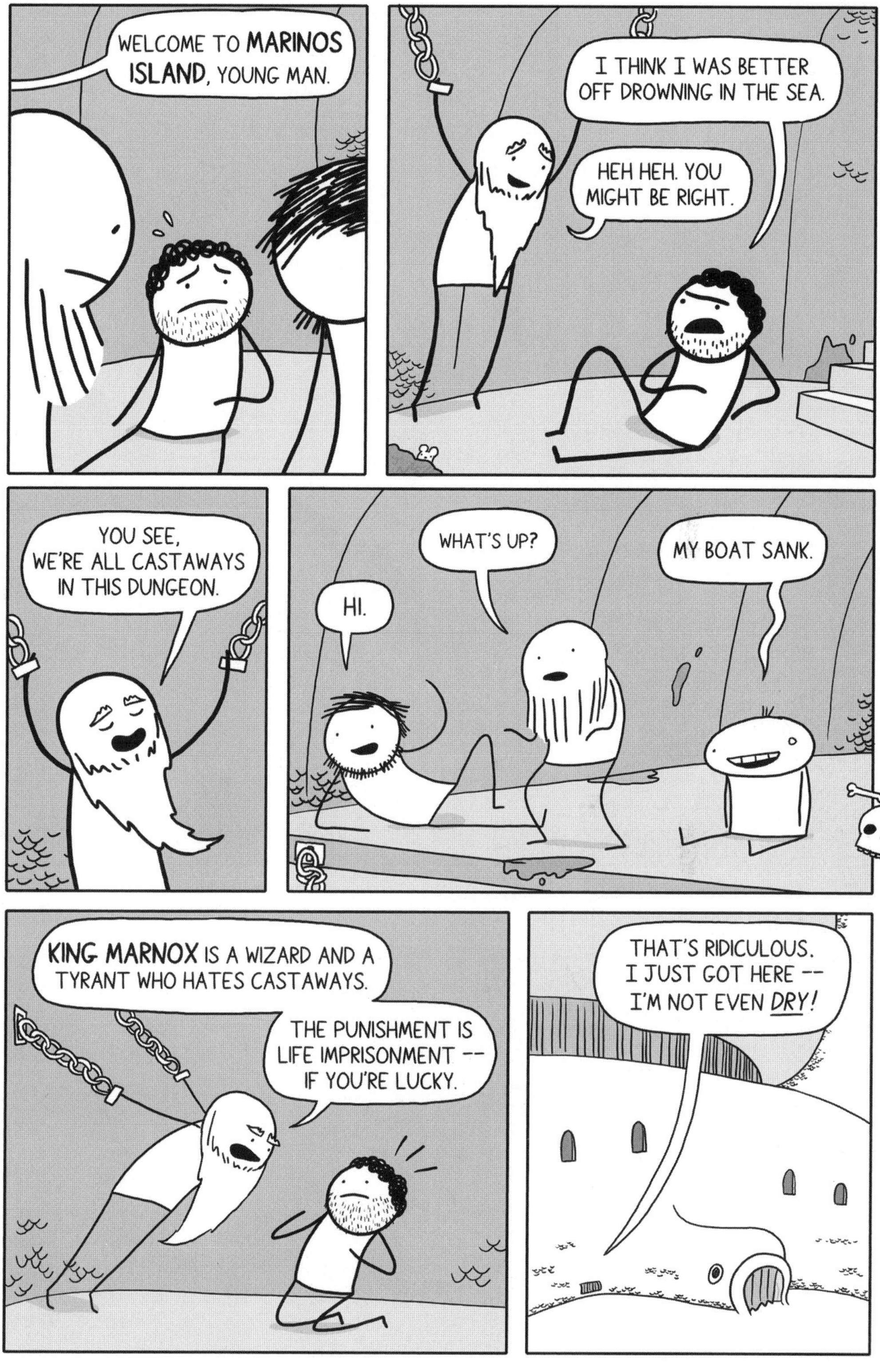
WELCOME TO **MARINOS ISLAND**, YOUNG MAN.
I THINK I WAS BETTER OFF DROWNING IN THE SEA.
HEH HEH. YOU MIGHT BE RIGHT.
YOU SEE, WE'RE ALL CASTAWAYS IN THIS DUNGEON.
HI.
WHAT'S UP?
MY BOAT SANK.
KING MARNOX IS A WIZARD AND A TYRANT WHO HATES CASTAWAYS.
THE PUNISHMENT IS LIFE IMPRISONMENT -- IF YOU'RE LUCKY.
THAT'S RIDICULOUS. I JUST GOT HERE -- I'M NOT EVEN *DRY*!

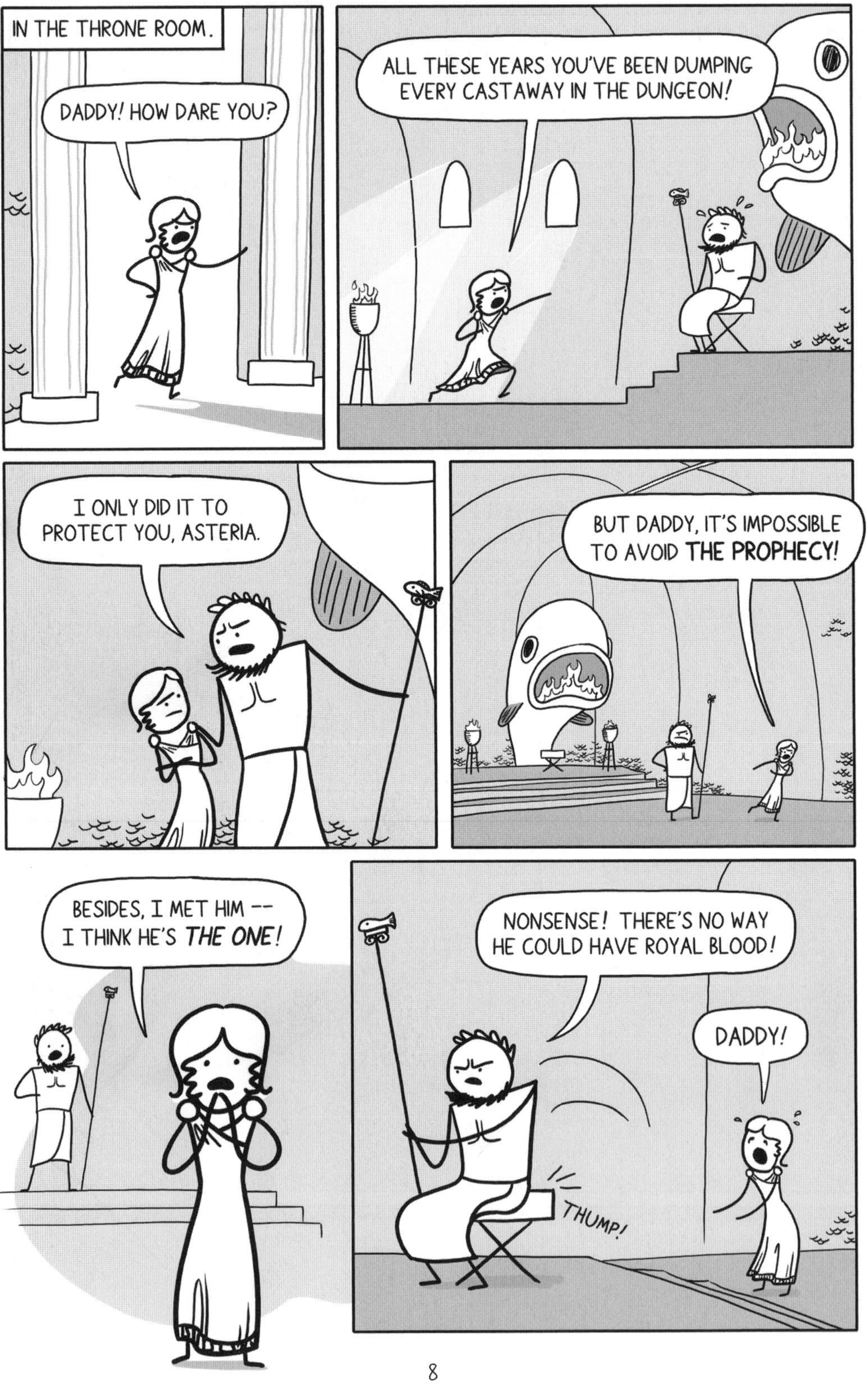
IN THE THRONE ROOM.
DADDY! HOW DARE YOU?
ALL THESE YEARS YOU'VE BEEN DUMPING EVERY CASTAWAY IN THE DUNGEON!
I ONLY DID IT TO PROTECT YOU, ASTERIA.
BUT DADDY, IT'S IMPOSSIBLE TO AVOID **THE PROPHECY**!
BESIDES, I MET HIM -- I THINK HE'S ***THE ONE***!
NONSENSE! THERE'S NO WAY HE COULD HAVE ROYAL BLOOD!
THUMP!
DADDY!

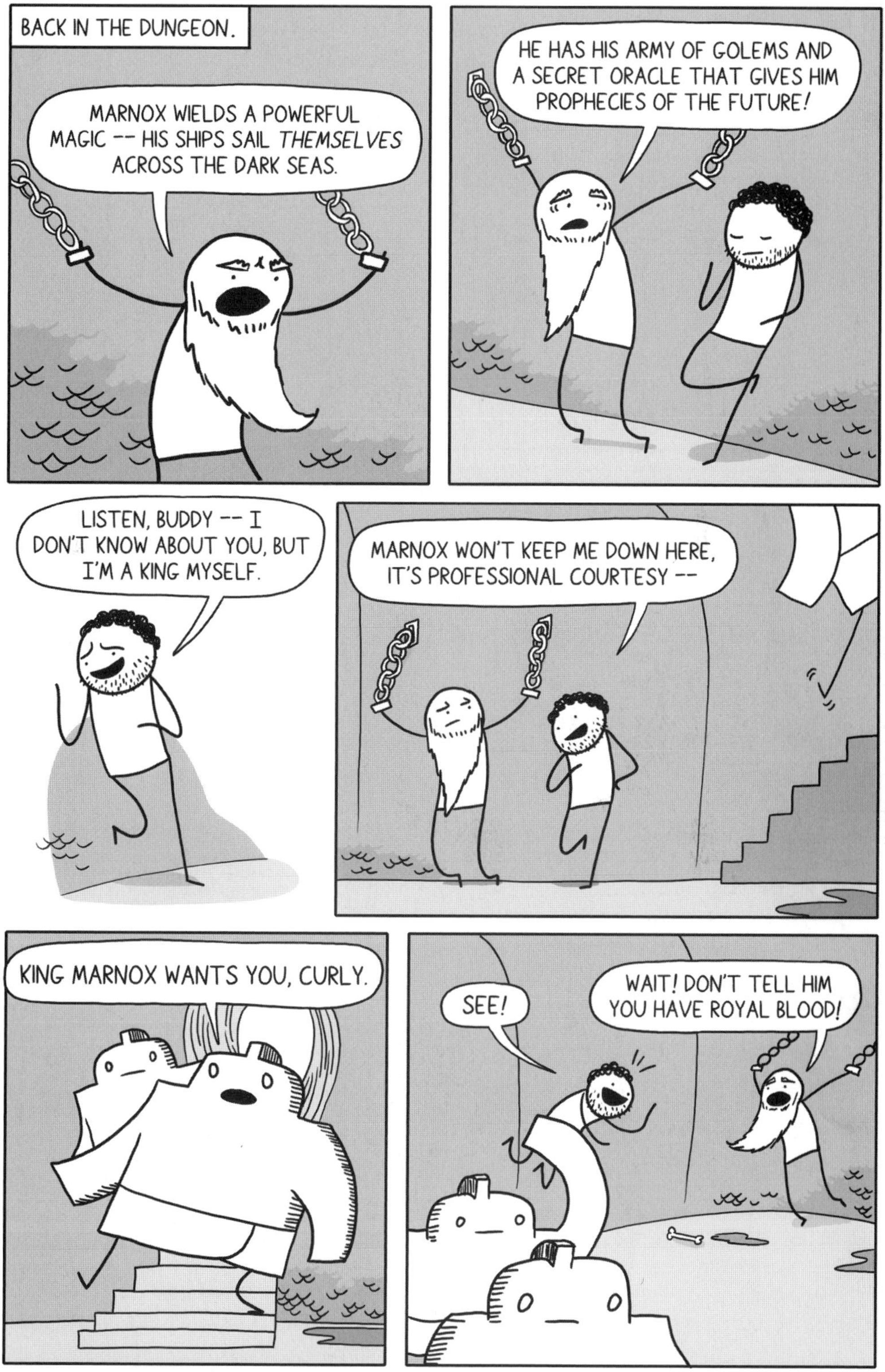
BACK IN THE DUNGEON.
MARNOX WIELDS A POWERFUL MAGIC -- HIS SHIPS SAIL *THEMSELVES* ACROSS THE DARK SEAS.
HE HAS HIS ARMY OF GOLEMS AND A SECRET ORACLE THAT GIVES HIM PROPHECIES OF THE FUTURE!
LISTEN, BUDDY -- I DON'T KNOW ABOUT YOU, BUT I'M A KING MYSELF.
MARNOX WON'T KEEP ME DOWN HERE, IT'S PROFESSIONAL COURTESY --
KING MARNOX WANTS YOU, CURLY.
SEE!
WAIT! DON'T TELL HIM YOU HAVE ROYAL BLOOD!

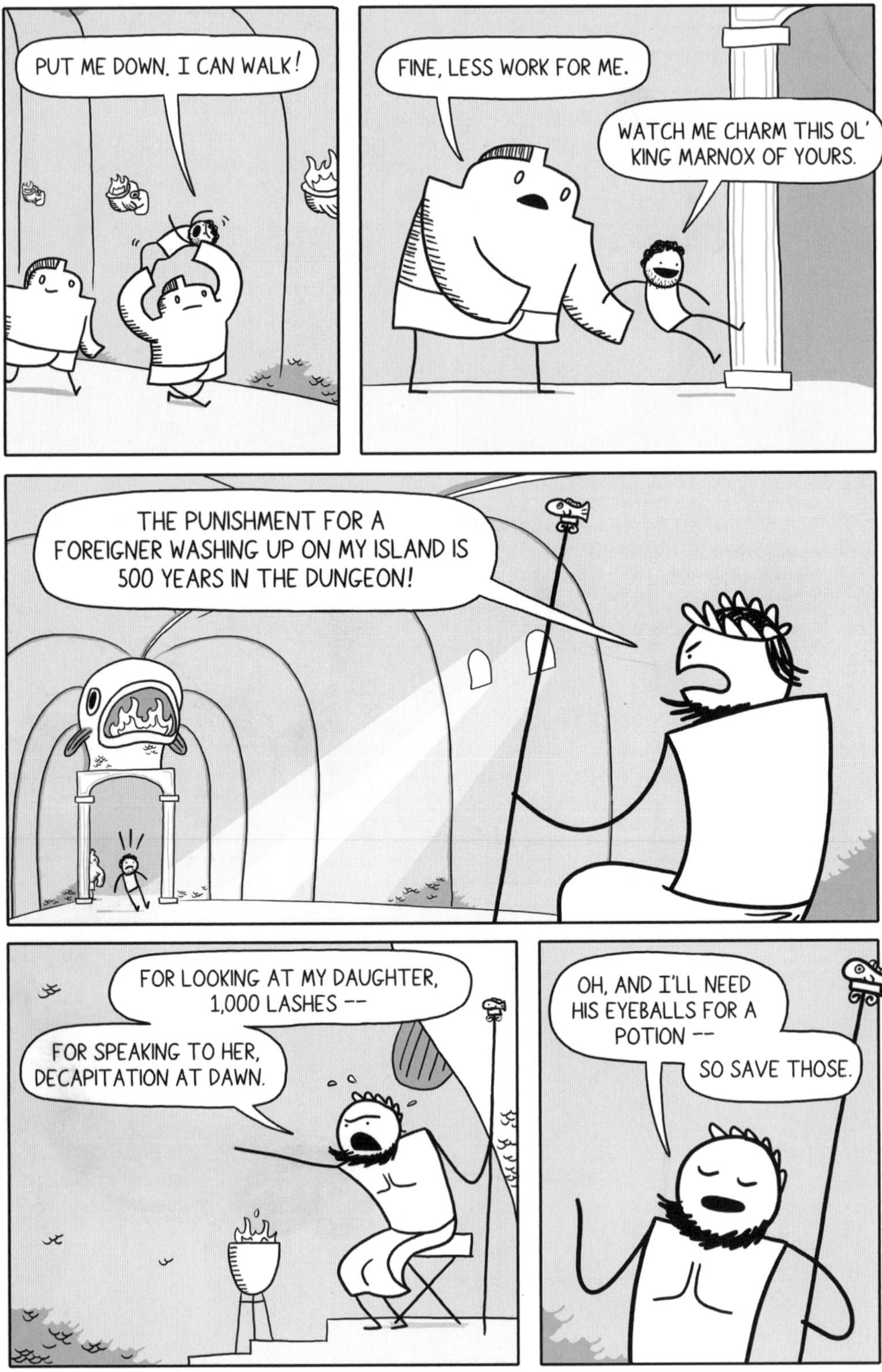
PUT ME DOWN. I CAN WALK!
FINE, LESS WORK FOR ME.
WATCH ME CHARM THIS OL' KING MARNOX OF YOURS.
THE PUNISHMENT FOR A FOREIGNER WASHING UP ON MY ISLAND IS 500 YEARS IN THE DUNGEON!
FOR LOOKING AT MY DAUGHTER, 1,000 LASHES --
FOR SPEAKING TO HER, DECAPITATION AT DAWN.
OH, AND I'LL NEED HIS EYEBALLS FOR A POTION --
SO SAVE THOSE.

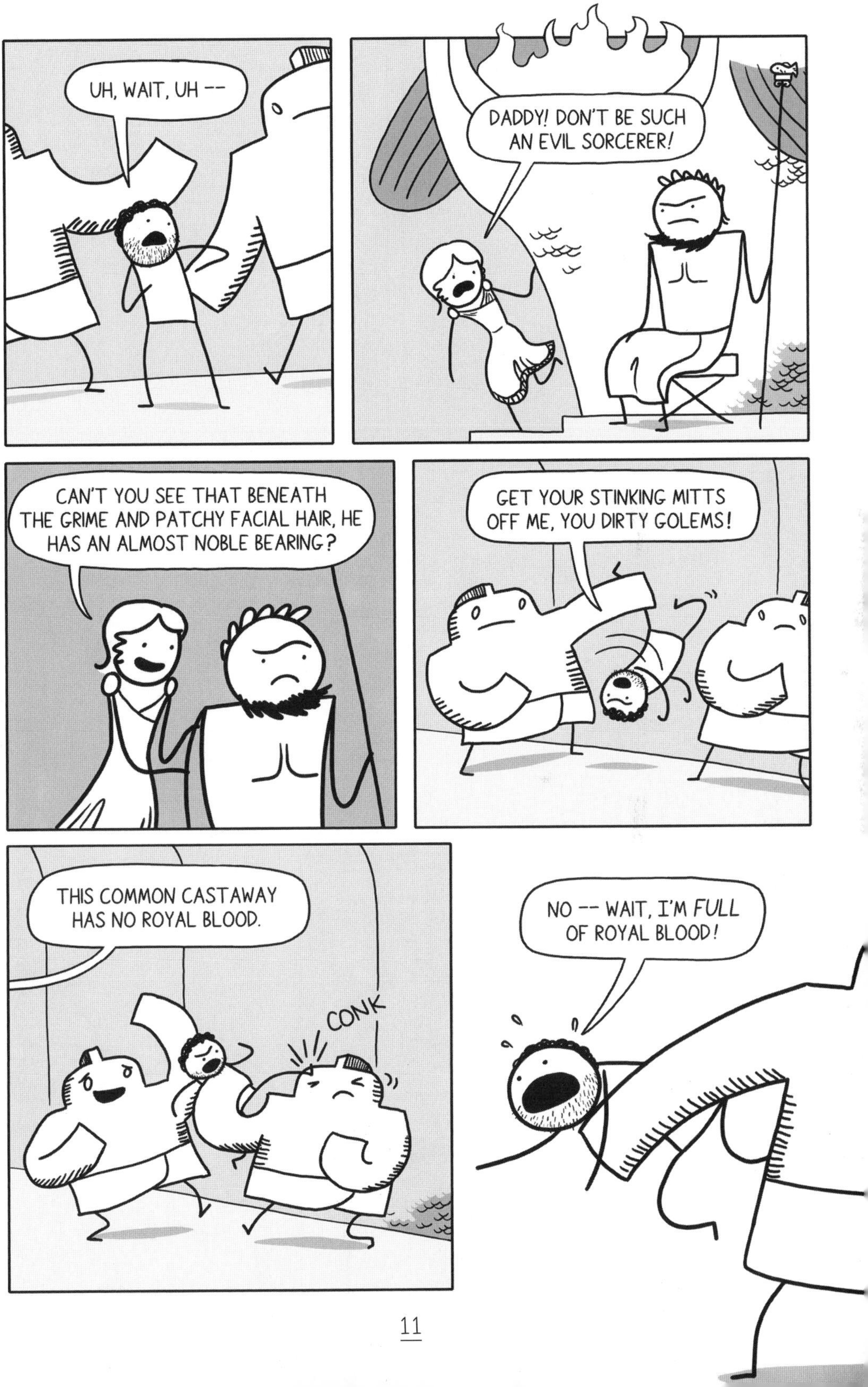
UH, WAIT, UH --
DADDY! DON'T BE SUCH AN EVIL SORCERER!
CAN'T YOU SEE THAT BENEATH THE GRIME AND PATCHY FACIAL HAIR, HE HAS AN ALMOST NOBLE BEARING?
GET YOUR STINKING MITTS OFF ME, YOU DIRTY GOLEMS!
THIS COMMON CASTAWAY HAS NO ROYAL BLOOD.
CONK
NO -- WAIT, I'M *FULL* OF ROYAL BLOOD!

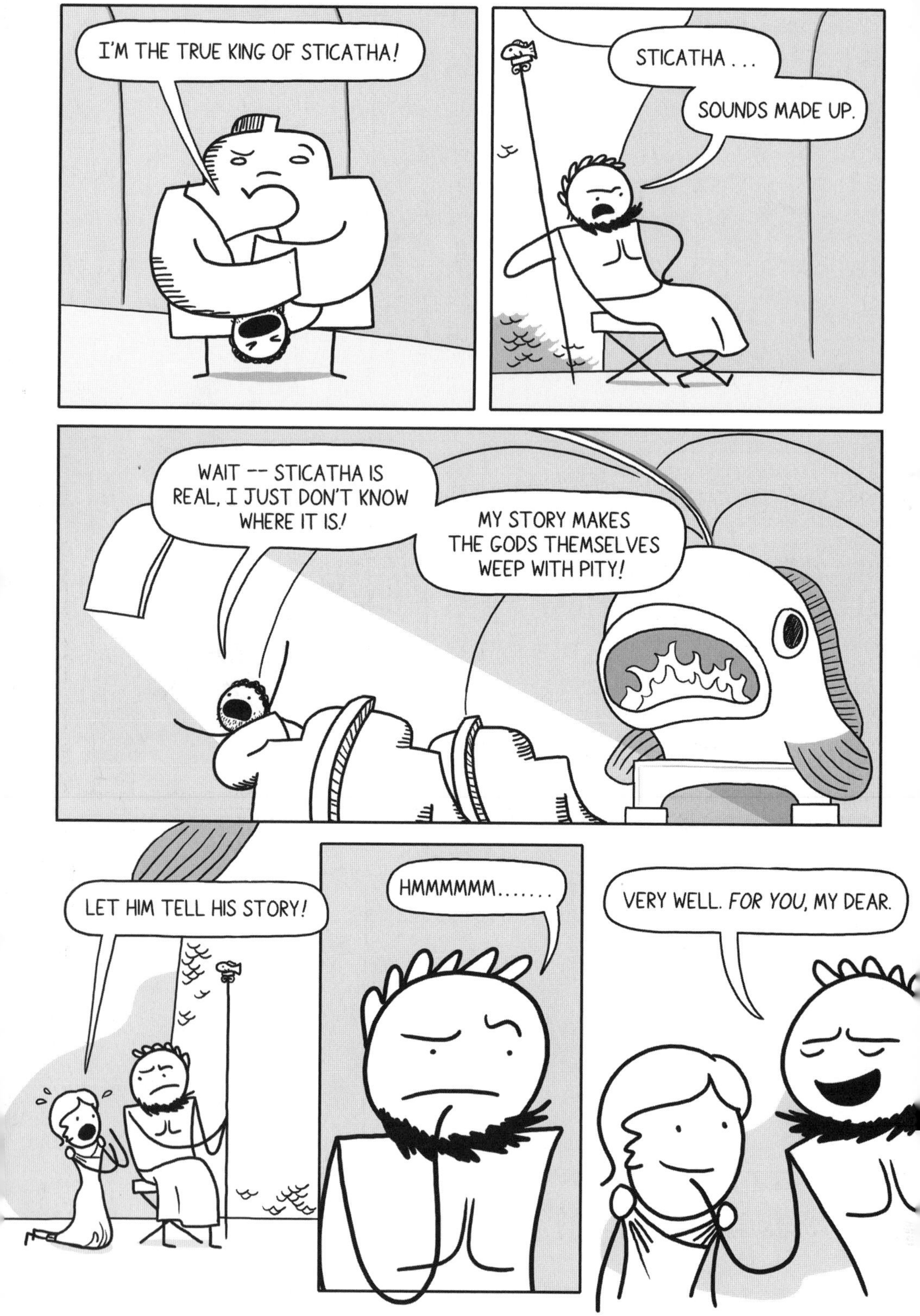
I'M THE TRUE KING OF STICATHA!
STICATHA . . .
SOUNDS MADE UP.
WAIT -- STICATHA IS REAL, I JUST DON'T KNOW WHERE IT IS!
MY STORY MAKES THE GODS THEMSELVES WEEP WITH PITY!
LET HIM TELL HIS STORY!
HMMMMMM.......
VERY WELL. *FOR YOU,* MY DEAR.

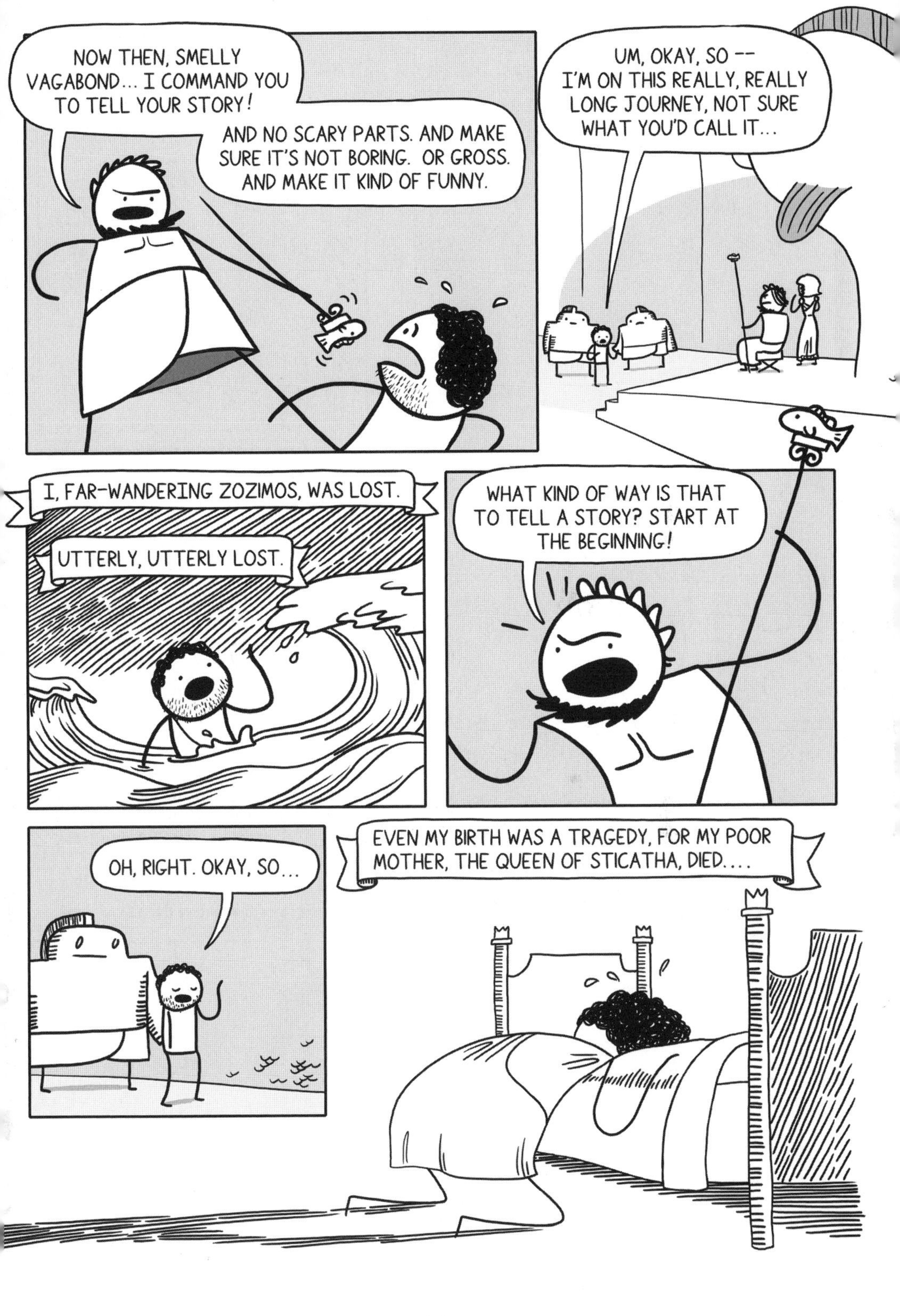

NOW THEN, SMELLY VAGABOND... I COMMAND YOU TO TELL YOUR STORY!
AND NO SCARY PARTS. AND MAKE SURE IT'S NOT BORING. OR GROSS. AND MAKE IT KIND OF FUNNY.
UM, OKAY, SO -- I'M ON THIS REALLY, REALLY LONG JOURNEY, NOT SURE WHAT YOU'D CALL IT...
I, FAR-WANDERING ZOZIMOS, WAS LOST.
UTTERLY, UTTERLY LOST.
WHAT KIND OF WAY IS THAT TO TELL A STORY? START AT THE BEGINNING!
OH, RIGHT. OKAY, SO...
EVEN MY BIRTH WAS A TRAGEDY, FOR MY POOR MOTHER, THE QUEEN OF STICATHA, DIED....

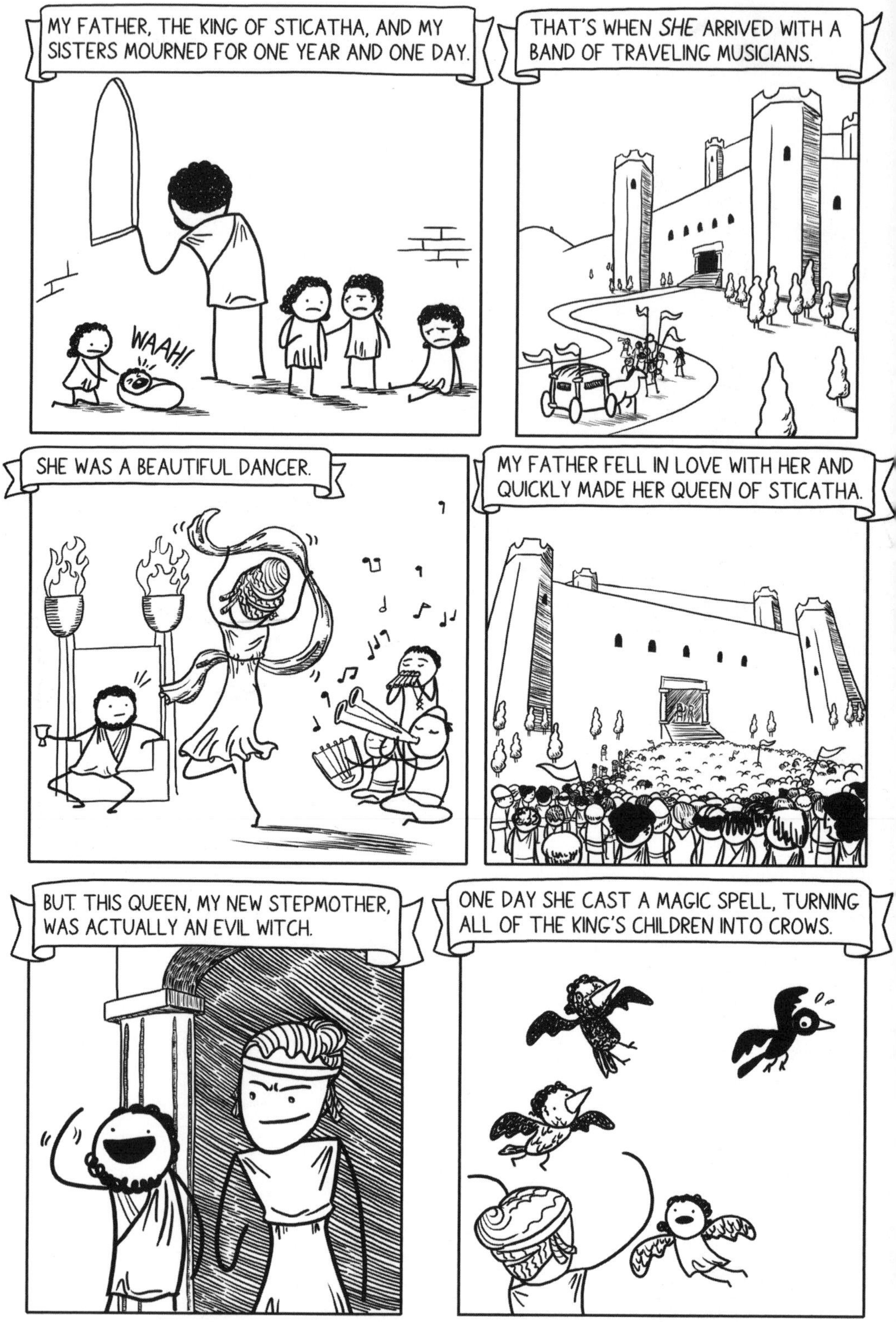
MY FATHER, THE KING OF STICATHA, AND MY SISTERS MOURNED FOR ONE YEAR AND ONE DAY.
WAAH!
THAT'S WHEN *SHE* ARRIVED WITH A BAND OF TRAVELING MUSICIANS.
SHE WAS A BEAUTIFUL DANCER.
MY FATHER FELL IN LOVE WITH HER AND QUICKLY MADE HER QUEEN OF STICATHA.
BUT THIS QUEEN, MY NEW STEPMOTHER, WAS ACTUALLY AN EVIL WITCH.
ONE DAY SHE CAST A MAGIC SPELL, TURNING ALL OF THE KING'S CHILDREN INTO CROWS.

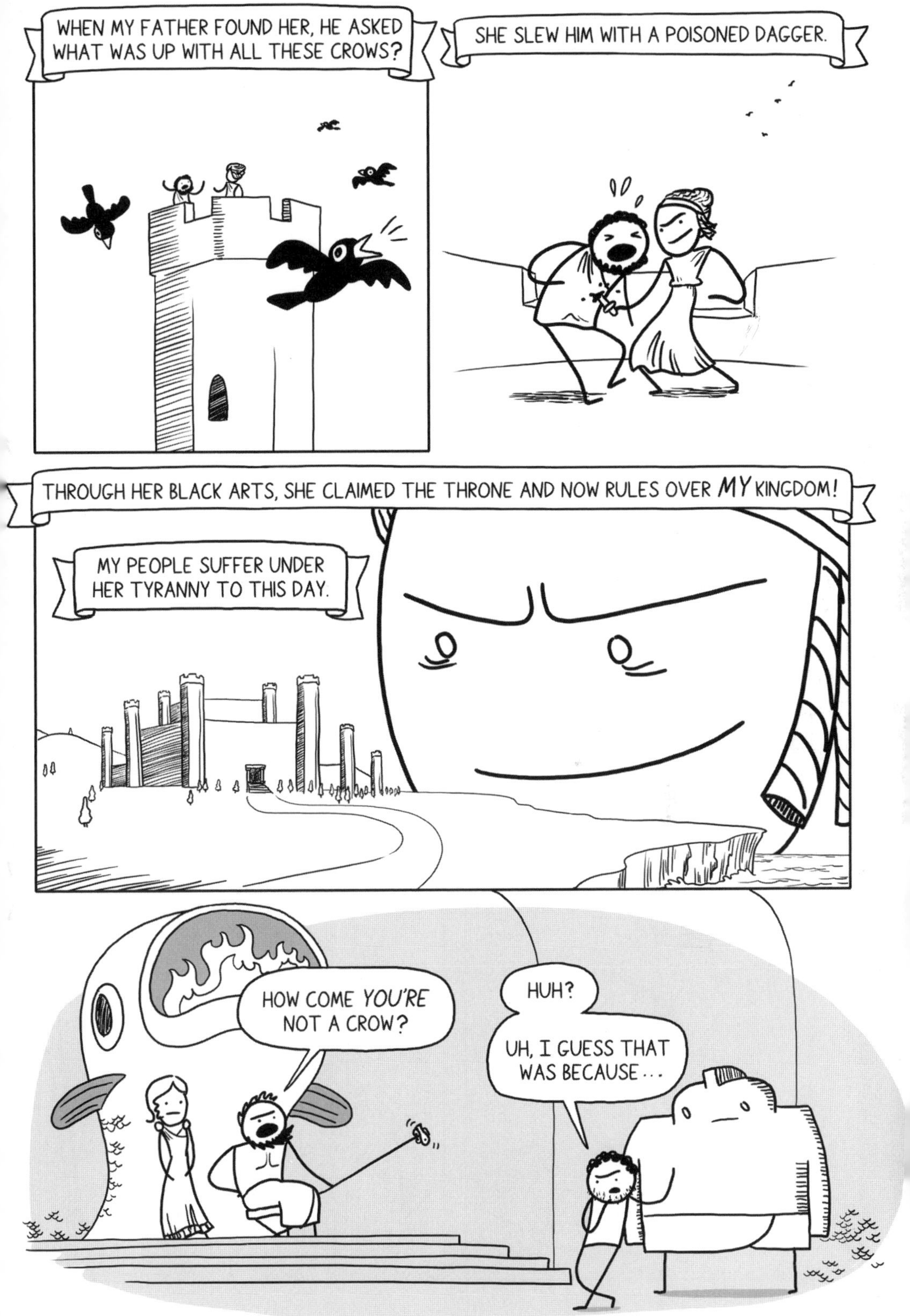
WHEN MY FATHER FOUND HER, HE ASKED WHAT WAS UP WITH ALL THESE CROWS?
SHE SLEW HIM WITH A POISONED DAGGER.
THROUGH HER BLACK ARTS, SHE CLAIMED THE THRONE AND NOW RULES OVER *MY* KINGDOM!
MY PEOPLE SUFFER UNDER HER TYRANNY TO THIS DAY.
HOW COME *YOU'RE* NOT A CROW?
HUH?
UH, I GUESS THAT WAS BECAUSE . . .

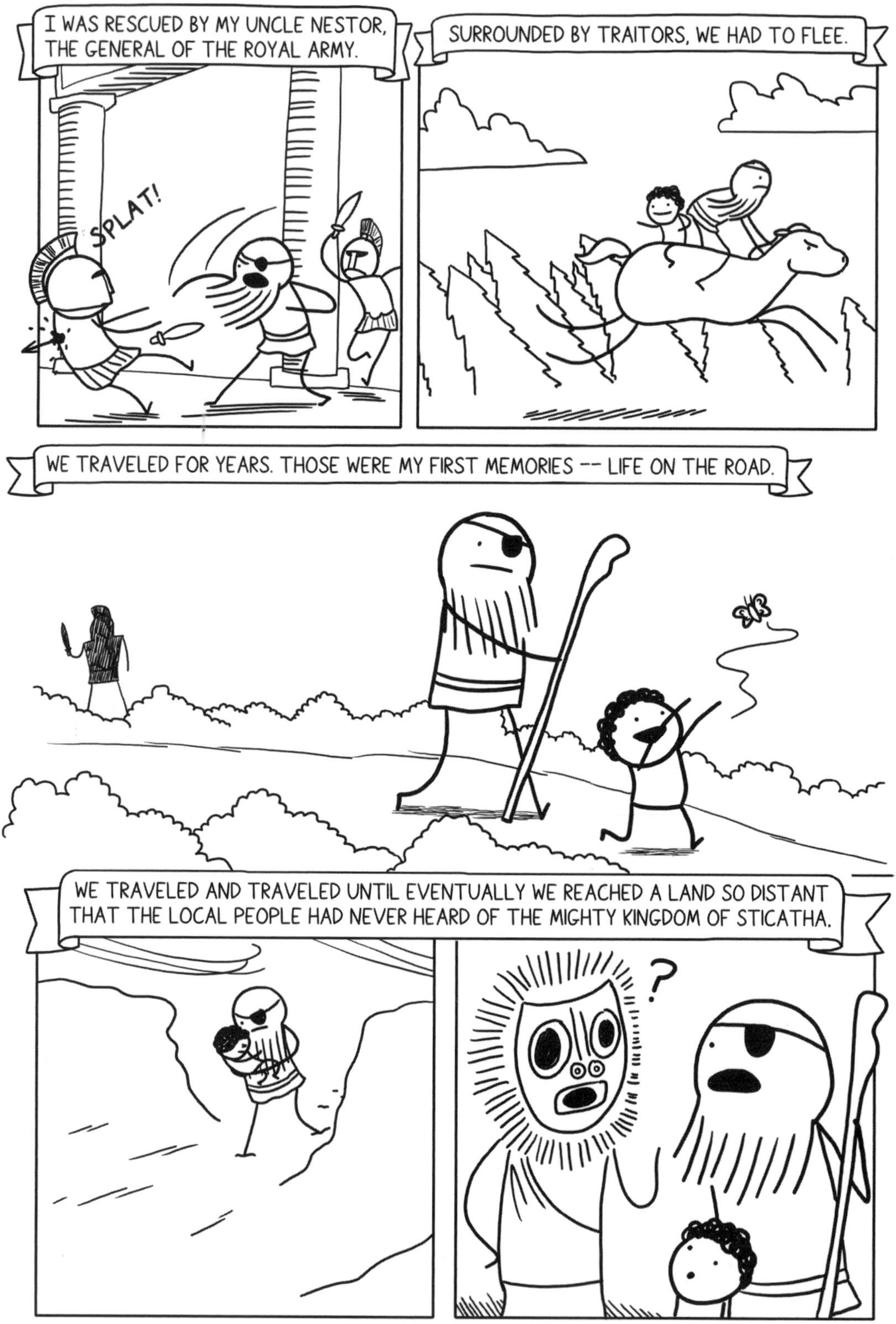
I WAS RESCUED BY MY UNCLE NESTOR, THE GENERAL OF THE ROYAL ARMY.
SPLAT!
SURROUNDED BY TRAITORS, WE HAD TO FLEE.
WE TRAVELED FOR YEARS. THOSE WERE MY FIRST MEMORIES -- LIFE ON THE ROAD.
WE TRAVELED AND TRAVELED UNTIL EVENTUALLY WE REACHED A LAND SO DISTANT THAT THE LOCAL PEOPLE HAD NEVER HEARD OF THE MIGHTY KINGDOM OF STICATHA.
?

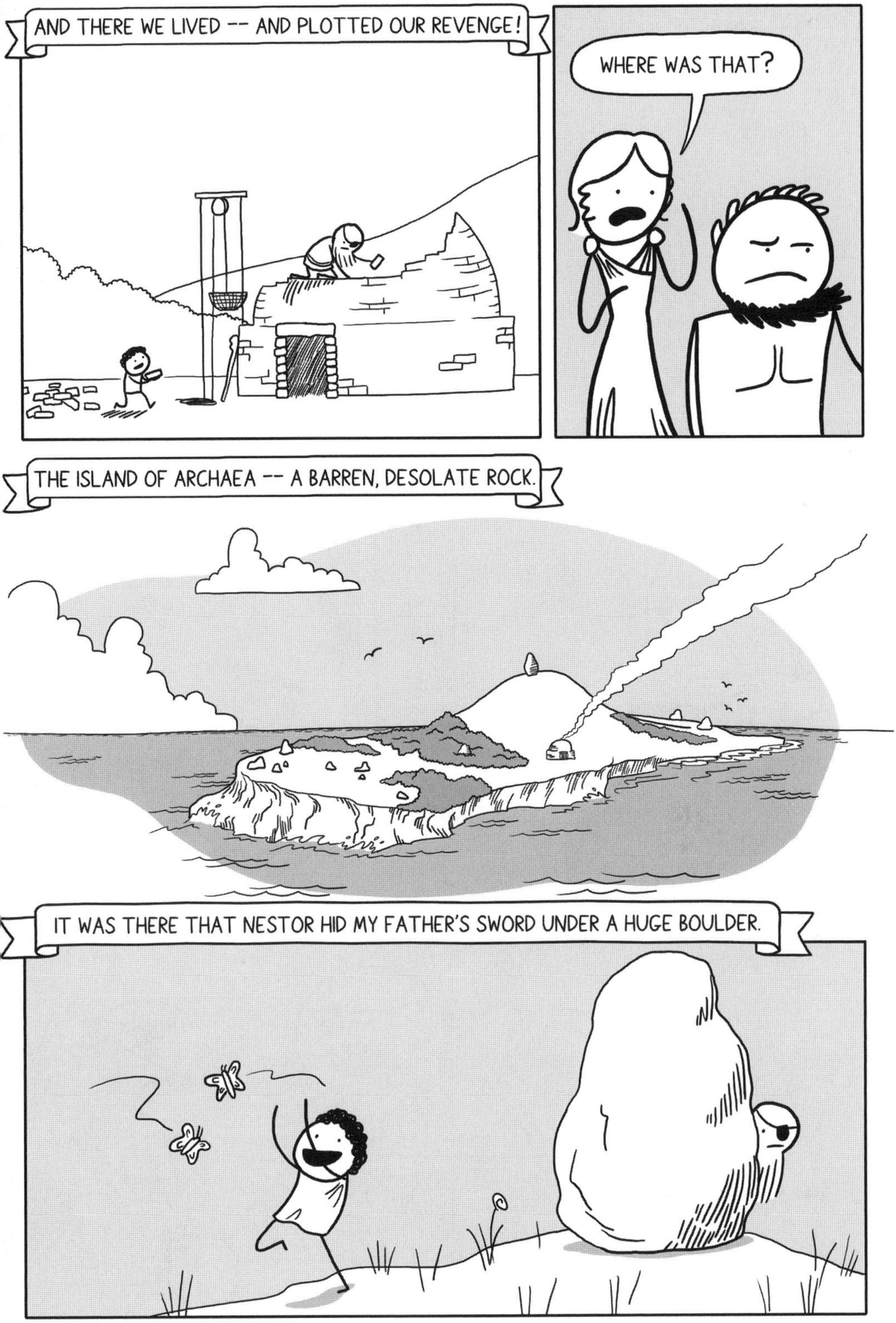
AND THERE WE LIVED -- AND PLOTTED OUR REVENGE!
WHERE WAS THAT?
THE ISLAND OF ARCHAEA -- A BARREN, DESOLATE ROCK.
IT WAS THERE THAT NESTOR HID MY FATHER'S SWORD UNDER A HUGE BOULDER.

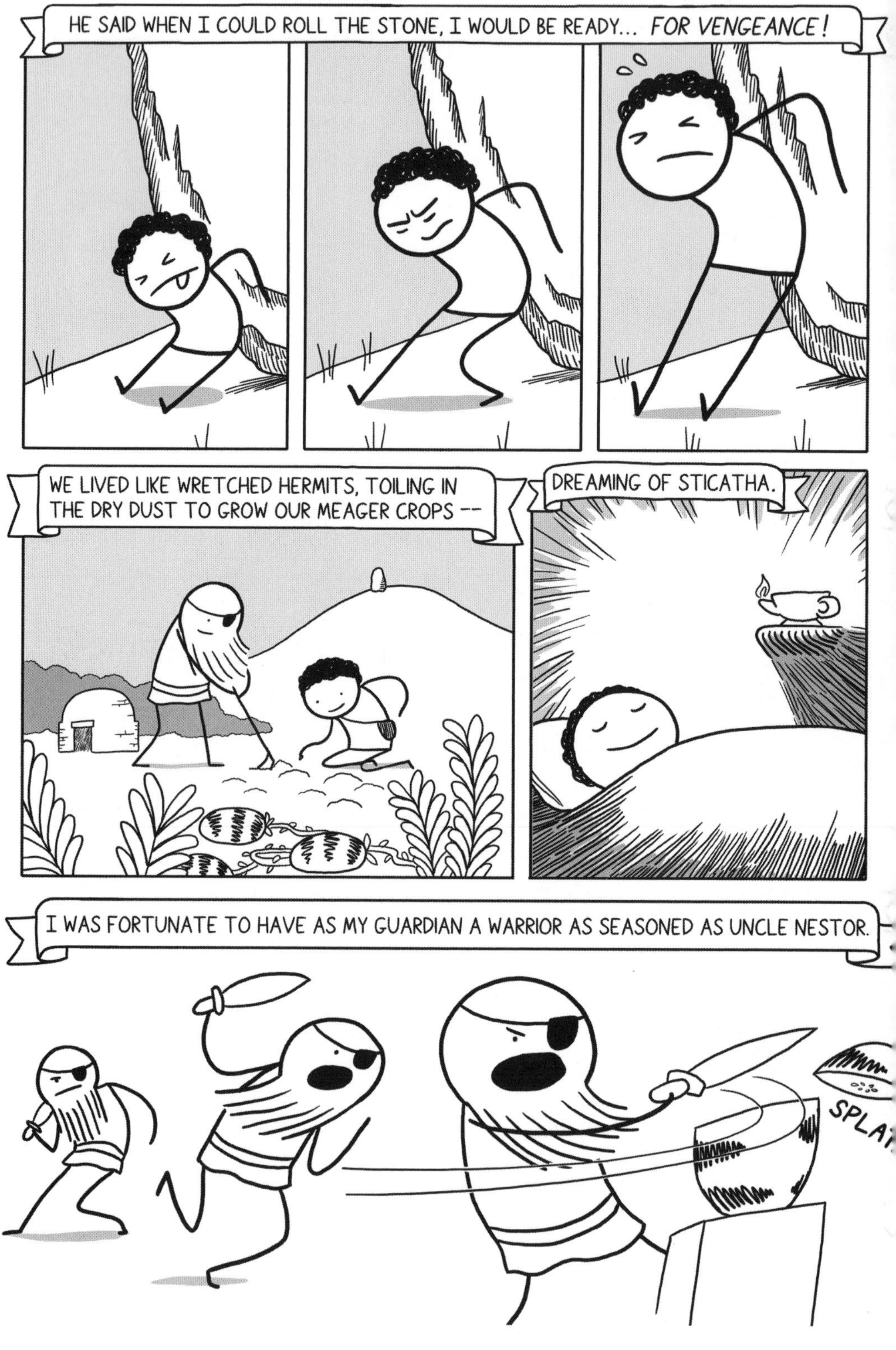
HE SAID WHEN I COULD ROLL THE STONE, I WOULD BE READY... *FOR VENGEANCE!*
WE LIVED LIKE WRETCHED HERMITS, TOILING IN THE DRY DUST TO GROW OUR MEAGER CROPS --
DREAMING OF STICATHA.
I WAS FORTUNATE TO HAVE AS MY GUARDIAN A WARRIOR AS SEASONED AS UNCLE NESTOR.
SPLA

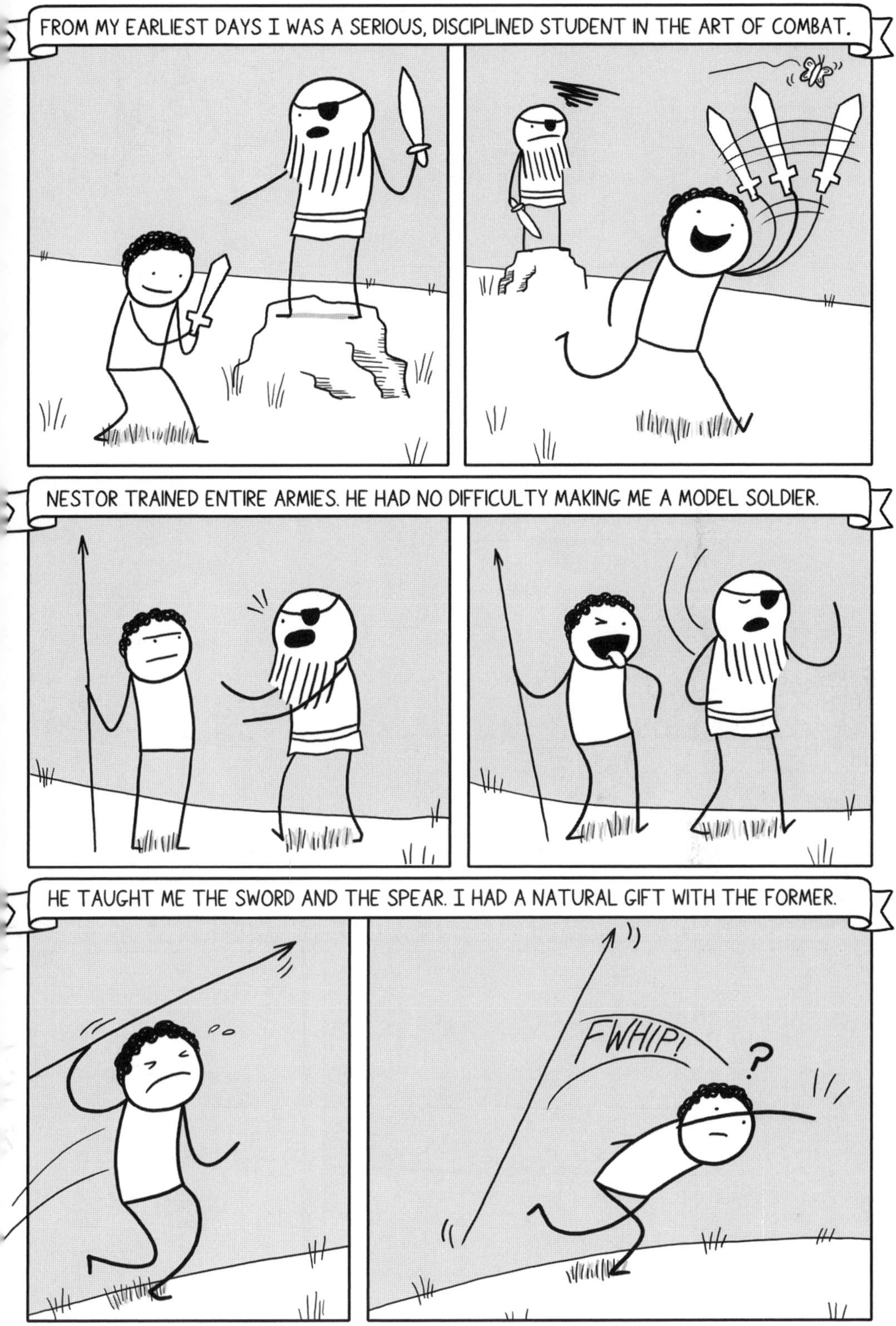
FROM MY EARLIEST DAYS I WAS A SERIOUS, DISCIPLINED STUDENT IN THE ART OF COMBAT.
NESTOR TRAINED ENTIRE ARMIES. HE HAD NO DIFFICULTY MAKING ME A MODEL SOLDIER.
HE TAUGHT ME THE SWORD AND THE SPEAR. I HAD A NATURAL GIFT WITH THE FORMER.
FWHIP!
?

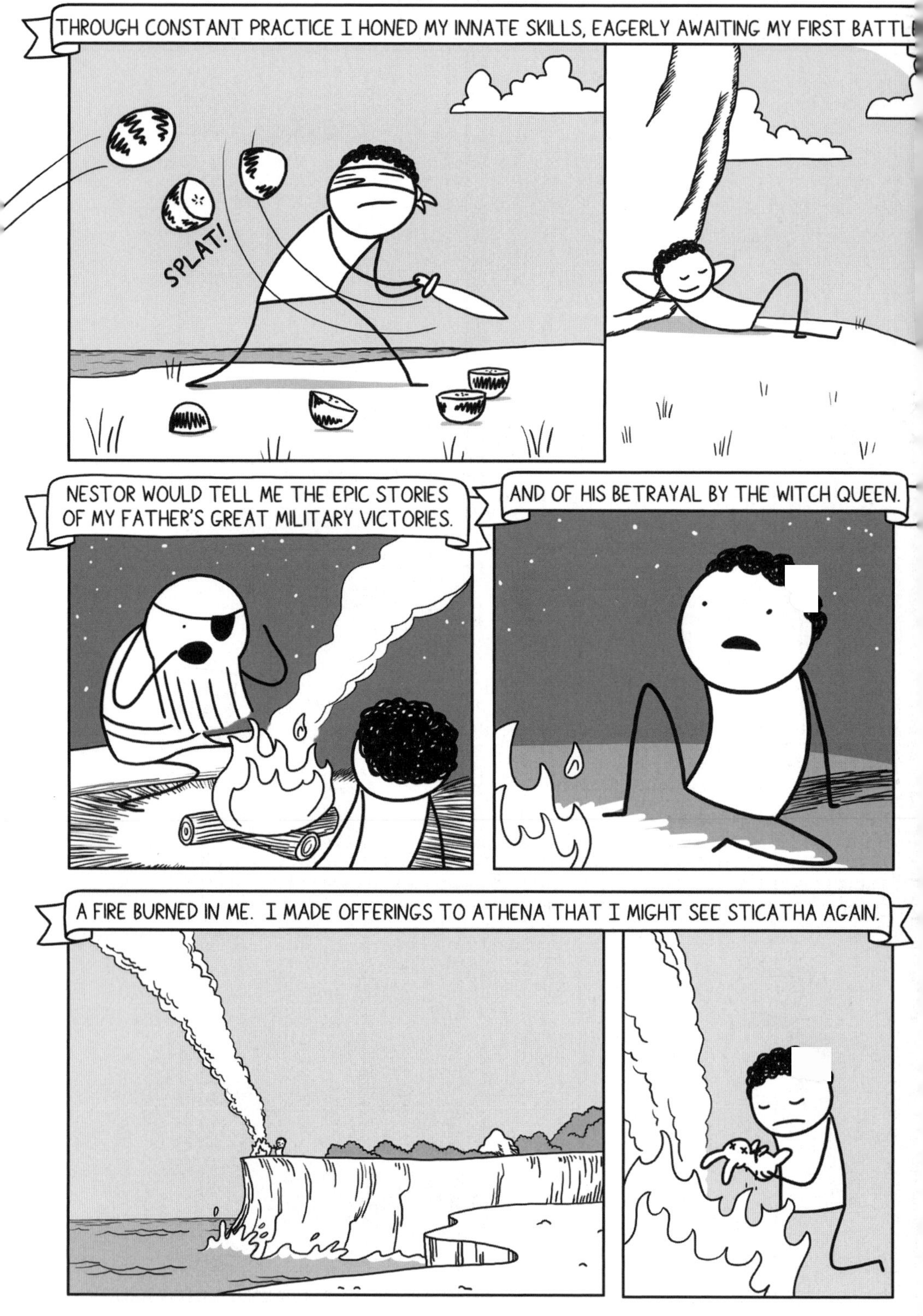
THROUGH CONSTANT PRACTICE I HONED MY INNATE SKILLS, EAGERLY AWAITING MY FIRST BATTL
SPLAT!
NESTOR WOULD TELL ME THE EPIC STORIES OF MY FATHER'S GREAT MILITARY VICTORIES.
AND OF HIS BETRAYAL BY THE WITCH QUEEN.
A FIRE BURNED IN ME. I MADE OFFERINGS TO ATHENA THAT I MIGHT SEE STICATHA AGAIN.

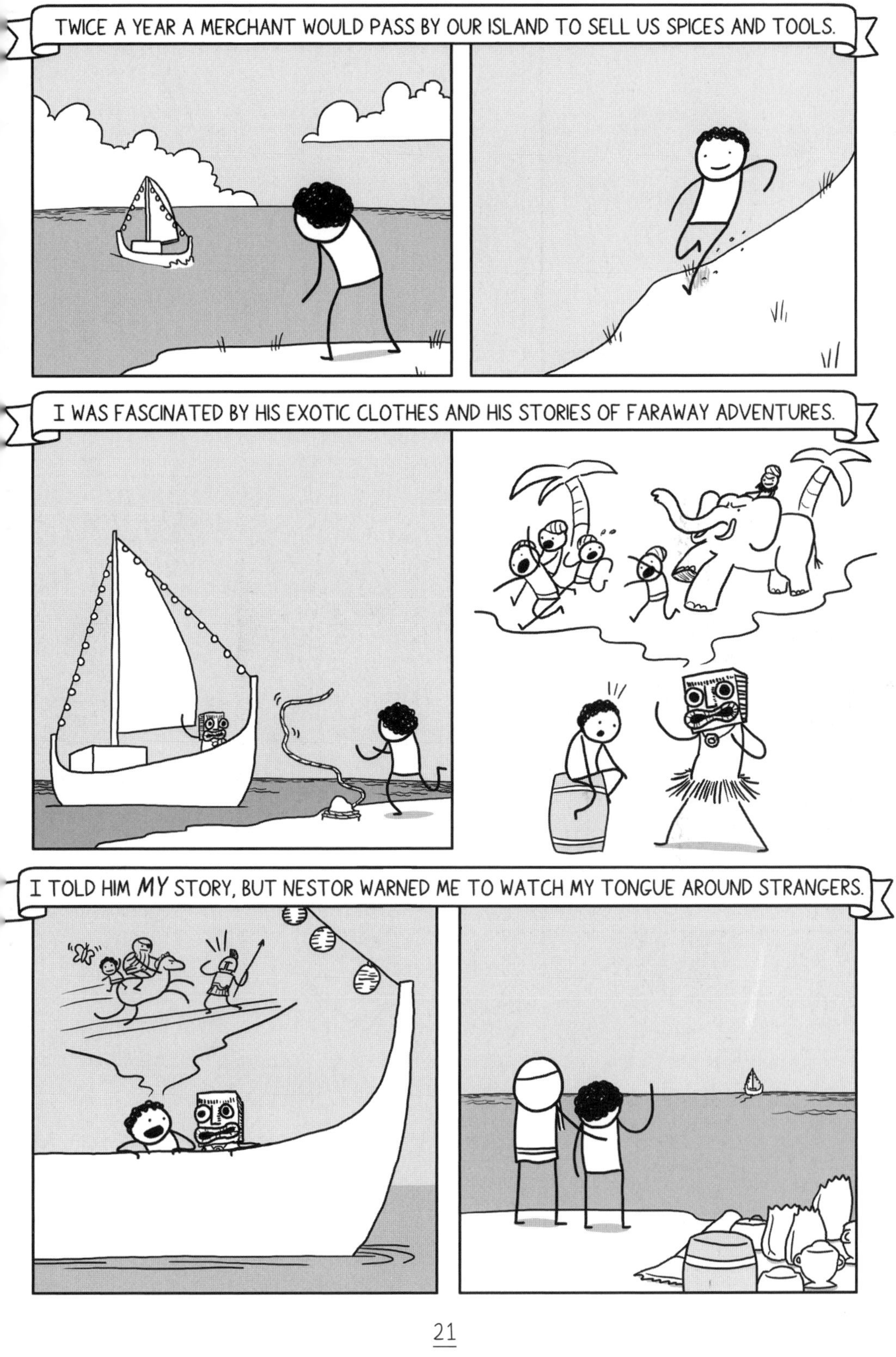
TWICE A YEAR A MERCHANT WOULD PASS BY OUR ISLAND TO SELL US SPICES AND TOOLS.
I WAS FASCINATED BY HIS EXOTIC CLOTHES AND HIS STORIES OF FARAWAY ADVENTURES.
I TOLD HIM *MY* STORY, BUT NESTOR WARNED ME TO WATCH MY TONGUE AROUND STRANGERS.

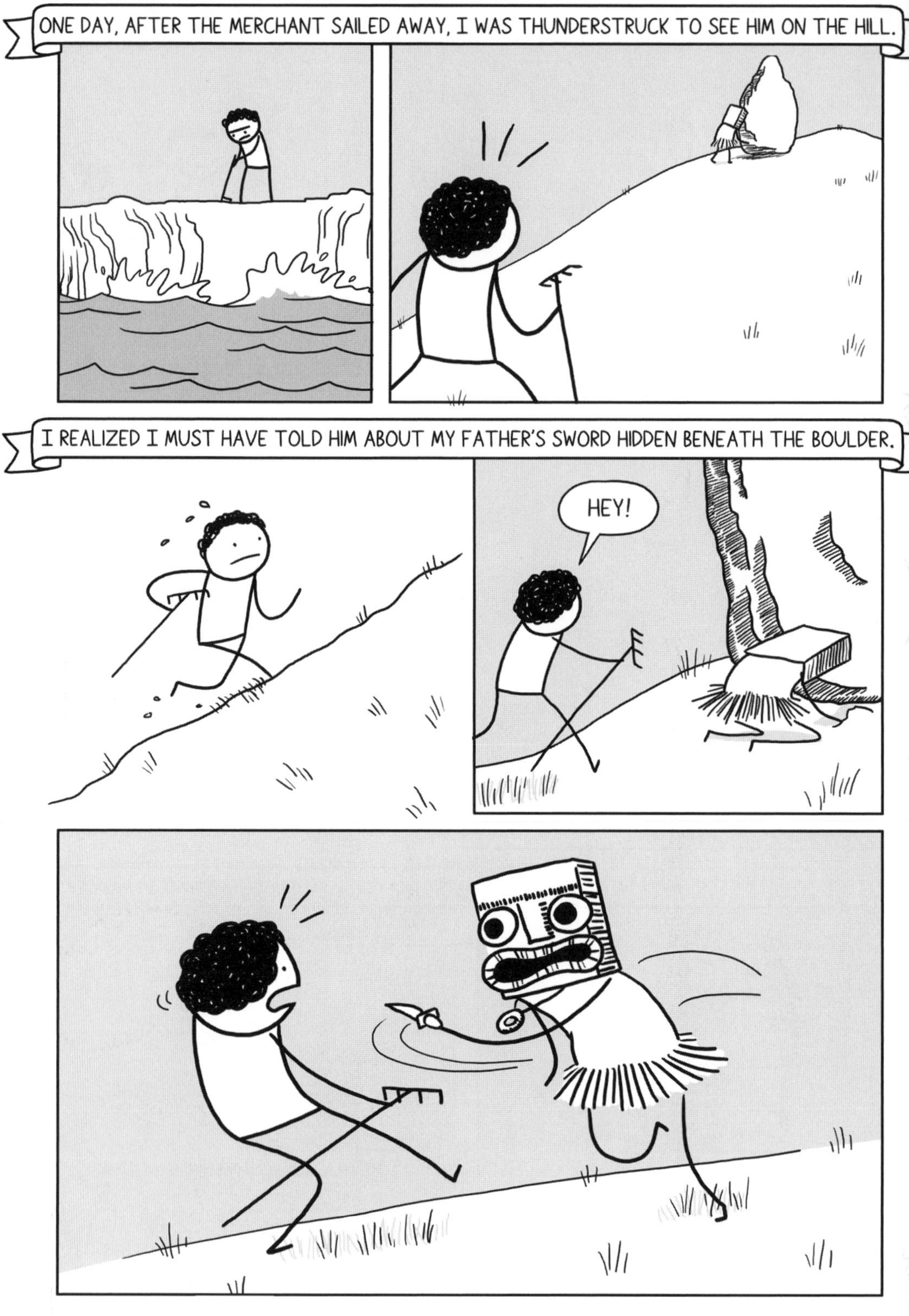
ONE DAY, AFTER THE MERCHANT SAILED AWAY, I WAS THUNDERSTRUCK TO SEE HIM ON THE HILL.
I REALIZED I MUST HAVE TOLD HIM ABOUT MY FATHER'S SWORD HIDDEN BENEATH THE BOULDER.
HEY!

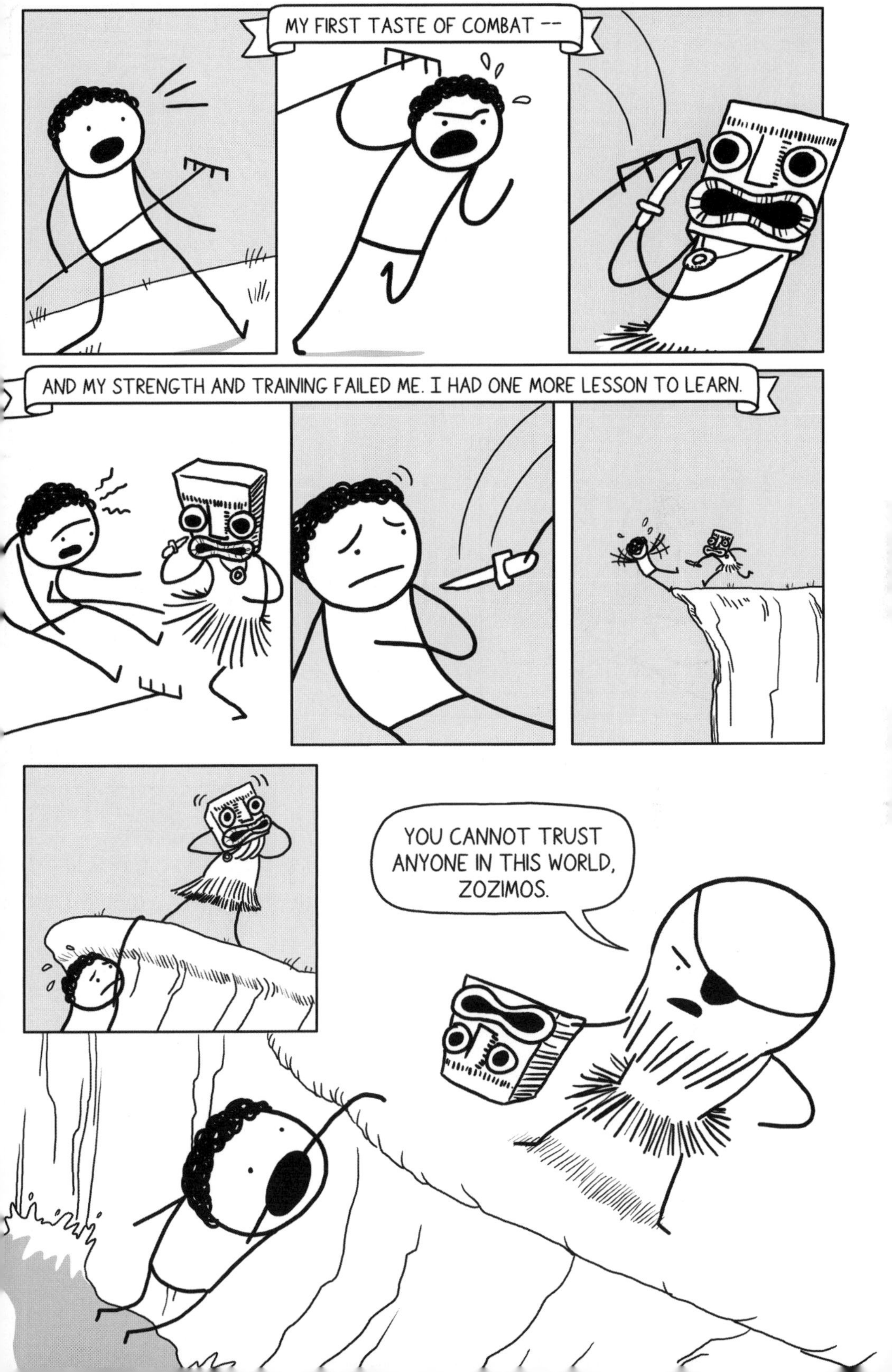
MY FIRST TASTE OF COMBAT --
AND MY STRENGTH AND TRAINING FAILED ME. I HAD ONE MORE LESSON TO LEARN.
YOU CANNOT TRUST ANYONE IN THIS WORLD, ZOZIMOS.

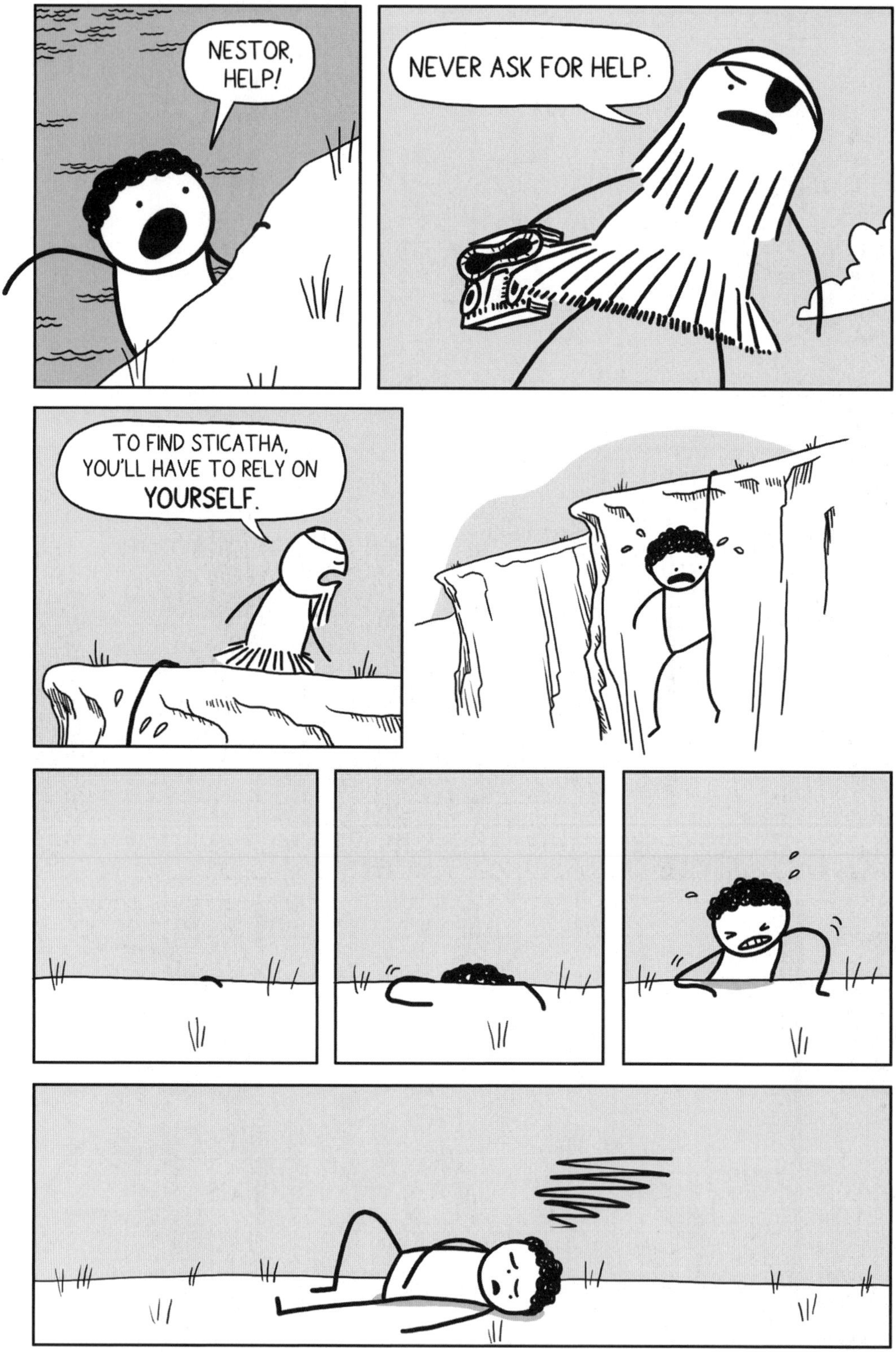
NESTOR, HELP!
NEVER ASK FOR HELP.
TO FIND STICATHA, YOU'LL HAVE TO RELY ON **YOURSELF**.

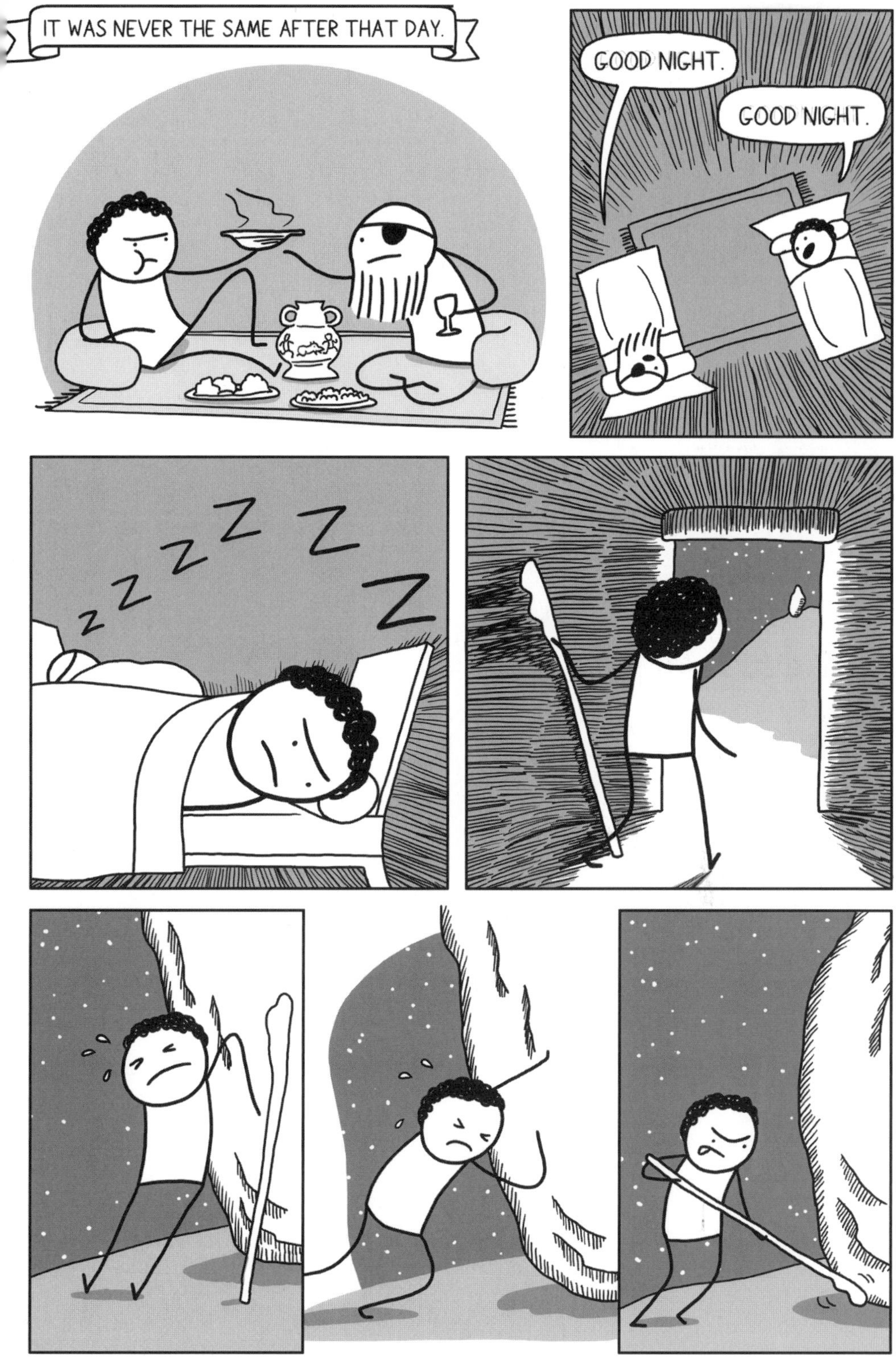
IT WAS NEVER THE SAME AFTER THAT DAY.
GOOD NIGHT.
GOOD NIGHT.
Z Z Z Z Z Z

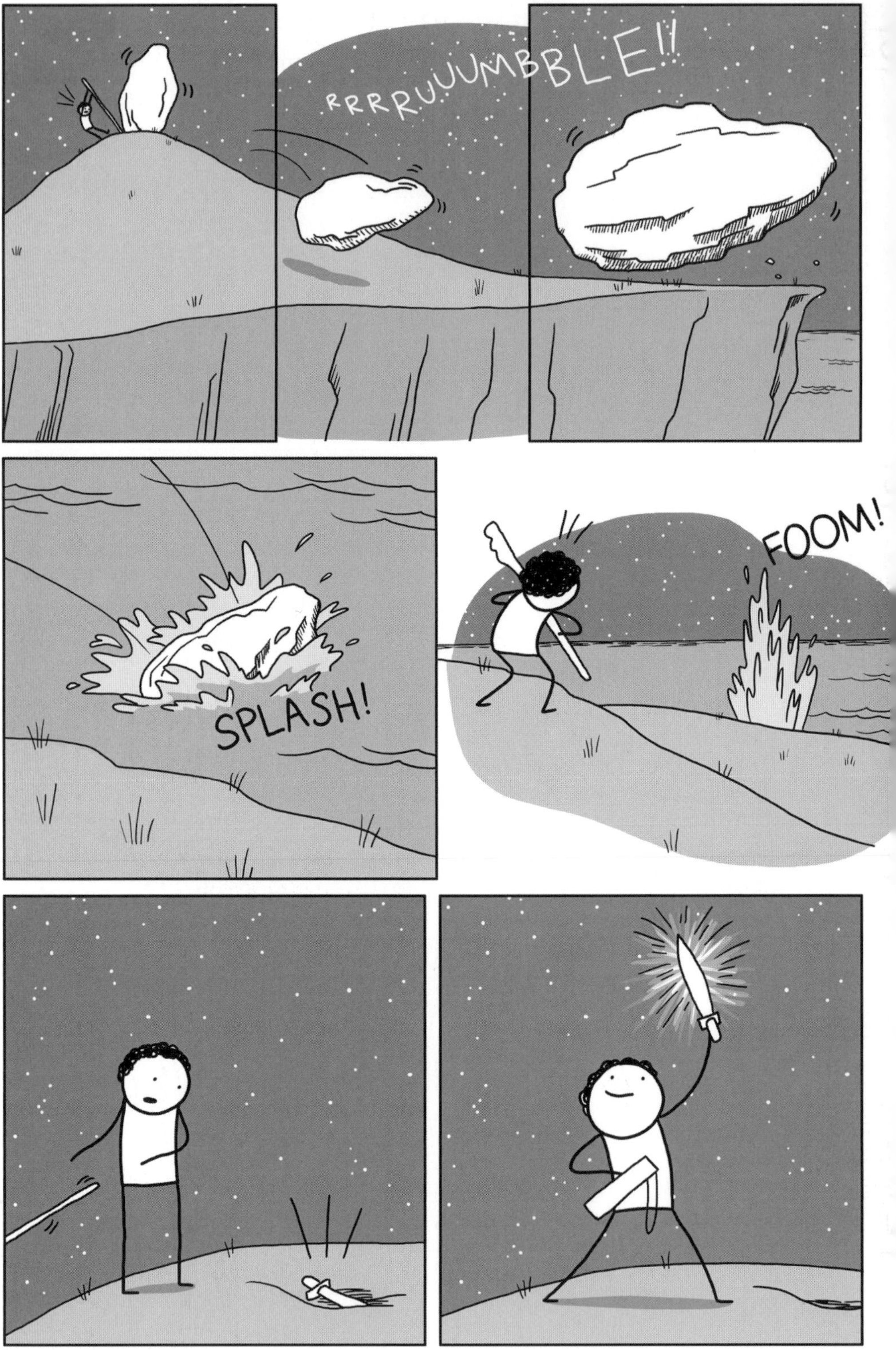
RRRRUUUMBBLE!!
SPLASH!
FOOM!

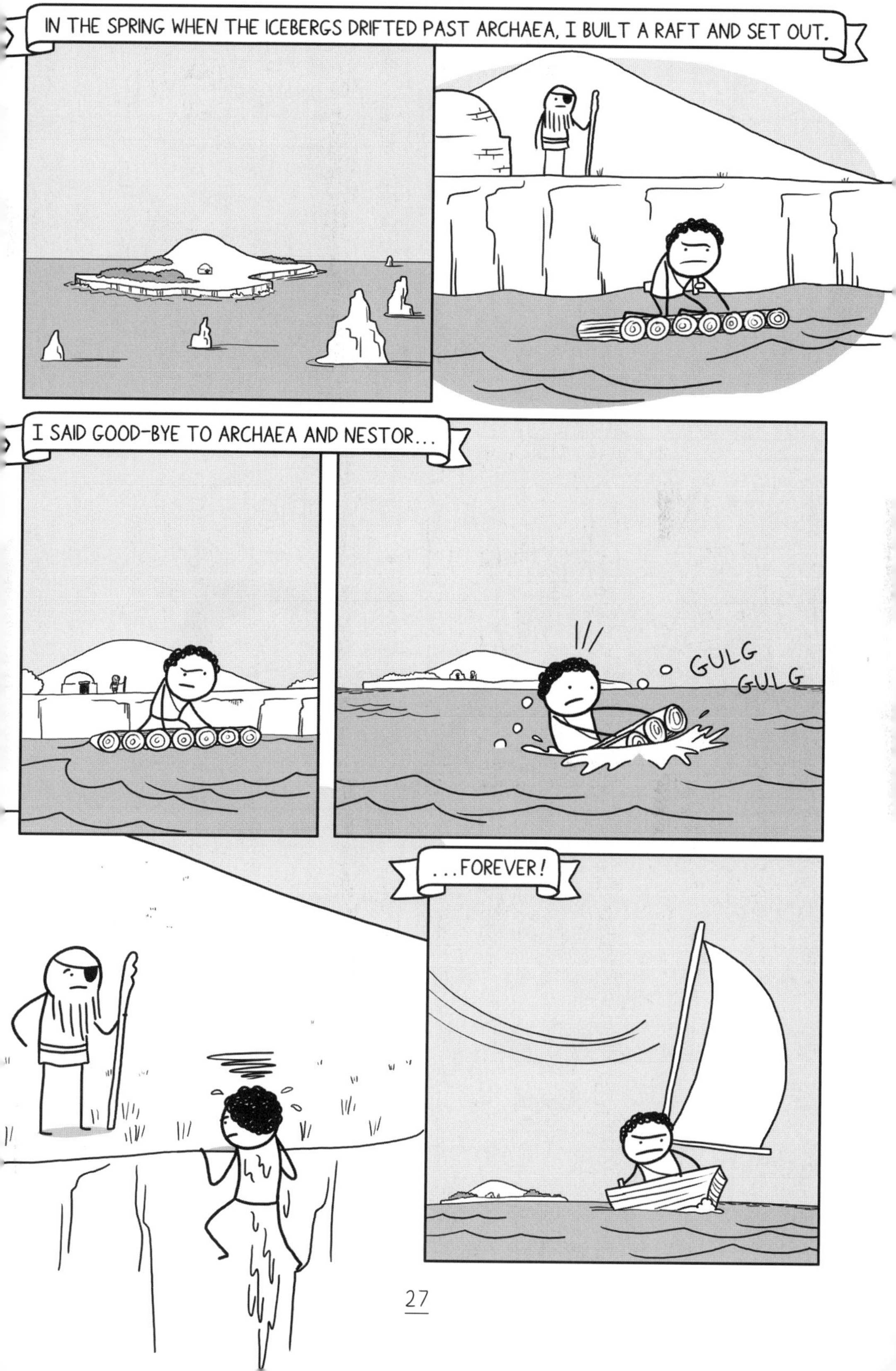
IN THE SPRING WHEN THE ICEBERGS DRIFTED PAST ARCHAEA, I BUILT A RAFT AND SET OUT.
I SAID GOOD-BYE TO ARCHAEA AND NESTOR...
GULG
GULG
...FOREVER!

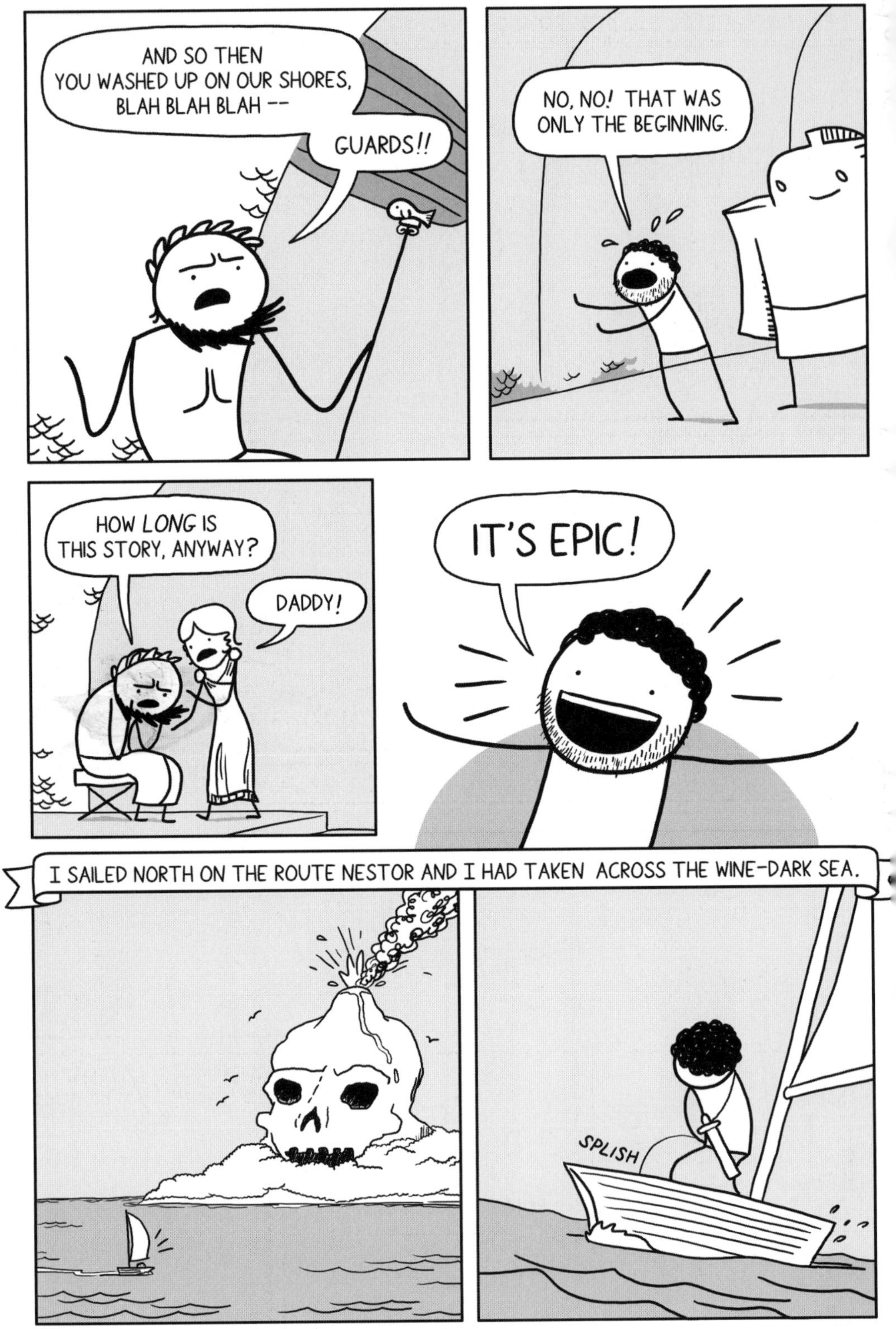
AND SO THEN YOU WASHED UP ON OUR SHORES, BLAH BLAH BLAH --
GUARDS!!
NO, NO! THAT WAS ONLY THE BEGINNING.
HOW LONG IS THIS STORY, ANYWAY?
DADDY!
IT'S EPIC!
I SAILED NORTH ON THE ROUTE NESTOR AND I HAD TAKEN ACROSS THE WINE-DARK SEA.
SPLISH

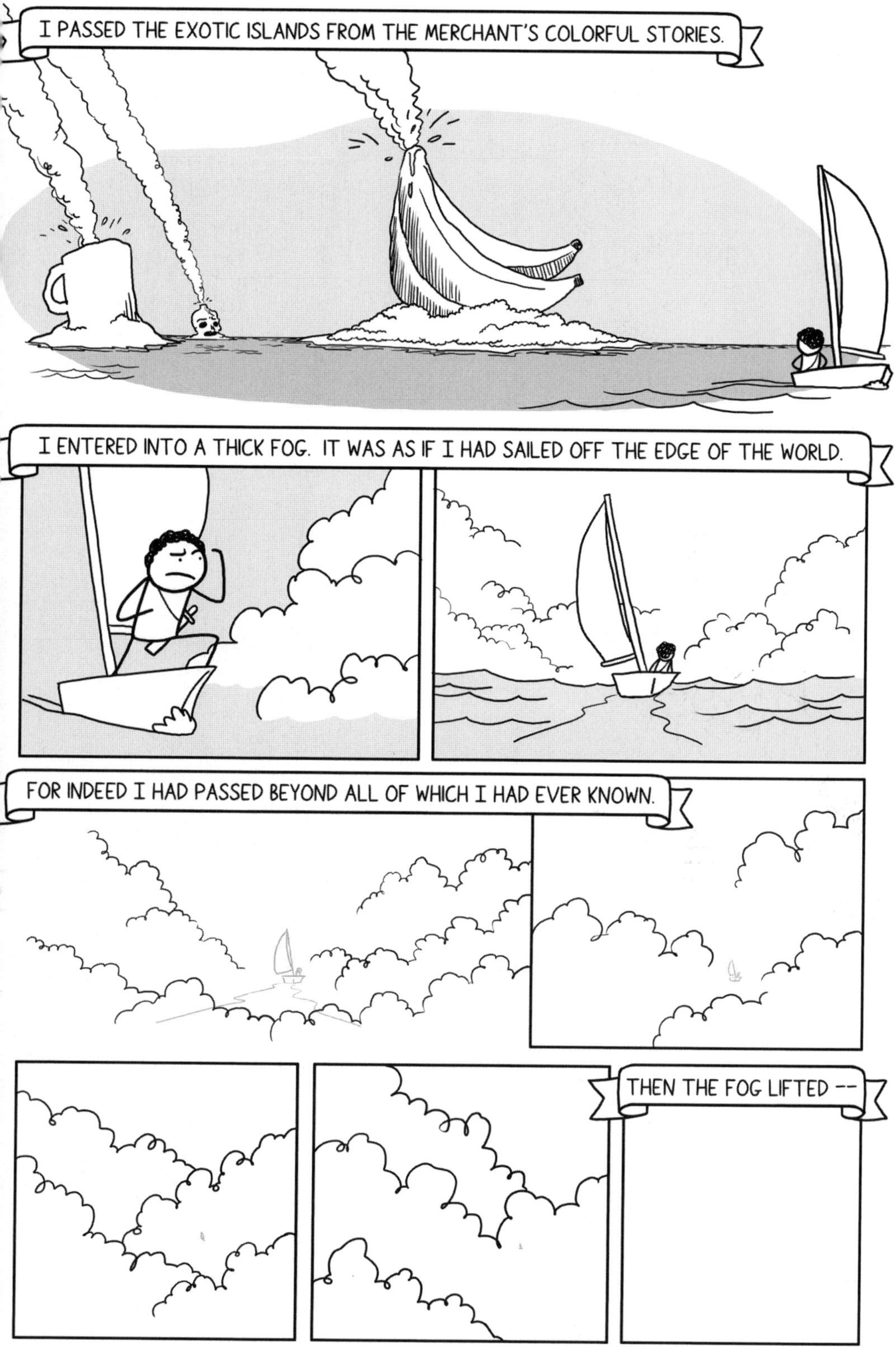
I PASSED THE EXOTIC ISLANDS FROM THE MERCHANT'S COLORFUL STORIES.
I ENTERED INTO A THICK FOG. IT WAS AS IF I HAD SAILED OFF THE EDGE OF THE WORLD.
FOR INDEED I HAD PASSED BEYOND ALL OF WHICH I HAD EVER KNOWN.
THEN THE FOG LIFTED --

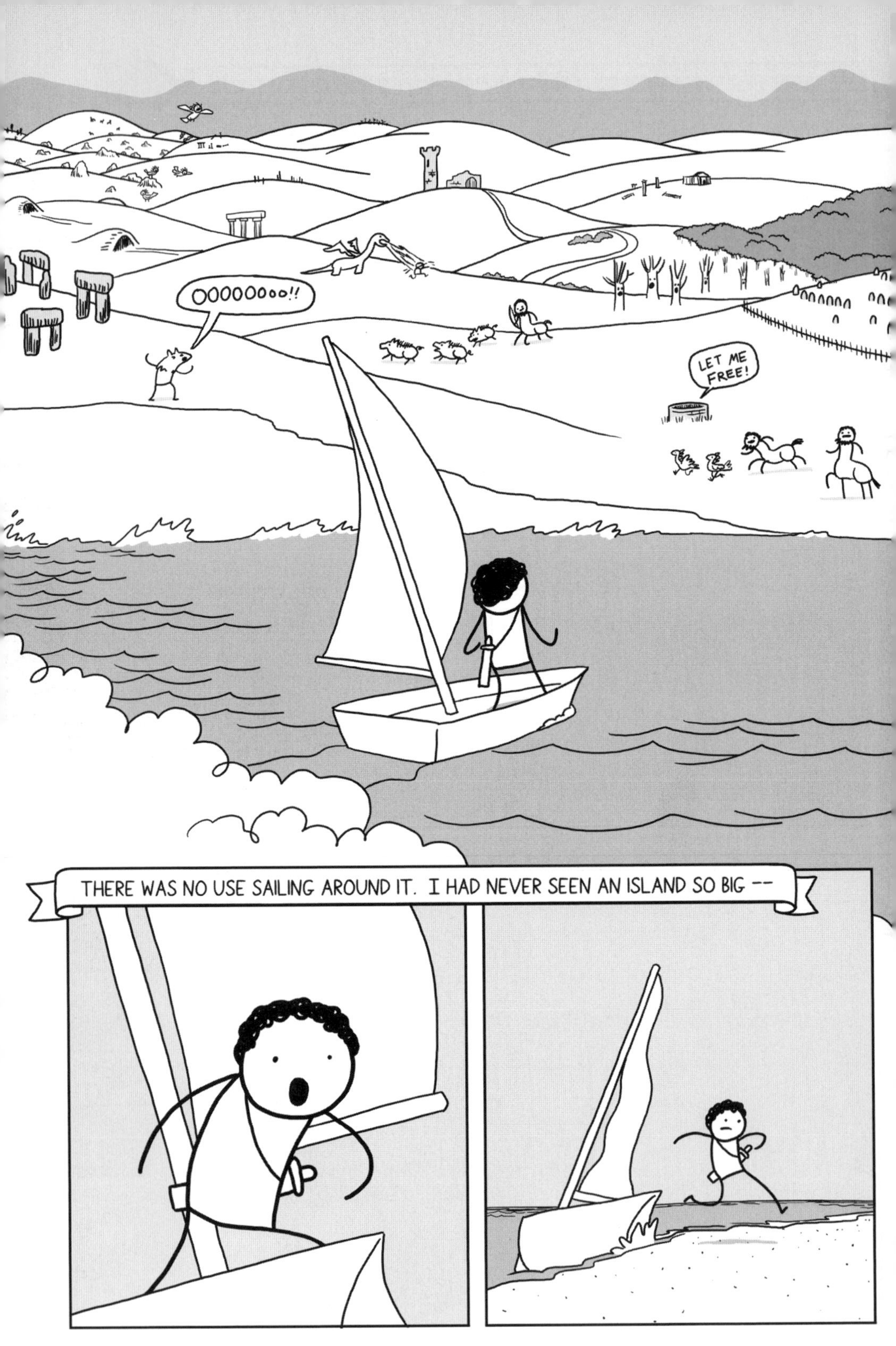
OOOOOOoo!!
LET ME FREE!
THERE WAS NO USE SAILING AROUND IT. I HAD NEVER SEEN AN ISLAND SO BIG --

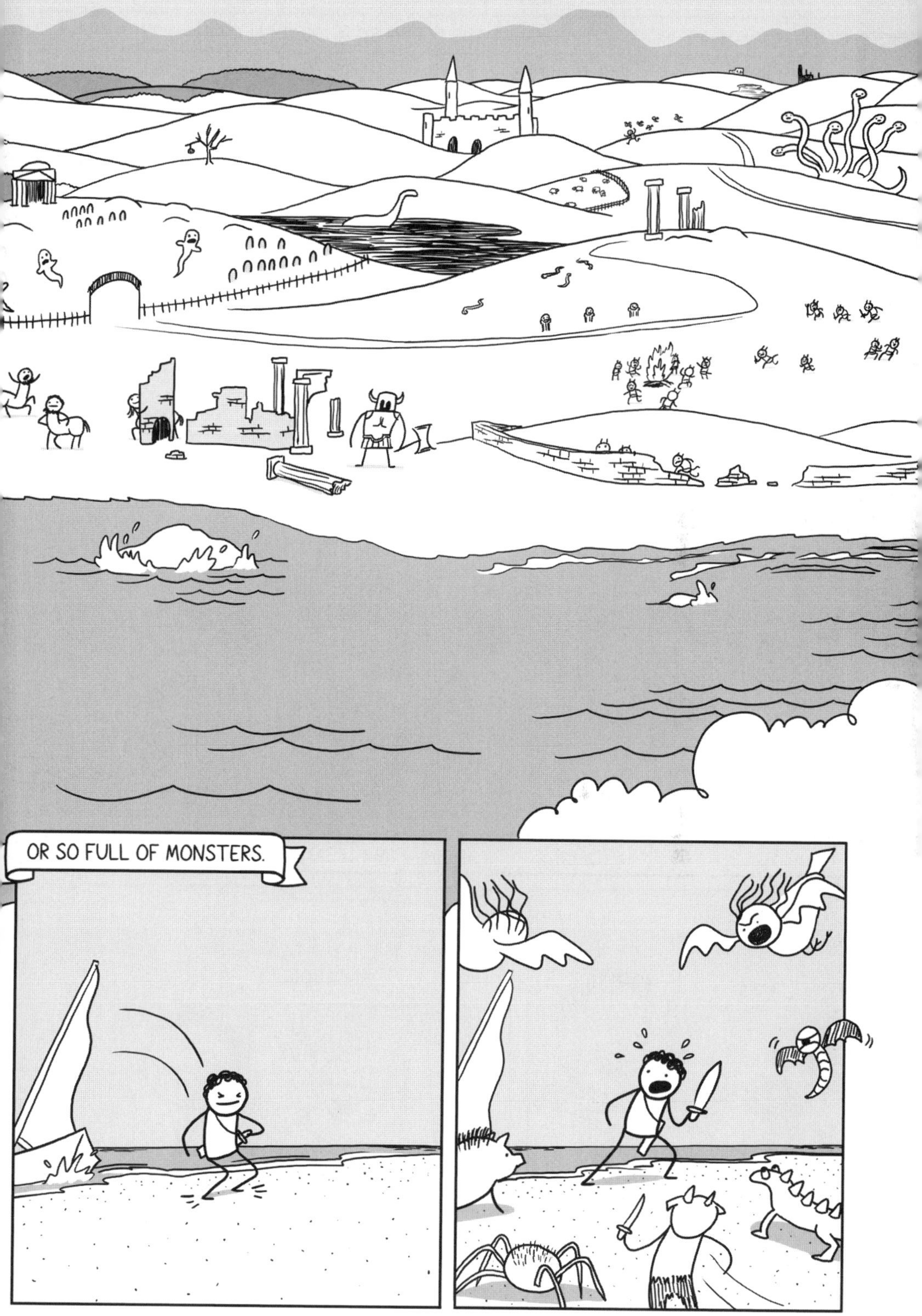
OR SO FULL OF MONSTERS.

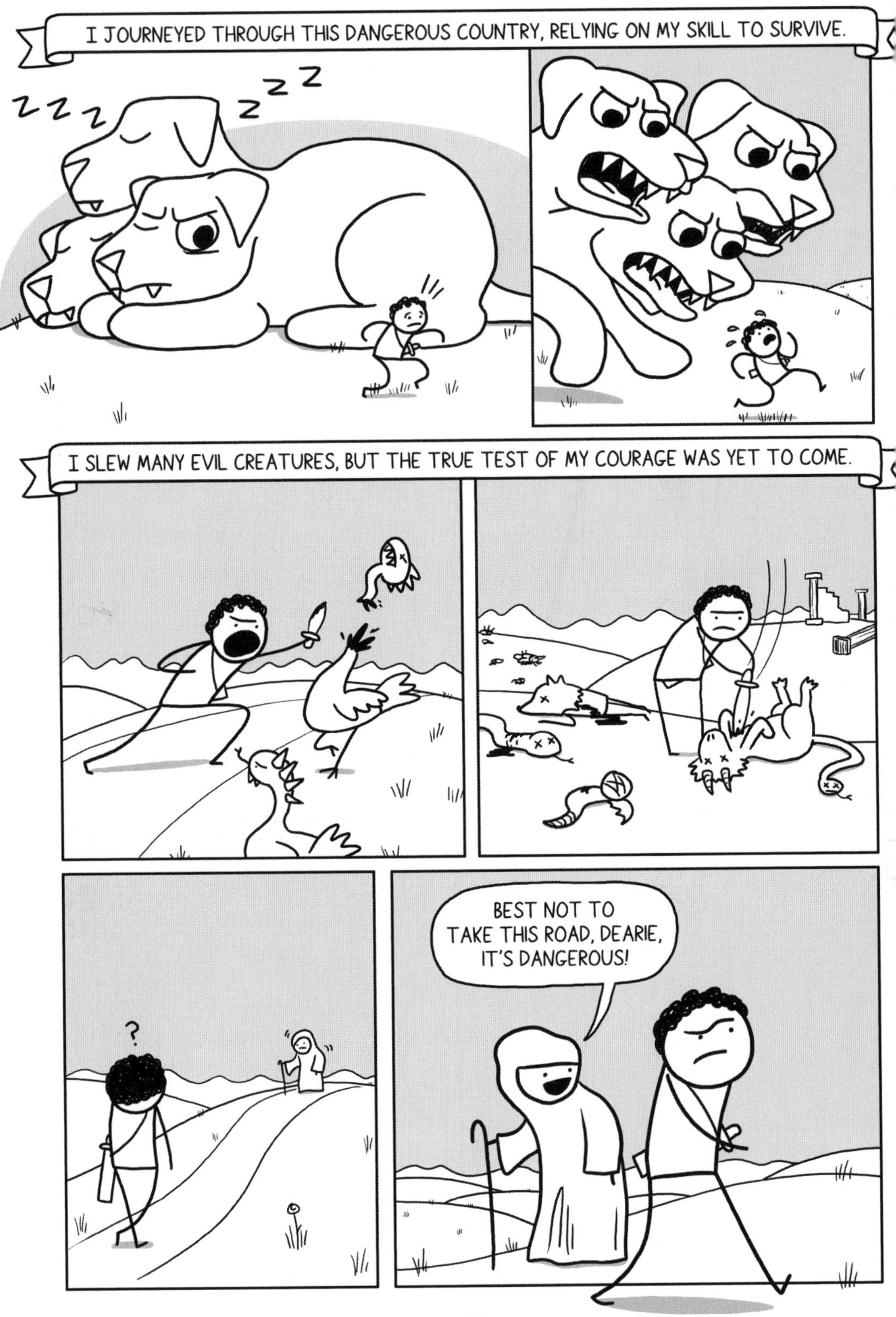
I JOURNEYED THROUGH THIS DANGEROUS COUNTRY, RELYING ON MY SKILL TO SURVIVE.
ZZZ ZZZ
I SLEW MANY EVIL CREATURES, BUT THE TRUE TEST OF MY COURAGE WAS YET TO COME.
?
BEST NOT TO TAKE THIS ROAD, DEARIE, IT'S DANGEROUS!

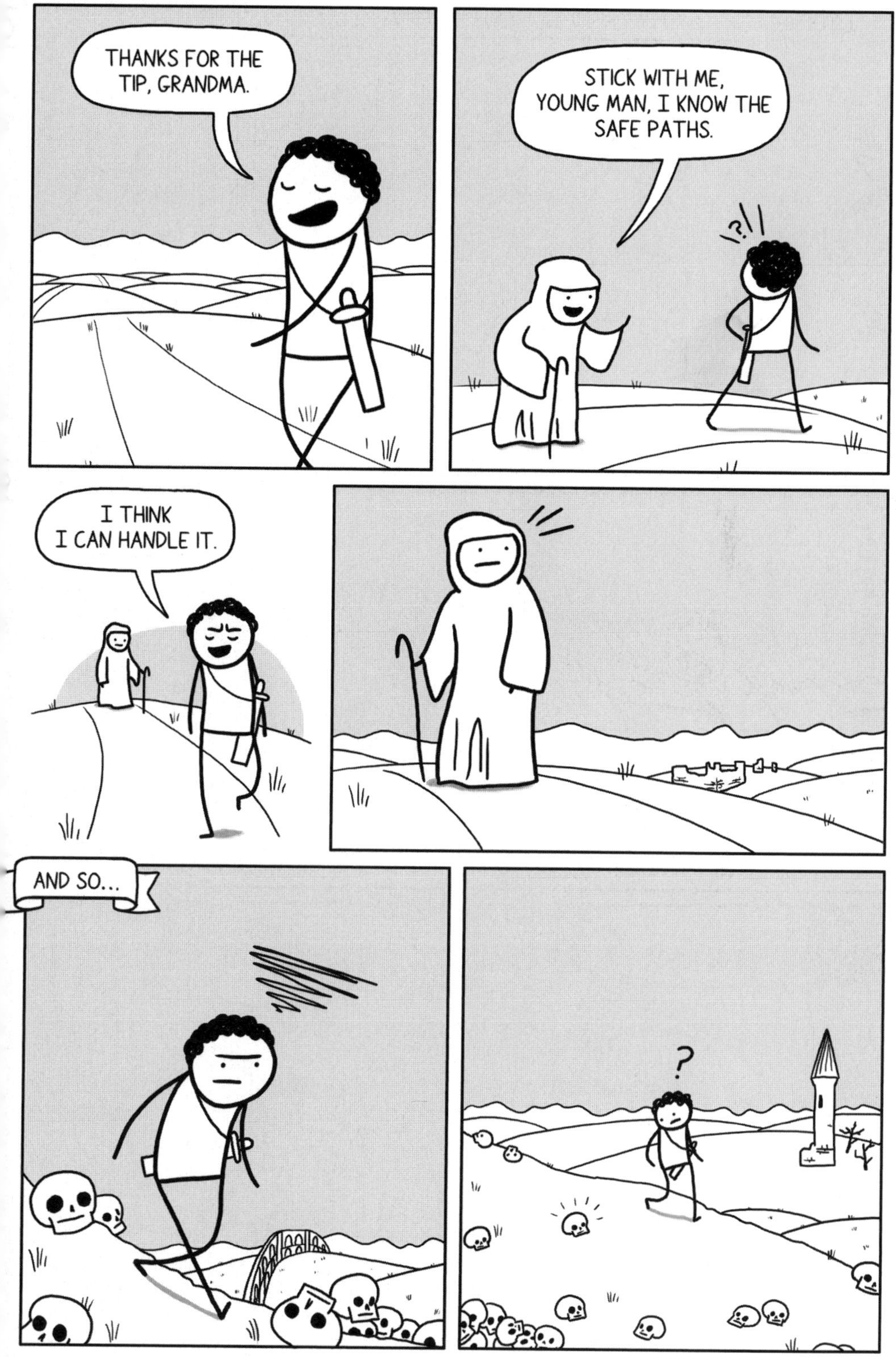
THANKS FOR THE TIP, GRANDMA.
STICK WITH ME, YOUNG MAN, I KNOW THE SAFE PATHS.
?
I THINK I CAN HANDLE IT.
AND SO...
?

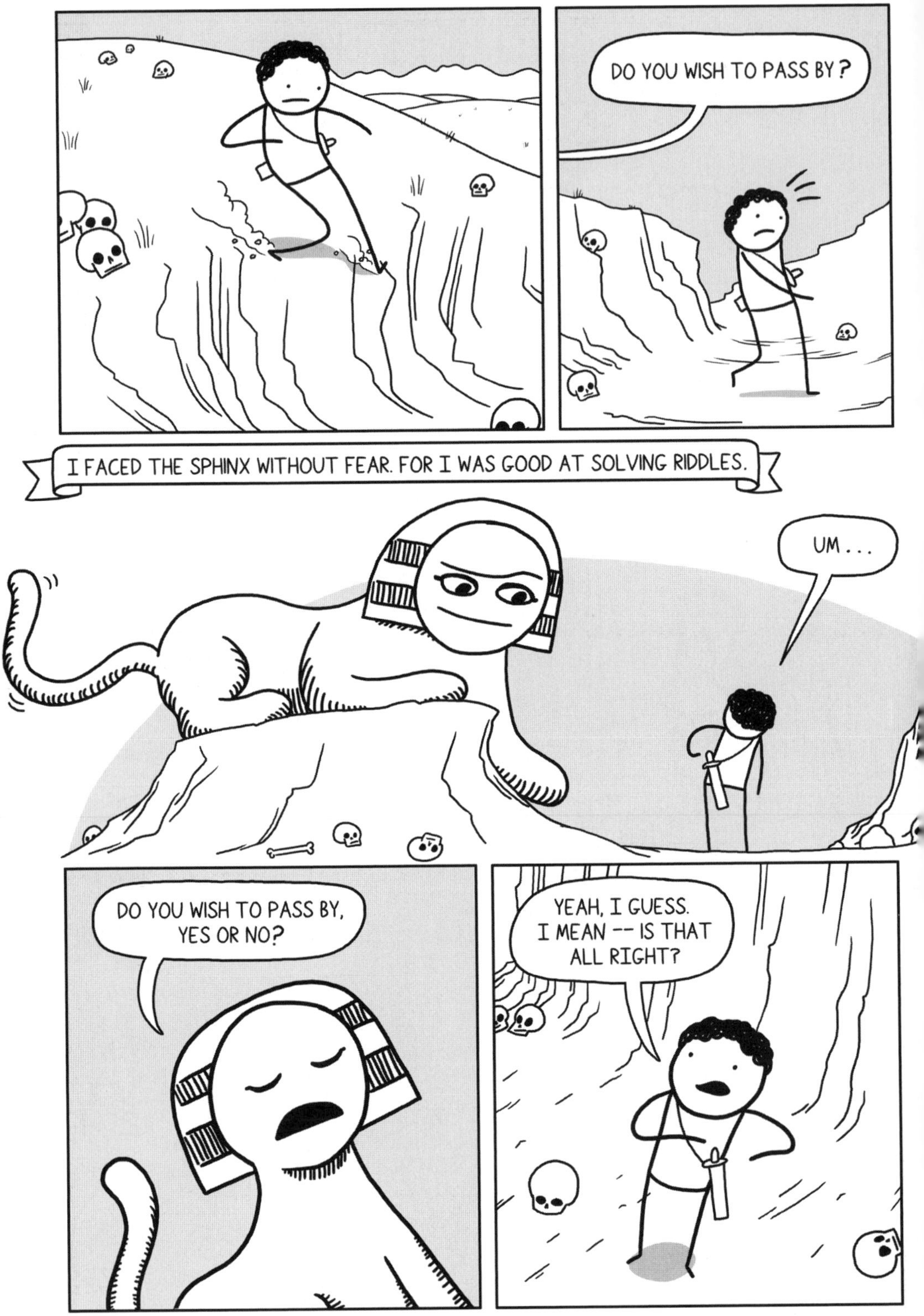
DO YOU WISH TO PASS BY?
I FACED THE SPHINX WITHOUT FEAR. FOR I WAS GOOD AT SOLVING RIDDLES.
UM . . .
DO YOU WISH TO PASS BY, YES OR NO?
YEAH, I GUESS. I MEAN -- IS THAT ALL RIGHT?

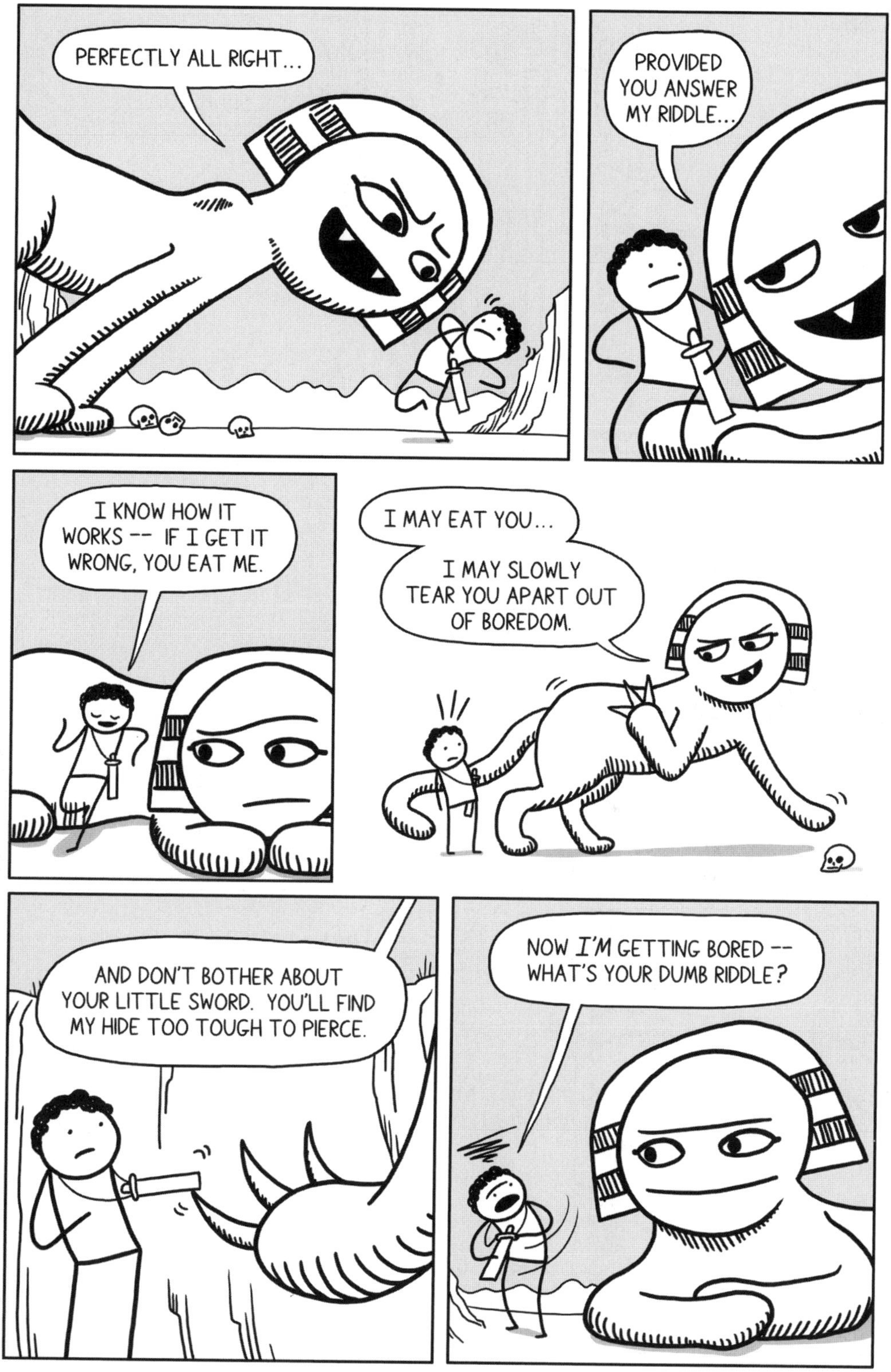
PERFECTLY ALL RIGHT...
PROVIDED YOU ANSWER MY RIDDLE...
I KNOW HOW IT WORKS -- IF I GET IT WRONG, YOU EAT ME.
I MAY EAT YOU...
I MAY SLOWLY TEAR YOU APART OUT OF BOREDOM.
AND DON'T BOTHER ABOUT YOUR LITTLE SWORD. YOU'LL FIND MY HIDE TOO TOUGH TO PIERCE.
NOW *I'M* GETTING BORED -- WHAT'S YOUR DUMB RIDDLE?

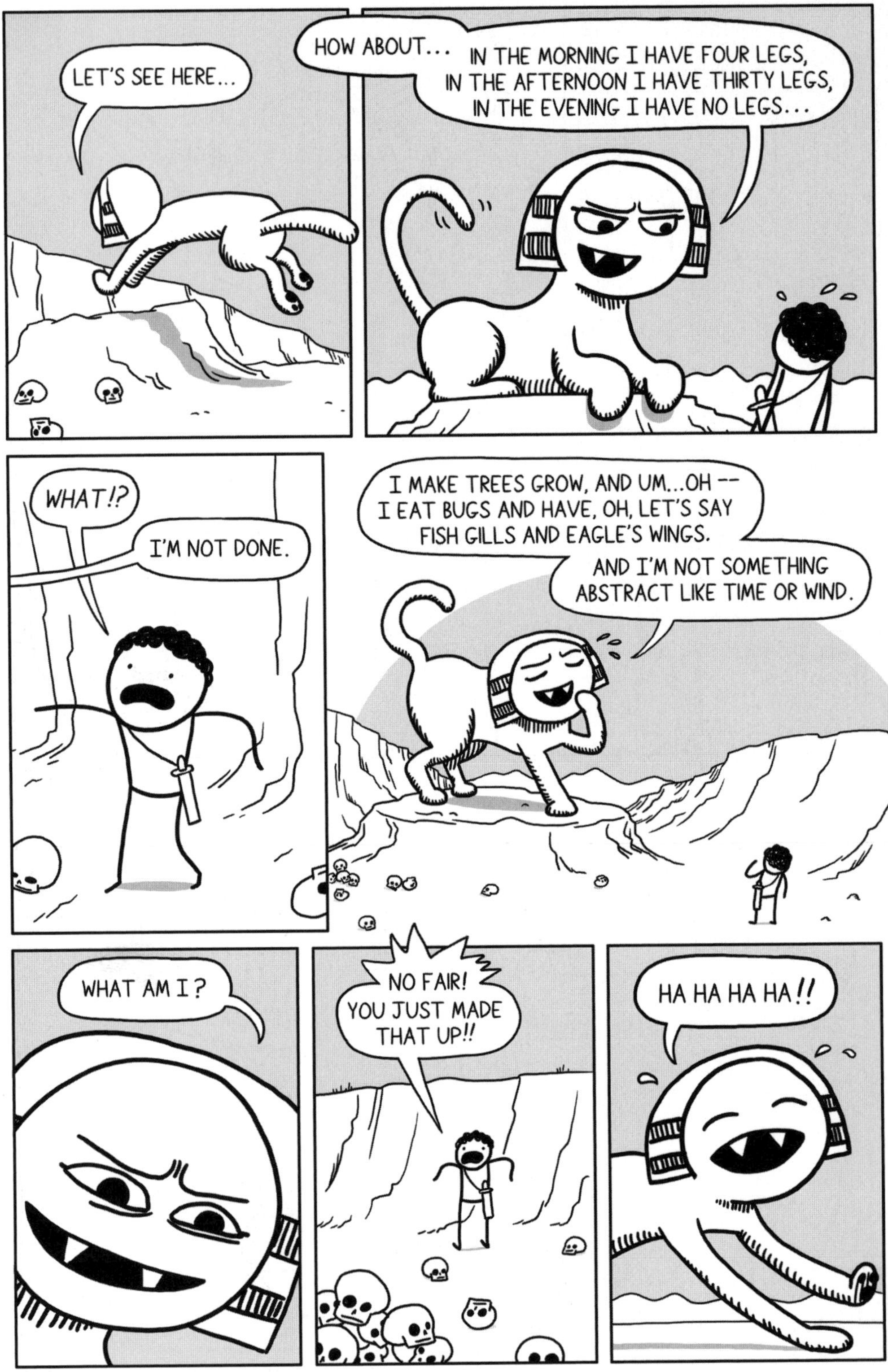
LET'S SEE HERE...
HOW ABOUT...
IN THE MORNING I HAVE FOUR LEGS, IN THE AFTERNOON I HAVE THIRTY LEGS, IN THE EVENING I HAVE NO LEGS...
WHAT!?
I'M NOT DONE.
I MAKE TREES GROW, AND UM...OH -- I EAT BUGS AND HAVE, OH, LET'S SAY FISH GILLS AND EAGLE'S WINGS.
AND I'M NOT SOMETHING ABSTRACT LIKE TIME OR WIND.
WHAT AM I?
NO FAIR! YOU JUST MADE THAT UP!!
HA HA HA HA!!

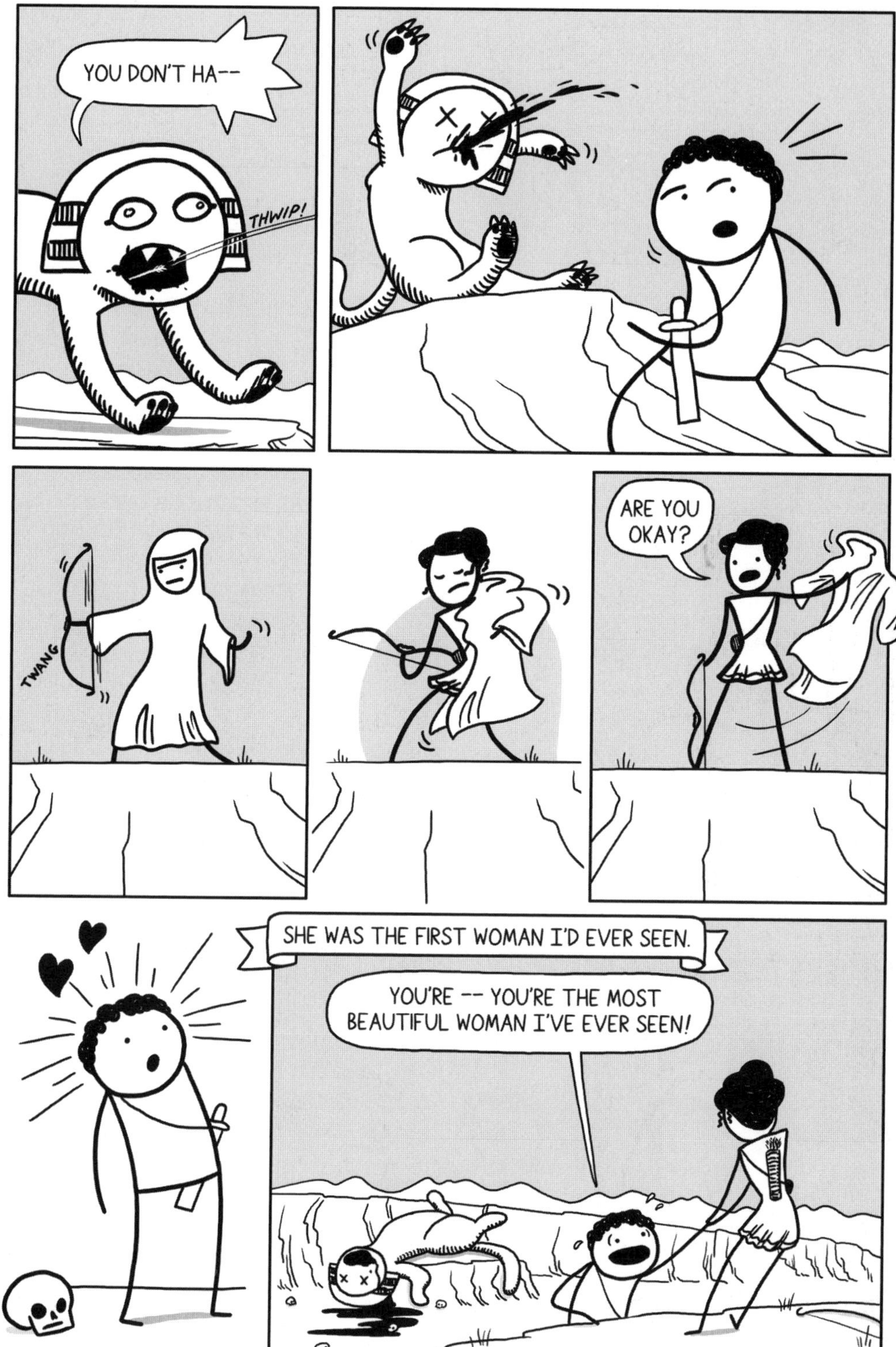
YOU DON'T HA--
THWIP!
TWANG
ARE YOU OKAY?
SHE WAS THE FIRST WOMAN I'D EVER SEEN.
YOU'RE -- YOU'RE THE MOST BEAUTIFUL WOMAN I'VE EVER SEEN!

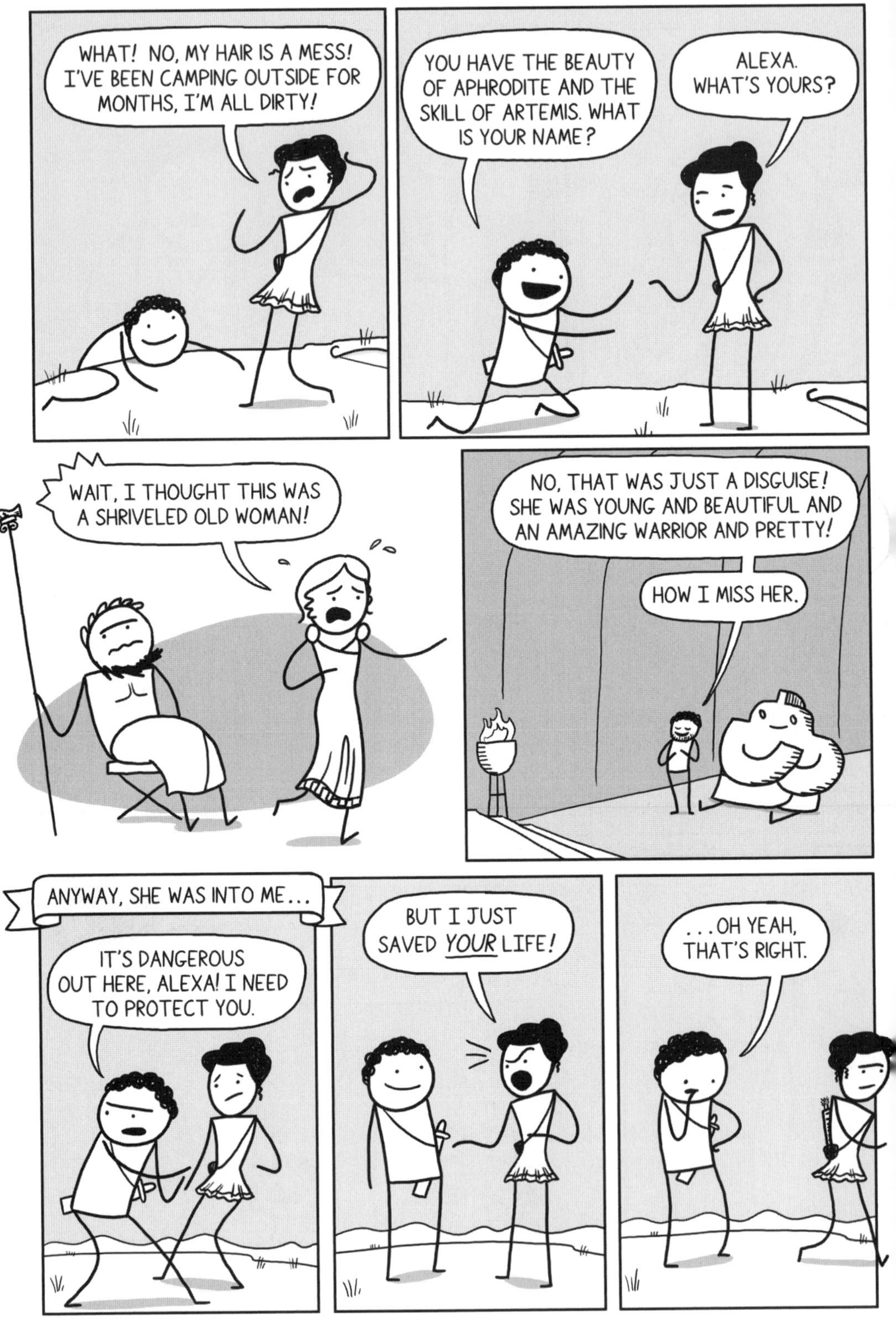
WHAT! NO, MY HAIR IS A MESS! I'VE BEEN CAMPING OUTSIDE FOR MONTHS, I'M ALL DIRTY!
YOU HAVE THE BEAUTY OF APHRODITE AND THE SKILL OF ARTEMIS. WHAT IS YOUR NAME?
ALEXA. WHAT'S YOURS?
WAIT, I THOUGHT THIS WAS A SHRIVELED OLD WOMAN!
NO, THAT WAS JUST A DISGUISE! SHE WAS YOUNG AND BEAUTIFUL AND AN AMAZING WARRIOR AND PRETTY!
HOW I MISS HER.
ANYWAY, SHE WAS INTO ME...
IT'S DANGEROUS OUT HERE, ALEXA! I NEED TO PROTECT YOU.
BUT I JUST SAVED YOUR LIFE!
...OH YEAH, THAT'S RIGHT.

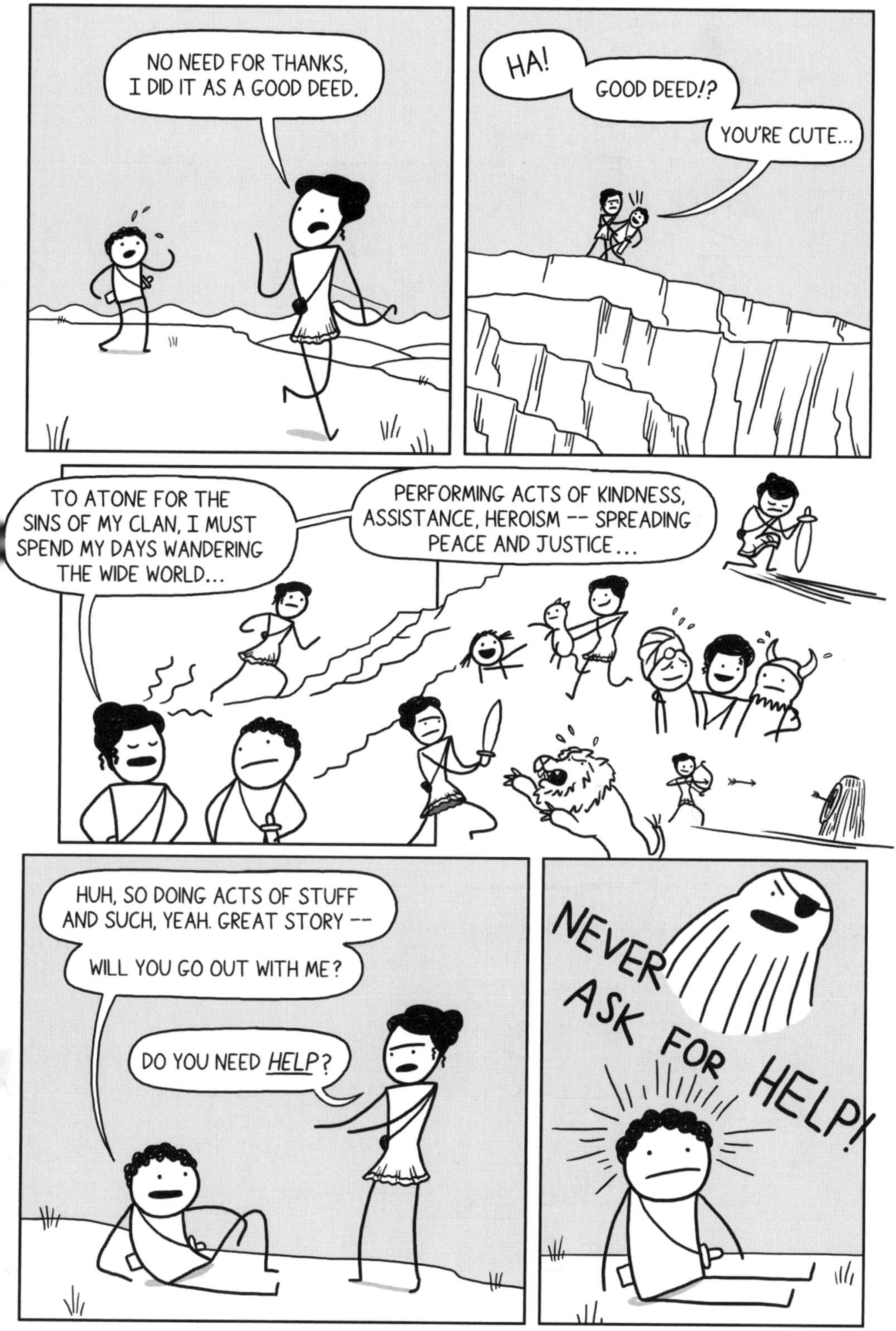
NO NEED FOR THANKS, I DID IT AS A GOOD DEED.
HA!
GOOD DEED!?
YOU'RE CUTE...
TO ATONE FOR THE SINS OF MY CLAN, I MUST SPEND MY DAYS WANDERING THE WIDE WORLD...
PERFORMING ACTS OF KINDNESS, ASSISTANCE, HEROISM -- SPREADING PEACE AND JUSTICE...
HUH, SO DOING ACTS OF STUFF AND SUCH, YEAH. GREAT STORY --
WILL YOU GO OUT WITH ME?
DO YOU NEED HELP?
NEVER ASK FOR HELP!

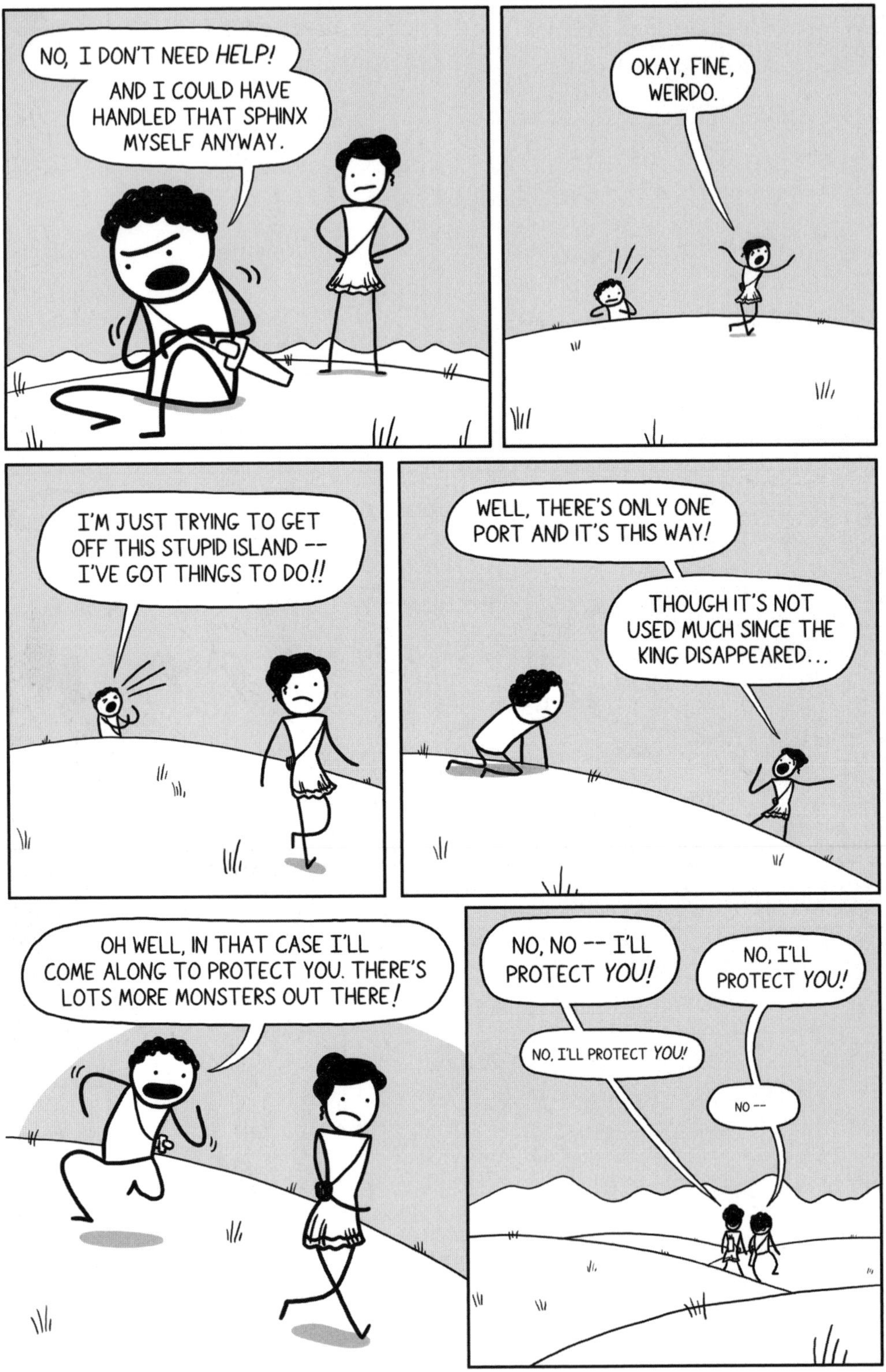
NO, I DON'T NEED *HELP!*
AND I COULD HAVE HANDLED THAT SPHINX MYSELF ANYWAY.
OKAY, FINE, WEIRDO.
I'M JUST TRYING TO GET OFF THIS STUPID ISLAND -- I'VE GOT THINGS TO DO!!
WELL, THERE'S ONLY ONE PORT AND IT'S THIS WAY!
THOUGH IT'S NOT USED MUCH SINCE THE KING DISAPPEARED...
OH WELL, IN THAT CASE I'LL COME ALONG TO PROTECT YOU. THERE'S LOTS MORE MONSTERS OUT THERE!
NO, NO -- I'LL PROTECT *YOU!*
NO, I'LL PROTECT *YOU!*
NO, I'LL PROTECT *YOU!*
NO --

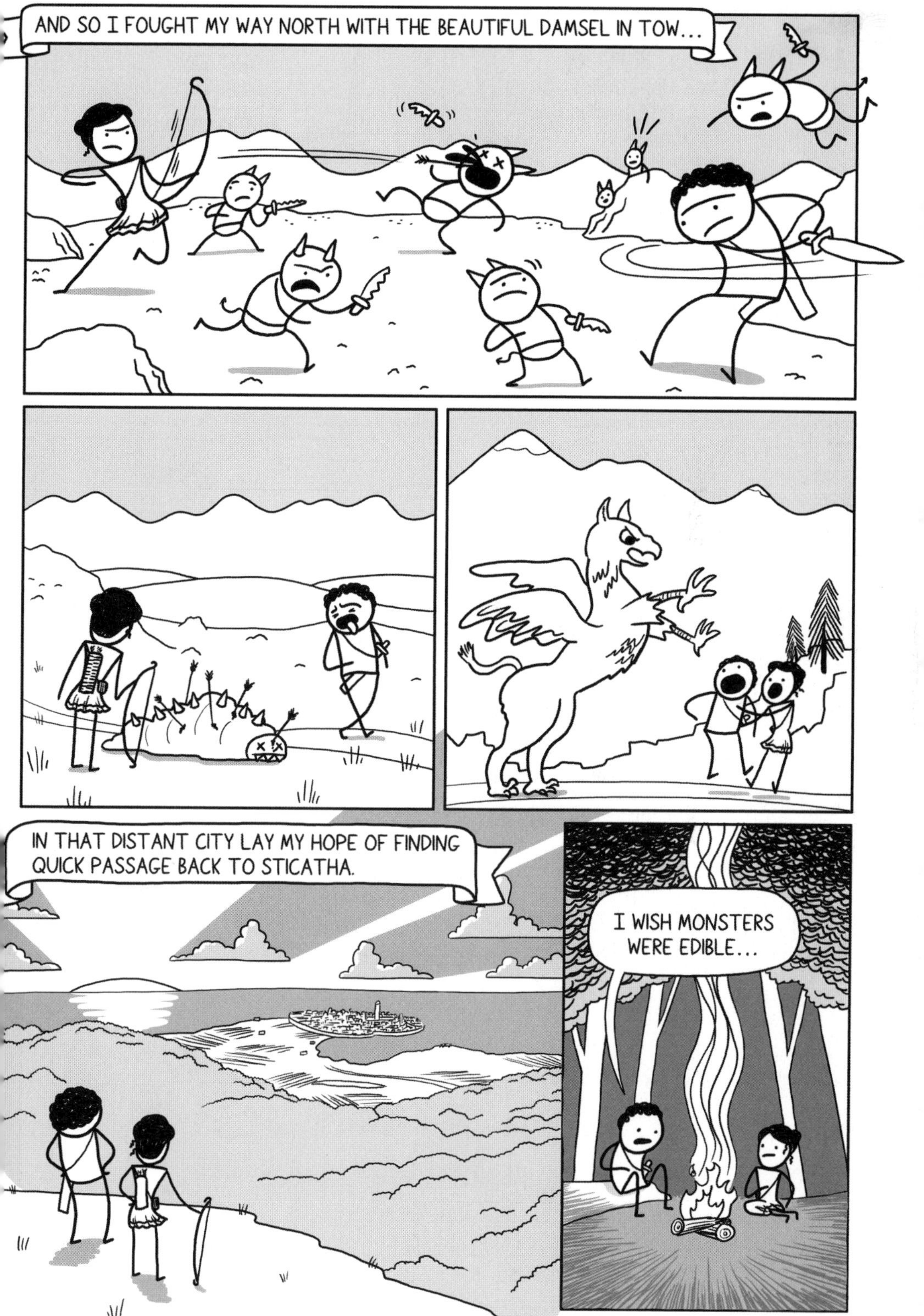
AND SO I FOUGHT MY WAY NORTH WITH THE BEAUTIFUL DAMSEL IN TOW...
IN THAT DISTANT CITY LAY MY HOPE OF FINDING QUICK PASSAGE BACK TO STICATHA.
I WISH MONSTERS WERE EDIBLE...

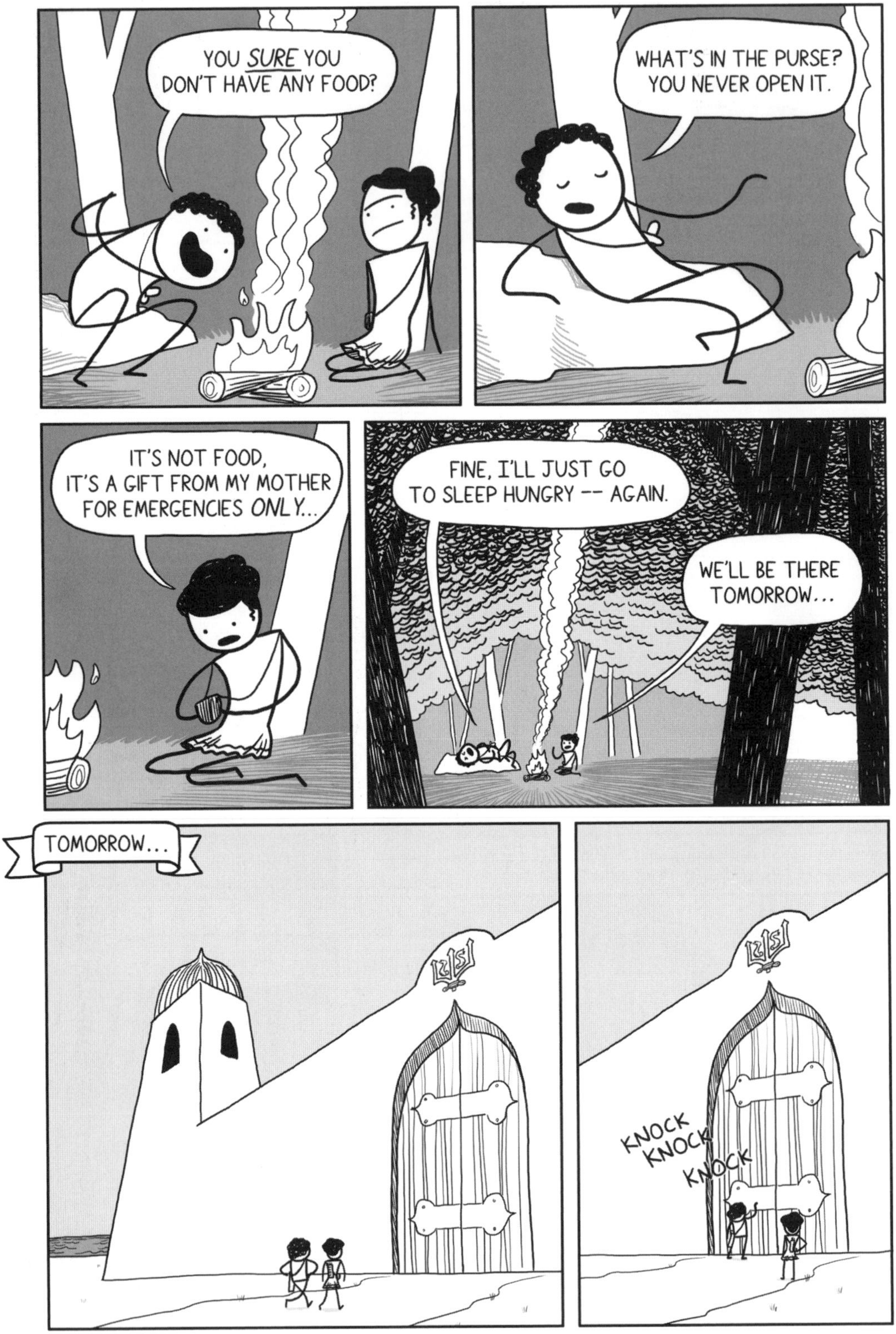
YOU SURE YOU DON'T HAVE ANY FOOD?
WHAT'S IN THE PURSE? YOU NEVER OPEN IT.
IT'S NOT FOOD, IT'S A GIFT FROM MY MOTHER FOR EMERGENCIES ONLY...
FINE, I'LL JUST GO TO SLEEP HUNGRY -- AGAIN.
WE'LL BE THERE TOMORROW...
TOMORROW...
KNOCK
KNOCK
KNOCK

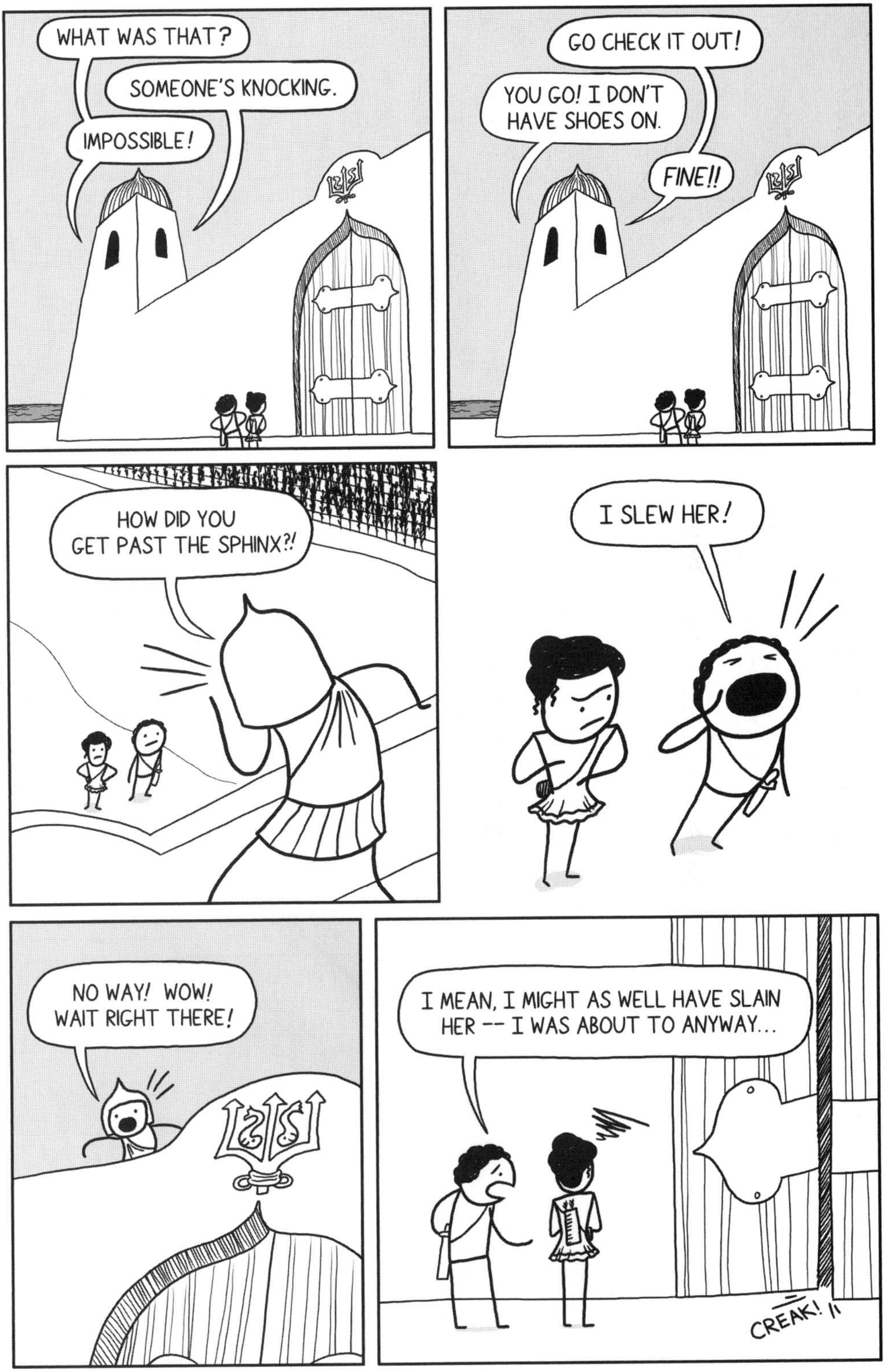
WHAT WAS THAT?
SOMEONE'S KNOCKING.
IMPOSSIBLE!
GO CHECK IT OUT!
YOU GO! I DON'T HAVE SHOES ON.
FINE!!
HOW DID YOU GET PAST THE SPHINX?!
I SLEW HER!
NO WAY! WOW! WAIT RIGHT THERE!
I MEAN, I MIGHT AS WELL HAVE SLAIN HER -- I WAS ABOUT TO ANYWAY...
CREAK!

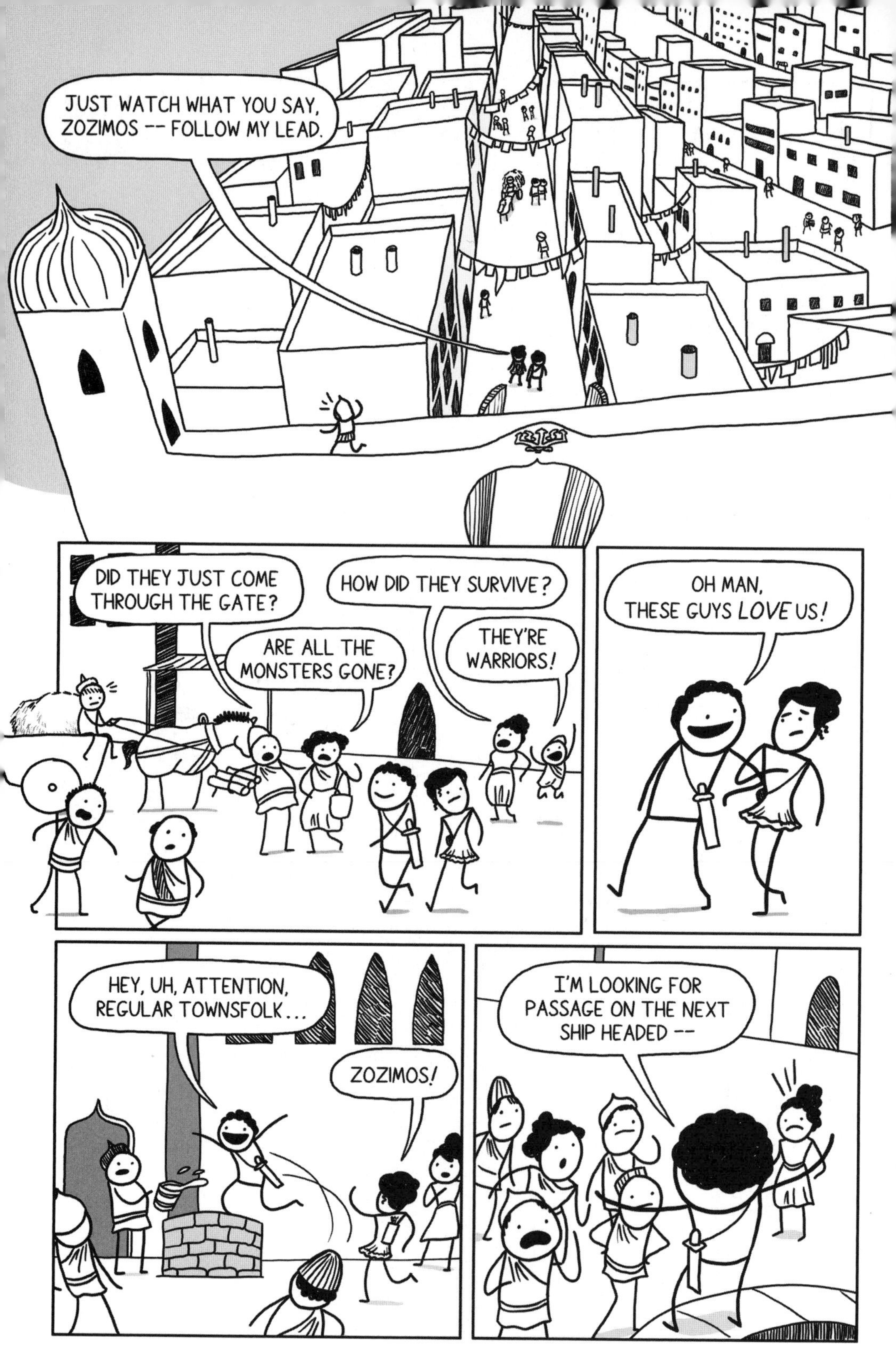
JUST WATCH WHAT YOU SAY, ZOZIMOS -- FOLLOW MY LEAD.
DID THEY JUST COME THROUGH THE GATE?
ARE ALL THE MONSTERS GONE?
HOW DID THEY SURVIVE?
THEY'RE WARRIORS!
OH MAN, THESE GUYS *LOVE* US!
HEY, UH, ATTENTION, REGULAR TOWNSFOLK...
ZOZIMOS!
I'M LOOKING FOR PASSAGE ON THE NEXT SHIP HEADED --

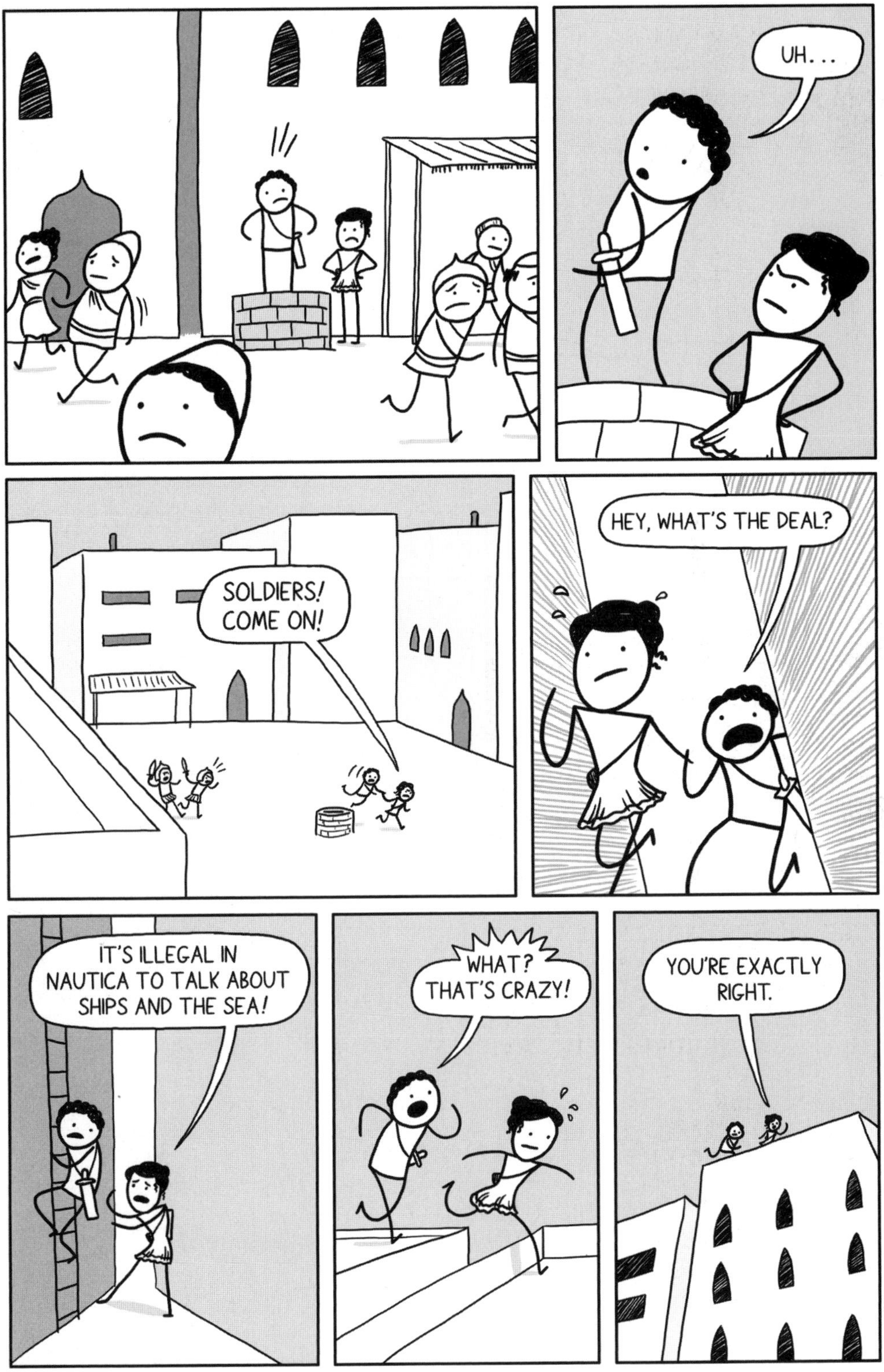
UH...
SOLDIERS! COME ON!
HEY, WHAT'S THE DEAL?
IT'S ILLEGAL IN NAUTICA TO TALK ABOUT SHIPS AND THE SEA!
WHAT? THAT'S CRAZY!
YOU'RE EXACTLY RIGHT.

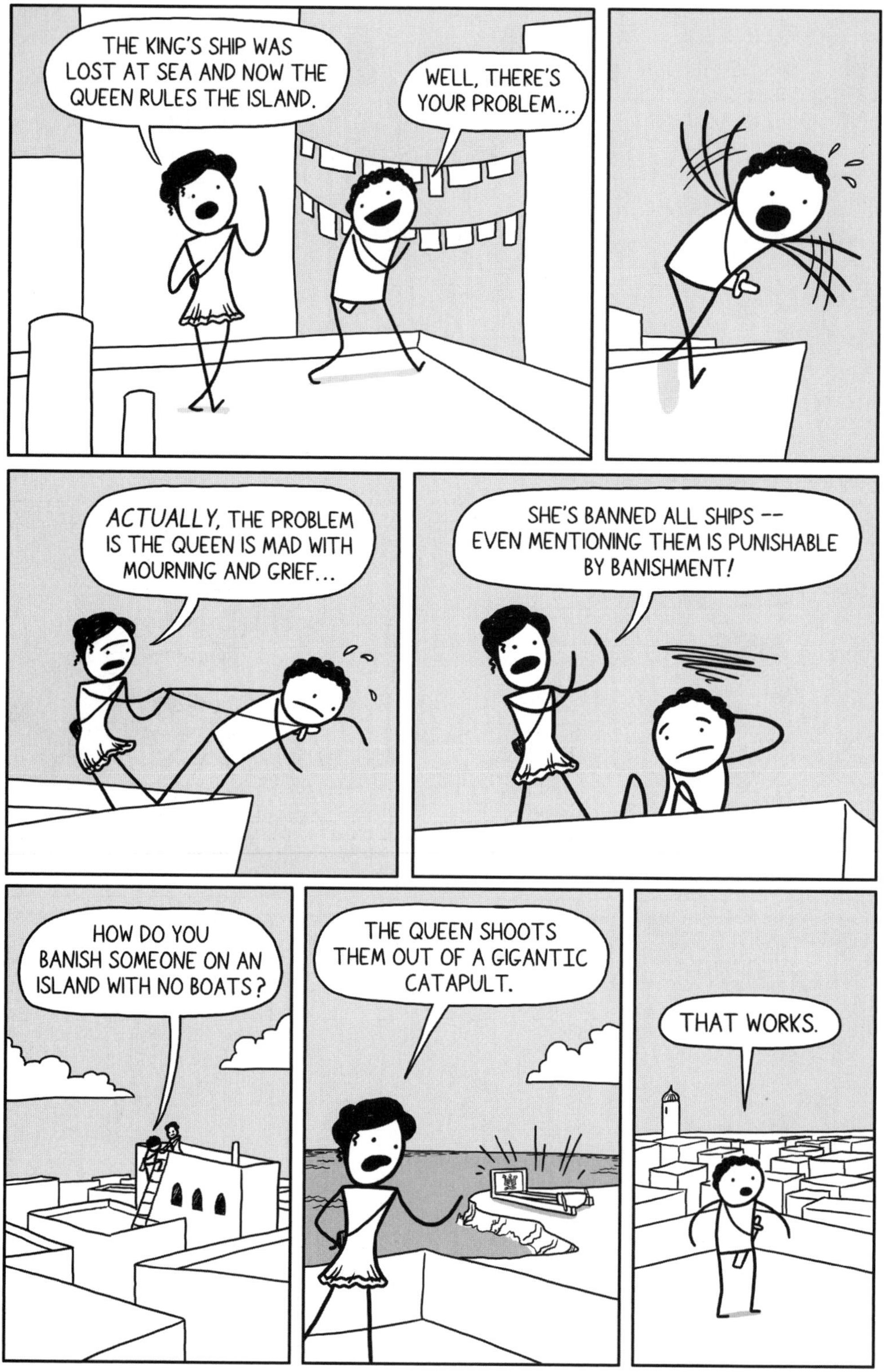
THE KING'S SHIP WAS LOST AT SEA AND NOW THE QUEEN RULES THE ISLAND.
WELL, THERE'S YOUR PROBLEM...
ACTUALLY, THE PROBLEM IS THE QUEEN IS MAD WITH MOURNING AND GRIEF...
SHE'S BANNED ALL SHIPS -- EVEN MENTIONING THEM IS PUNISHABLE BY BANISHMENT!
HOW DO YOU BANISH SOMEONE ON AN ISLAND WITH NO BOATS?
THE QUEEN SHOOTS THEM OUT OF A GIGANTIC CATAPULT.
THAT WORKS.

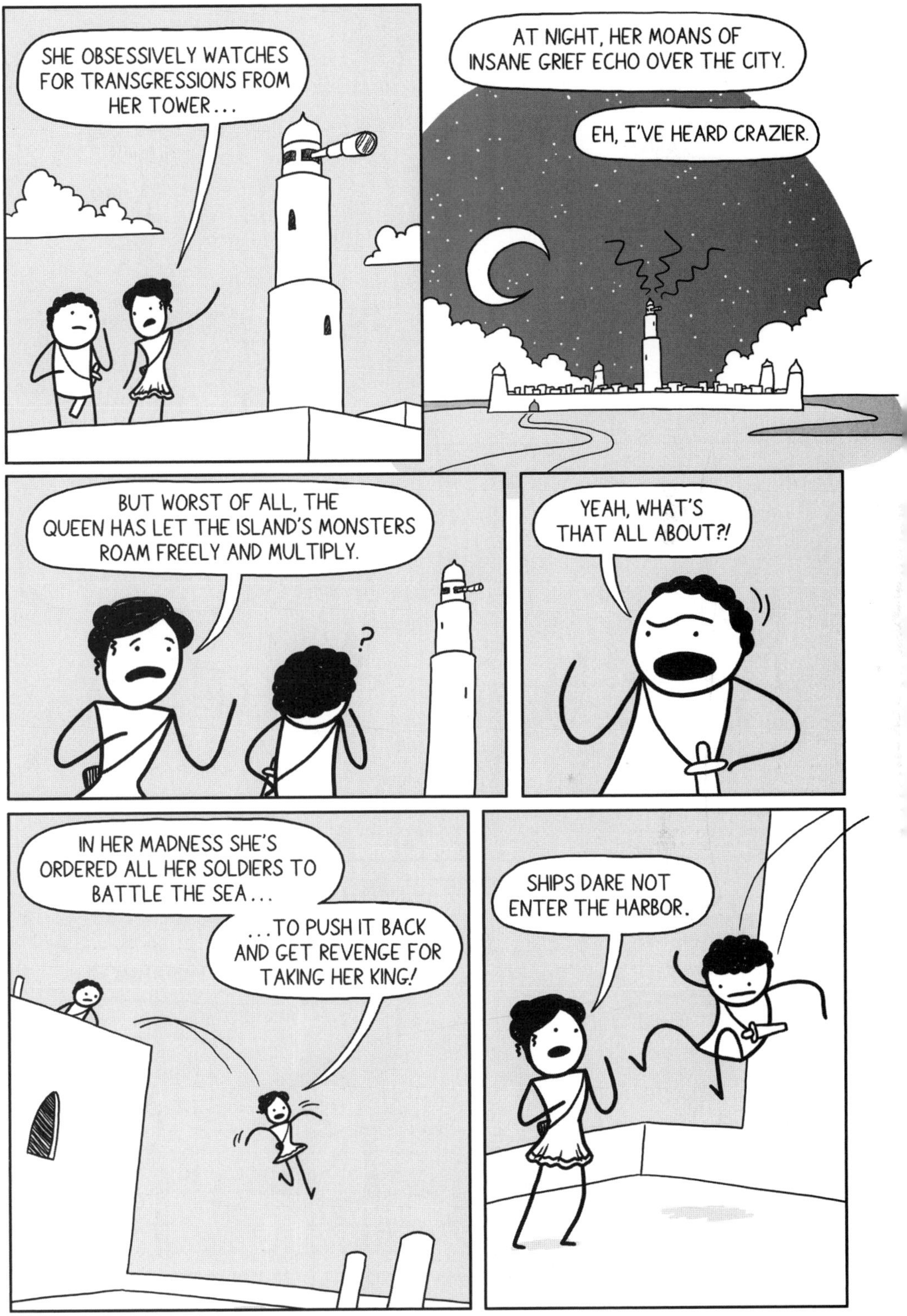
SHE OBSESSIVELY WATCHES FOR TRANSGRESSIONS FROM HER TOWER...
AT NIGHT, HER MOANS OF INSANE GRIEF ECHO OVER THE CITY.
EH, I'VE HEARD CRAZIER.
BUT WORST OF ALL, THE QUEEN HAS LET THE ISLAND'S MONSTERS ROAM FREELY AND MULTIPLY.
YEAH, WHAT'S THAT ALL ABOUT?!
IN HER MADNESS SHE'S ORDERED ALL HER SOLDIERS TO BATTLE THE SEA...
...TO PUSH IT BACK AND GET REVENGE FOR TAKING HER KING!
SHIPS DARE NOT ENTER THE HARBOR.

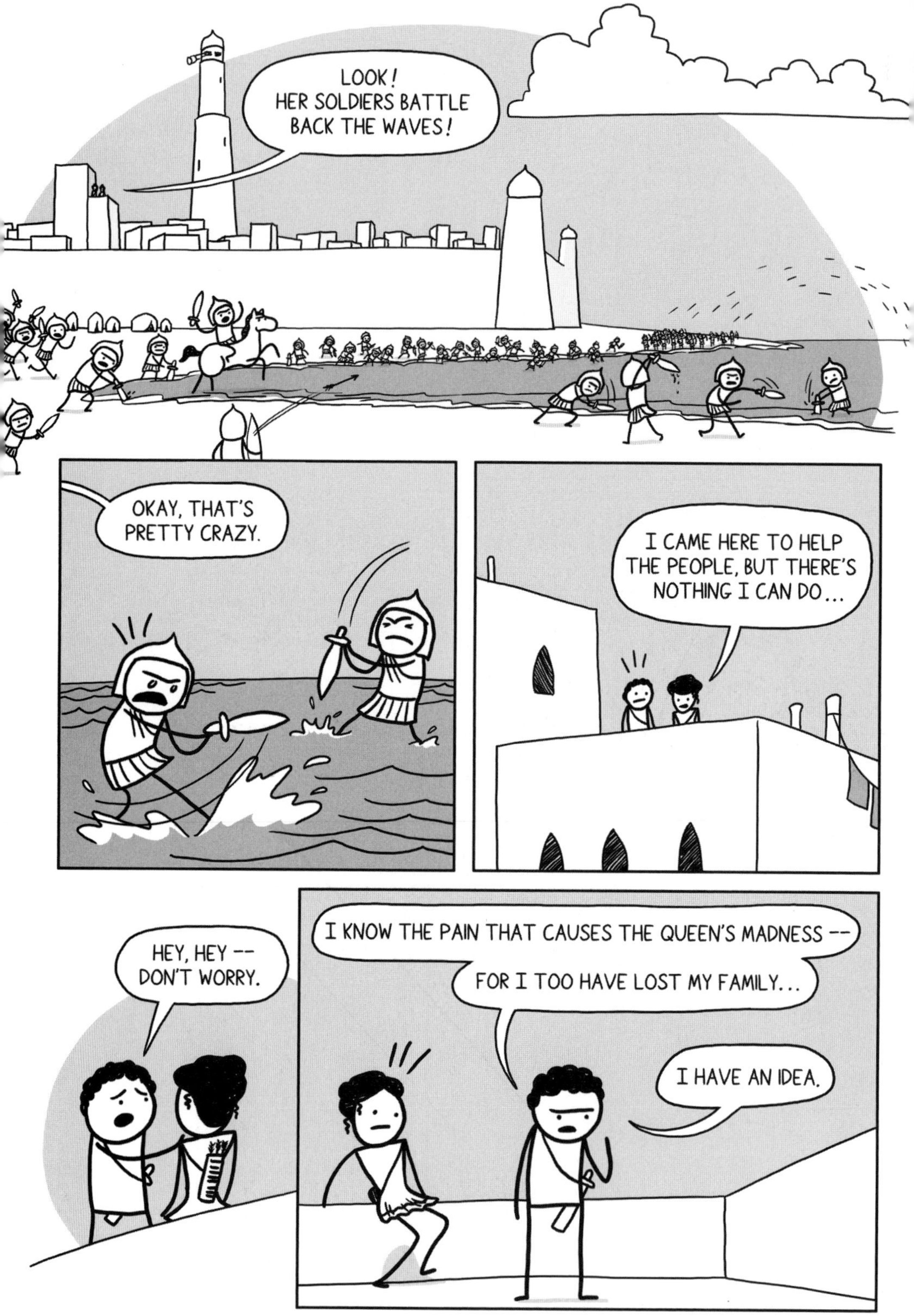
LOOK!
HER SOLDIERS BATTLE BACK THE WAVES!
OKAY, THAT'S PRETTY CRAZY.
I CAME HERE TO HELP THE PEOPLE, BUT THERE'S NOTHING I CAN DO...
HEY, HEY -- DON'T WORRY.
I KNOW THE PAIN THAT CAUSES THE QUEEN'S MADNESS --
FOR I TOO HAVE LOST MY FAMILY...
I HAVE AN IDEA.

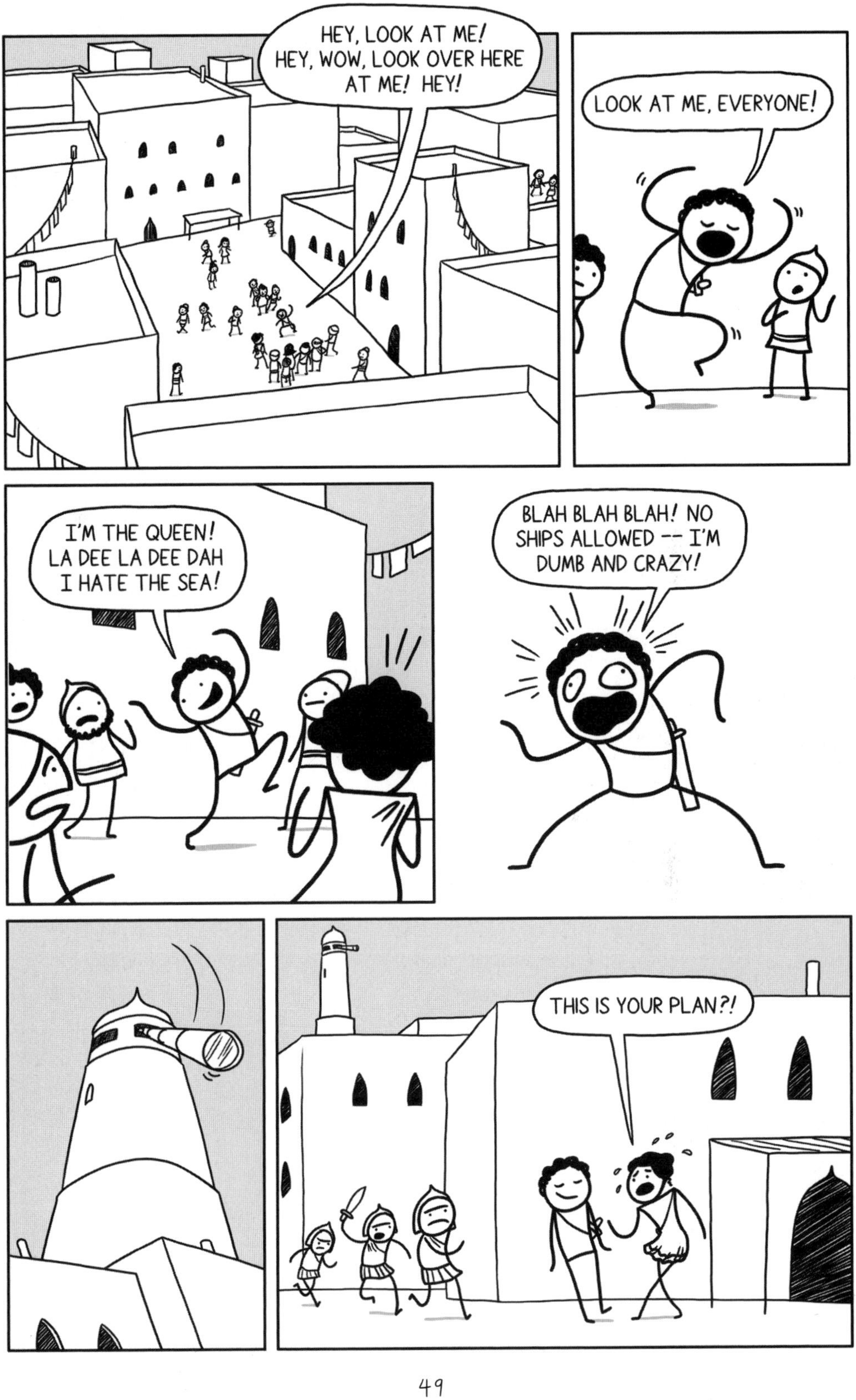
HEY, LOOK AT ME! HEY, WOW, LOOK OVER HERE AT ME! HEY!
LOOK AT ME, EVERYONE!
I'M THE QUEEN! LA DEE LA DEE DAH I HATE THE SEA!
BLAH BLAH BLAH! NO SHIPS ALLOWED -- I'M DUMB AND CRAZY!
THIS IS YOUR PLAN?!

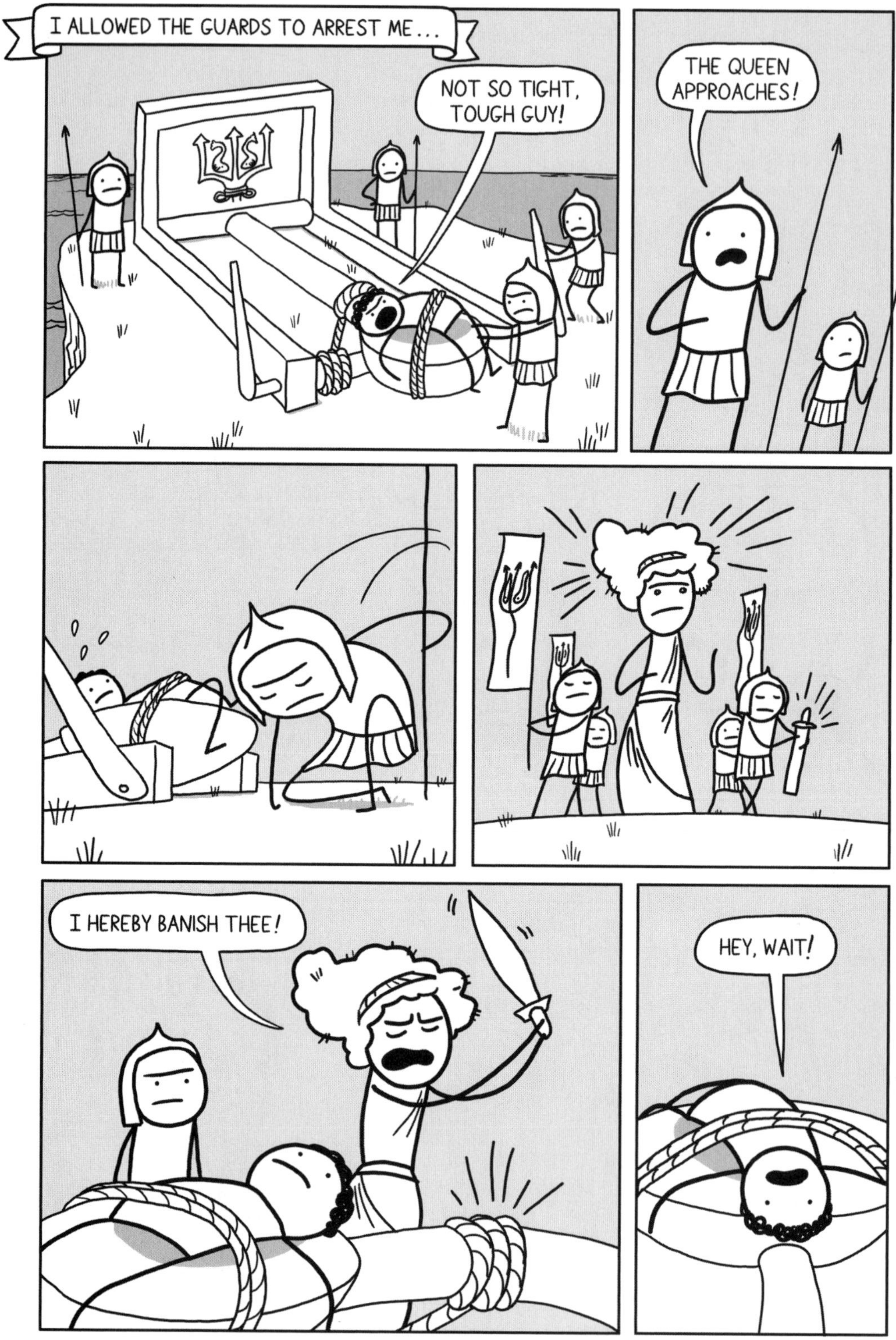
I ALLOWED THE GUARDS TO ARREST ME...
NOT SO TIGHT, TOUGH GUY!
THE QUEEN APPROACHES!
I HEREBY BANISH THEE!
HEY, WAIT!

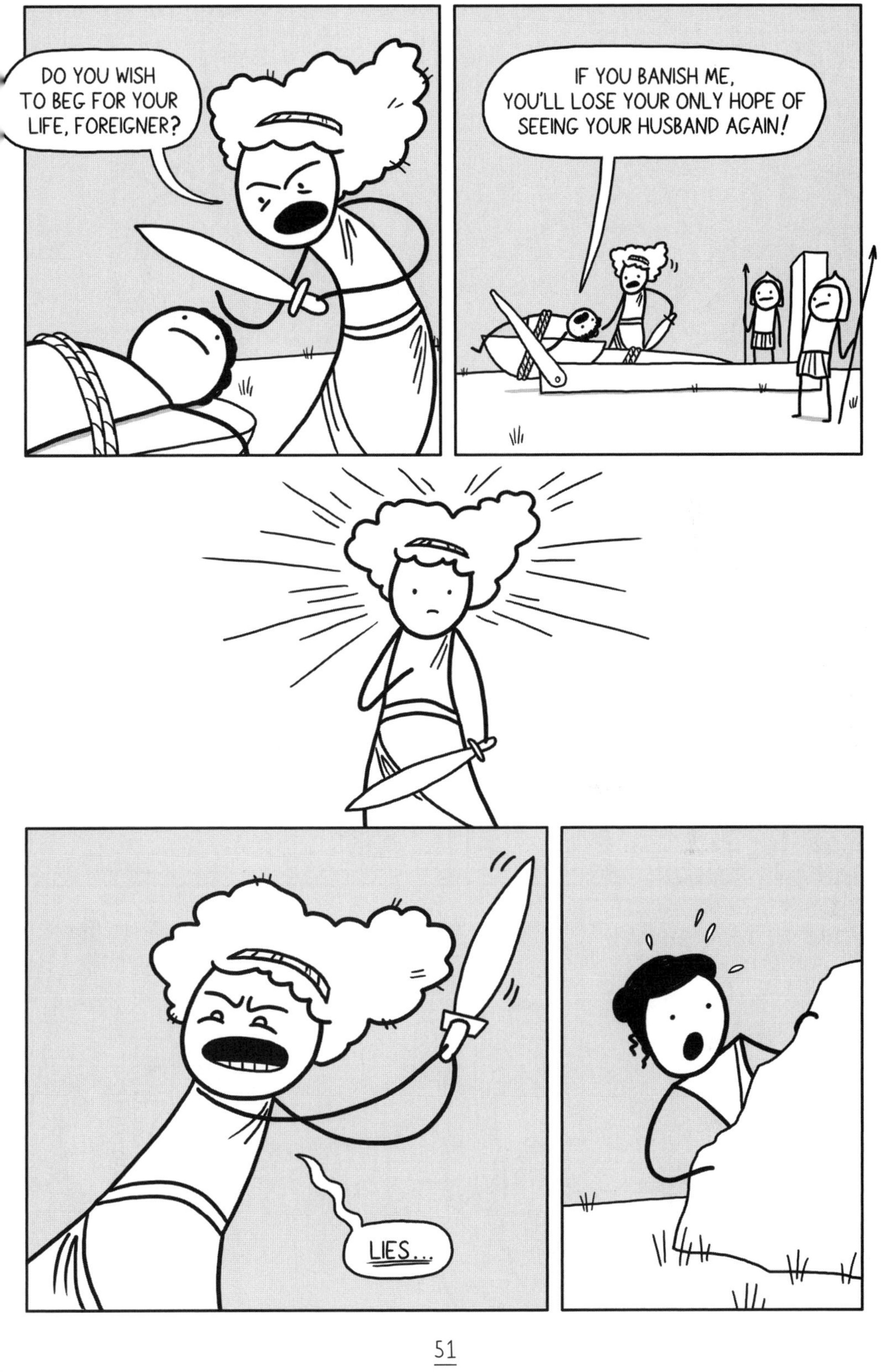
DO YOU WISH TO BEG FOR YOUR LIFE, FOREIGNER?
IF YOU BANISH ME, YOU'LL LOSE YOUR ONLY HOPE OF SEEING YOUR HUSBAND AGAIN!
LIES...

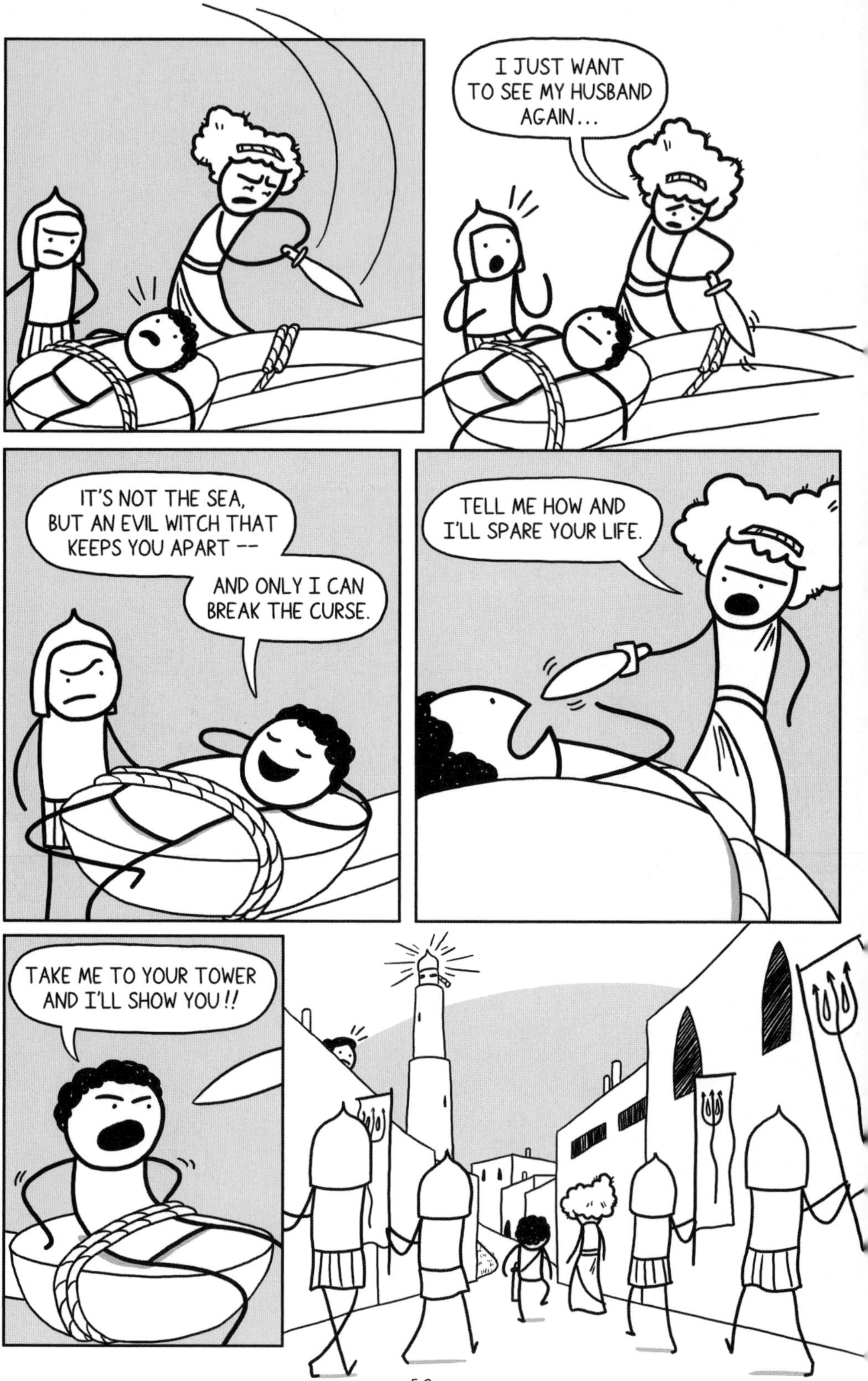
I JUST WANT TO SEE MY HUSBAND AGAIN...
IT'S NOT THE SEA, BUT AN EVIL WITCH THAT KEEPS YOU APART --
AND ONLY I CAN BREAK THE CURSE.
TELL ME HOW AND I'LL SPARE YOUR LIFE.
TAKE ME TO YOUR TOWER AND I'LL SHOW YOU!!

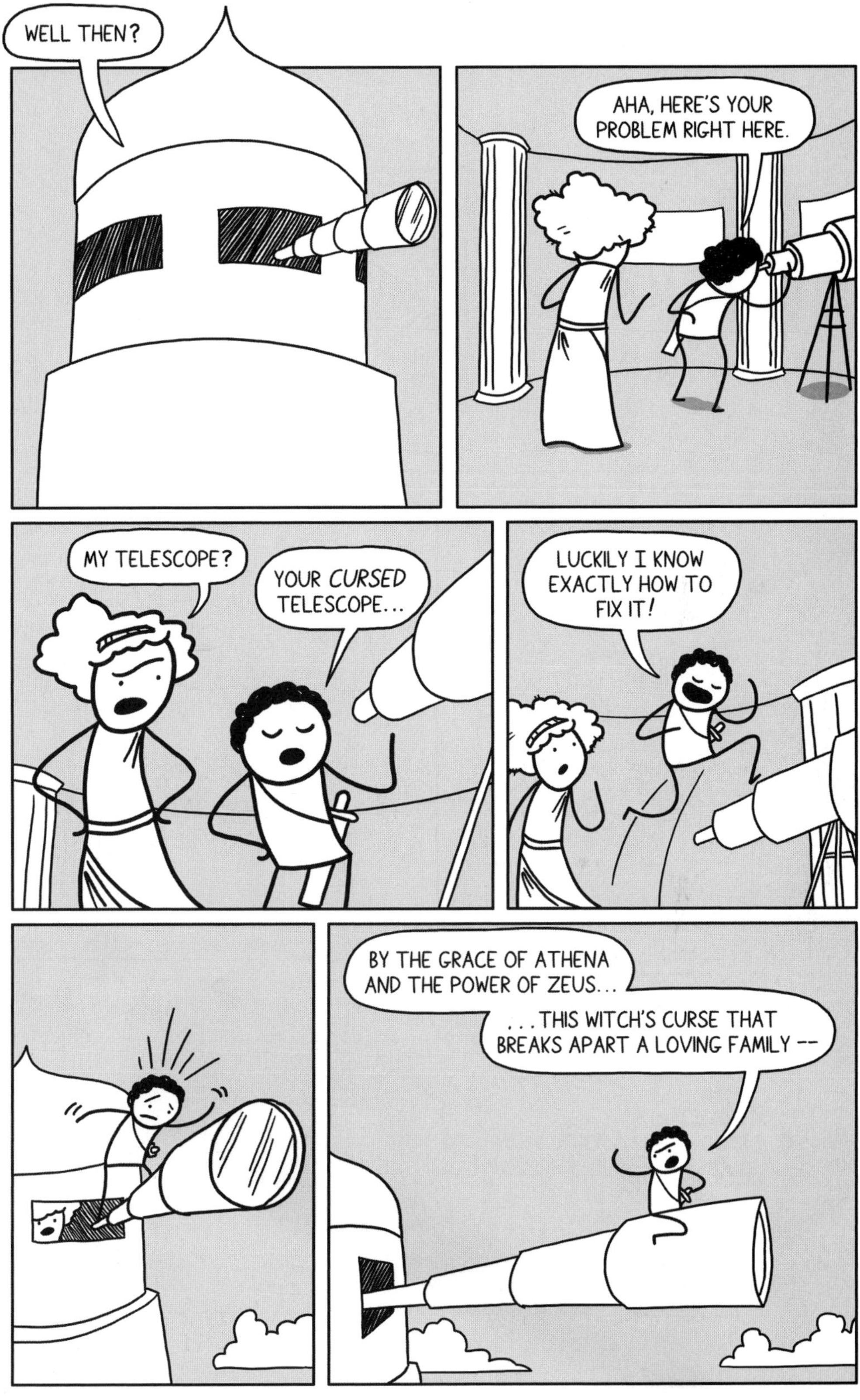
WELL THEN?
AHA, HERE'S YOUR PROBLEM RIGHT HERE.
MY TELESCOPE?
YOUR *CURSED* TELESCOPE...
LUCKILY I KNOW EXACTLY HOW TO FIX IT!
BY THE GRACE OF ATHENA AND THE POWER OF ZEUS...
...THIS WITCH'S CURSE THAT BREAKS APART A LOVING FAMILY --

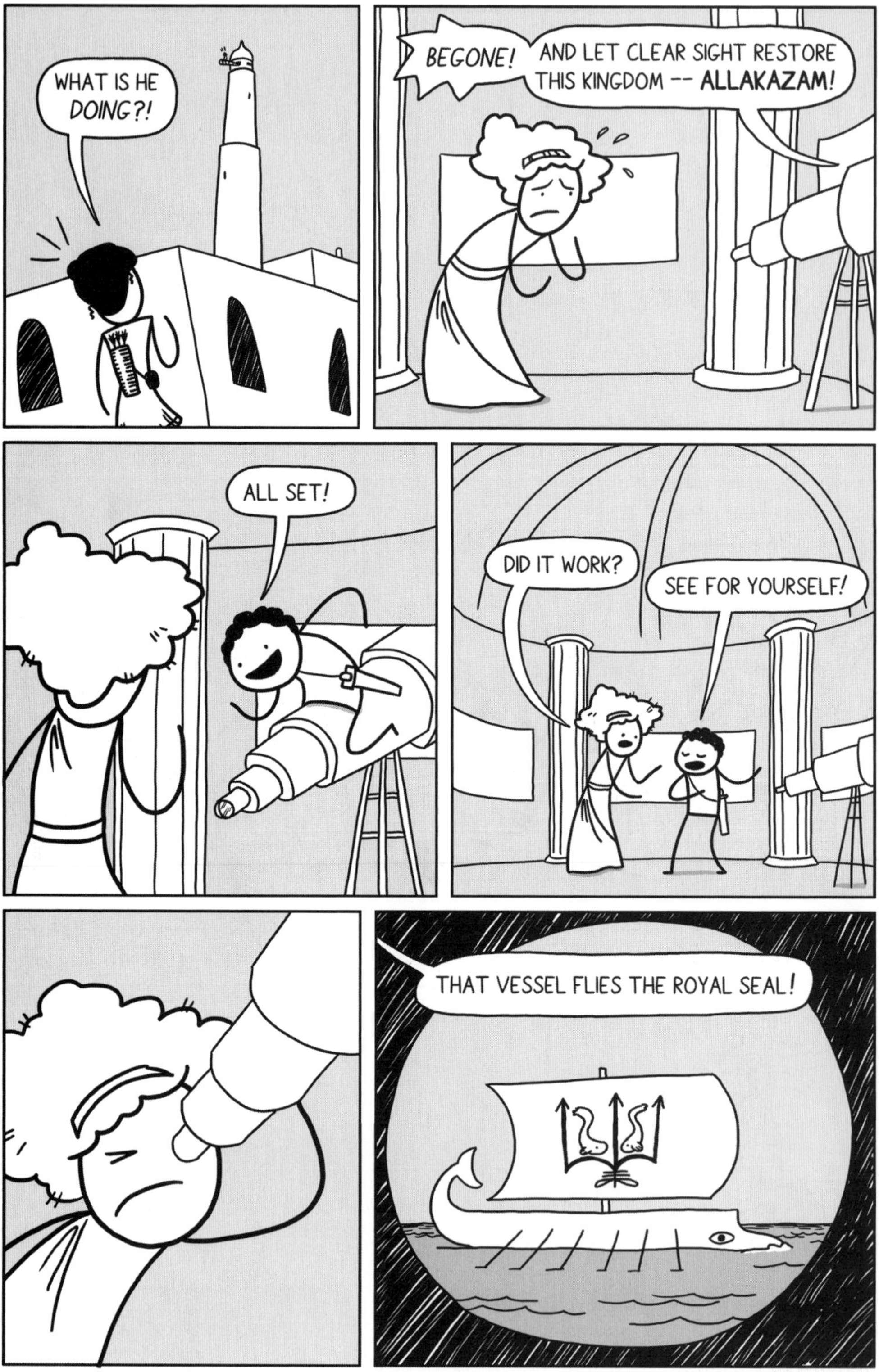
WHAT IS HE DOING?!
BEGONE!
AND LET CLEAR SIGHT RESTORE THIS KINGDOM -- **ALLAKAZAM!**
ALL SET!
DID IT WORK?
SEE FOR YOURSELF!
THAT VESSEL FLIES THE ROYAL SEAL!

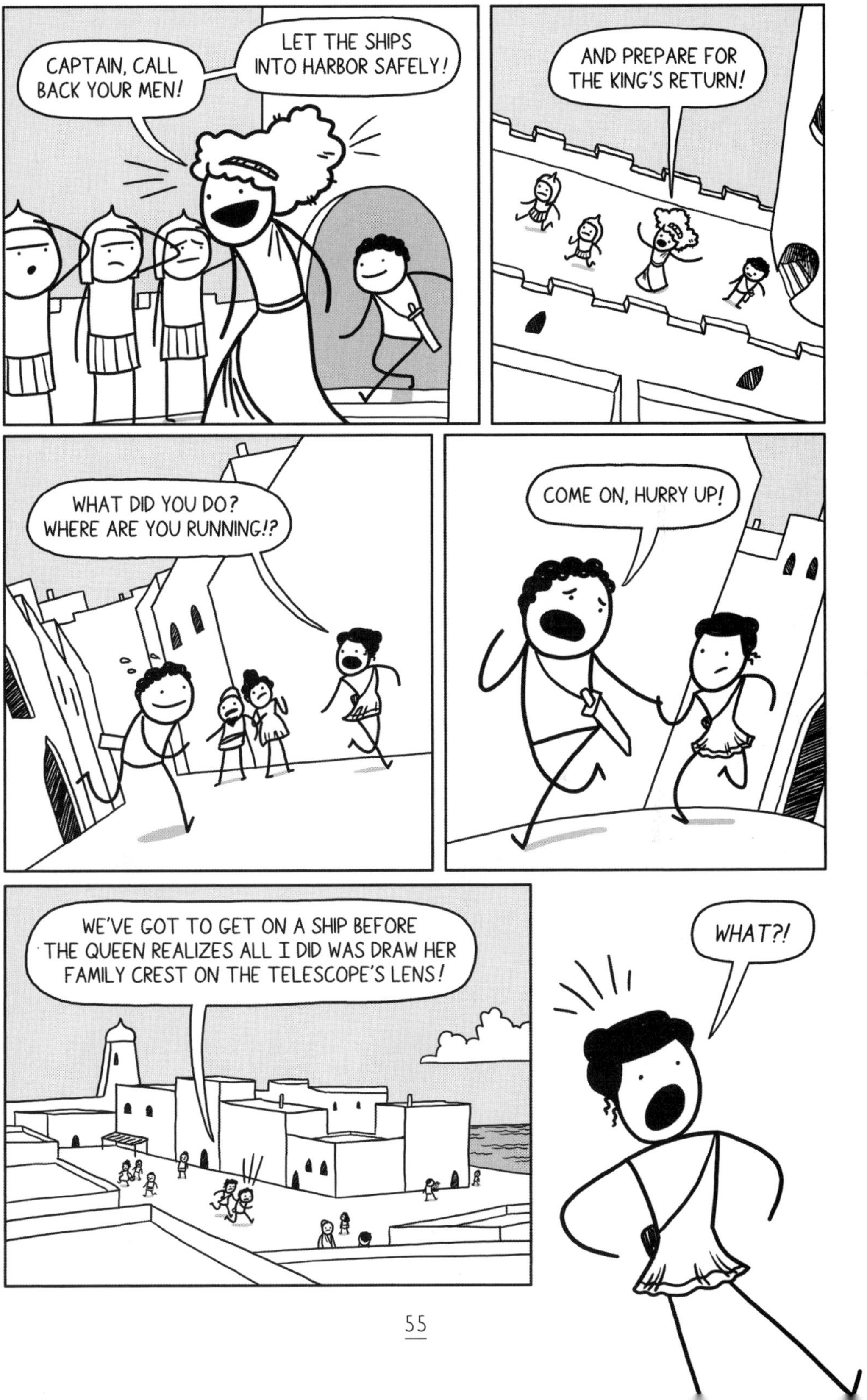
CAPTAIN, CALL BACK YOUR MEN!
LET THE SHIPS INTO HARBOR SAFELY!
AND PREPARE FOR THE KING'S RETURN!
WHAT DID YOU DO? WHERE ARE YOU RUNNING!?
COME ON, HURRY UP!
WE'VE GOT TO GET ON A SHIP BEFORE THE QUEEN REALIZES ALL I DID WAS DRAW HER FAMILY CREST ON THE TELESCOPE'S LENS!
WHAT?!

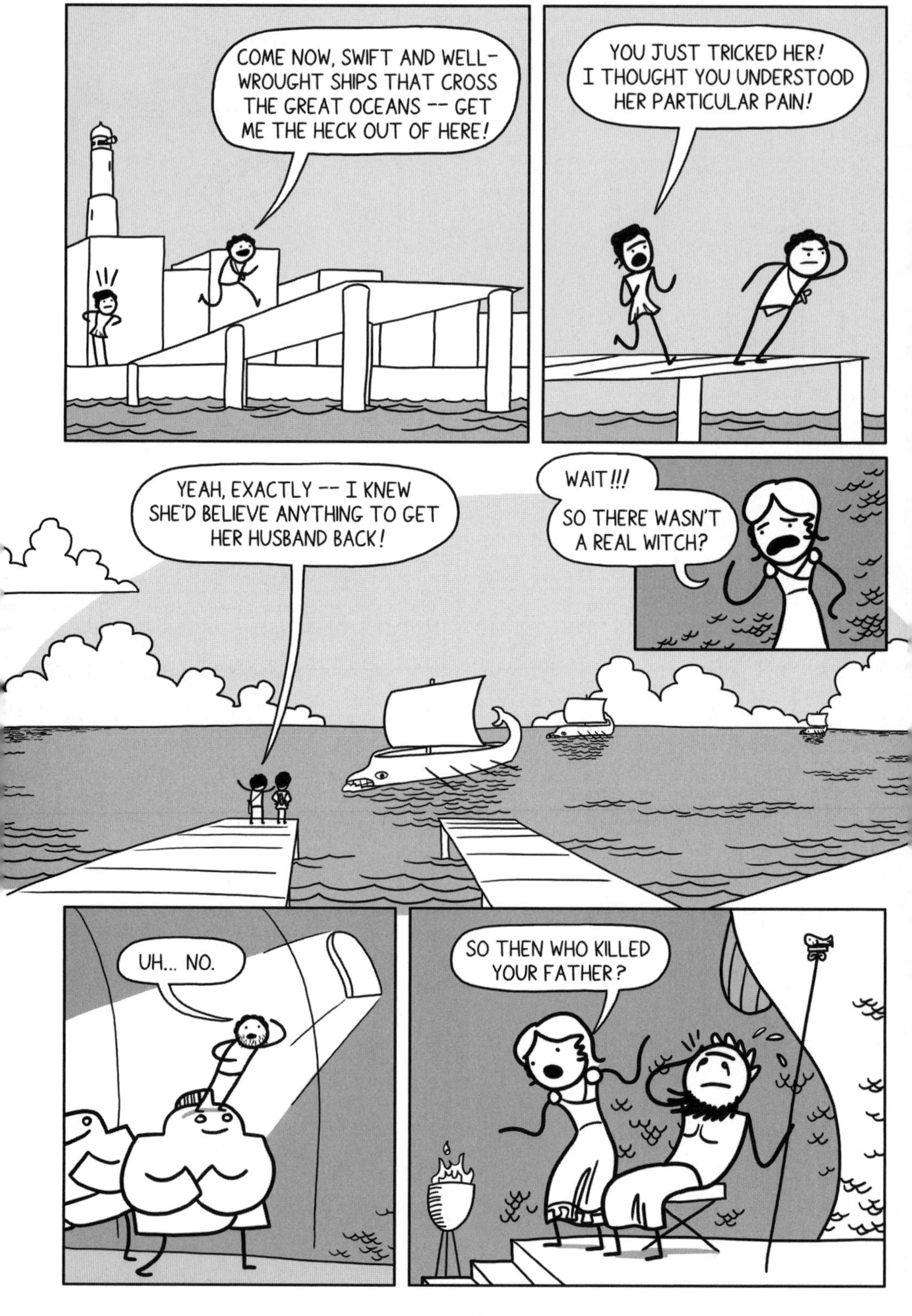
COME NOW, SWIFT AND WELL-WROUGHT SHIPS THAT CROSS THE GREAT OCEANS -- GET ME THE HECK OUT OF HERE!
YOU JUST TRICKED HER! I THOUGHT YOU UNDERSTOOD HER PARTICULAR PAIN!
YEAH, EXACTLY -- I KNEW SHE'D BELIEVE ANYTHING TO GET HER HUSBAND BACK!
WAIT!!!
SO THERE WASN'T A REAL WITCH?
UH... NO.
SO THEN WHO KILLED YOUR FATHER?

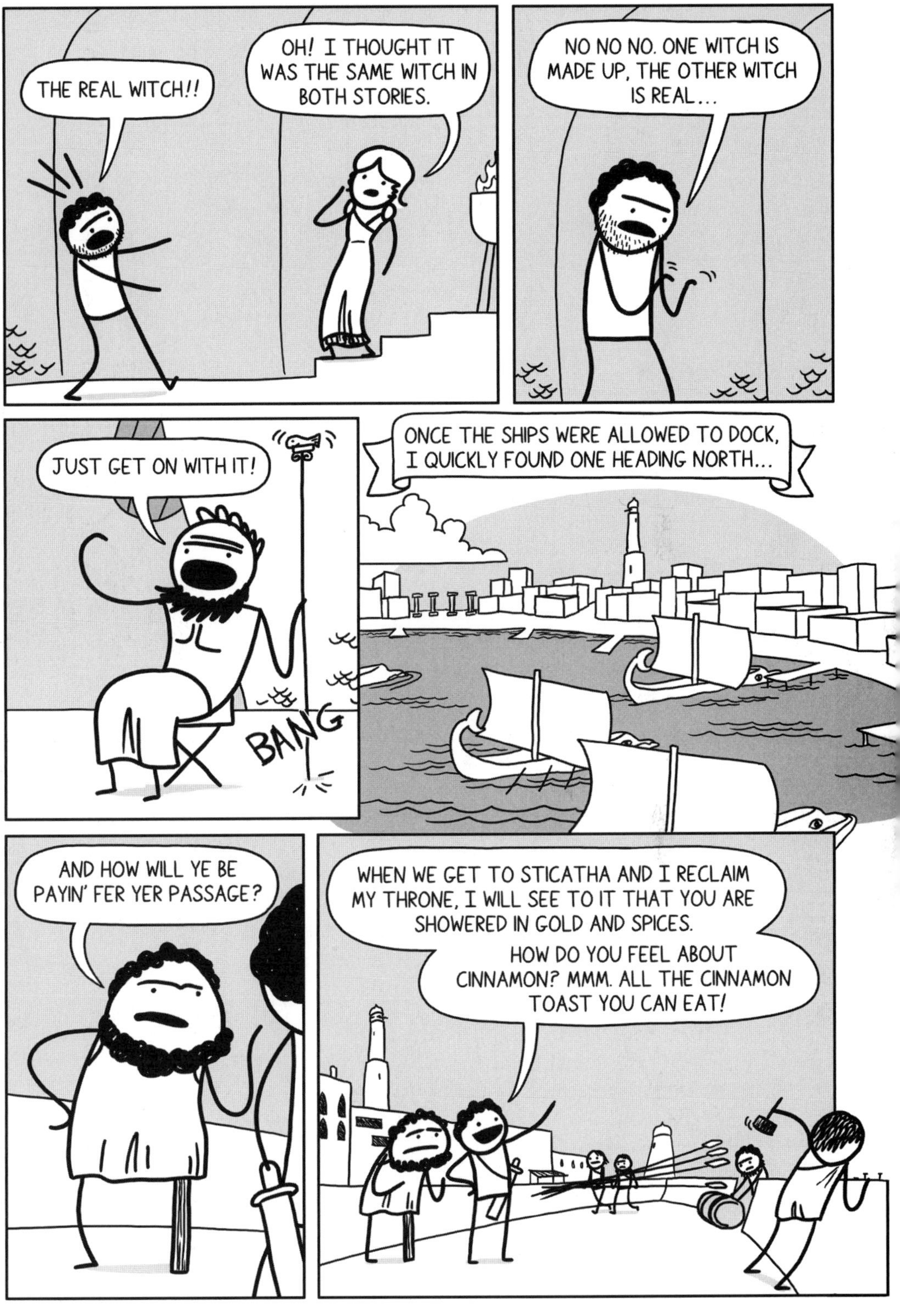
THE REAL WITCH!!
OH! I THOUGHT IT WAS THE SAME WITCH IN BOTH STORIES.
NO NO NO. ONE WITCH IS MADE UP, THE OTHER WITCH IS REAL...
JUST GET ON WITH IT!
BANG
ONCE THE SHIPS WERE ALLOWED TO DOCK, I QUICKLY FOUND ONE HEADING NORTH...
AND HOW WILL YE BE PAYIN' FER YER PASSAGE?
WHEN WE GET TO STICATHA AND I RECLAIM MY THRONE, I WILL SEE TO IT THAT YOU ARE SHOWERED IN GOLD AND SPICES.
HOW DO YOU FEEL ABOUT CINNAMON? MMM. ALL THE CINNAMON TOAST YOU CAN EAT!

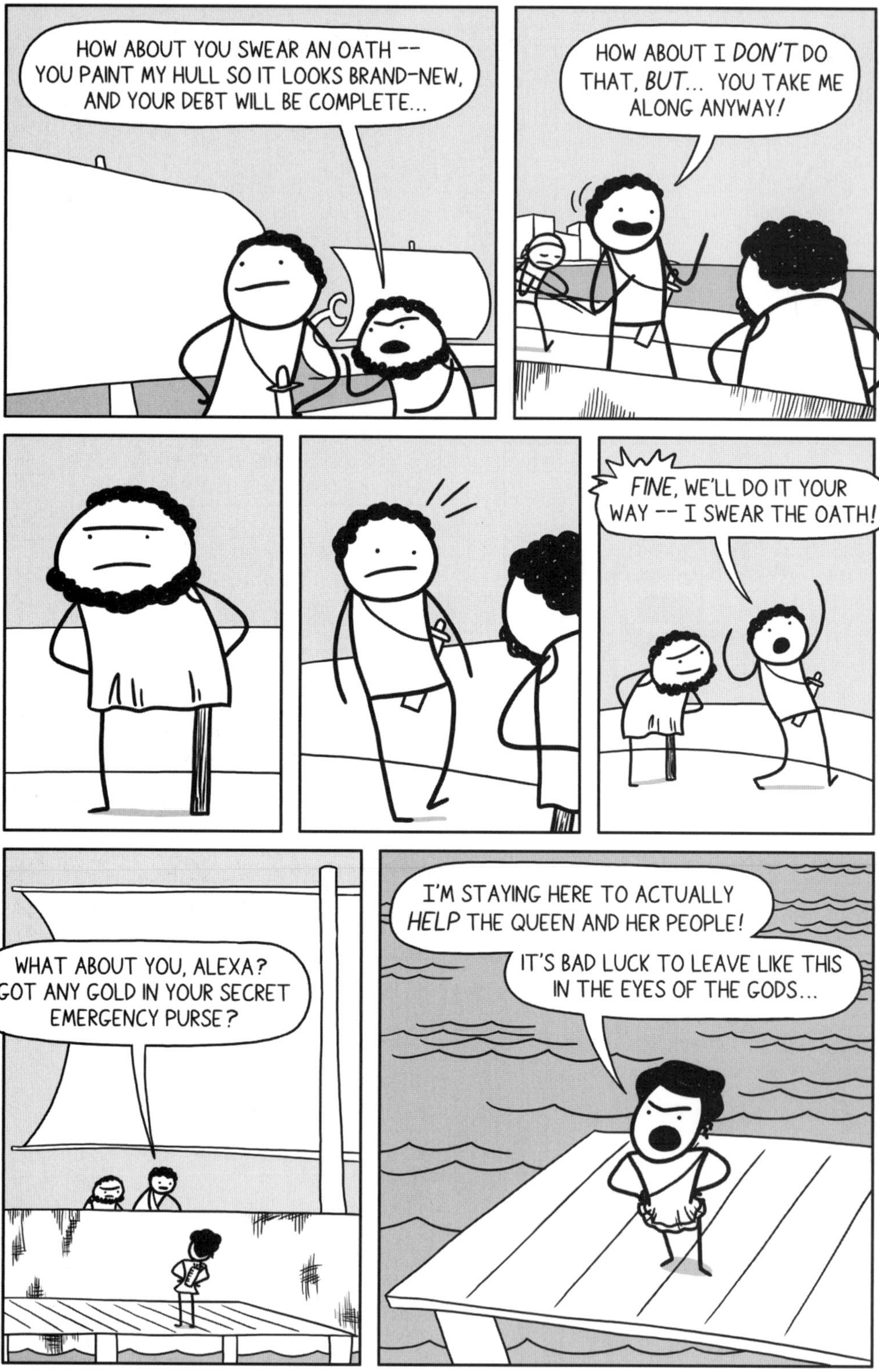
HOW ABOUT YOU SWEAR AN OATH -- YOU PAINT MY HULL SO IT LOOKS BRAND-NEW, AND YOUR DEBT WILL BE COMPLETE...
HOW ABOUT I *DON'T* DO THAT, *BUT*... YOU TAKE ME ALONG ANYWAY!
FINE, WE'LL DO IT YOUR WAY -- I SWEAR THE OATH!
WHAT ABOUT YOU, ALEXA? GOT ANY GOLD IN YOUR SECRET EMERGENCY PURSE?
I'M STAYING HERE TO ACTUALLY *HELP* THE QUEEN AND HER PEOPLE!
IT'S BAD LUCK TO LEAVE LIKE THIS IN THE EYES OF THE GODS...

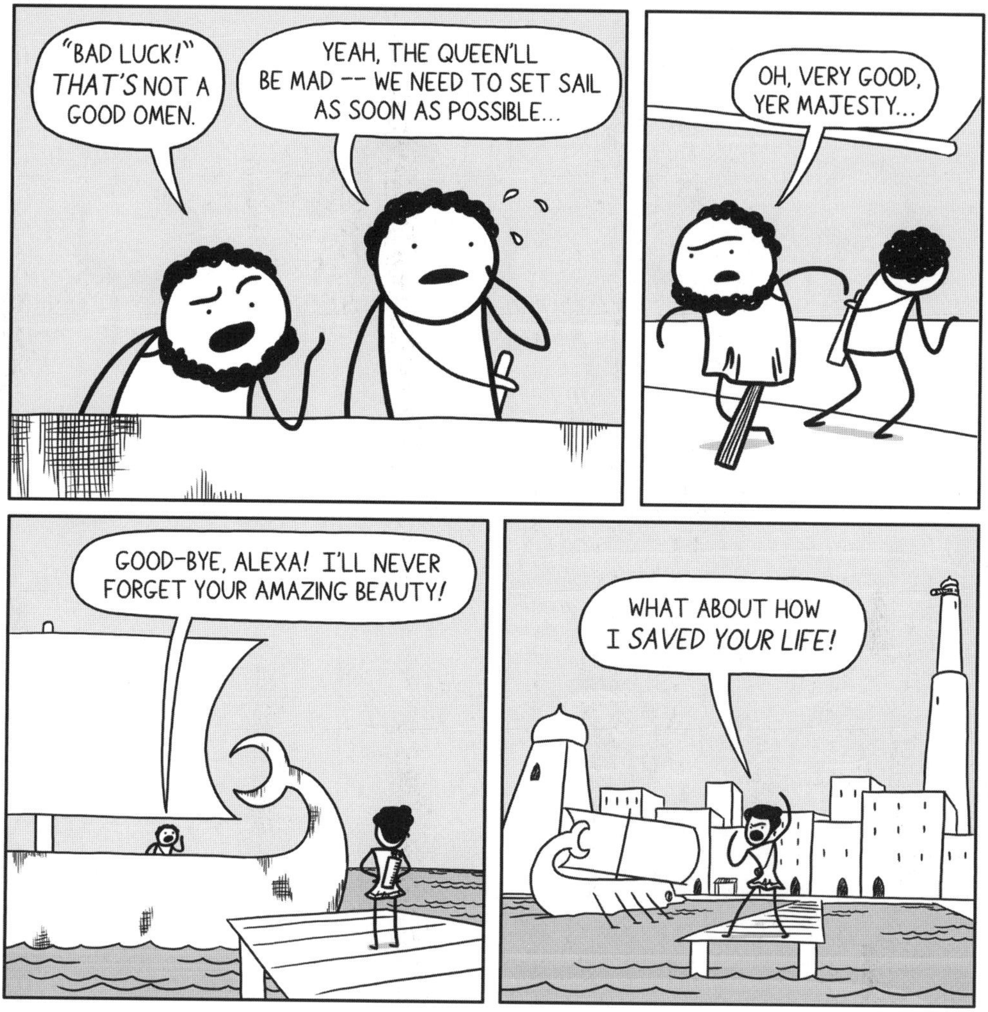
"BAD LUCK!" THAT'S NOT A GOOD OMEN.
YEAH, THE QUEEN'LL BE MAD -- WE NEED TO SET SAIL AS SOON AS POSSIBLE...
OH, VERY GOOD, YER MAJESTY...
GOOD-BYE, ALEXA! I'LL NEVER FORGET YOUR AMAZING BEAUTY!
WHAT ABOUT HOW I SAVED YOUR LIFE!

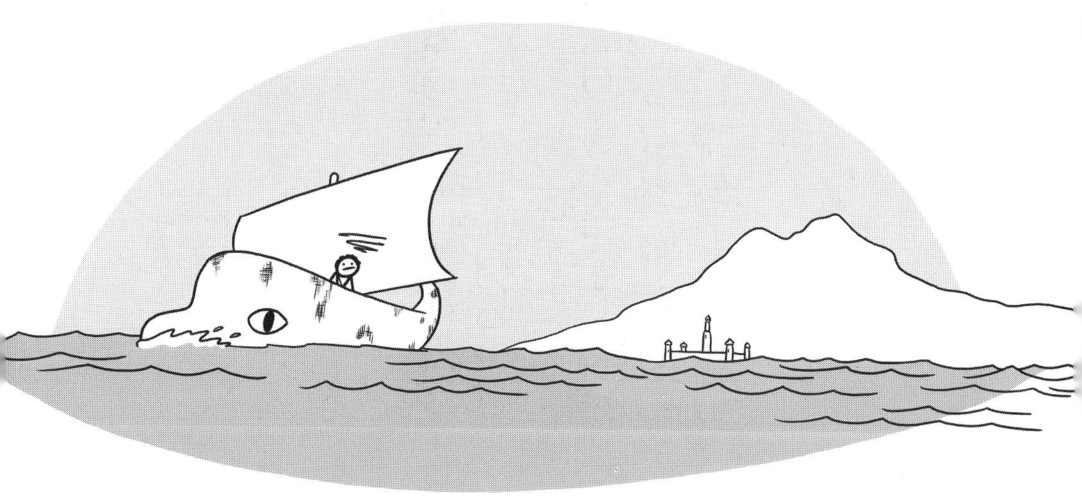

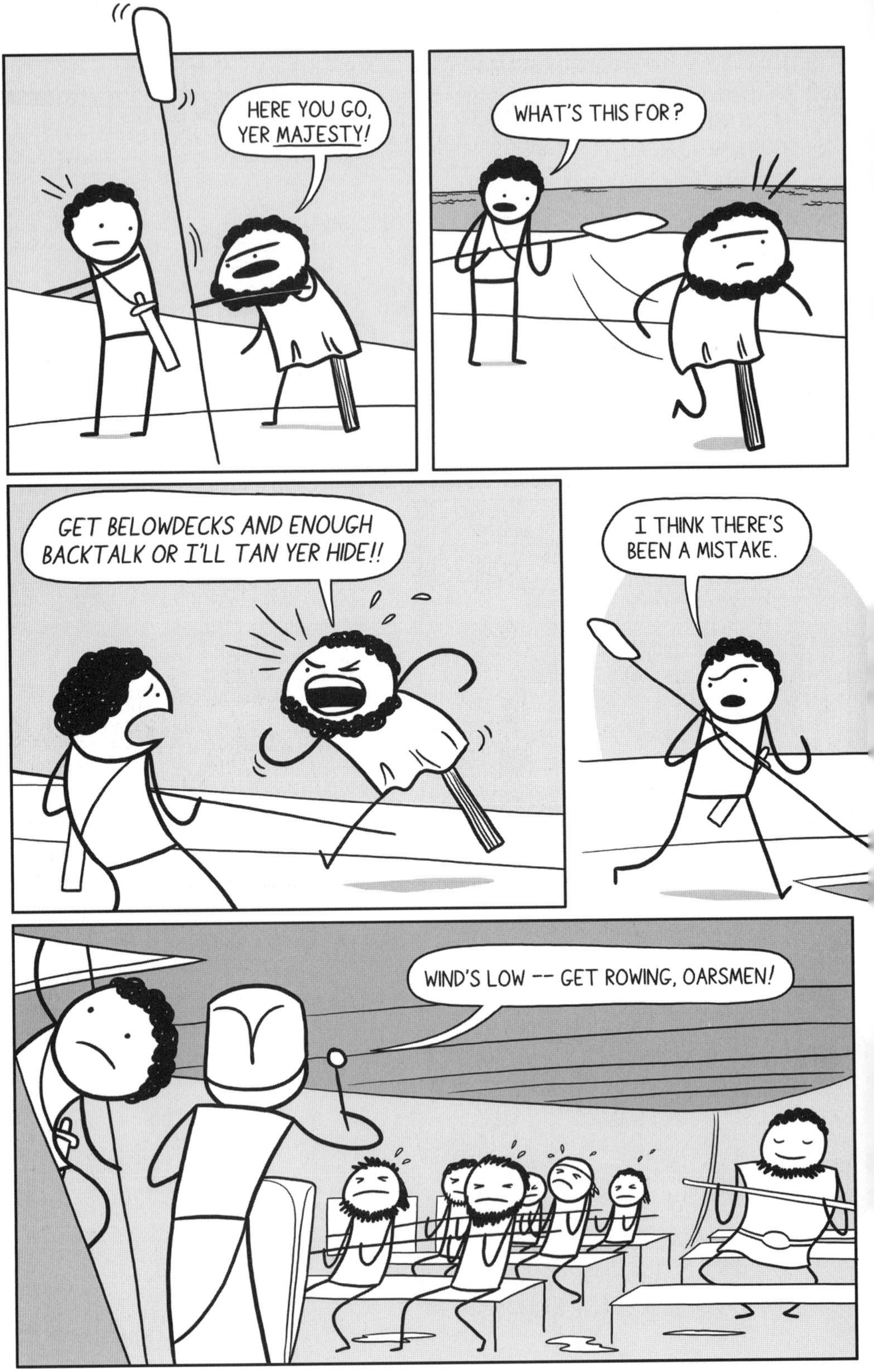
HERE YOU GO, YER MAJESTY!
WHAT'S THIS FOR?
GET BELOWDECKS AND ENOUGH BACKTALK OR I'LL TAN YER HIDE!!
I THINK THERE'S BEEN A MISTAKE.
WIND'S LOW -- GET ROWING, OARSMEN!

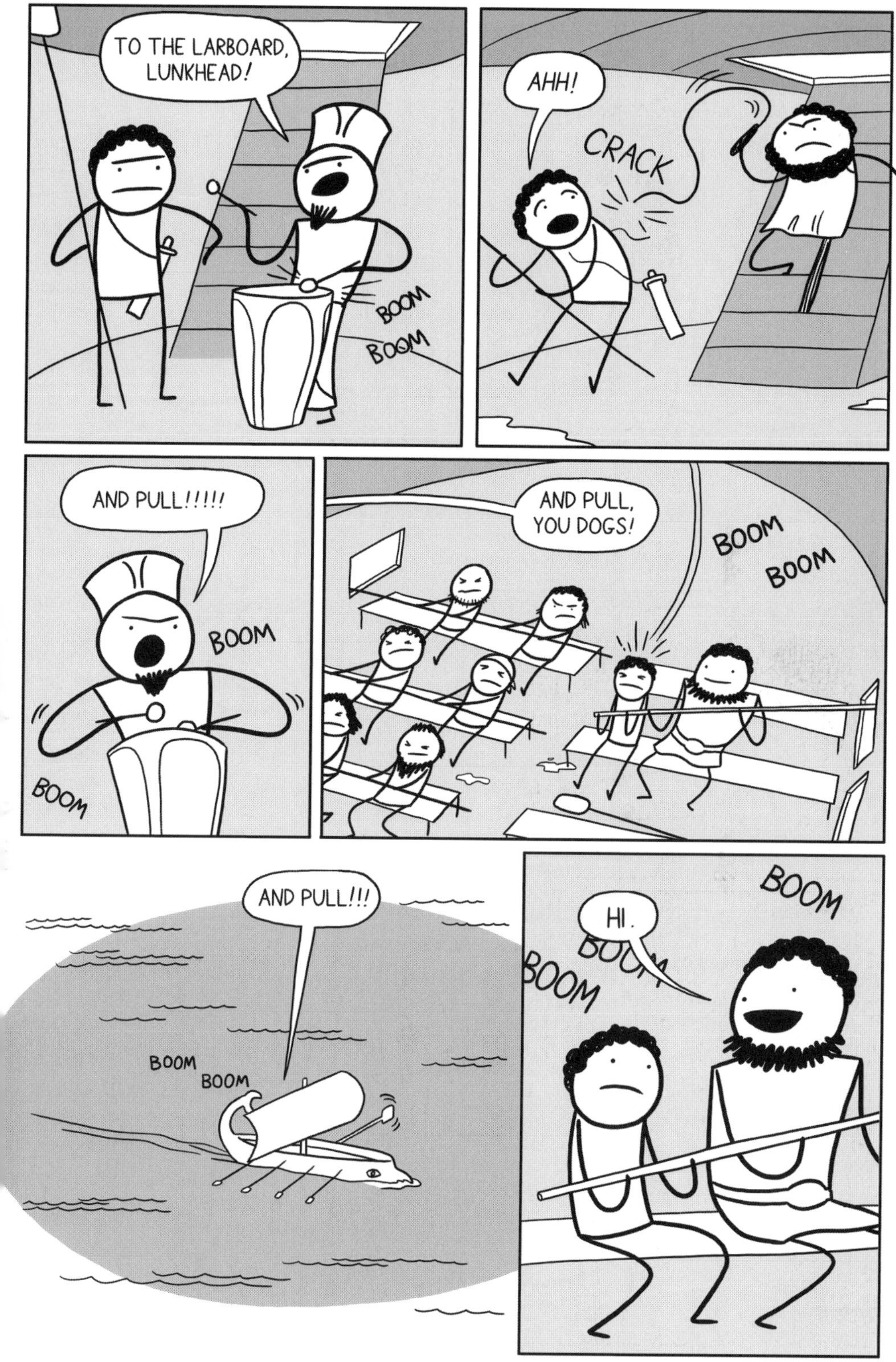

TO THE LARBOARD, LUNKHEAD!
BOOM
BOOM
AHH!
CRACK
AND PULL!!!!!
BOOM
BOOM
AND PULL, YOU DOGS!
BOOM
BOOM
AND PULL!!!
BOOM
BOOM
HI.
BOOM
BOOM
BOOM

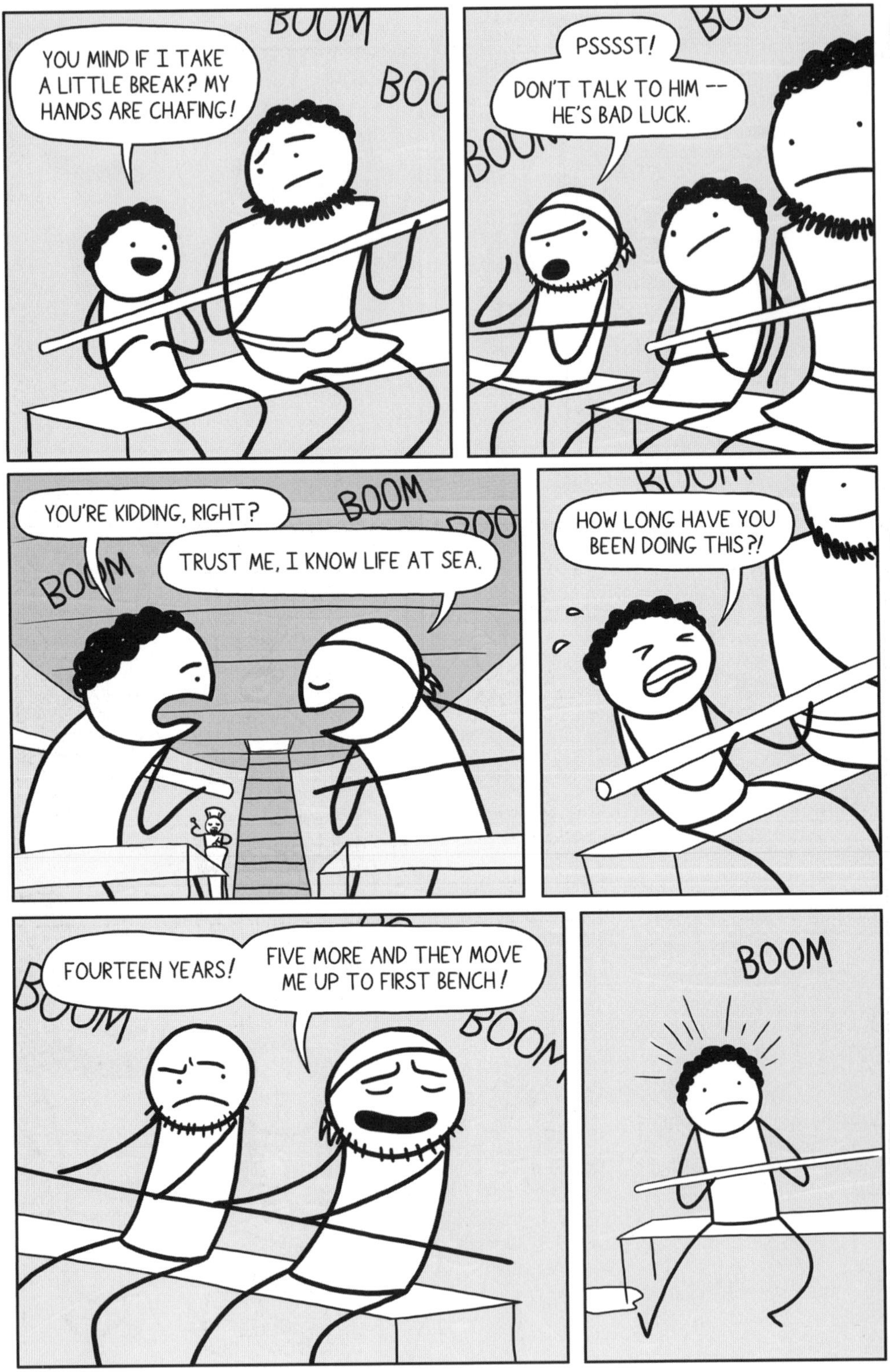
BOOM
YOU MIND IF I TAKE A LITTLE BREAK? MY HANDS ARE CHAFING!
BOO
PSSSST!
DON'T TALK TO HIM -- HE'S BAD LUCK.
YOU'RE KIDDING, RIGHT?
BOOM
TRUST ME, I KNOW LIFE AT SEA.
HOW LONG HAVE YOU BEEN DOING THIS?!
FOURTEEN YEARS!
FIVE MORE AND THEY MOVE ME UP TO FIRST BENCH!
BOOM

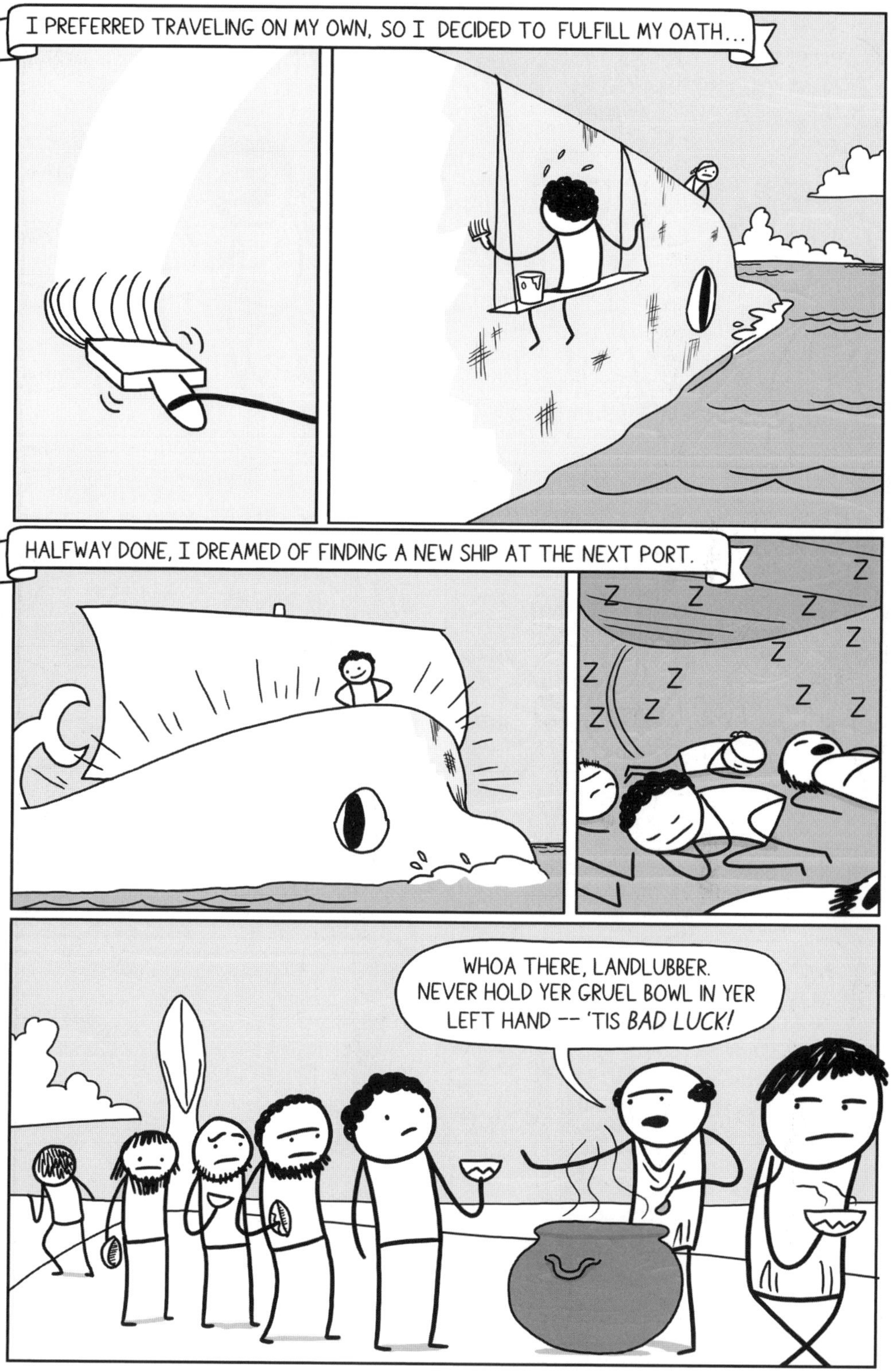
I PREFERRED TRAVELING ON MY OWN, SO I DECIDED TO FULFILL MY OATH...
HALFWAY DONE, I DREAMED OF FINDING A NEW SHIP AT THE NEXT PORT.
Z Z Z Z Z Z Z Z Z Z Z Z
WHOA THERE, LANDLUBBER. NEVER HOLD YER GRUEL BOWL IN YER LEFT HAND -- 'TIS BAD LUCK!

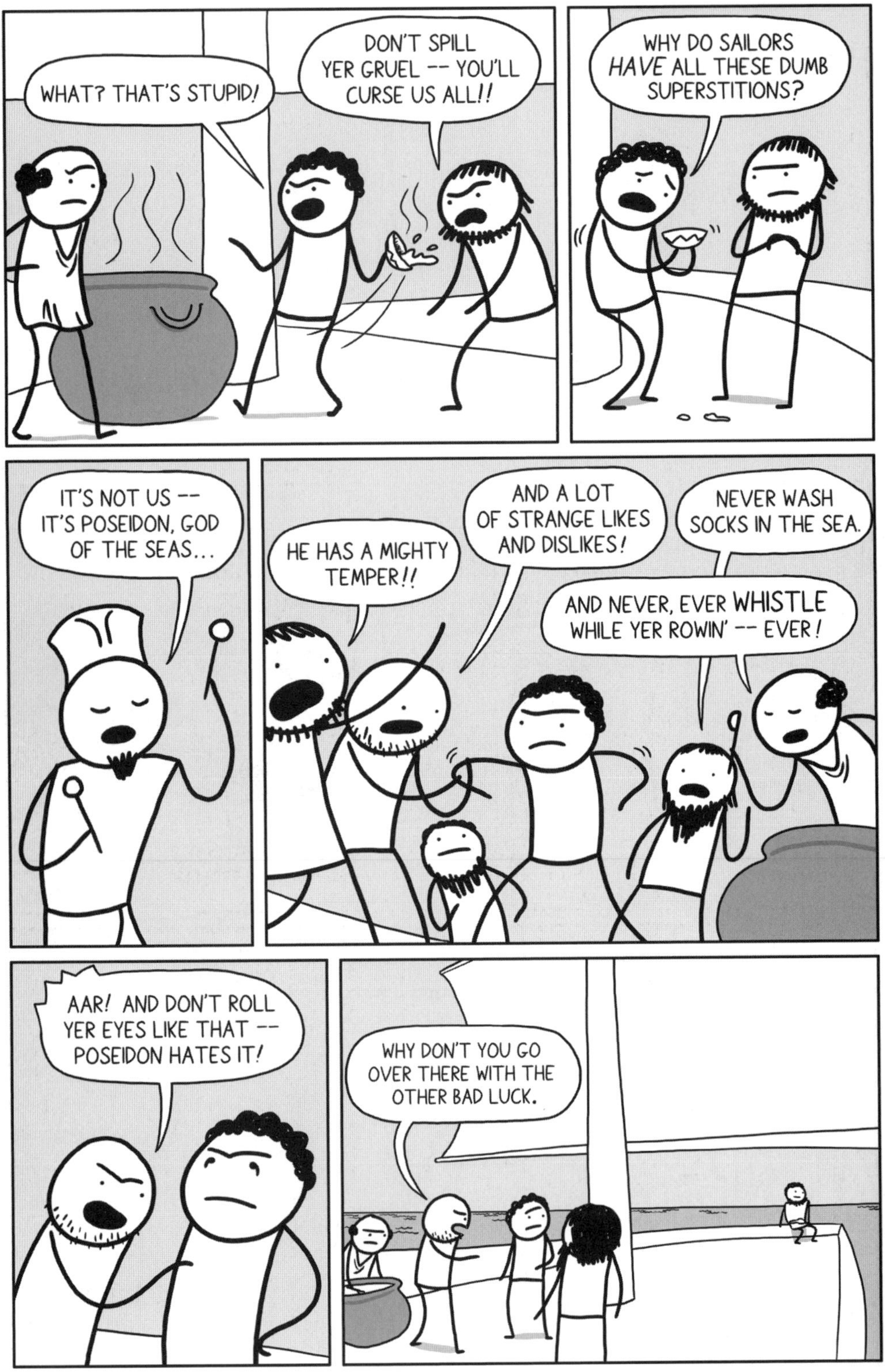
WHAT? THAT'S STUPID!
DON'T SPILL YER GRUEL -- YOU'LL CURSE US ALL!!
WHY DO SAILORS HAVE ALL THESE DUMB SUPERSTITIONS?
IT'S NOT US -- IT'S POSEIDON, GOD OF THE SEAS...
HE HAS A MIGHTY TEMPER!!
AND A LOT OF STRANGE LIKES AND DISLIKES!
NEVER WASH SOCKS IN THE SEA.
AND NEVER, EVER WHISTLE WHILE YER ROWIN' -- EVER!
AAR! AND DON'T ROLL YER EYES LIKE THAT -- POSEIDON HATES IT!
WHY DON'T YOU GO OVER THERE WITH THE OTHER BAD LUCK.

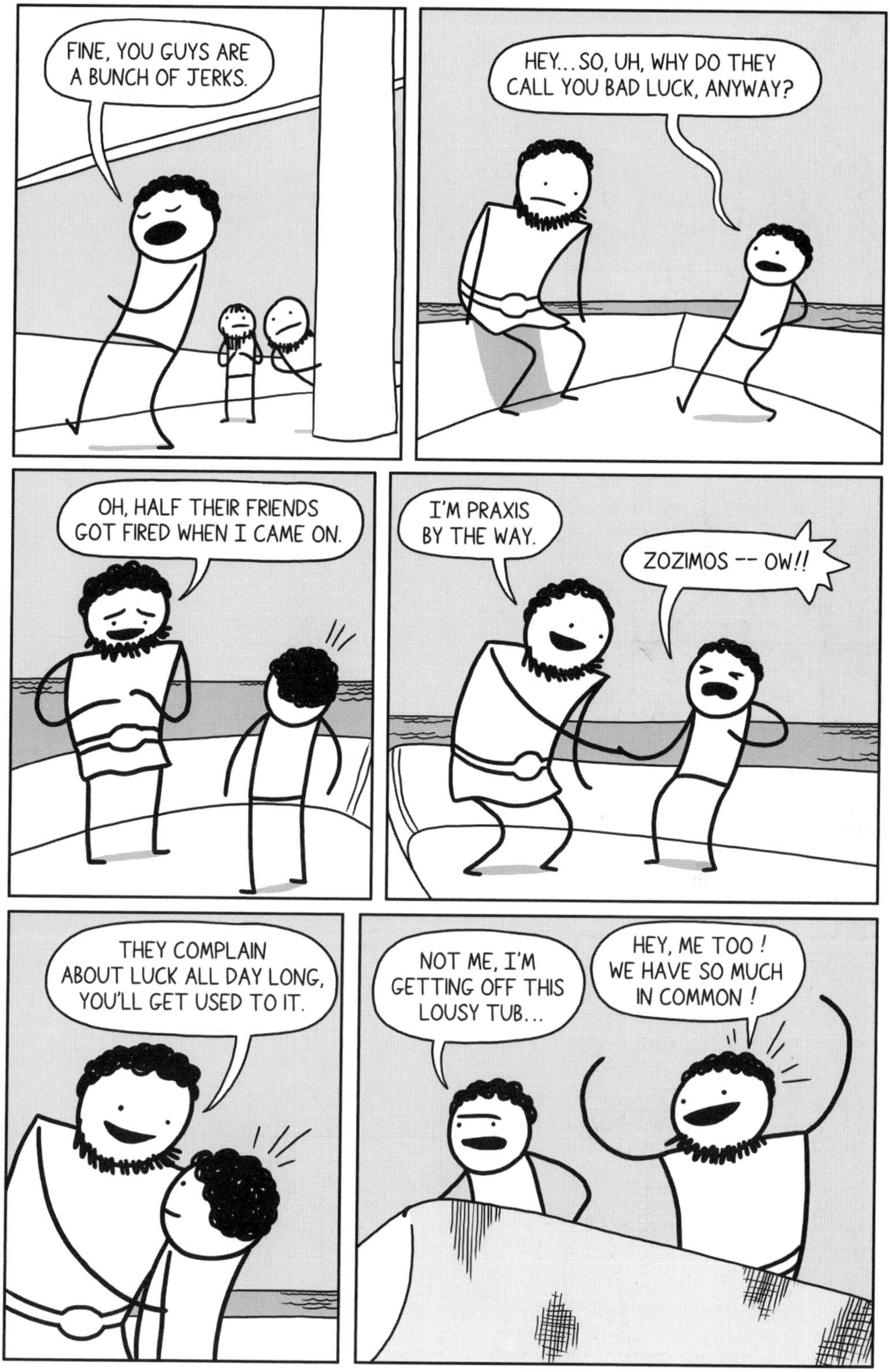

FINE, YOU GUYS ARE A BUNCH OF JERKS.
HEY... SO, UH, WHY DO THEY CALL YOU BAD LUCK, ANYWAY?
OH, HALF THEIR FRIENDS GOT FIRED WHEN I CAME ON.
I'M PRAXIS BY THE WAY.
ZOZIMOS -- OW!!
THEY COMPLAIN ABOUT LUCK ALL DAY LONG, YOU'LL GET USED TO IT.
NOT ME, I'M GETTING OFF THIS LOUSY TUB...
HEY, ME TOO! WE HAVE SO MUCH IN COMMON!

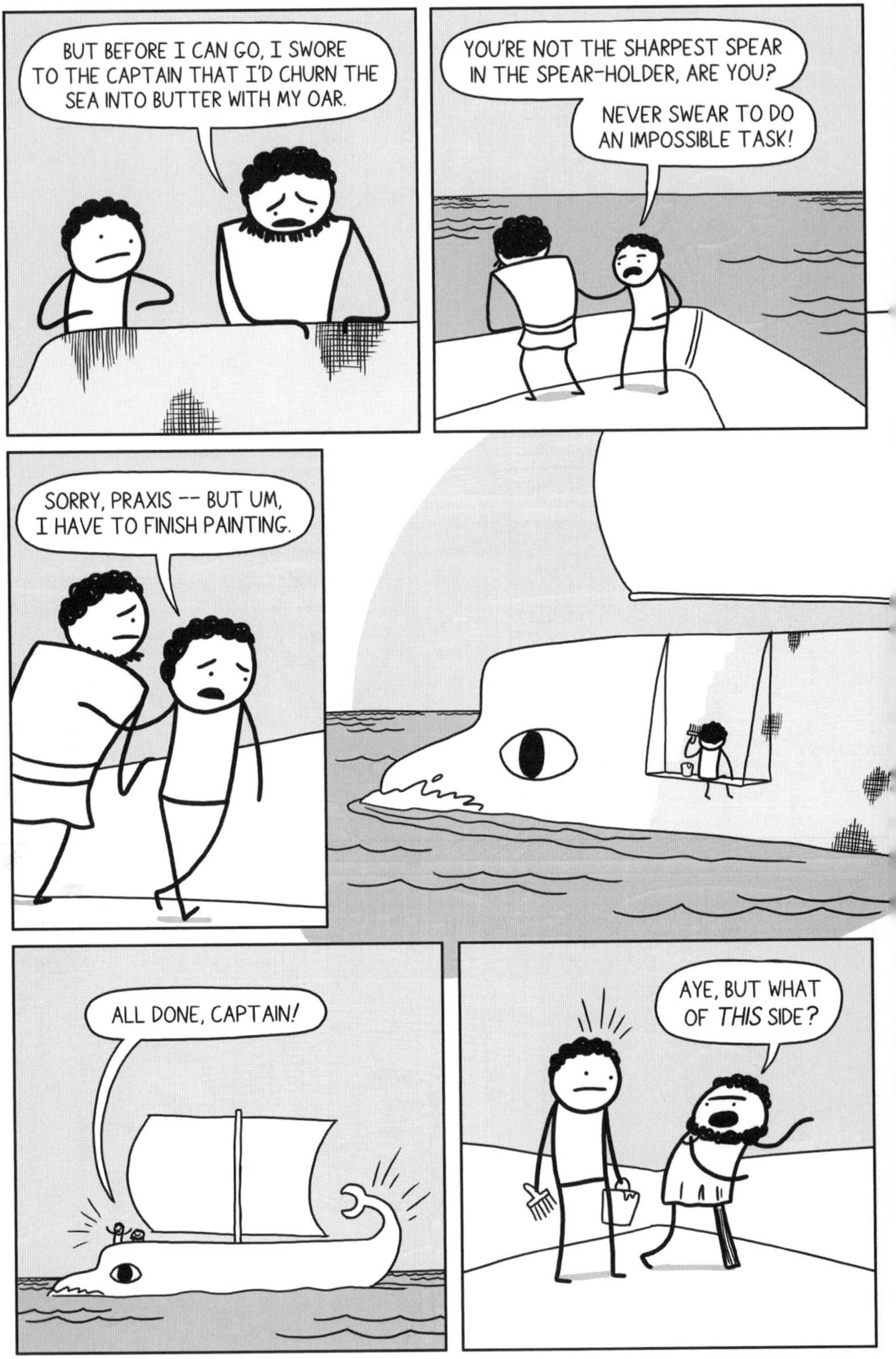
BUT BEFORE I CAN GO, I SWORE TO THE CAPTAIN THAT I'D CHURN THE SEA INTO BUTTER WITH MY OAR.
YOU'RE NOT THE SHARPEST SPEAR IN THE SPEAR-HOLDER, ARE YOU?
NEVER SWEAR TO DO AN IMPOSSIBLE TASK!
SORRY, PRAXIS -- BUT UM, I HAVE TO FINISH PAINTING.
ALL DONE, CAPTAIN!
AYE, BUT WHAT OF *THIS* SIDE?

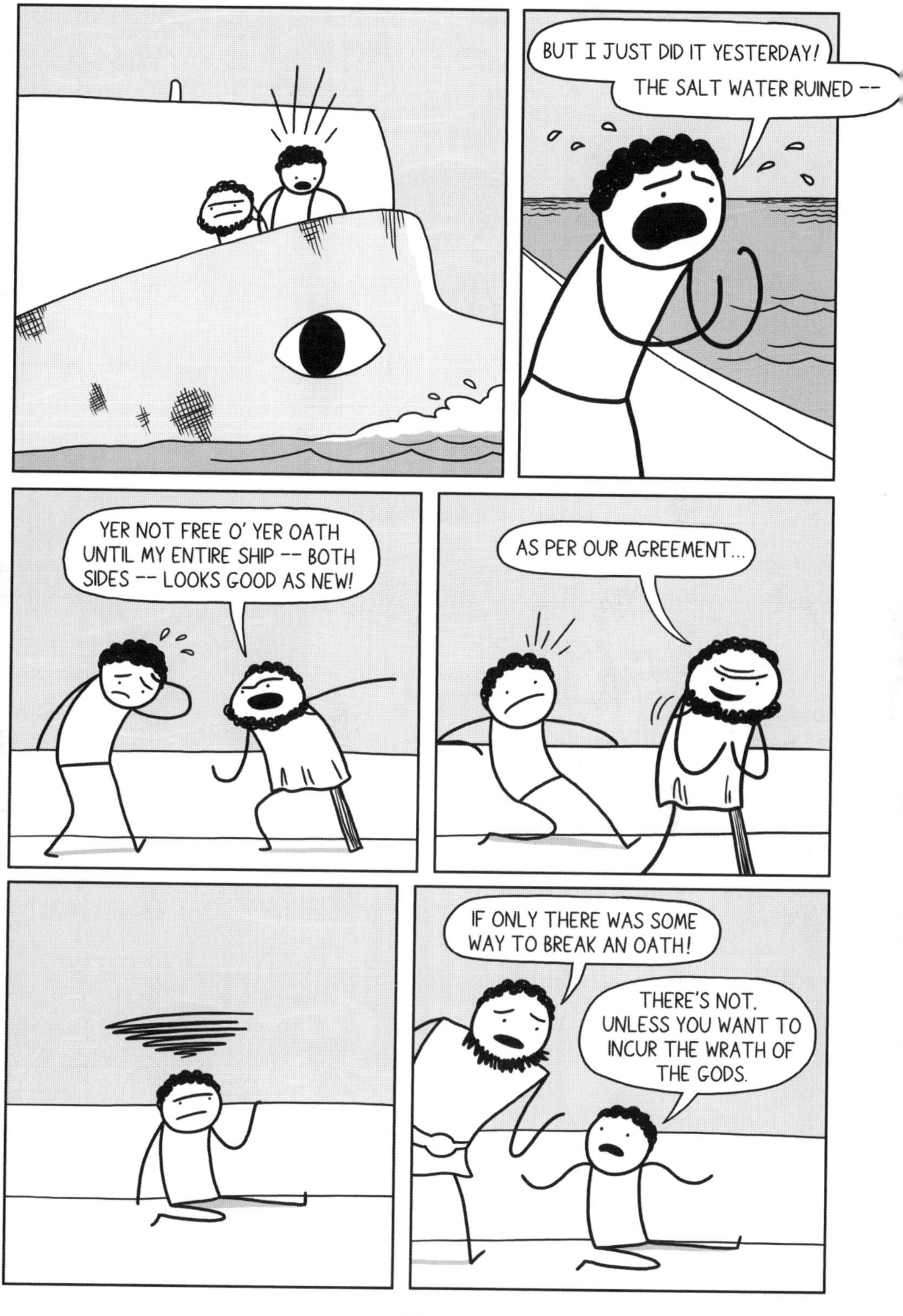
BUT I JUST DID IT YESTERDAY!
THE SALT WATER RUINED --
YER NOT FREE O' YER OATH UNTIL MY ENTIRE SHIP -- BOTH SIDES -- LOOKS GOOD AS NEW!
AS PER OUR AGREEMENT...
IF ONLY THERE WAS SOME WAY TO BREAK AN OATH!
THERE'S NOT. UNLESS YOU WANT TO INCUR THE WRATH OF THE GODS.

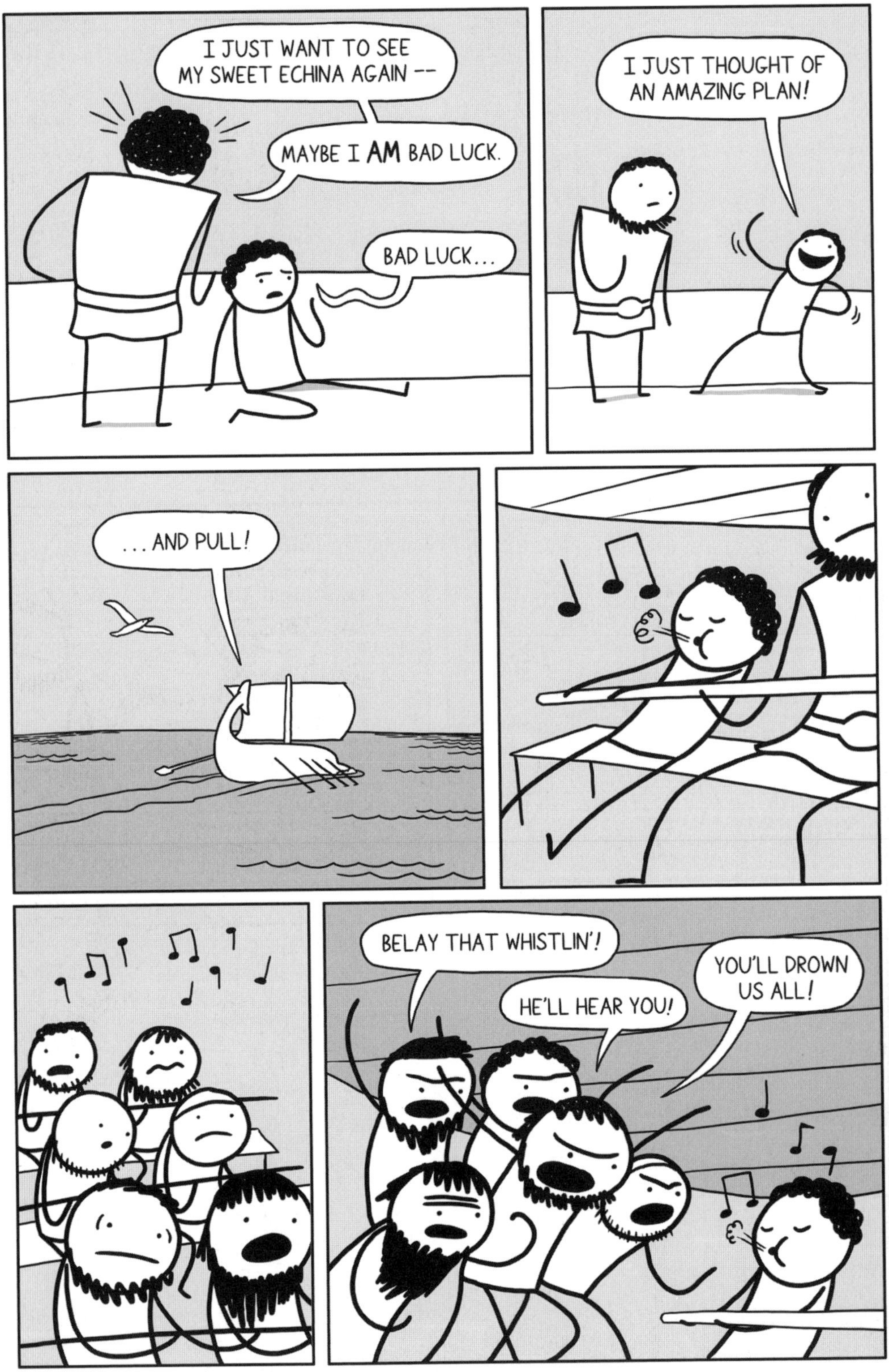
I JUST WANT TO SEE MY SWEET ECHINA AGAIN --
MAYBE I AM BAD LUCK.
BAD LUCK...
I JUST THOUGHT OF AN AMAZING PLAN!
...AND PULL!
BELAY THAT WHISTLIN'!
HE'LL HEAR YOU!
YOU'LL DROWN US ALL!

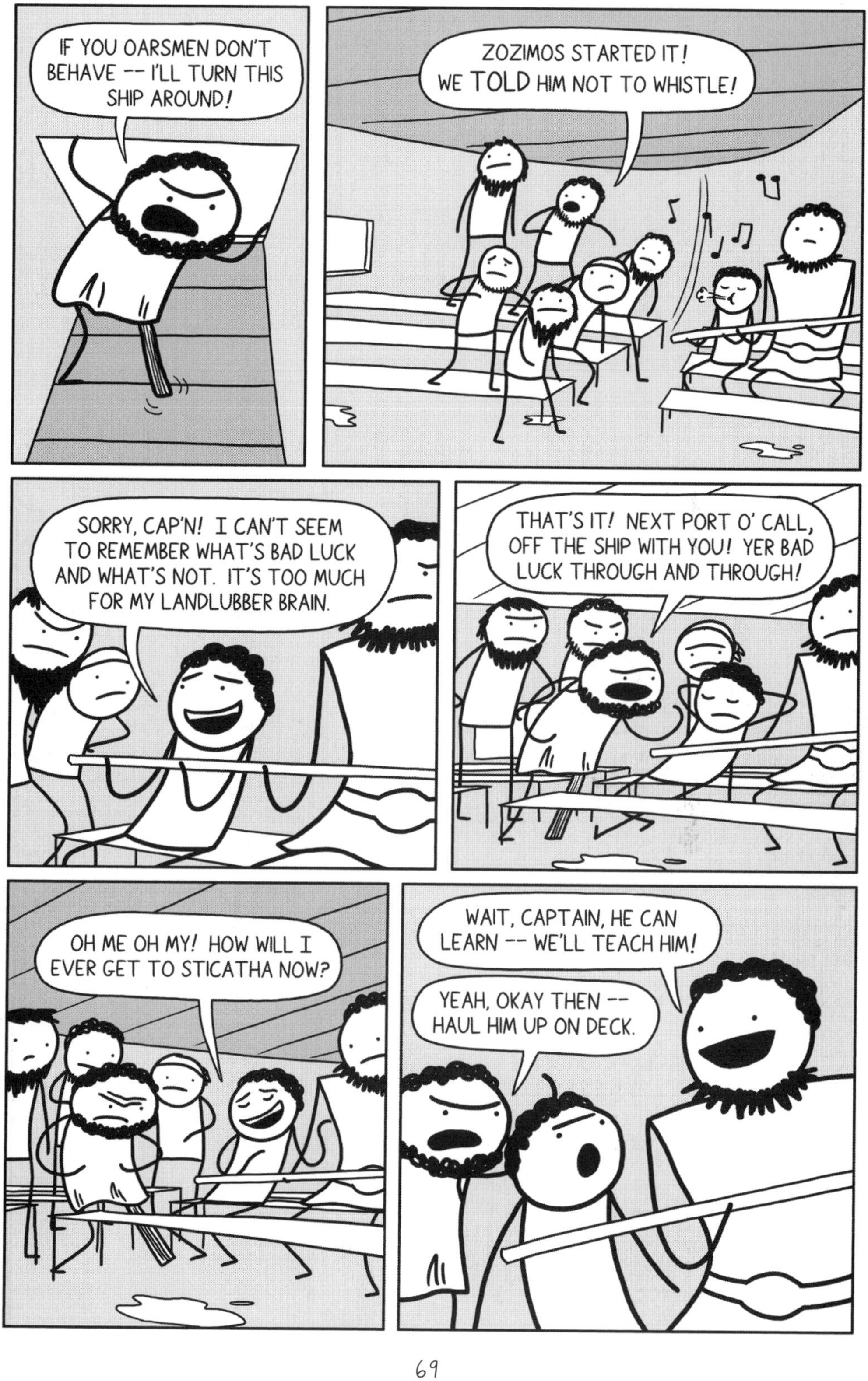
IF YOU OARSMEN DON'T BEHAVE -- I'LL TURN THIS SHIP AROUND!
ZOZIMOS STARTED IT! WE TOLD HIM NOT TO WHISTLE!
SORRY, CAP'N! I CAN'T SEEM TO REMEMBER WHAT'S BAD LUCK AND WHAT'S NOT. IT'S TOO MUCH FOR MY LANDLUBBER BRAIN.
THAT'S IT! NEXT PORT O' CALL, OFF THE SHIP WITH YOU! YER BAD LUCK THROUGH AND THROUGH!
OH ME OH MY! HOW WILL I EVER GET TO STICATHA NOW?
WAIT, CAPTAIN, HE CAN LEARN -- WE'LL TEACH HIM!
YEAH, OKAY THEN -- HAUL HIM UP ON DECK.

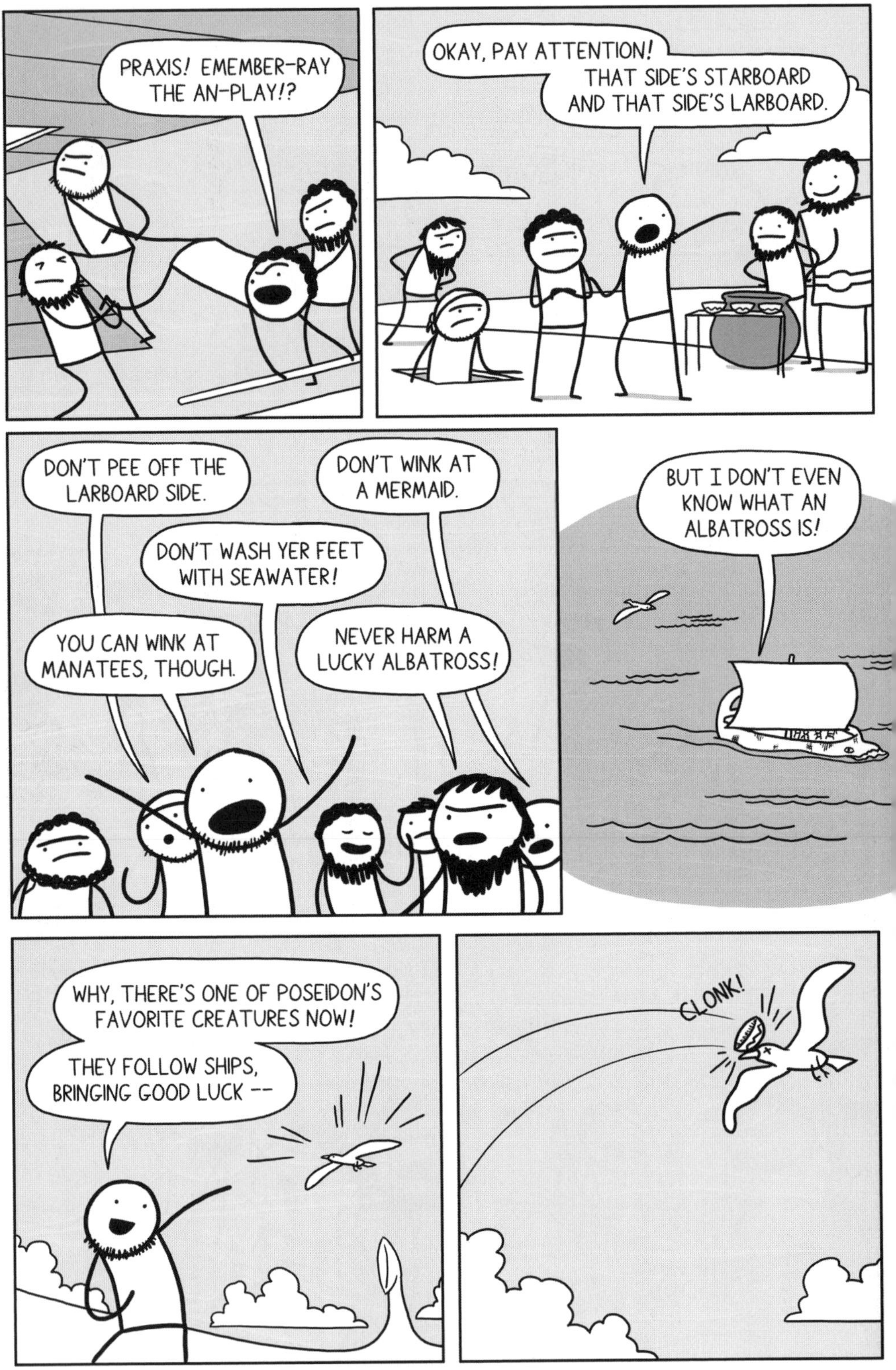
PRAXIS! EMEMBER-RAY THE AN-PLAY!?
OKAY, PAY ATTENTION!
THAT SIDE'S STARBOARD AND THAT SIDE'S LARBOARD.
DON'T PEE OFF THE LARBOARD SIDE.
DON'T WINK AT A MERMAID.
DON'T WASH YER FEET WITH SEAWATER!
YOU CAN WINK AT MANATEES, THOUGH.
NEVER HARM A LUCKY ALBATROSS!
BUT I DON'T EVEN KNOW WHAT AN ALBATROSS IS!
WHY, THERE'S ONE OF POSEIDON'S FAVORITE CREATURES NOW!
THEY FOLLOW SHIPS, BRINGING GOOD LUCK --
CLONK!

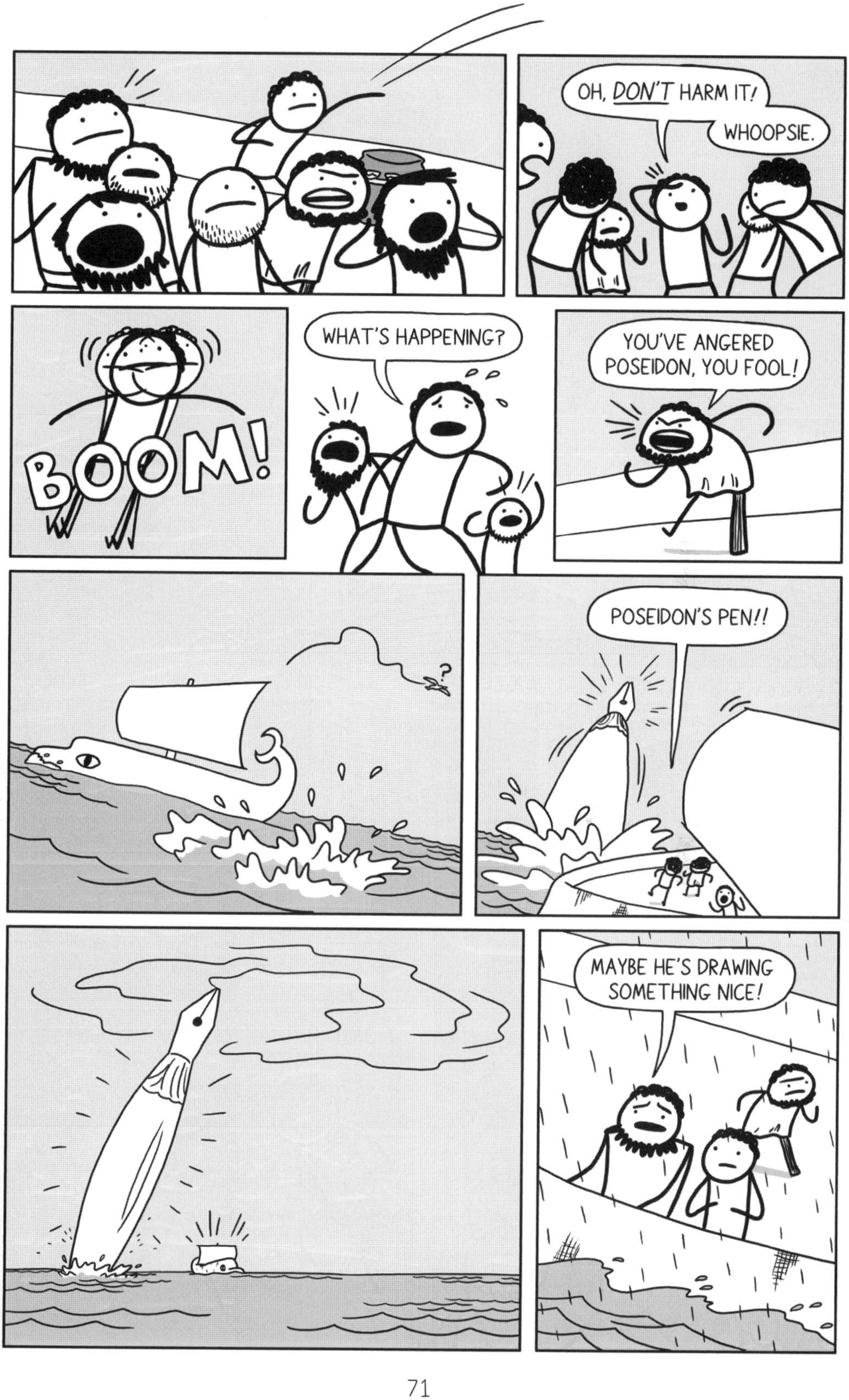
OH, DON'T HARM IT!
WHOOPSIE.
BOOM!
WHAT'S HAPPENING?
YOU'VE ANGERED POSEIDON, YOU FOOL!
POSEIDON'S PEN!!
MAYBE HE'S DRAWING SOMETHING NICE!

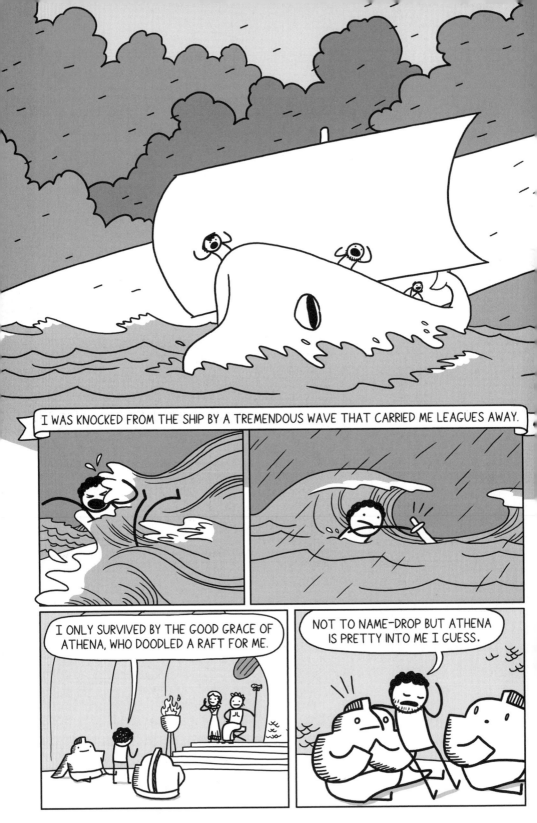

I WAS KNOCKED FROM THE SHIP BY A TREMENDOUS WAVE THAT CARRIED ME LEAGUES AWAY.

I ONLY SURVIVED BY THE GOOD GRACE OF ATHENA, WHO DOODLED A RAFT FOR ME.

NOT TO NAME-DROP BUT ATHENA IS PRETTY INTO ME I GUESS.

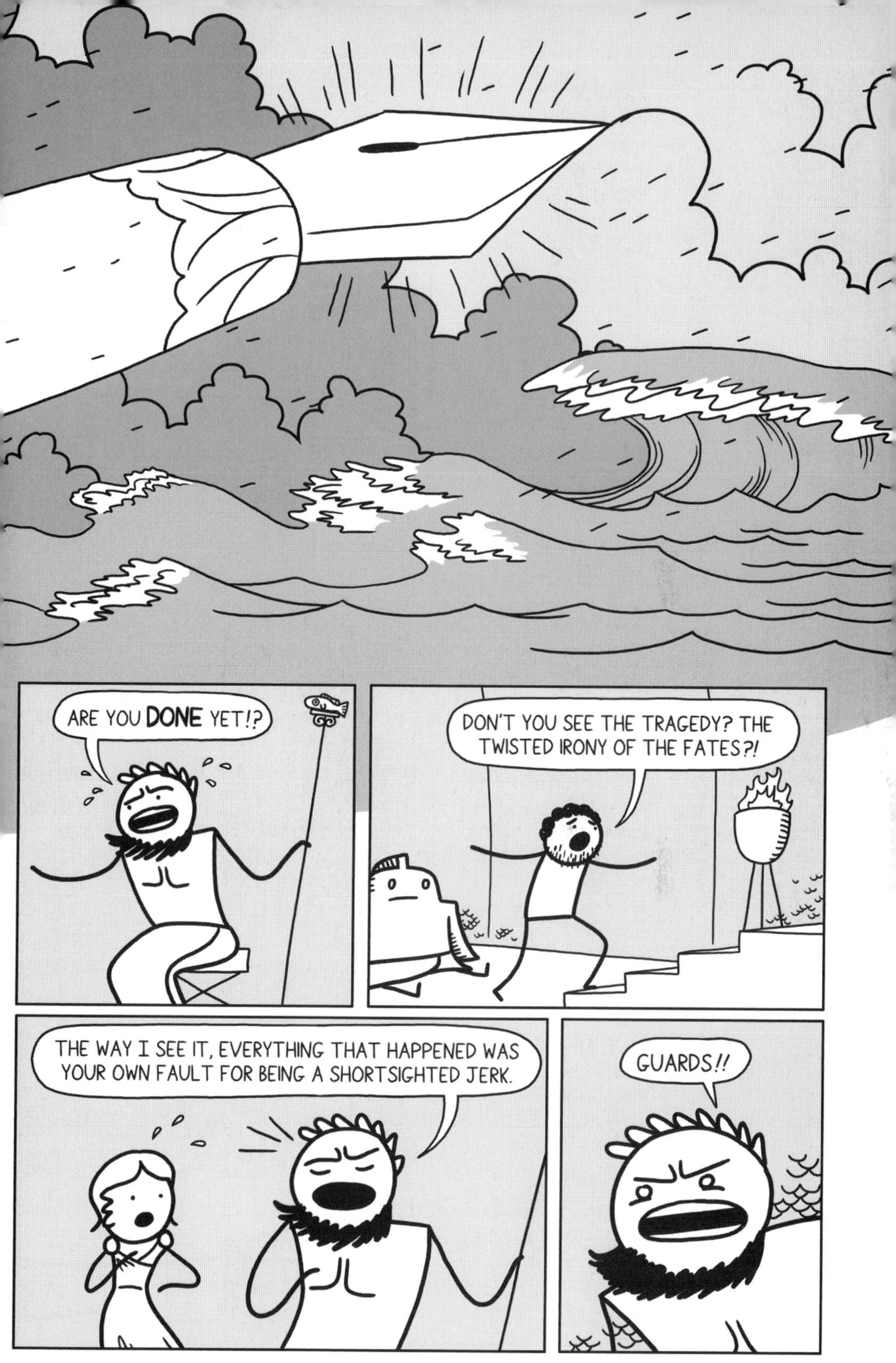
ARE YOU DONE YET!?
DON'T YOU SEE THE TRAGEDY? THE TWISTED IRONY OF THE FATES?!
THE WAY I SEE IT, EVERYTHING THAT HAPPENED WAS YOUR OWN FAULT FOR BEING A SHORTSIGHTED JERK.
GUARDS!!

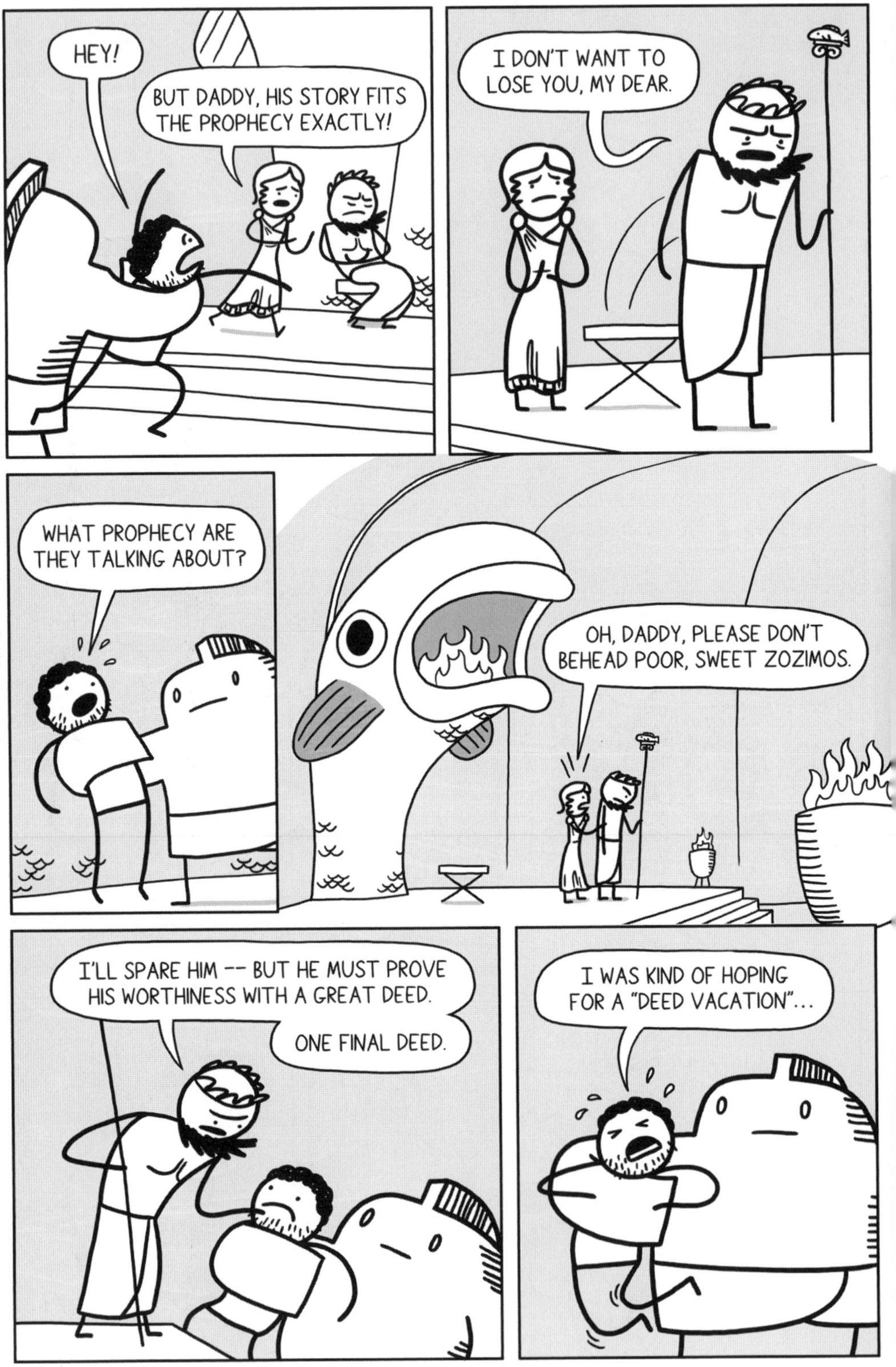
HEY!
BUT DADDY, HIS STORY FITS THE PROPHECY EXACTLY!
I DON'T WANT TO LOSE YOU, MY DEAR.
WHAT PROPHECY ARE THEY TALKING ABOUT?
OH, DADDY, PLEASE DON'T BEHEAD POOR, SWEET ZOZIMOS.
I'LL SPARE HIM -- BUT HE MUST PROVE HIS WORTHINESS WITH A GREAT DEED.
ONE FINAL DEED.
I WAS KIND OF HOPING FOR A "DEED VACATION"...

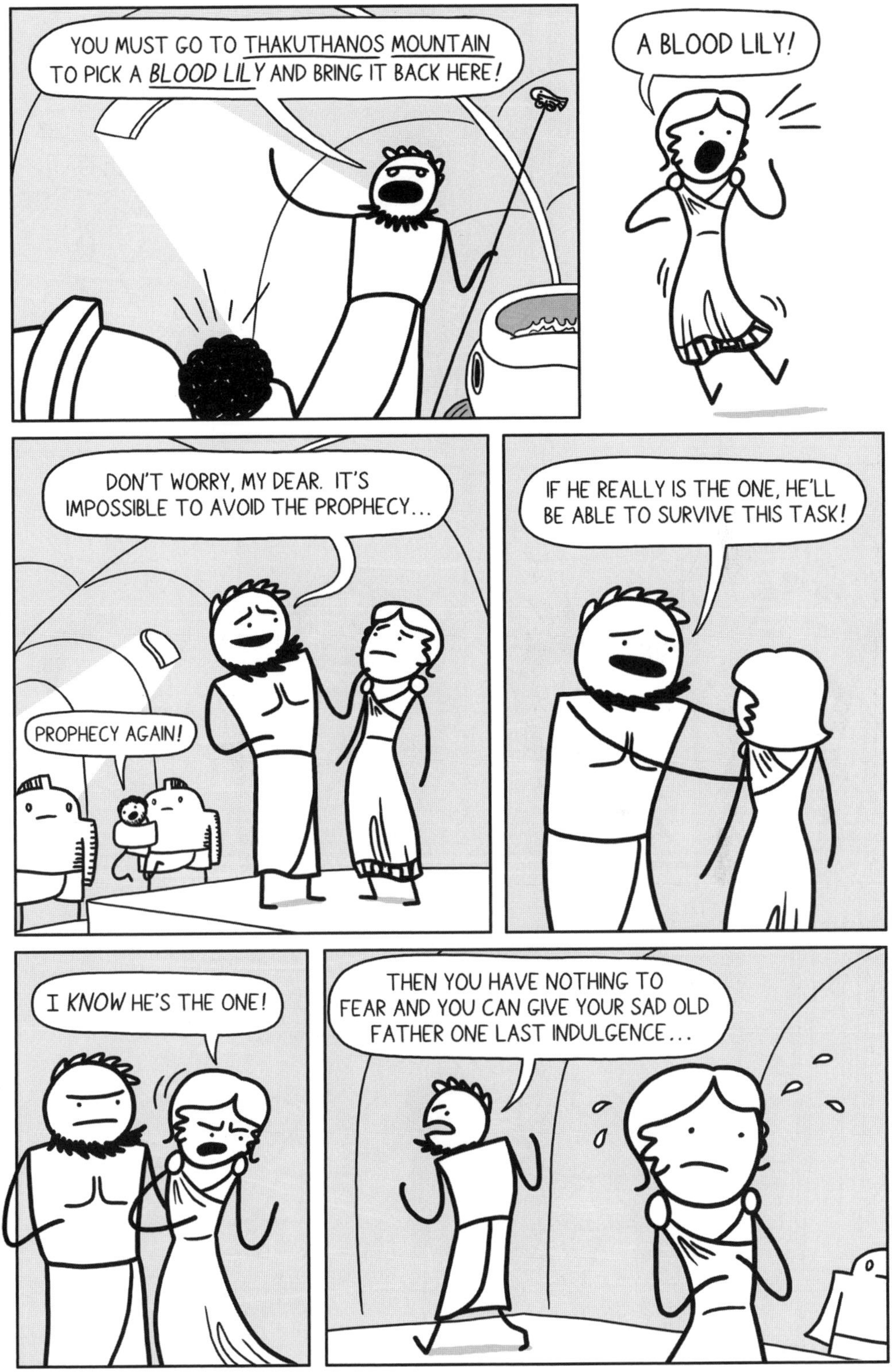
YOU MUST GO TO THAKUTHANOS MOUNTAIN TO PICK A BLOOD LILY AND BRING IT BACK HERE!
A BLOOD LILY!
DON'T WORRY, MY DEAR. IT'S IMPOSSIBLE TO AVOID THE PROPHECY...
PROPHECY AGAIN!
IF HE REALLY IS THE ONE, HE'LL BE ABLE TO SURVIVE THIS TASK!
I KNOW HE'S THE ONE!
THEN YOU HAVE NOTHING TO FEAR AND YOU CAN GIVE YOUR SAD OLD FATHER ONE LAST INDULGENCE...

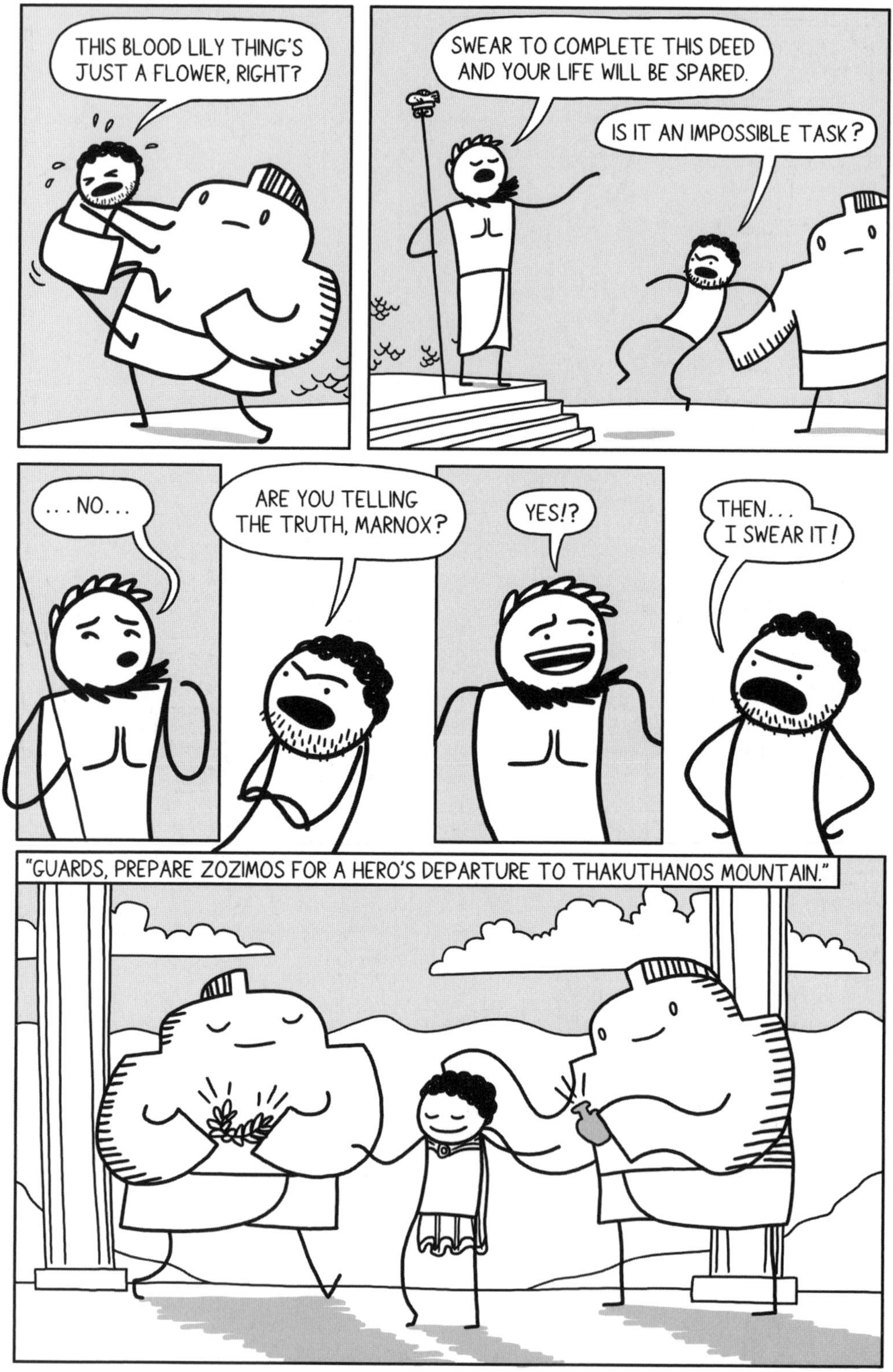
THIS BLOOD LILY THING'S JUST A FLOWER, RIGHT?
SWEAR TO COMPLETE THIS DEED AND YOUR LIFE WILL BE SPARED.
IS IT AN IMPOSSIBLE TASK?
...NO...
ARE YOU TELLING THE TRUTH, MARNOX?
YES!?
THEN... I SWEAR IT!
"GUARDS, PREPARE ZOZIMOS FOR A HERO'S DEPARTURE TO THAKUTHANOS MOUNTAIN."

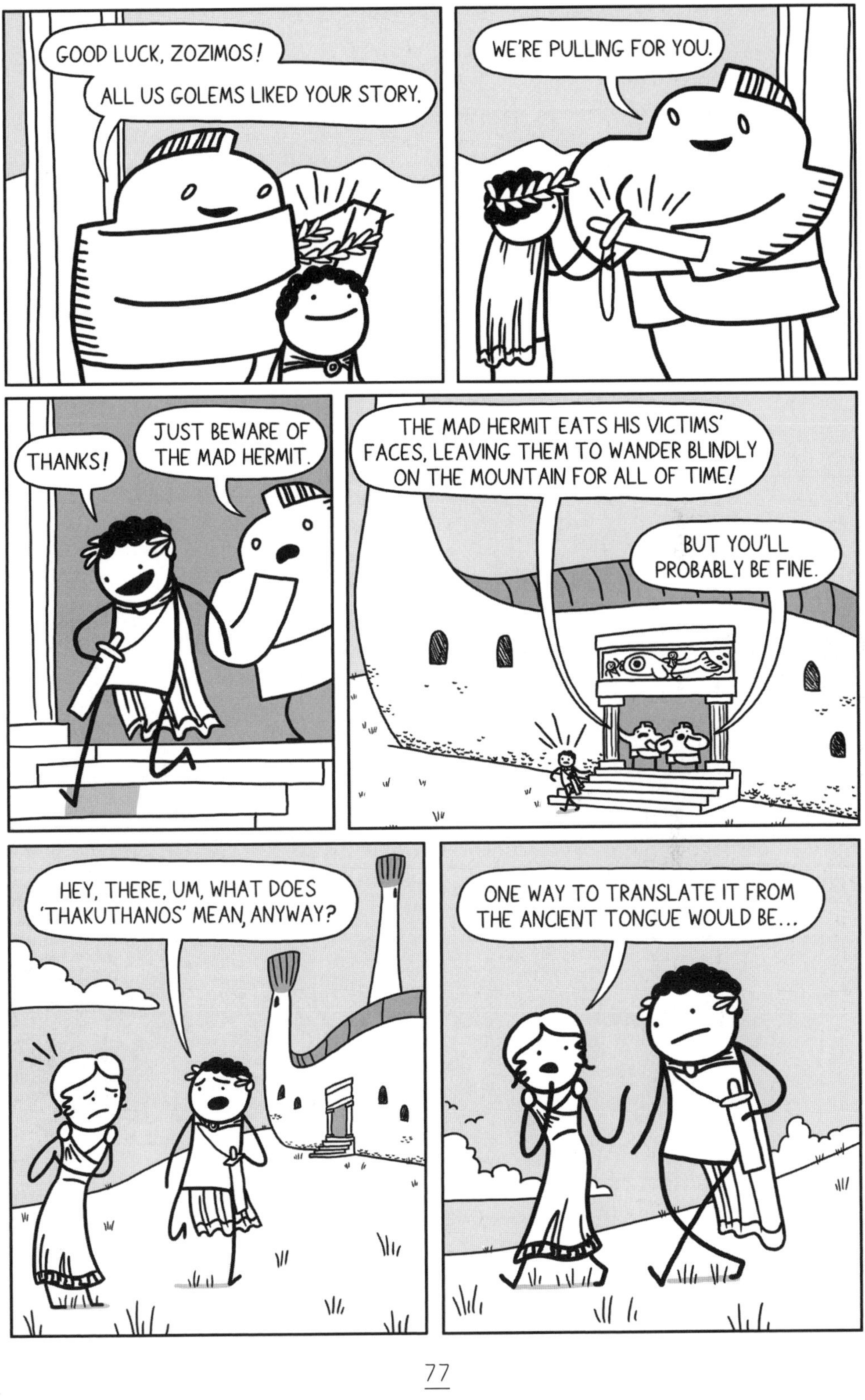
GOOD LUCK, ZOZIMOS!
ALL US GOLEMS LIKED YOUR STORY.
WE'RE PULLING FOR YOU.
THANKS!
JUST BEWARE OF THE MAD HERMIT.
THE MAD HERMIT EATS HIS VICTIMS' FACES, LEAVING THEM TO WANDER BLINDLY ON THE MOUNTAIN FOR ALL OF TIME!
BUT YOU'LL PROBABLY BE FINE.
HEY, THERE, UM, WHAT DOES 'THAKUTHANOS' MEAN, ANYWAY?
ONE WAY TO TRANSLATE IT FROM THE ANCIENT TONGUE WOULD BE...

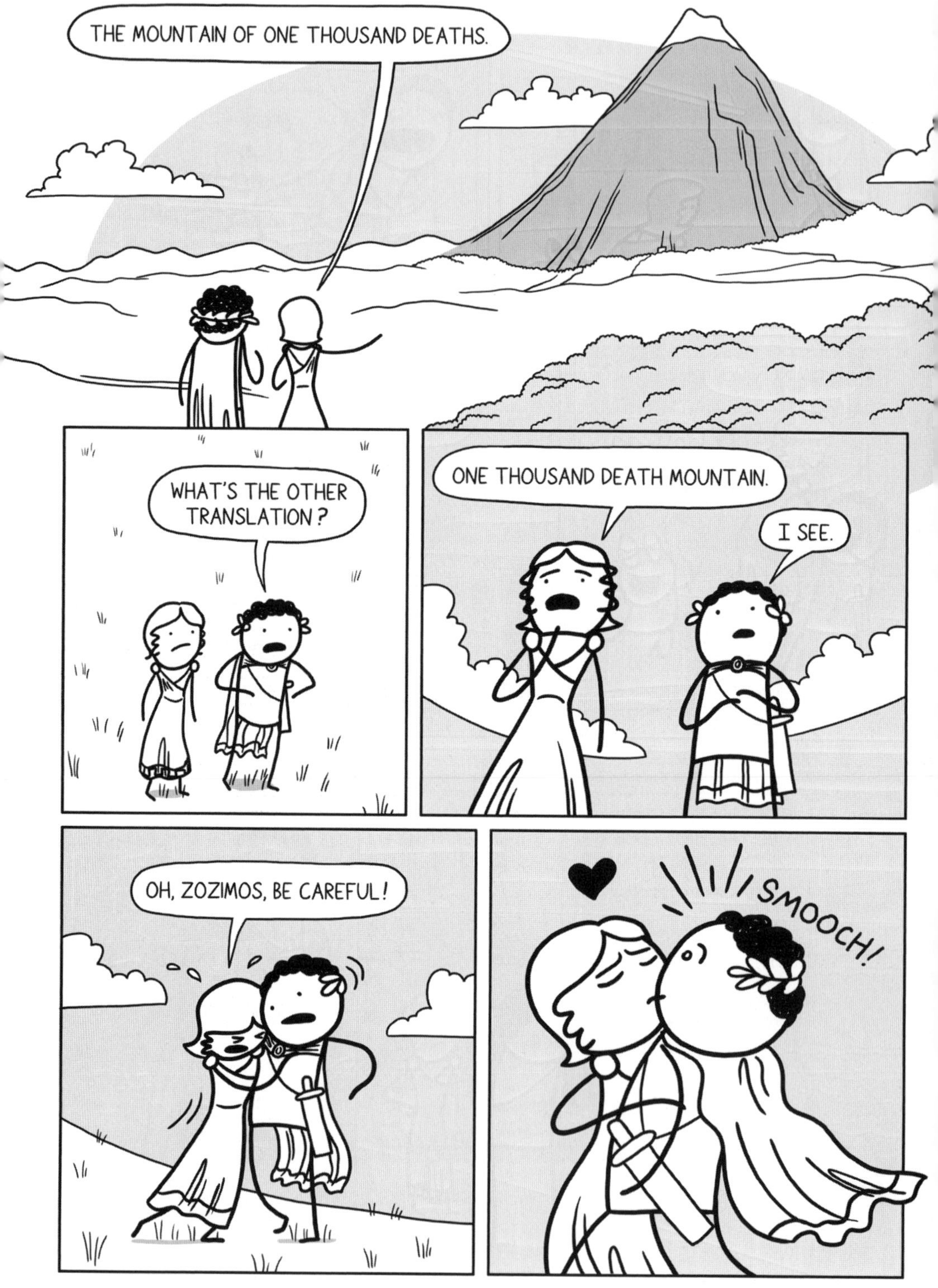
THE MOUNTAIN OF ONE THOUSAND DEATHS.
WHAT'S THE OTHER TRANSLATION?
ONE THOUSAND DEATH MOUNTAIN.
I SEE.
OH, ZOZIMOS, BE CAREFUL!
SMOOCH!

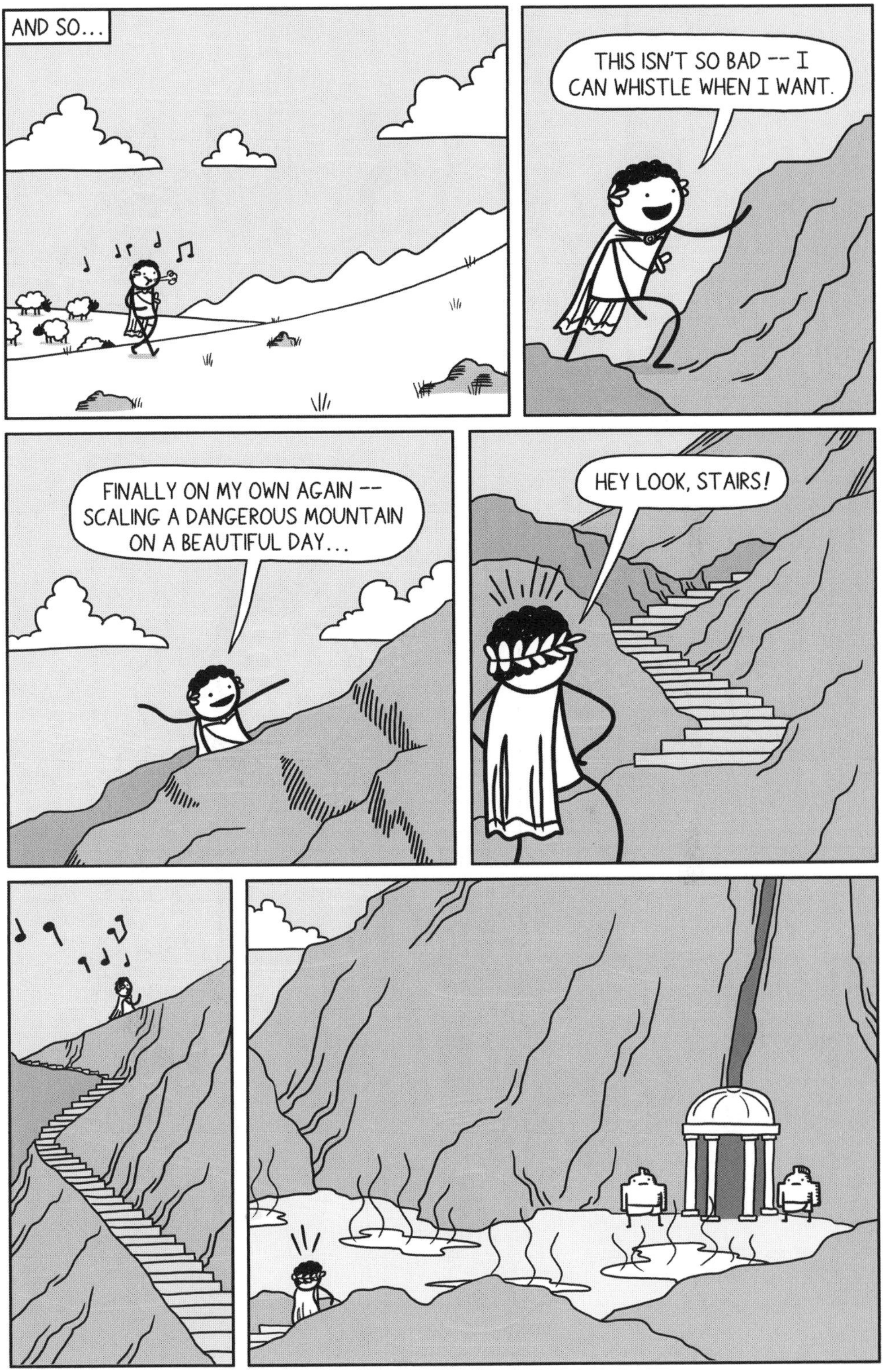
AND SO...
THIS ISN'T SO BAD -- I CAN WHISTLE WHEN I WANT.
FINALLY ON MY OWN AGAIN -- SCALING A DANGEROUS MOUNTAIN ON A BEAUTIFUL DAY...
HEY LOOK, STAIRS!

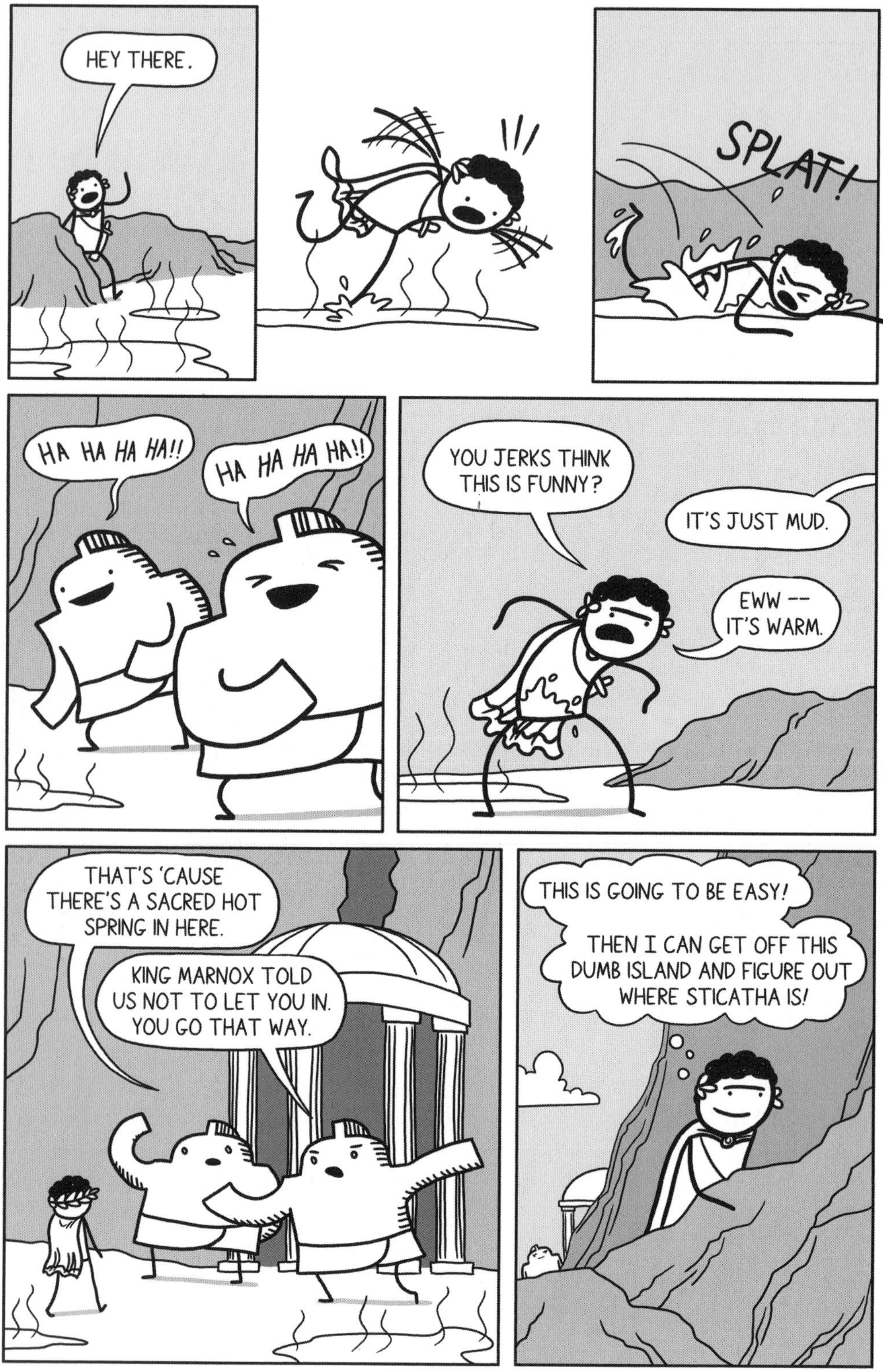
HEY THERE.
SPLAT!
HA HA HA HA!!
HA HA HA HA!!
YOU JERKS THINK THIS IS FUNNY?
IT'S JUST MUD.
EWW -- IT'S WARM.
THAT'S 'CAUSE THERE'S A SACRED HOT SPRING IN HERE.
KING MARNOX TOLD US NOT TO LET YOU IN. YOU GO THAT WAY.
THIS IS GOING TO BE EASY!
THEN I CAN GET OFF THIS DUMB ISLAND AND FIGURE OUT WHERE STICATHA IS!

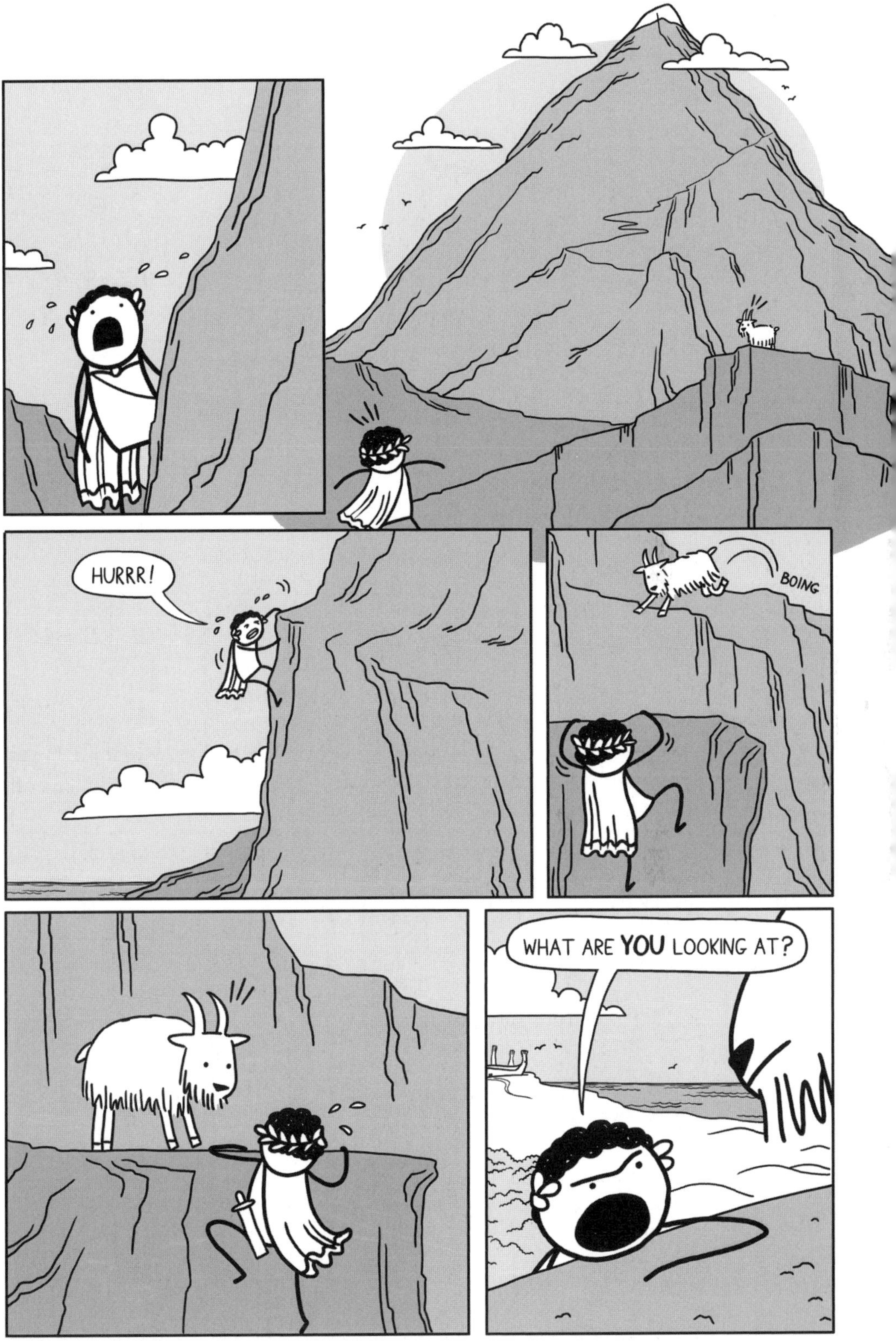
HURRR!
BOING
WHAT ARE **YOU** LOOKING AT?

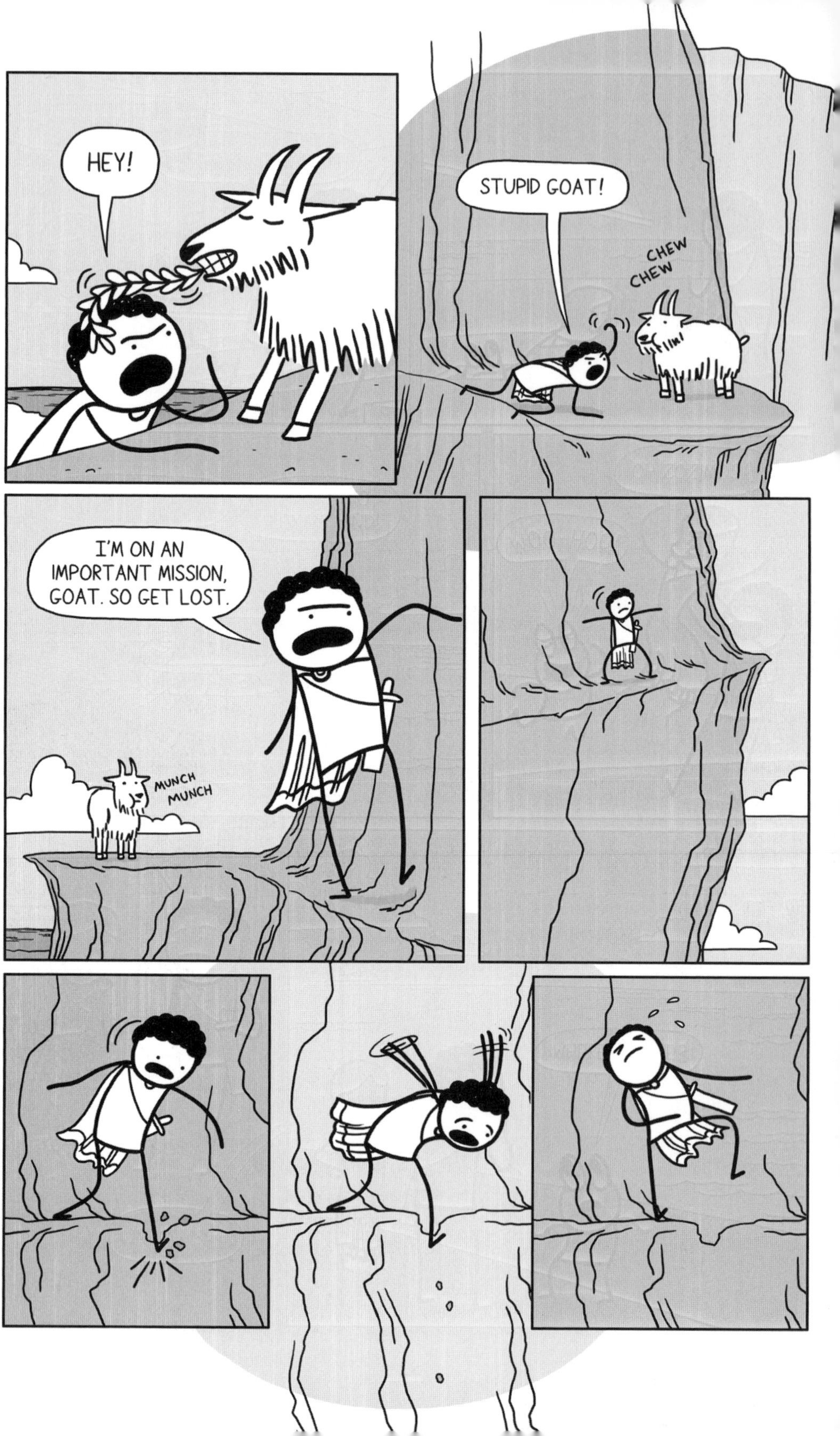
HEY!
STUPID GOAT!
CHEW CHEW
I'M ON AN IMPORTANT MISSION, GOAT. SO GET LOST.
MUNCH MUNCH

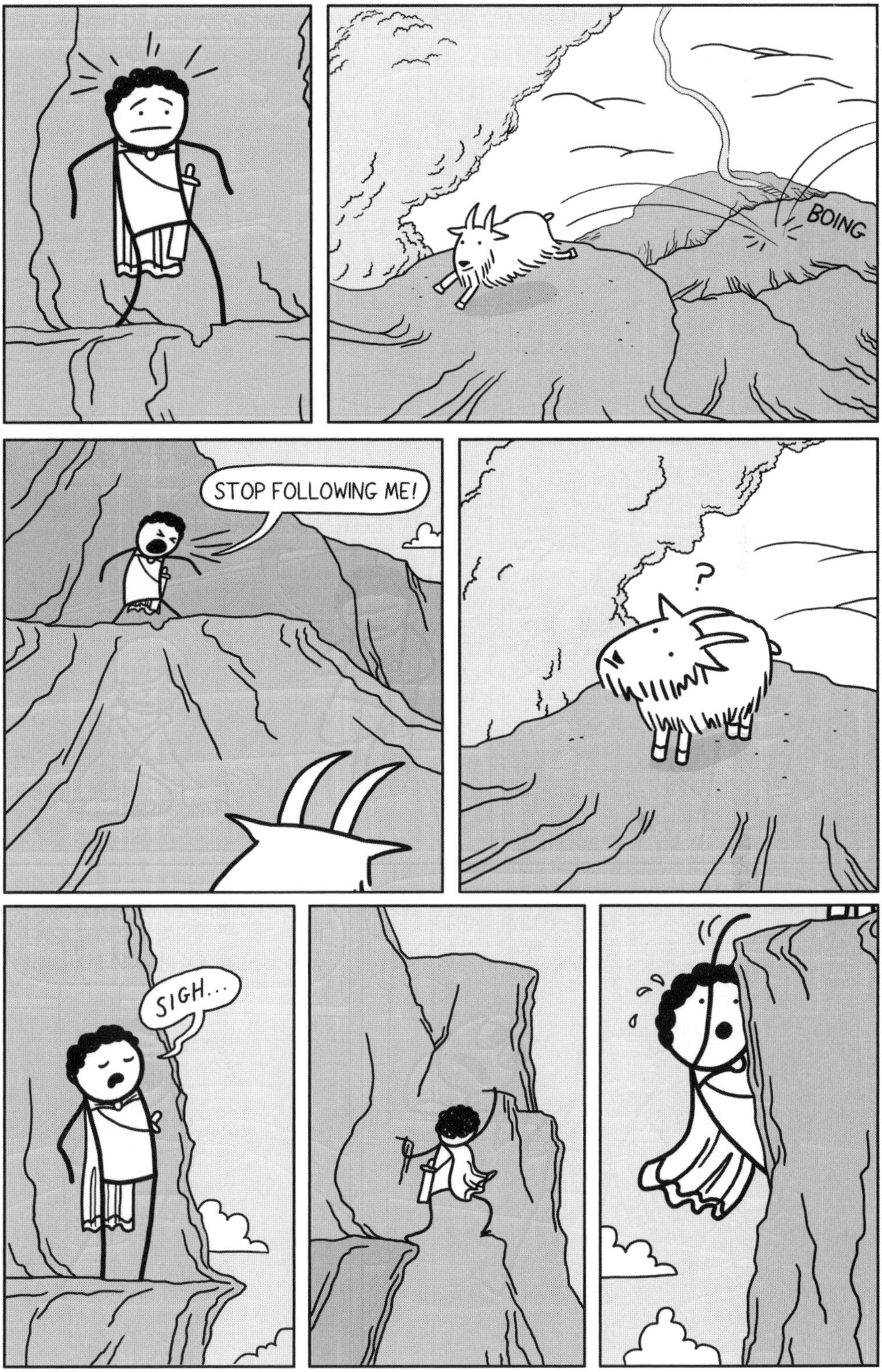
BOING
STOP FOLLOWING ME!
?
SIGH...

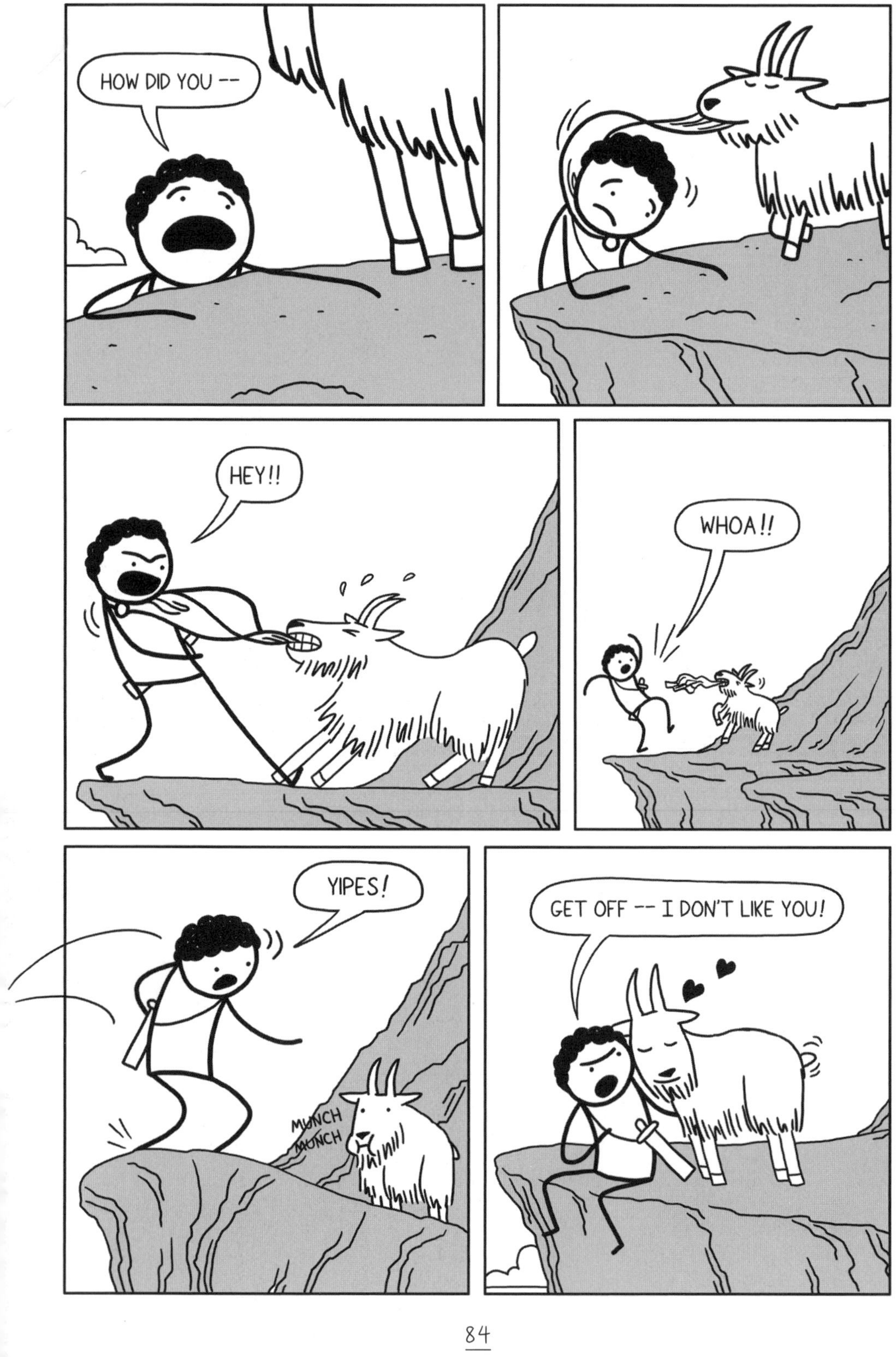
HOW DID YOU --
HEY!!
WHOA!!
YIPES!
MUNCH
MUNCH
GET OFF -- I DON'T LIKE YOU!

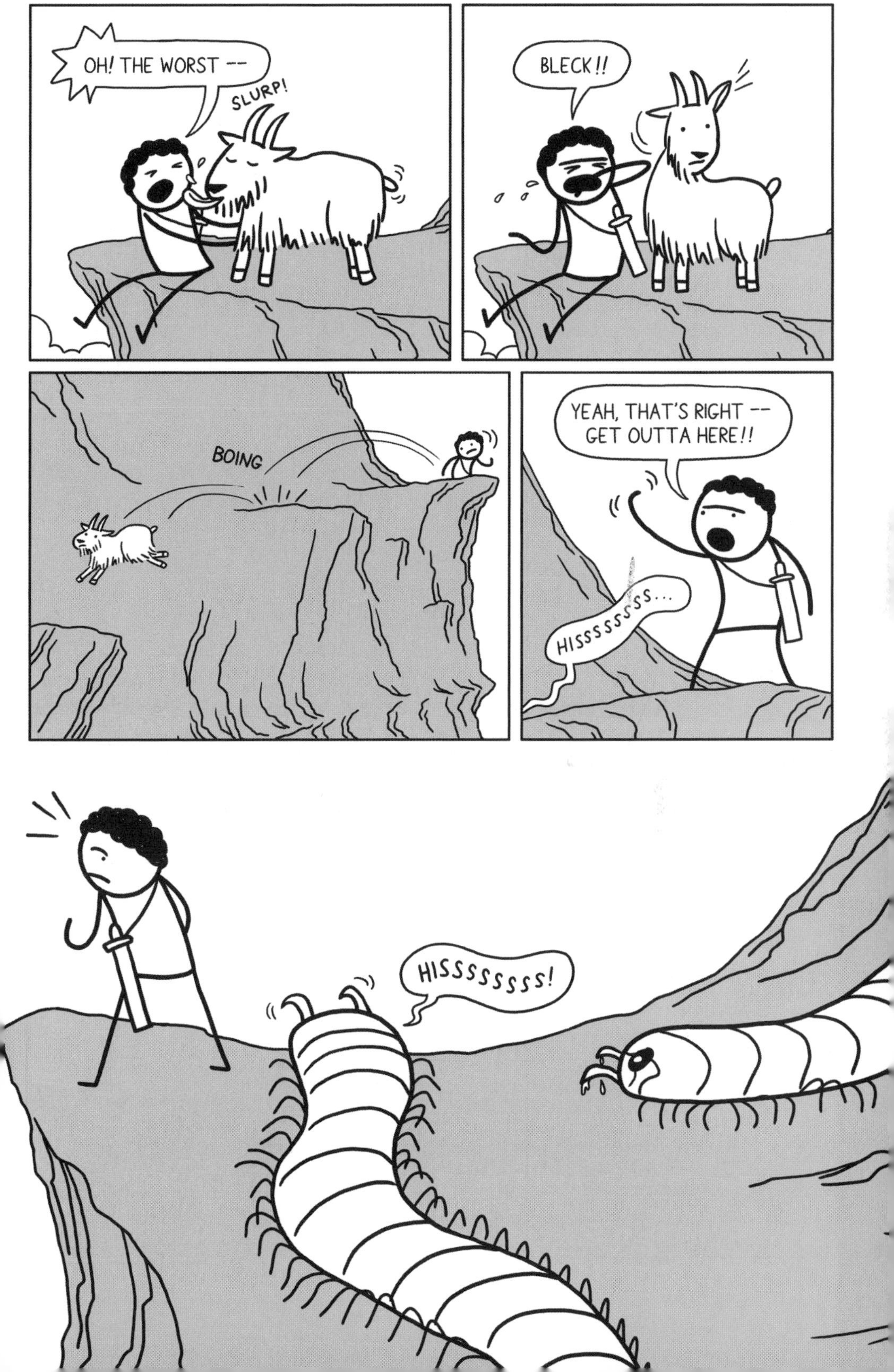
OH! THE WORST --
SLURP!
BLECK!!
BOING
YEAH, THAT'S RIGHT -- GET OUTTA HERE!!
HISSSSSSSSS...
HISSSSSSSSS!

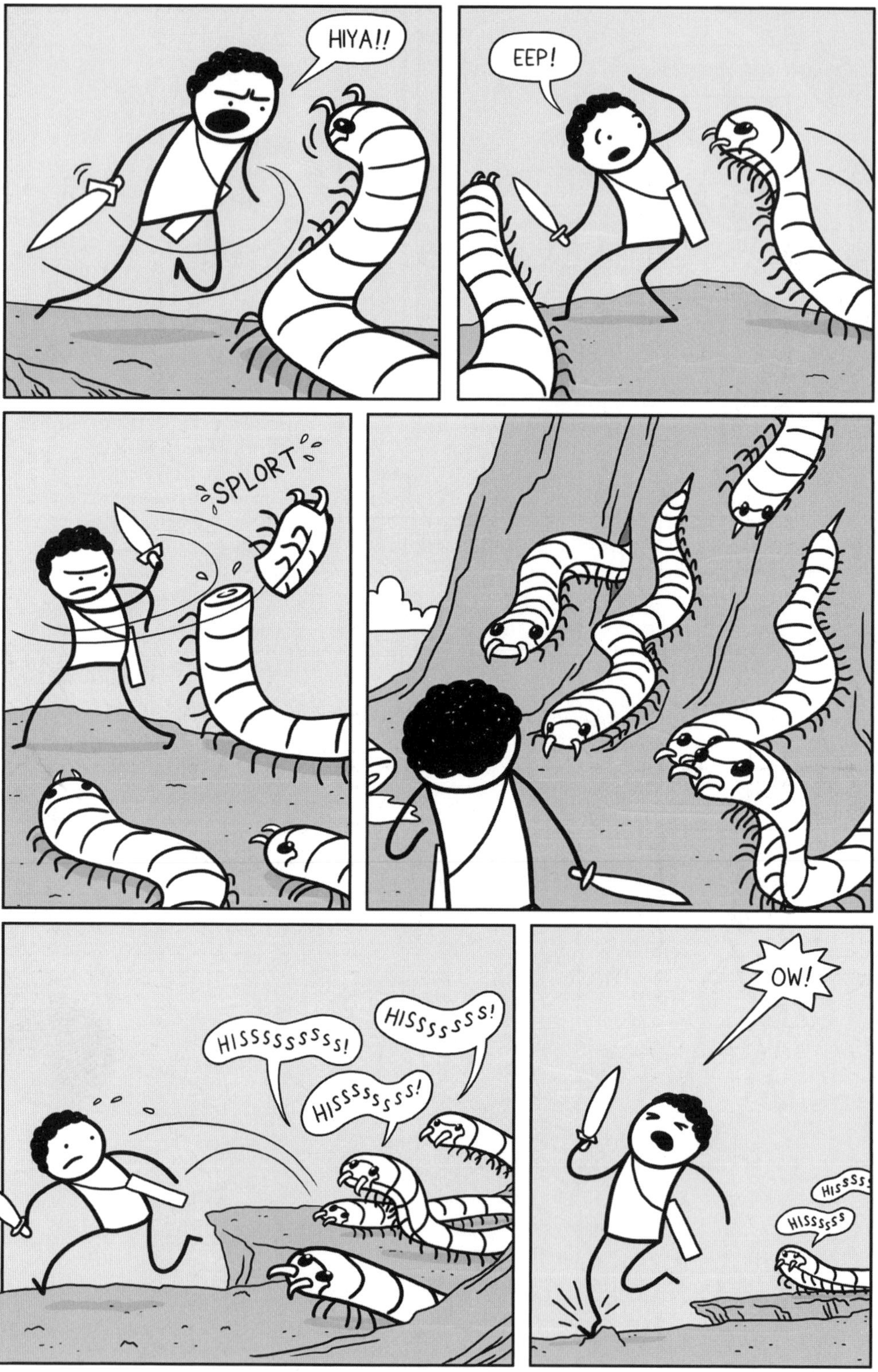

HIYA!!
EEP!
SPLORT
HISSSSSSSSSSs!
HISSSSSSSS!
HISSSSSSSSS!
OW!
HISSSS
HISSSSSS

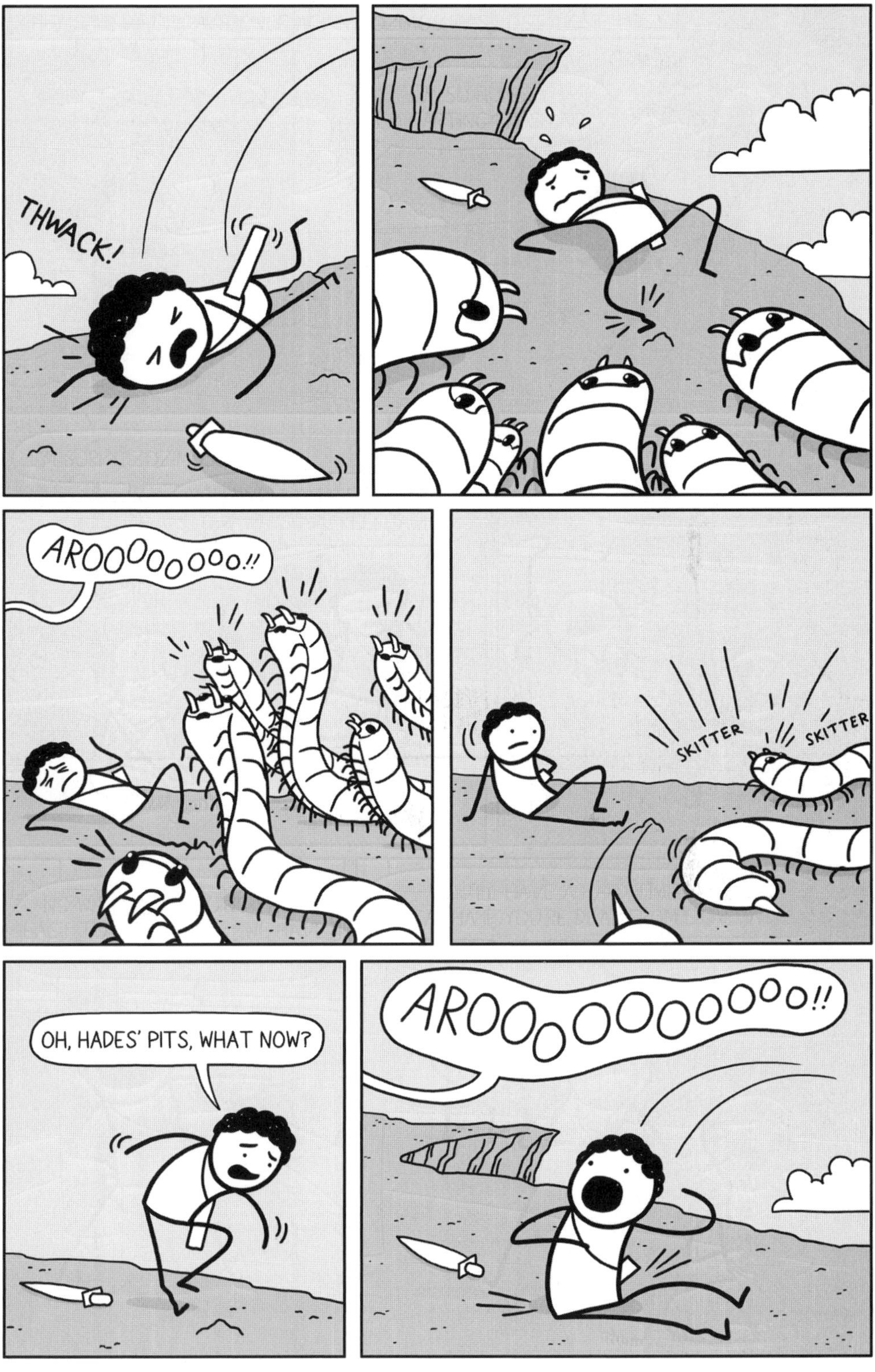
THWACK!
AROOOOOOOOO!!
SKITTER
SKITTER
OH, HADES' PITS, WHAT NOW?
AROOOOOOOOOOOOO!!

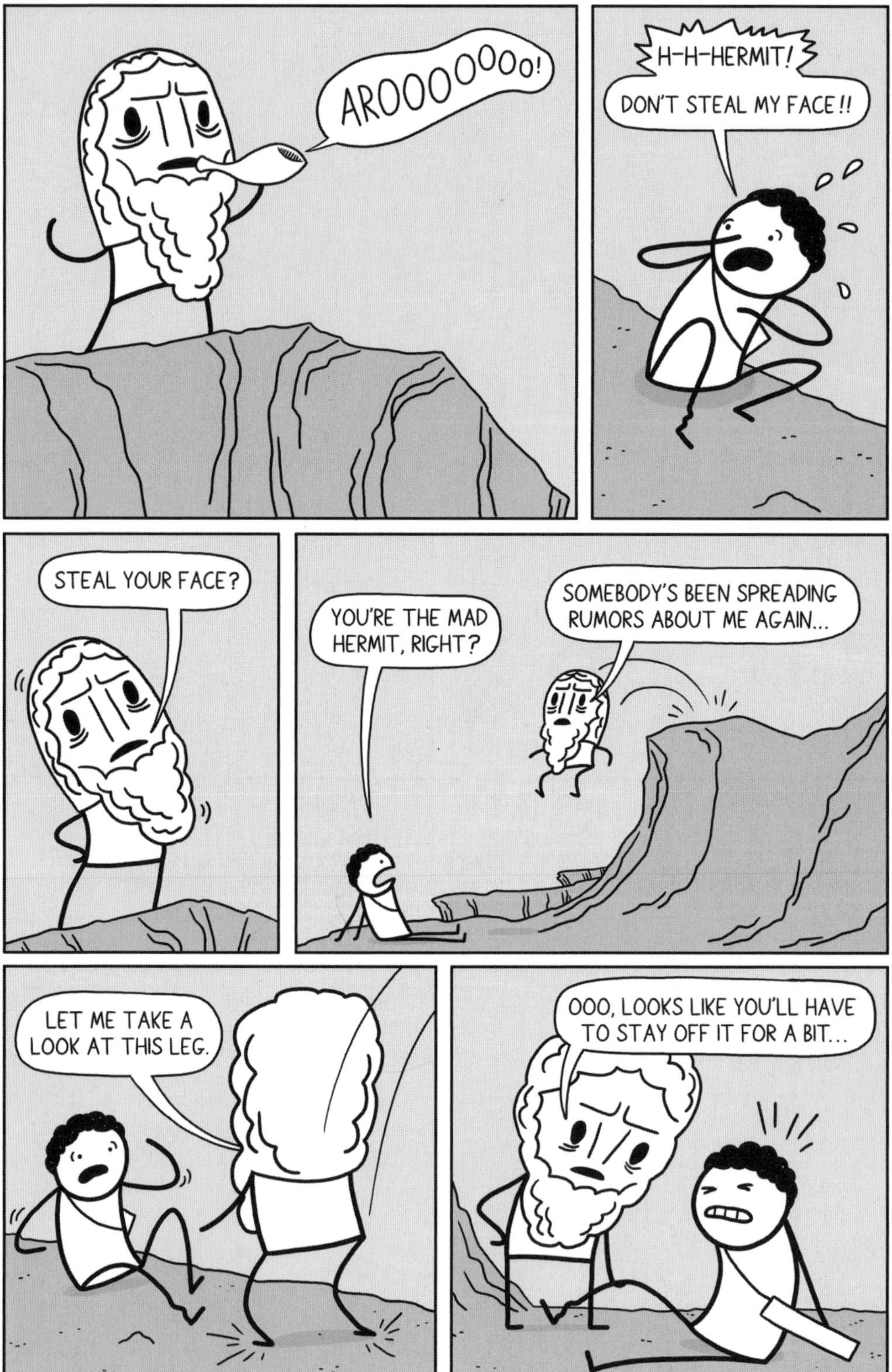
AROOOOOOOo!
H-H-HERMIT!
DON'T STEAL MY FACE!!
STEAL YOUR FACE?
YOU'RE THE MAD HERMIT, RIGHT?
SOMEBODY'S BEEN SPREADING RUMORS ABOUT ME AGAIN...
LET ME TAKE A LOOK AT THIS LEG.
OOO, LOOKS LIKE YOU'LL HAVE TO STAY OFF IT FOR A BIT...

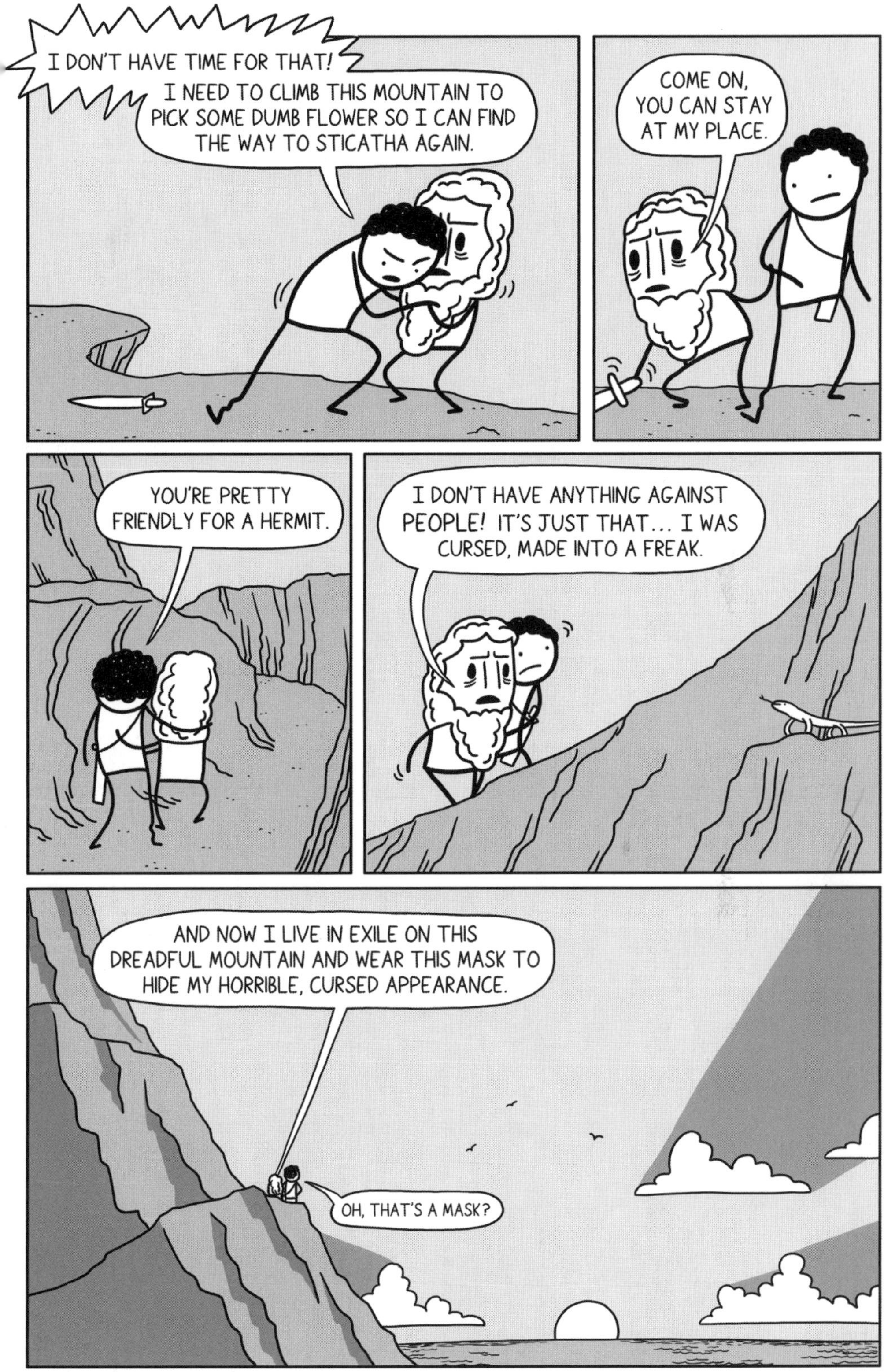
I DON'T HAVE TIME FOR THAT!
I NEED TO CLIMB THIS MOUNTAIN TO PICK SOME DUMB FLOWER SO I CAN FIND THE WAY TO STICATHA AGAIN.
COME ON, YOU CAN STAY AT MY PLACE.
YOU'RE PRETTY FRIENDLY FOR A HERMIT.
I DON'T HAVE ANYTHING AGAINST PEOPLE! IT'S JUST THAT... I WAS CURSED, MADE INTO A FREAK.
AND NOW I LIVE IN EXILE ON THIS DREADFUL MOUNTAIN AND WEAR THIS MASK TO HIDE MY HORRIBLE, CURSED APPEARANCE.
OH, THAT'S A MASK?

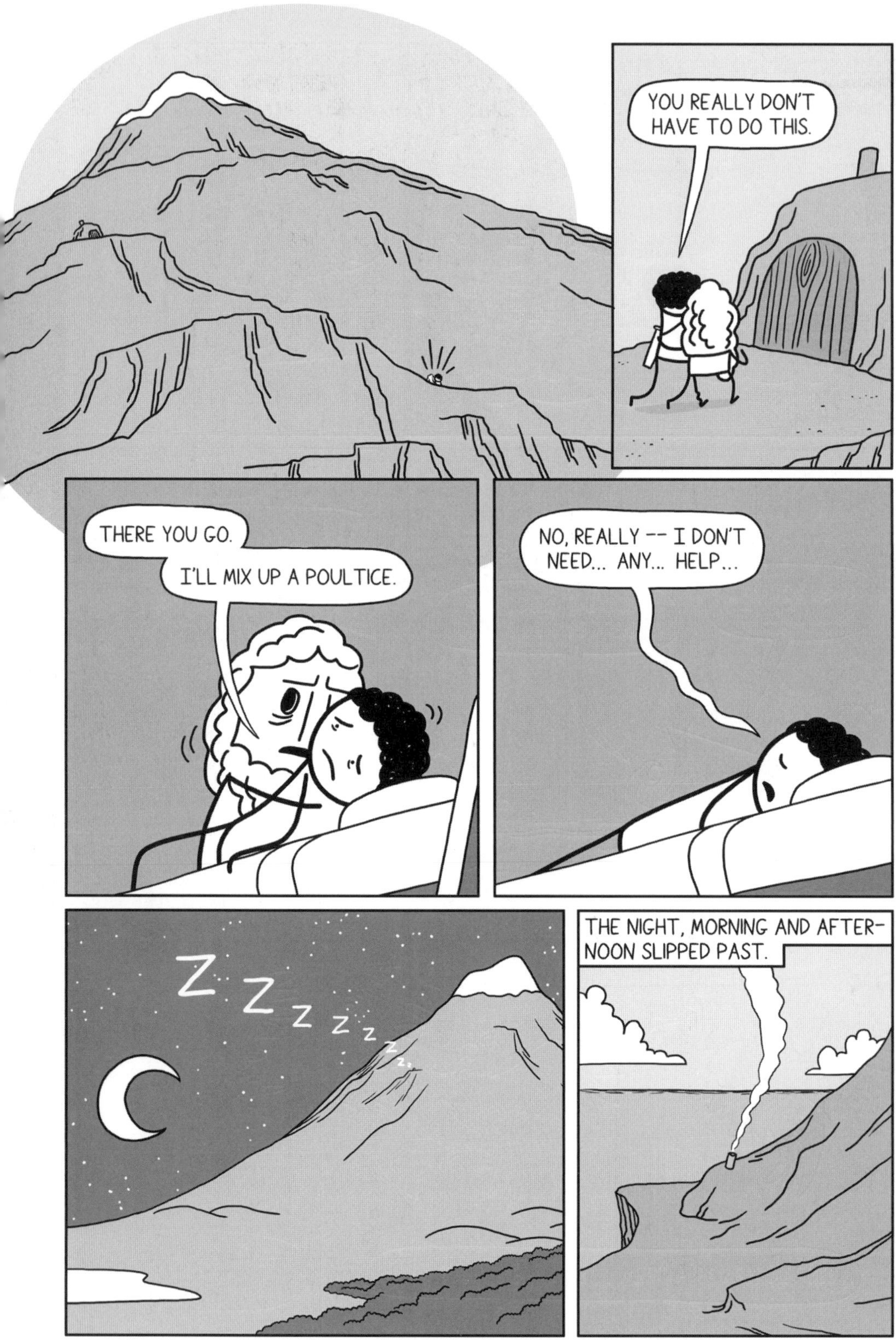
YOU REALLY DON'T HAVE TO DO THIS.
THERE YOU GO.
I'LL MIX UP A POULTICE.
NO, REALLY -- I DON'T NEED... ANY... HELP...
Z Z Z Z Z Z Z z
THE NIGHT, MORNING AND AFTER-NOON SLIPPED PAST.

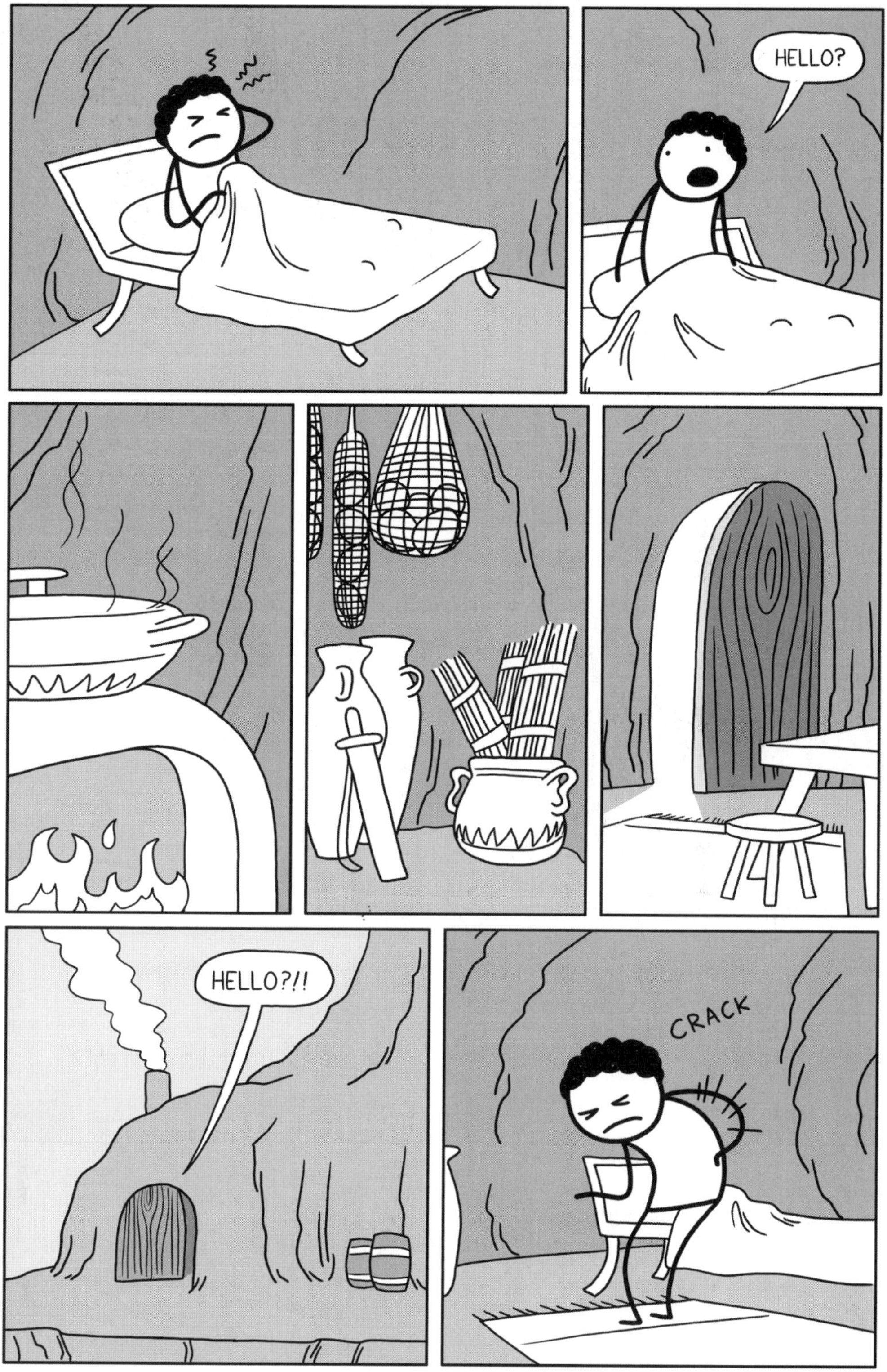
HELLO?
HELLO?!!
CRACK

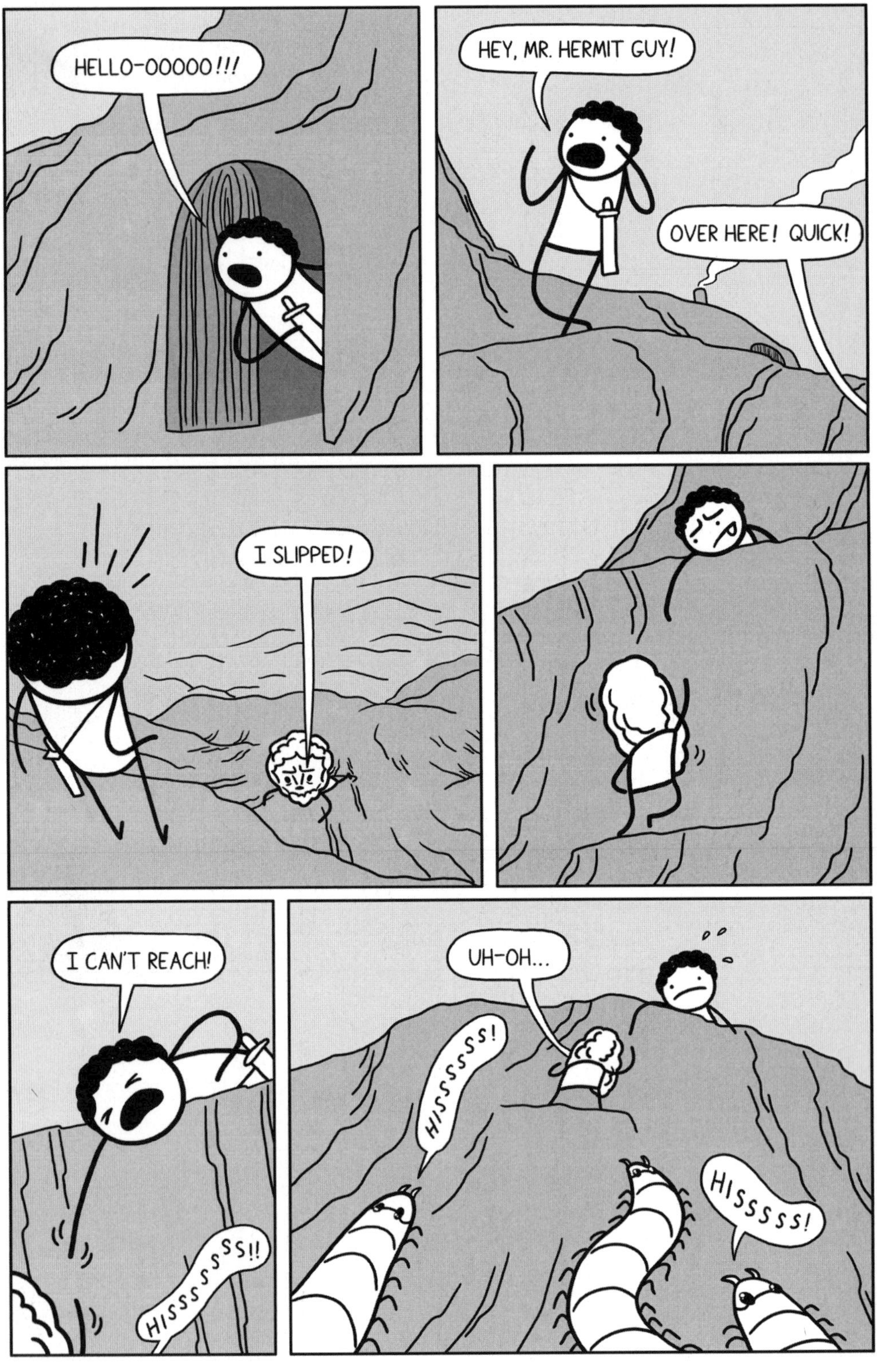
HELLO-OOOOO!!!
HEY, MR. HERMIT GUY!
OVER HERE! QUICK!
I SLIPPED!
I CAN'T REACH!
HISSSSSSS!!
UH-OH...
HISSSSSS!
HISSSSS!

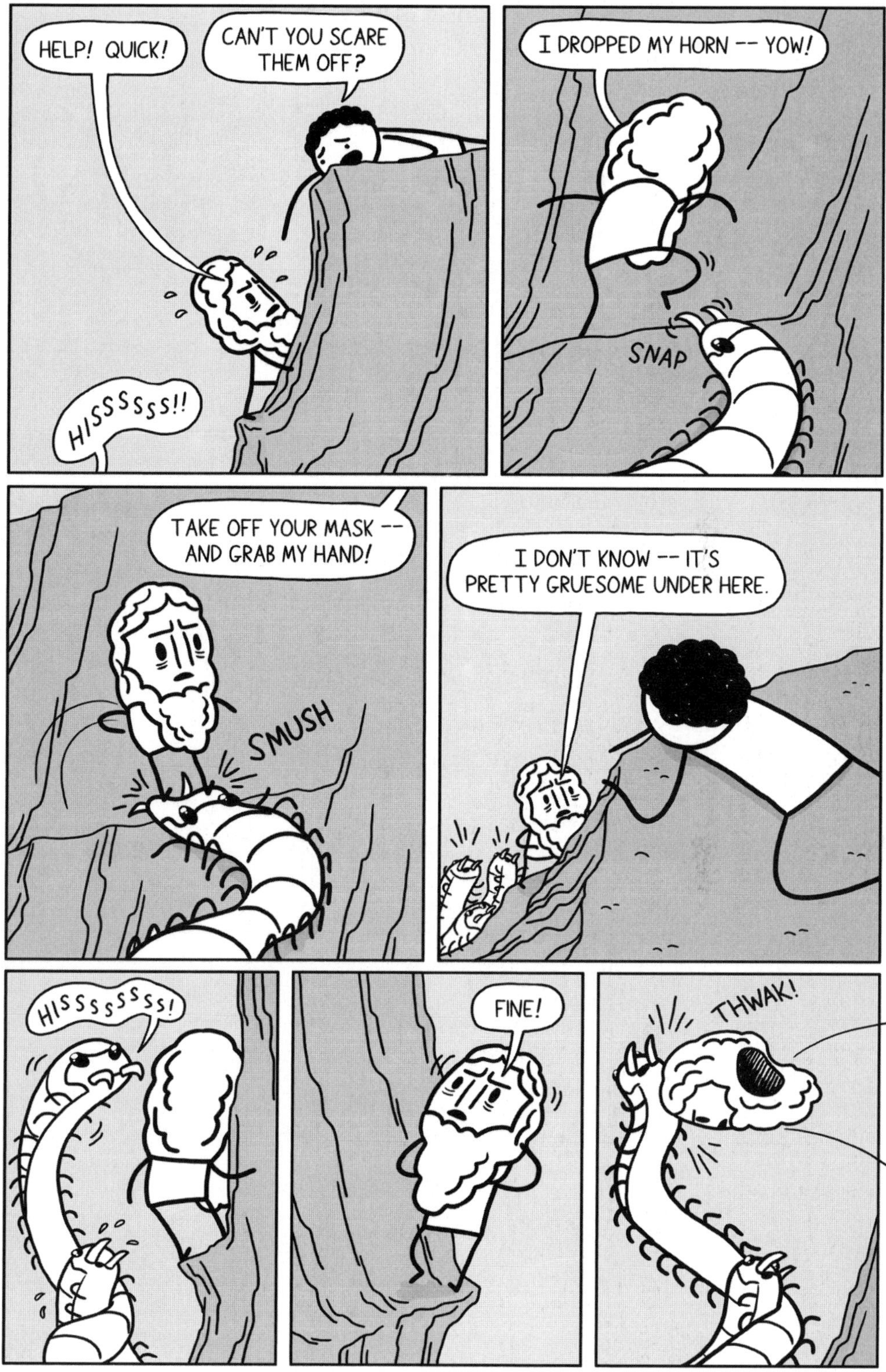
HELP! QUICK!
CAN'T YOU SCARE THEM OFF?
HISSSSSS!!
I DROPPED MY HORN -- YOW!
SNAP
TAKE OFF YOUR MASK -- AND GRAB MY HAND!
SMUSH
I DON'T KNOW -- IT'S PRETTY GRUESOME UNDER HERE.
HISSSSSSSSS!
FINE!
THWAK!

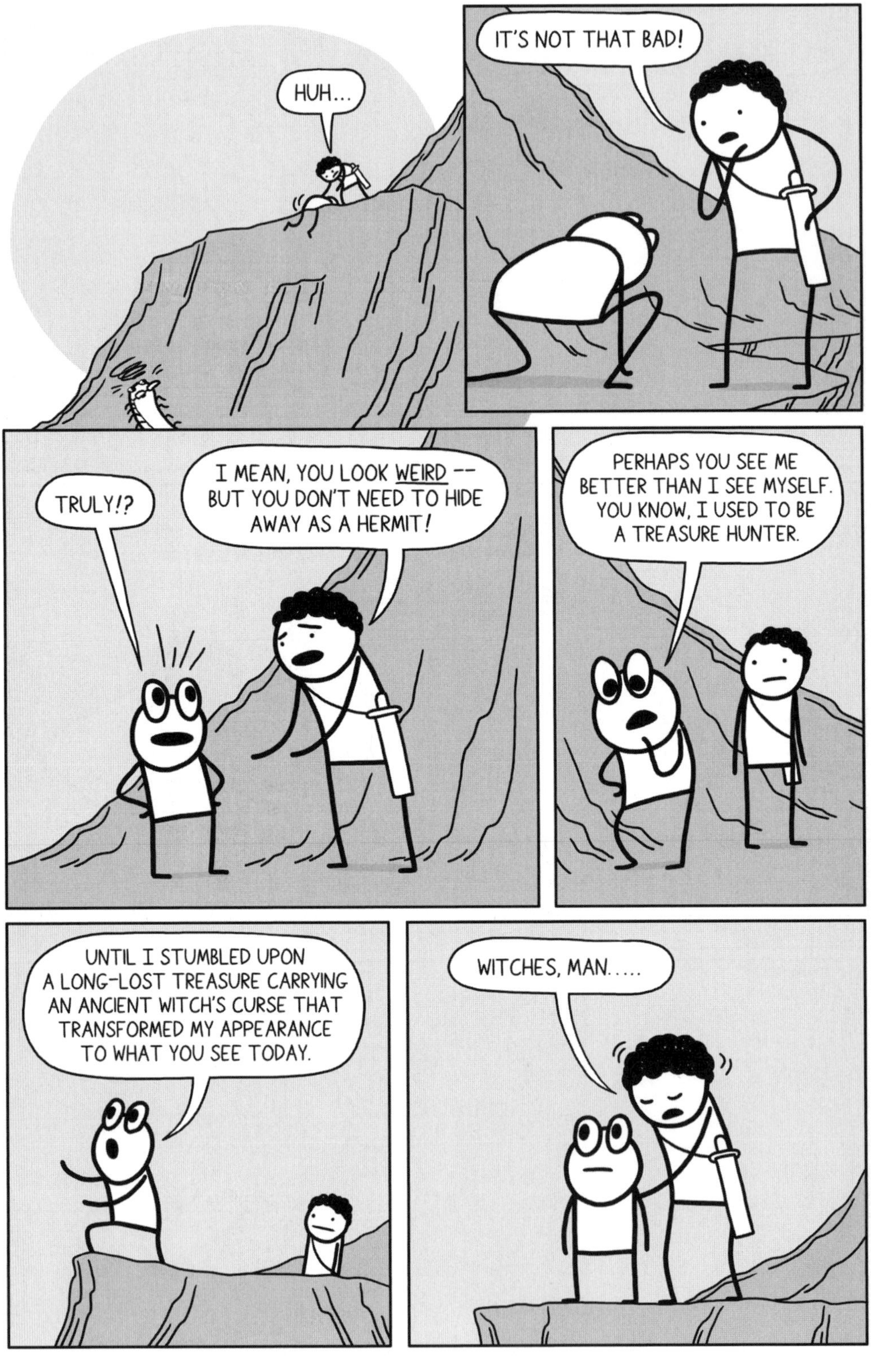
HUH...
IT'S NOT THAT BAD!
TRULY!?
I MEAN, YOU LOOK WEIRD -- BUT YOU DON'T NEED TO HIDE AWAY AS A HERMIT!
PERHAPS YOU SEE ME BETTER THAN I SEE MYSELF. YOU KNOW, I USED TO BE A TREASURE HUNTER.
UNTIL I STUMBLED UPON A LONG-LOST TREASURE CARRYING AN ANCIENT WITCH'S CURSE THAT TRANSFORMED MY APPEARANCE TO WHAT YOU SEE TODAY.
WITCHES, MAN.....

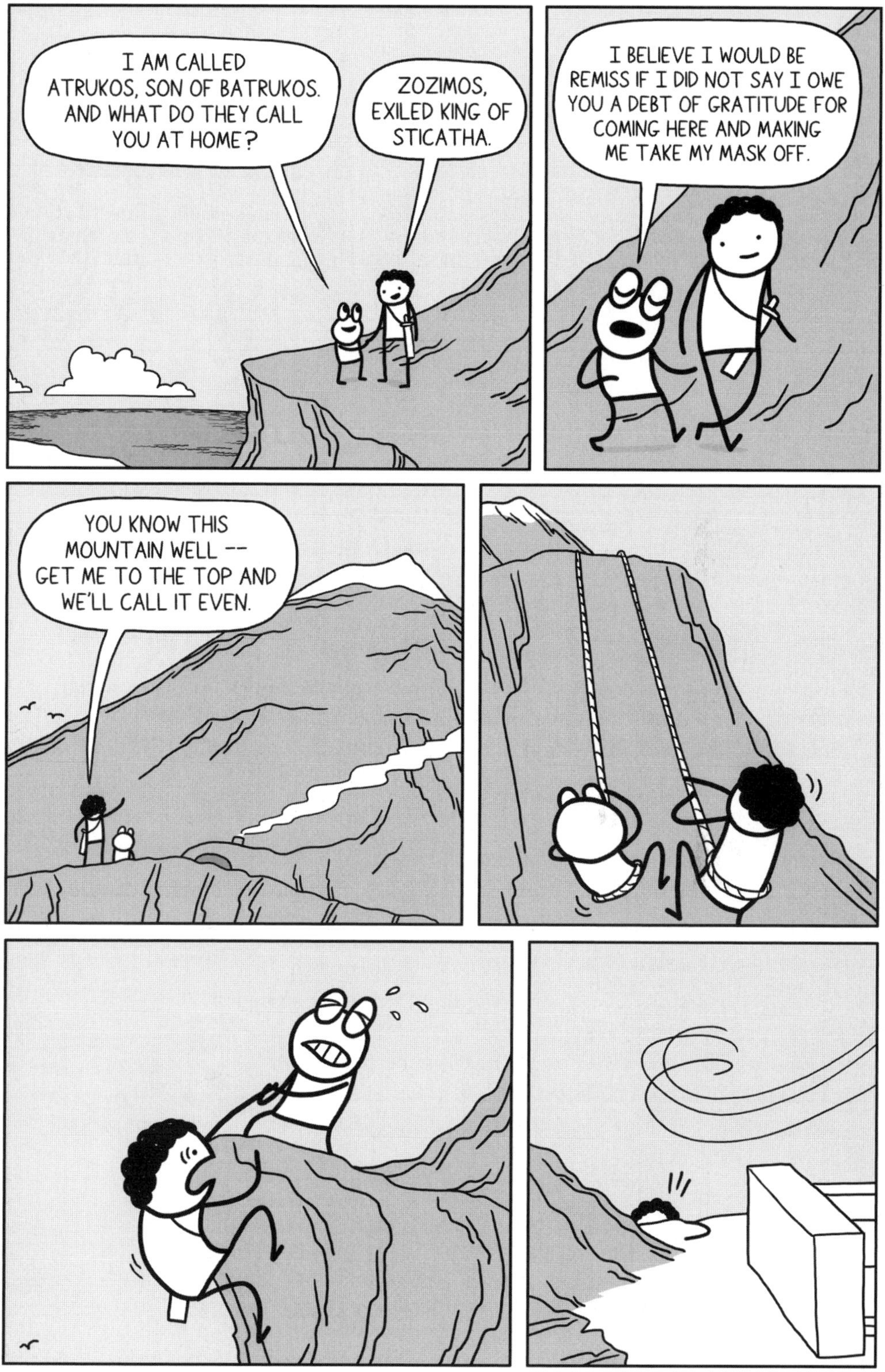
I AM CALLED ATRUKOS, SON OF BATRUKOS. AND WHAT DO THEY CALL YOU AT HOME?
ZOZIMOS, EXILED KING OF STICATHA.
I BELIEVE I WOULD BE REMISS IF I DID NOT SAY I OWE YOU A DEBT OF GRATITUDE FOR COMING HERE AND MAKING ME TAKE MY MASK OFF.
YOU KNOW THIS MOUNTAIN WELL -- GET ME TO THE TOP AND WE'LL CALL IT EVEN.

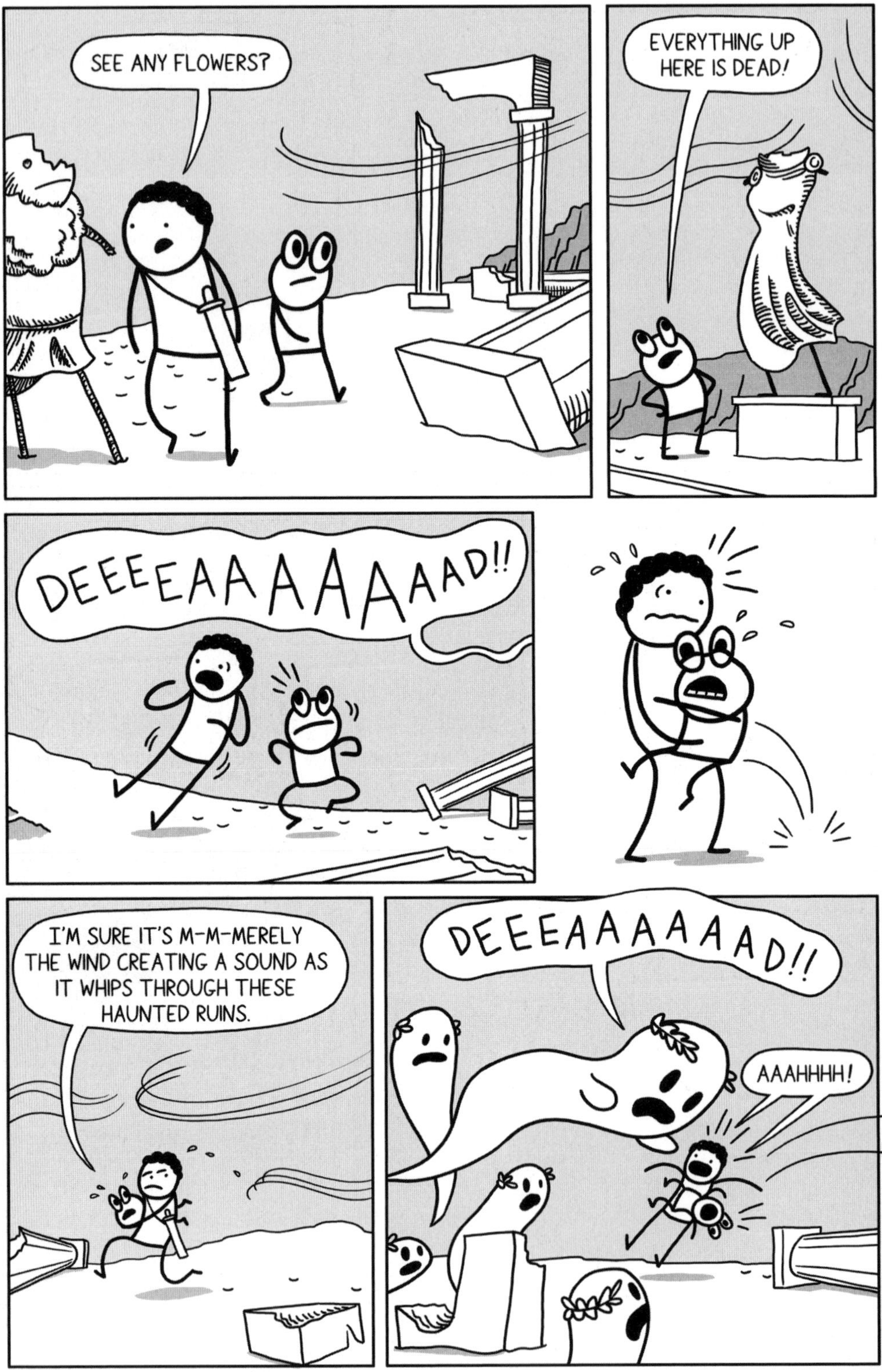
SEE ANY FLOWERS?
EVERYTHING UP HERE IS DEAD!
DEEEEAAAAAAAD!!
I'M SURE IT'S M-M-MERELY THE WIND CREATING A SOUND AS IT WHIPS THROUGH THESE HAUNTED RUINS.
DEEEAAAAAAAD!!
AAAHHHH!

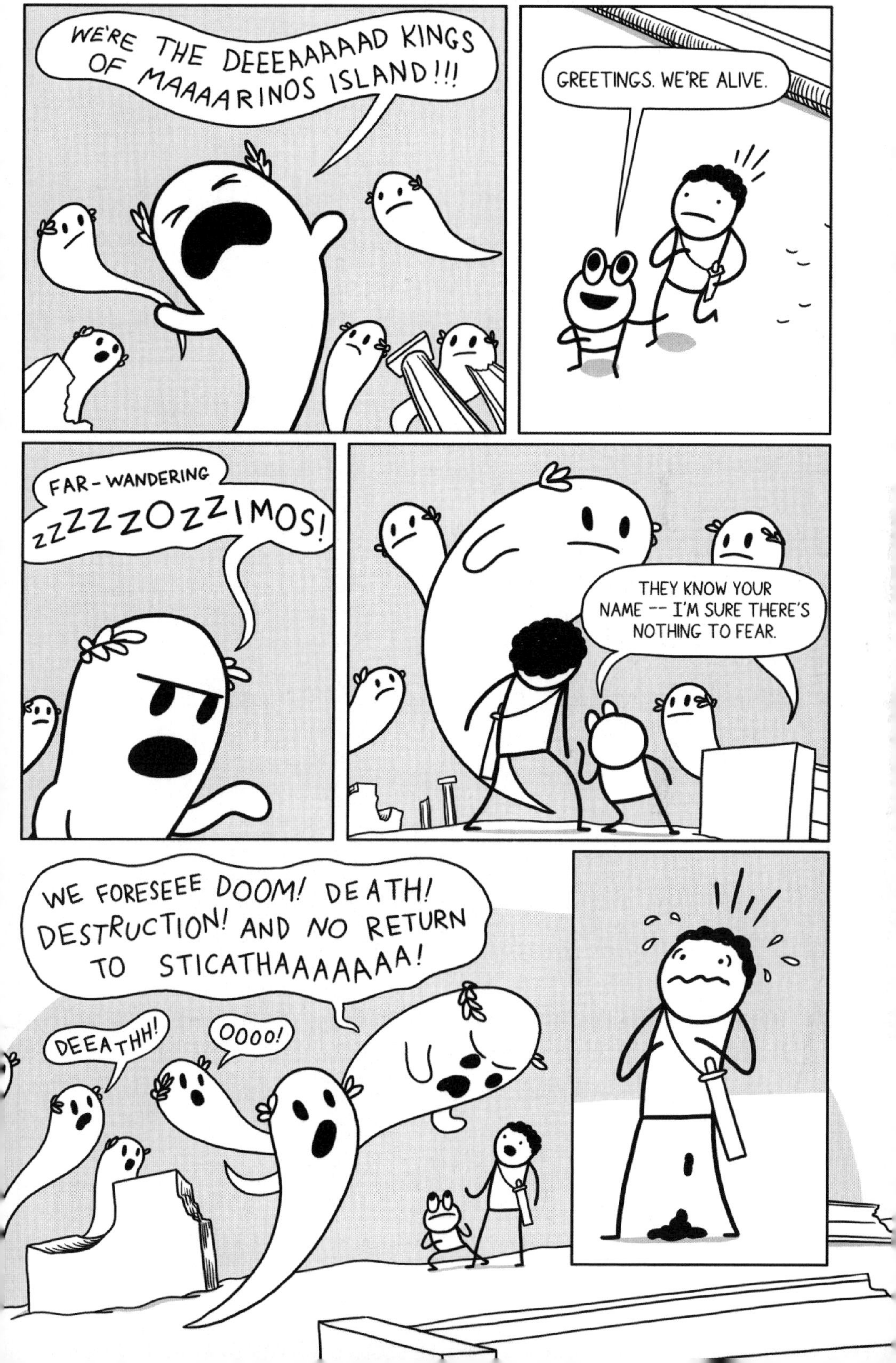
WE'RE THE DEEEAAAAAD KINGS OF MAAAARINOS ISLAND!!!
GREETINGS. WE'RE ALIVE.
FAR-WANDERING zzZZZZOZZZIMOS!
THEY KNOW YOUR NAME -- I'M SURE THERE'S NOTHING TO FEAR.
WE FORESEEE DOOM! DEATH! DESTRUCTION! AND NO RETURN TO STICATHAAAAAAA!
DEEATHH!
OOOO!

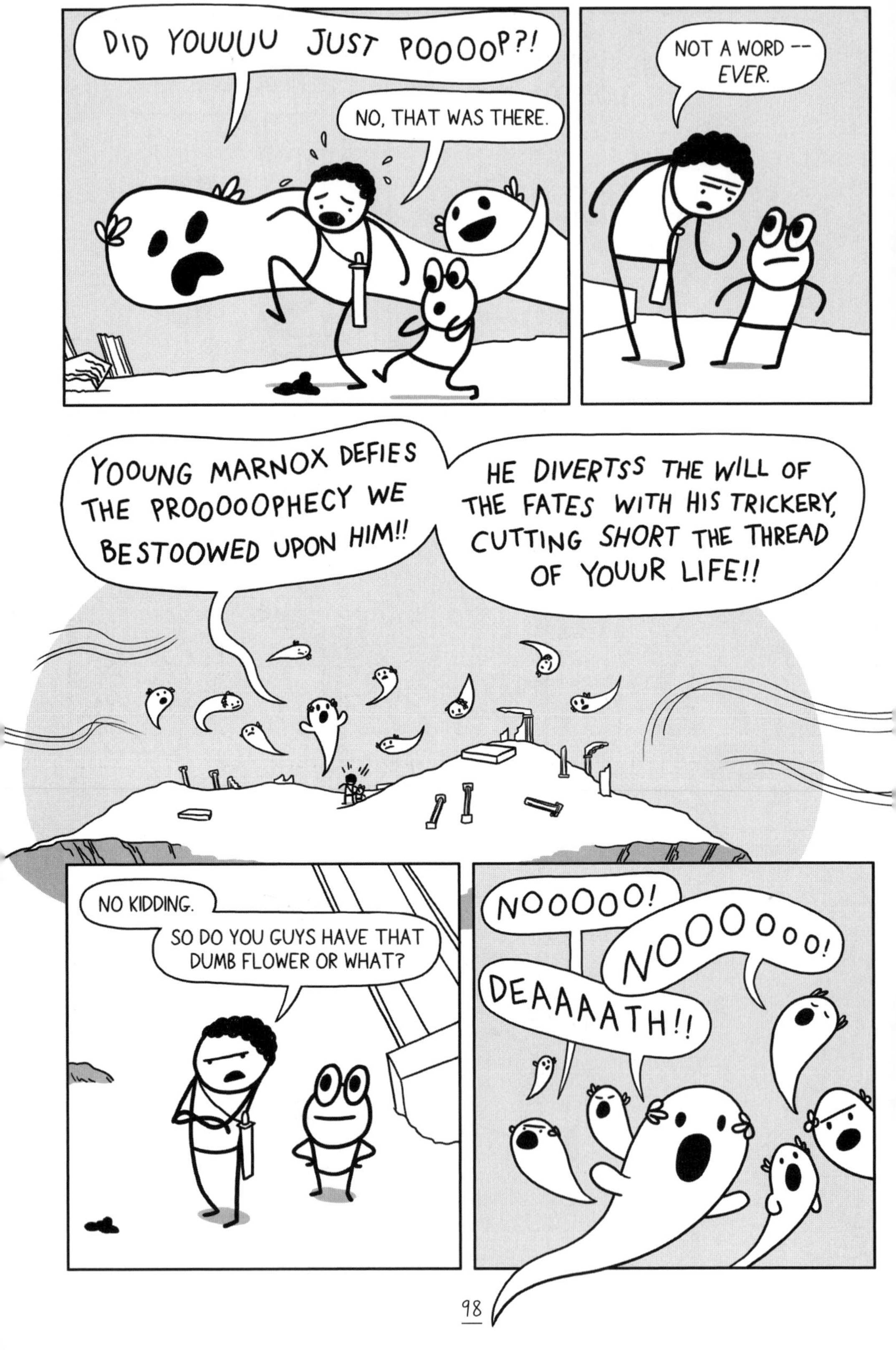
DID YOUUUU JUST POOOOP?!
NO, THAT WAS THERE.
NOT A WORD -- EVER.
YOOUNG MARNOX DEFIES THE PROOOOOPHECY WE BESTOOWED UPON HIM!!
HE DIVERTSS THE WILL OF THE FATES WITH HIS TRICKERY, CUTTING SHORT THE THREAD OF YOUUR LIFE!!
NO KIDDING.
SO DO YOU GUYS HAVE THAT DUMB FLOWER OR WHAT?
NOOOOO!
NOOOOOO!
DEAAAATH!!

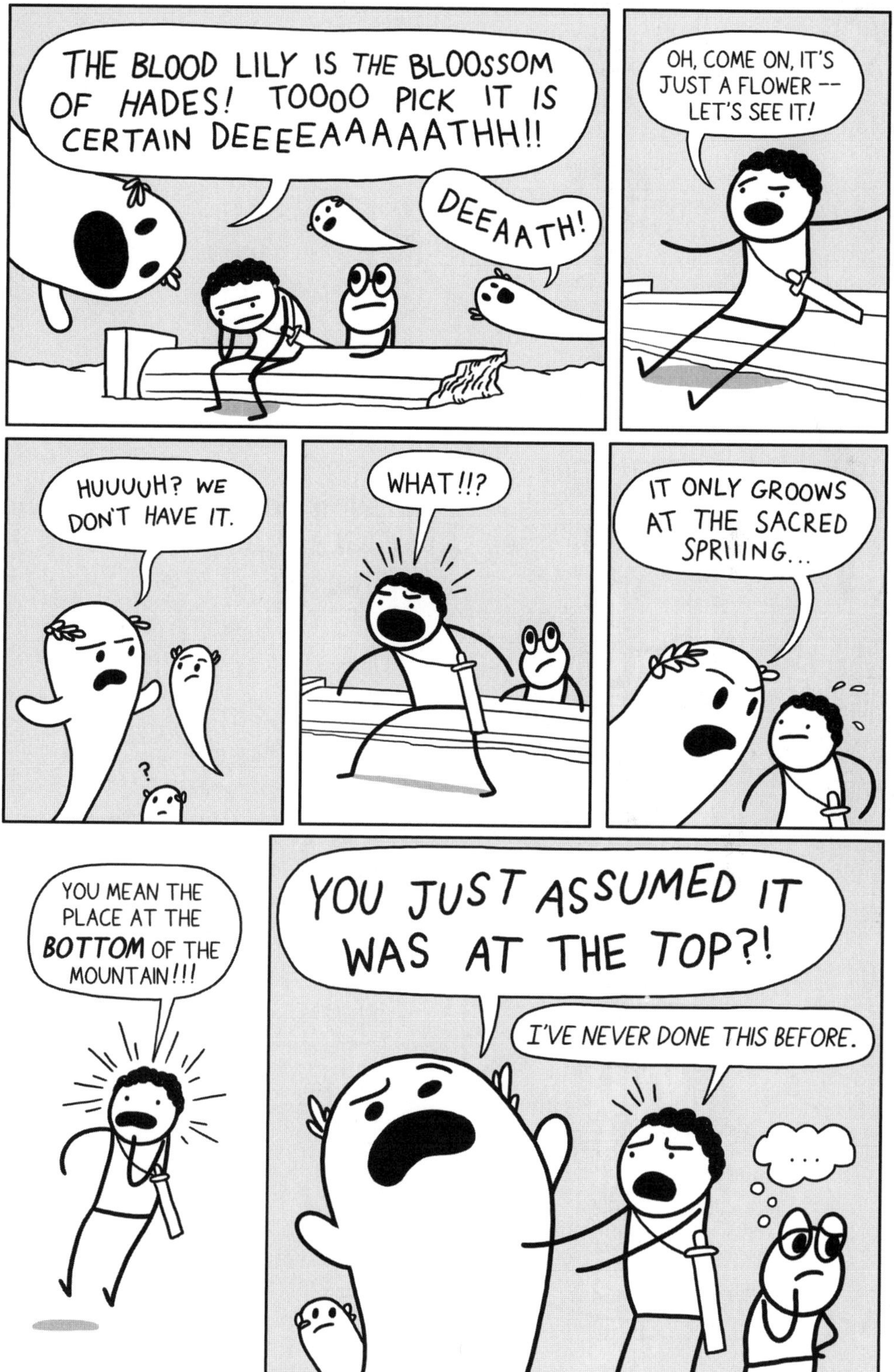
THE BLOOD LILY IS THE BLOOSSOM OF HADES! TOOOO PICK IT IS CERTAIN DEEEEAAAAATHH!!
DEEAATH!
OH, COME ON, IT'S JUST A FLOWER -- LET'S SEE IT!
HUUUUH? WE DON'T HAVE IT.
?
WHAT!!?
IT ONLY GROOWS AT THE SACRED SPRIIING...
YOU MEAN THE PLACE AT THE **BOTTOM** OF THE MOUNTAIN!!!
YOU JUST ASSUMED IT WAS AT THE TOP?!
I'VE NEVER DONE THIS BEFORE.
...

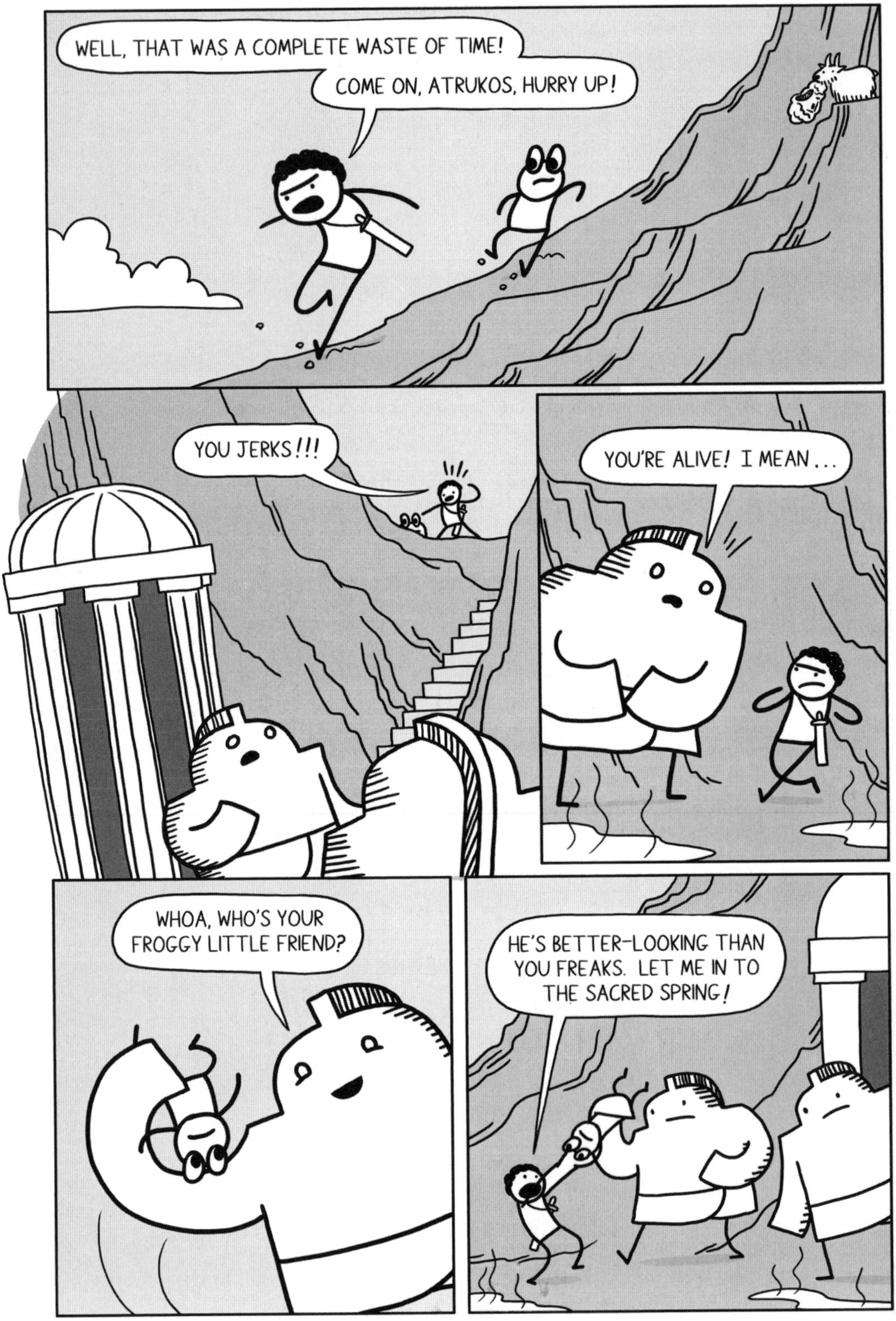
WELL, THAT WAS A COMPLETE WASTE OF TIME!
COME ON, ATRUKOS, HURRY UP!
YOU JERKS!!!
YOU'RE ALIVE! I MEAN . . .
WHOA, WHO'S YOUR FROGGY LITTLE FRIEND?
HE'S BETTER-LOOKING THAN YOU FREAKS. LET ME IN TO THE SACRED SPRING!

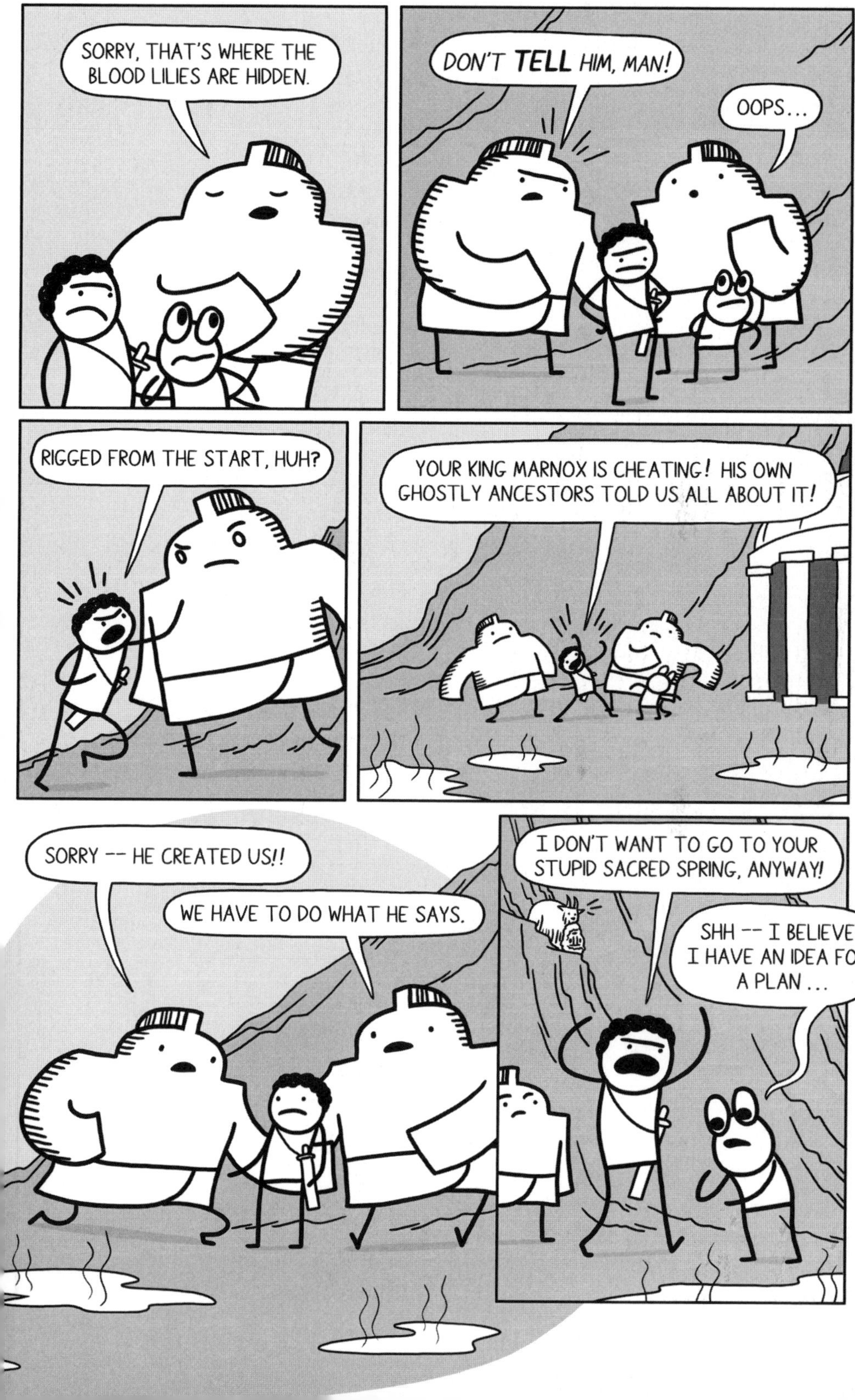
SORRY, THAT'S WHERE THE BLOOD LILIES ARE HIDDEN.
DON'T **TELL** HIM, MAN!
OOPS...
RIGGED FROM THE START, HUH?
YOUR KING MARNOX IS CHEATING! HIS OWN GHOSTLY ANCESTORS TOLD US ALL ABOUT IT!
SORRY -- HE CREATED US!!
WE HAVE TO DO WHAT HE SAYS.
I DON'T WANT TO GO TO YOUR STUPID SACRED SPRING, ANYWAY!
SHH -- I BELIEVE I HAVE AN IDEA FOR A PLAN ...

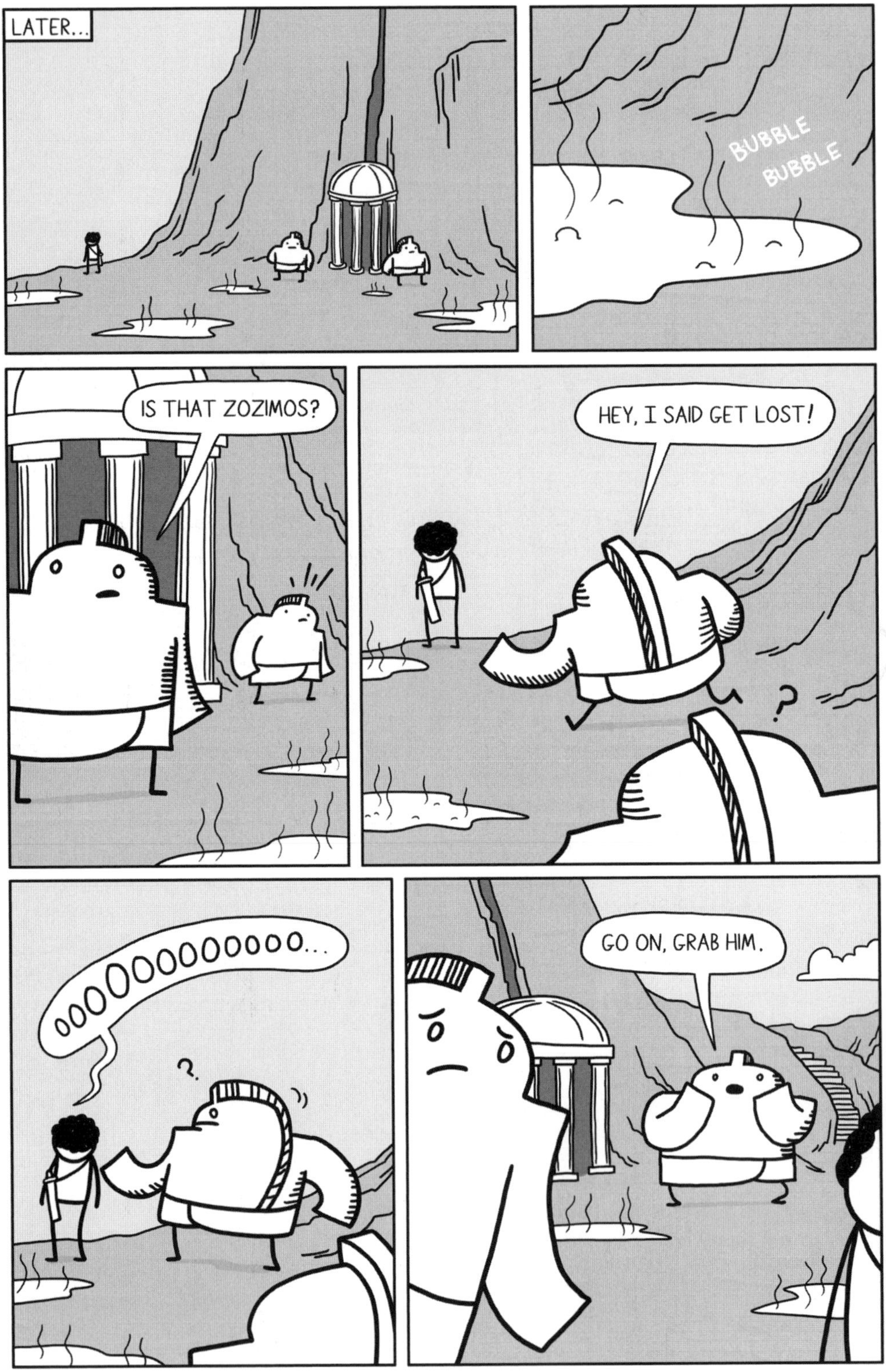
LATER...
BUBBLE
BUBBLE
IS THAT ZOZIMOS?
HEY, I SAID GET LOST!
?
oooOOOOOOOOoo...
?
GO ON, GRAB HIM.

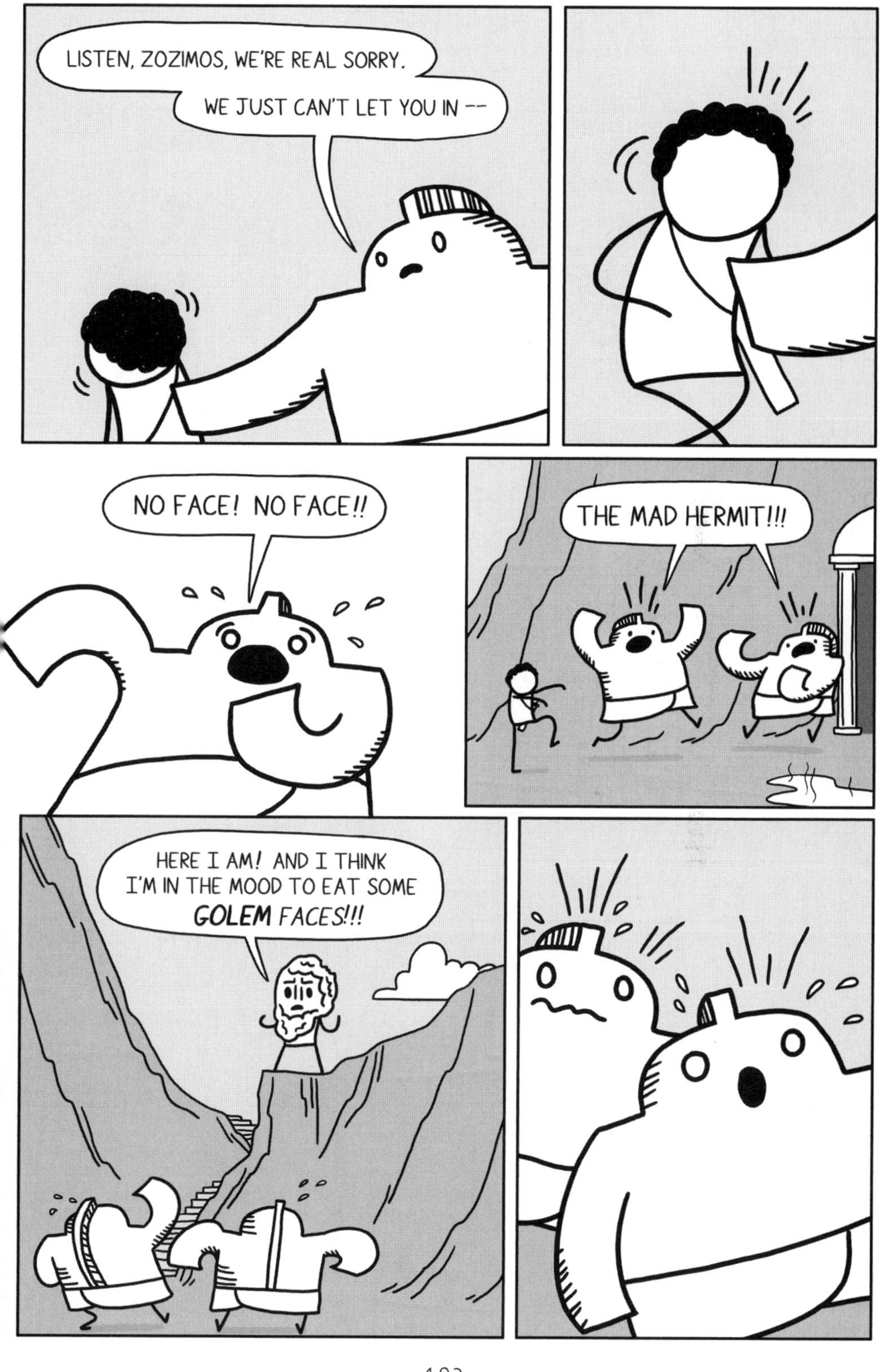
LISTEN, ZOZIMOS, WE'RE REAL SORRY.
WE JUST CAN'T LET YOU IN --
NO FACE! NO FACE!!
THE MAD HERMIT!!!
HERE I AM! AND I THINK I'M IN THE MOOD TO EAT SOME **GOLEM** FACES!!!

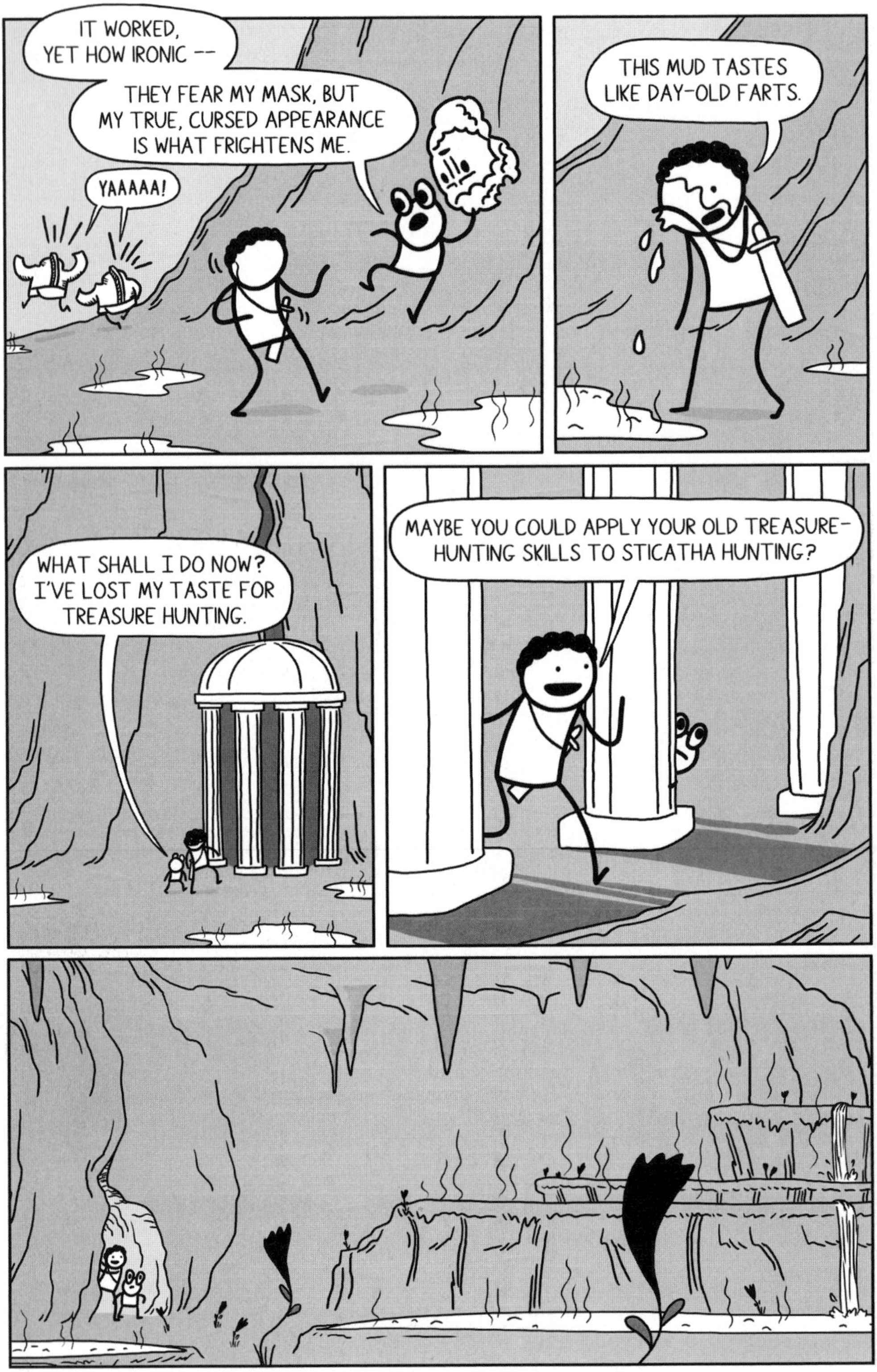
IT WORKED, YET HOW IRONIC --
THEY FEAR MY MASK, BUT MY TRUE, CURSED APPEARANCE IS WHAT FRIGHTENS ME.
YAAAAA!
THIS MUD TASTES LIKE DAY-OLD FARTS.
WHAT SHALL I DO NOW? I'VE LOST MY TASTE FOR TREASURE HUNTING.
MAYBE YOU COULD APPLY YOUR OLD TREASURE-HUNTING SKILLS TO STICATHA HUNTING?

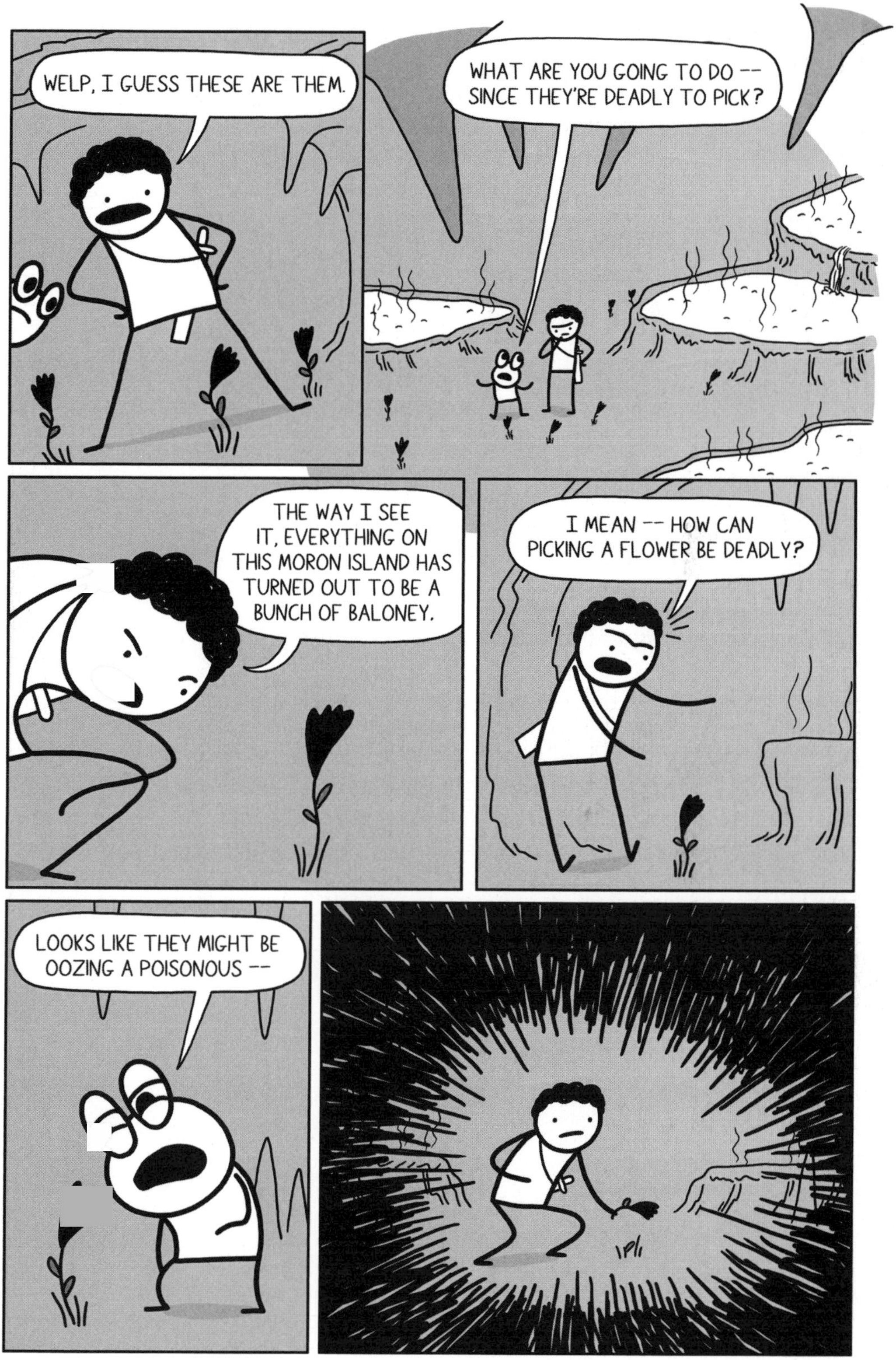
WELP, I GUESS THESE ARE THEM.
WHAT ARE YOU GOING TO DO -- SINCE THEY'RE DEADLY TO PICK?
THE WAY I SEE IT, EVERYTHING ON THIS MORON ISLAND HAS TURNED OUT TO BE A BUNCH OF BALONEY.
I MEAN -- HOW CAN PICKING A FLOWER BE DEADLY?
LOOKS LIKE THEY MIGHT BE OOZING A POISONOUS --

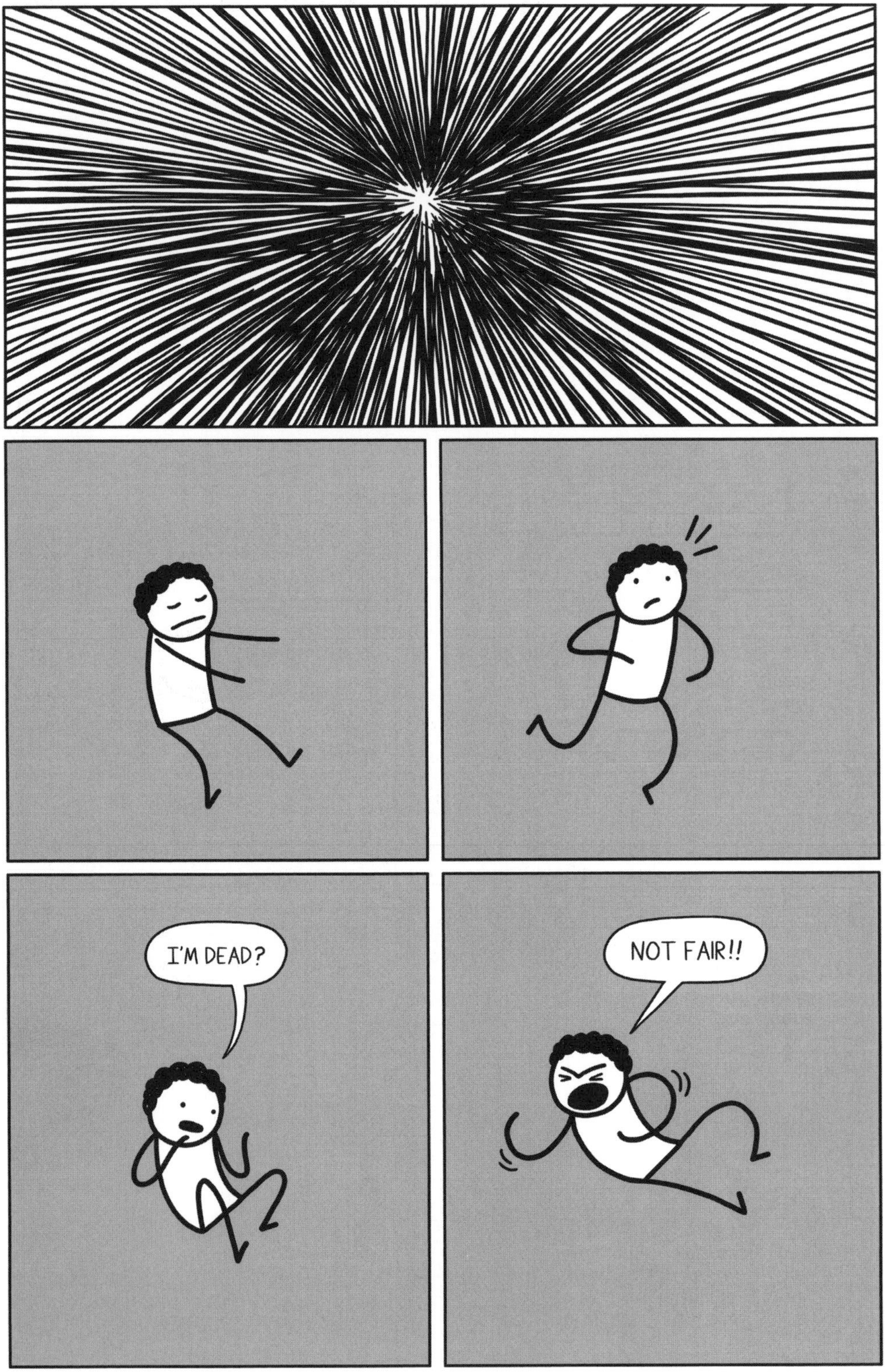
I'M DEAD?
NOT FAIR!!

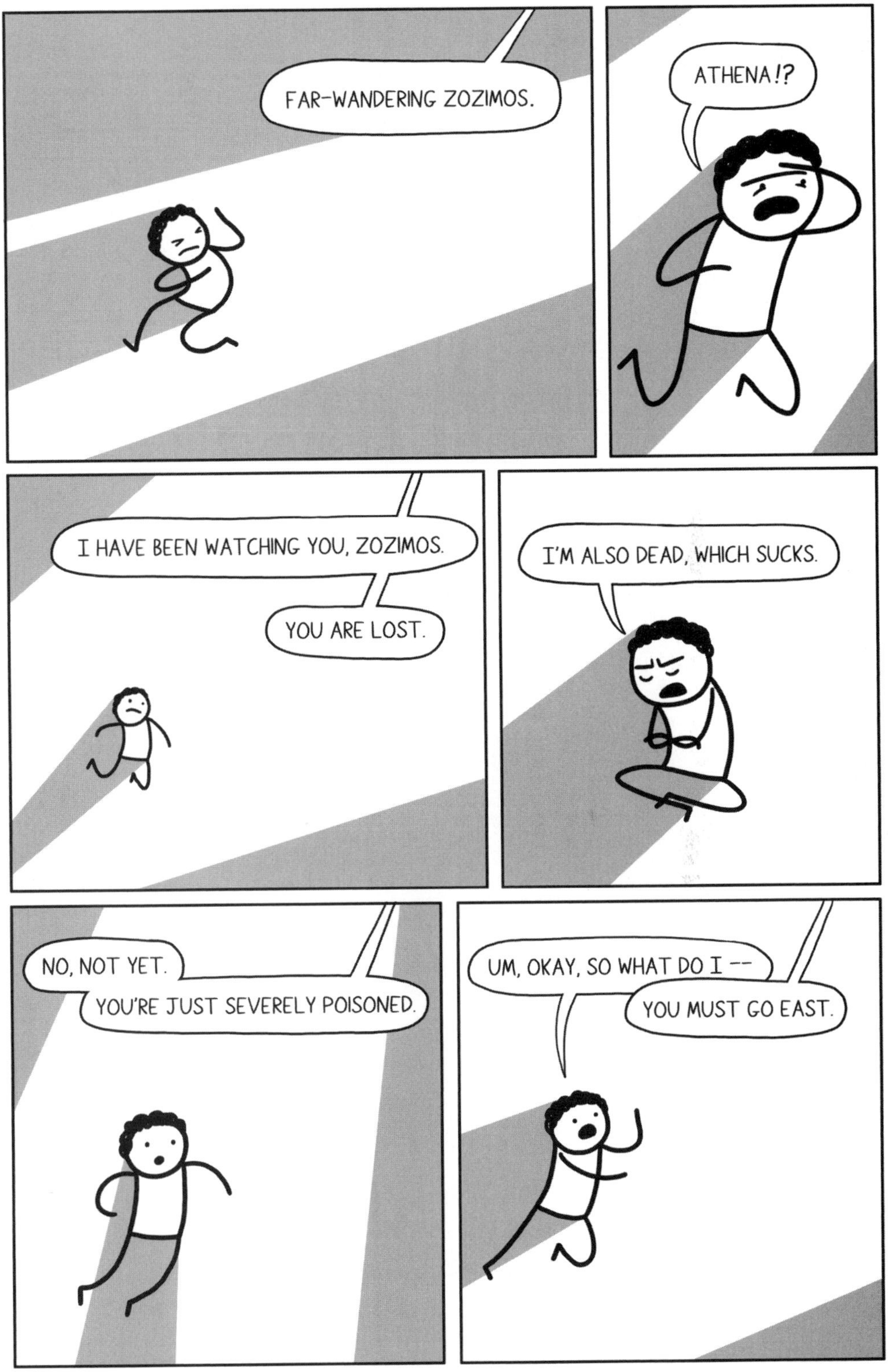
FAR-WANDERING ZOZIMOS.
ATHENA!?
I HAVE BEEN WATCHING YOU, ZOZIMOS.
YOU ARE LOST.
I'M ALSO DEAD, WHICH SUCKS.
NO, NOT YET.
YOU'RE JUST SEVERELY POISONED.
UM, OKAY, SO WHAT DO I --
YOU MUST GO EAST.

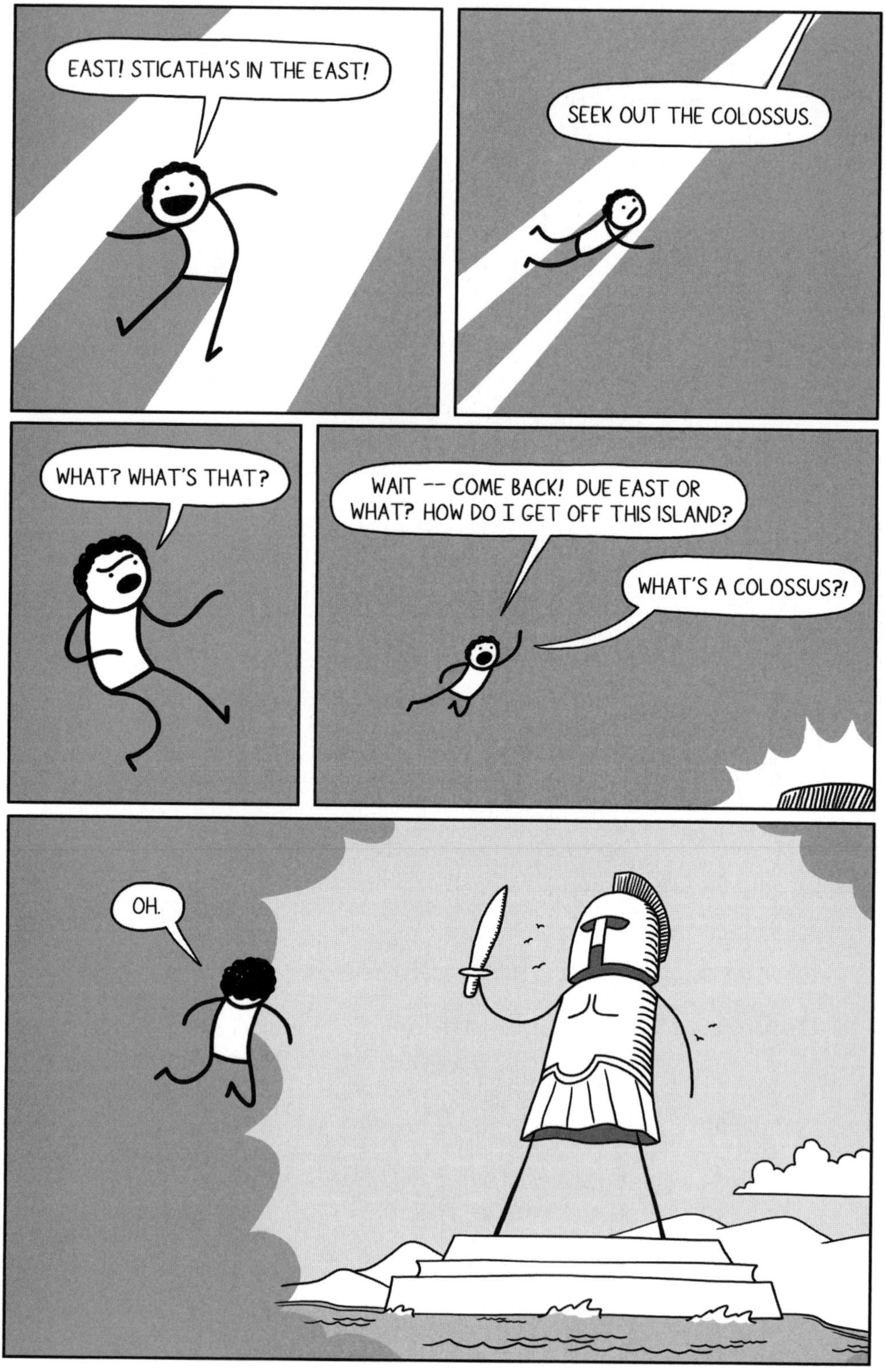
EAST! STICATHA'S IN THE EAST!
SEEK OUT THE COLOSSUS.
WHAT? WHAT'S THAT?
WAIT -- COME BACK! DUE EAST OR WHAT? HOW DO I GET OFF THIS ISLAND?
WHAT'S A COLOSSUS?!
OH.

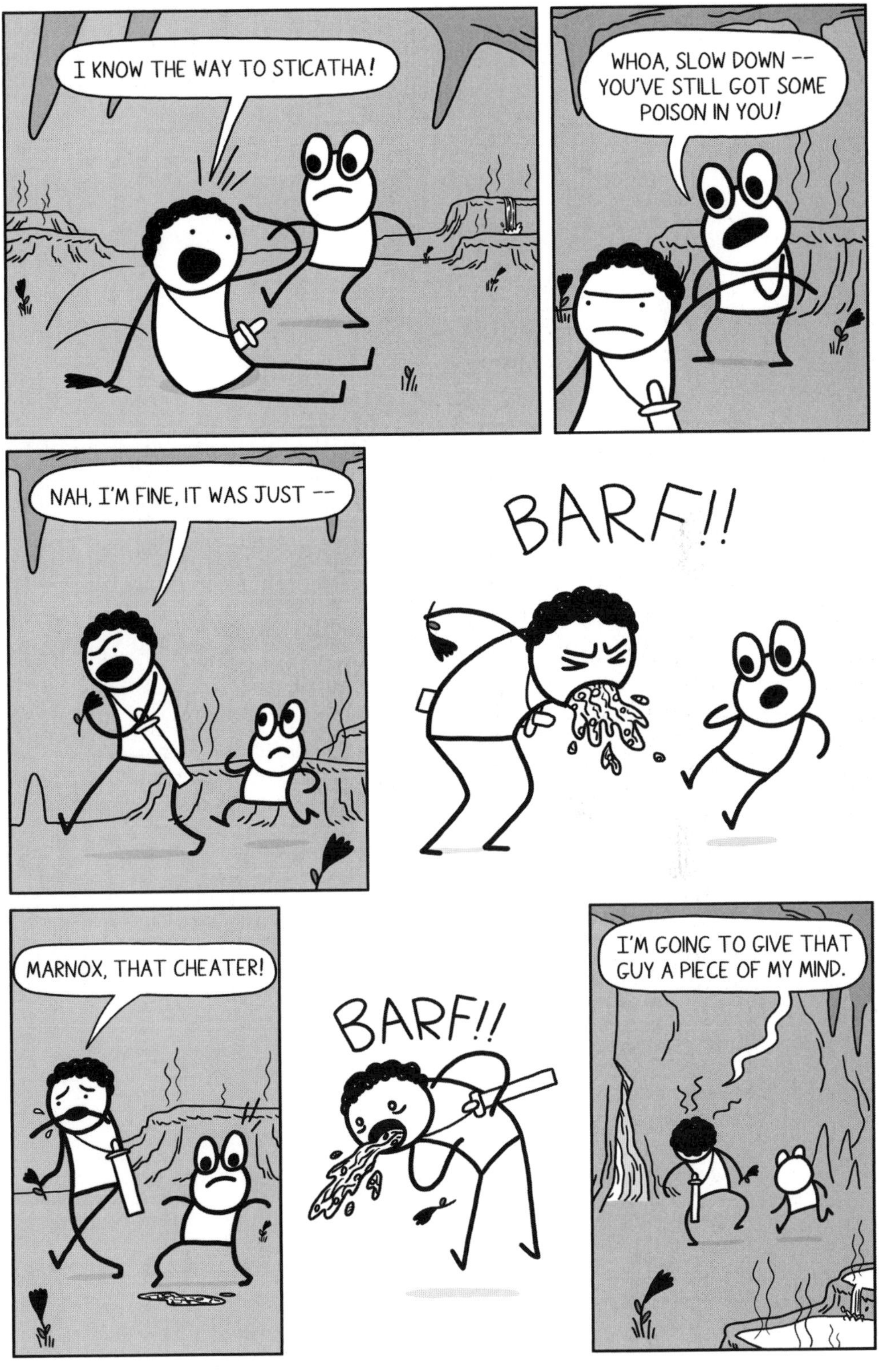
I KNOW THE WAY TO STICATHA!
WHOA, SLOW DOWN -- YOU'VE STILL GOT SOME POISON IN YOU!
NAH, I'M FINE, IT WAS JUST --
BARF!!
MARNOX, THAT CHEATER!
BARF!!
I'M GOING TO GIVE THAT GUY A PIECE OF MY MIND.

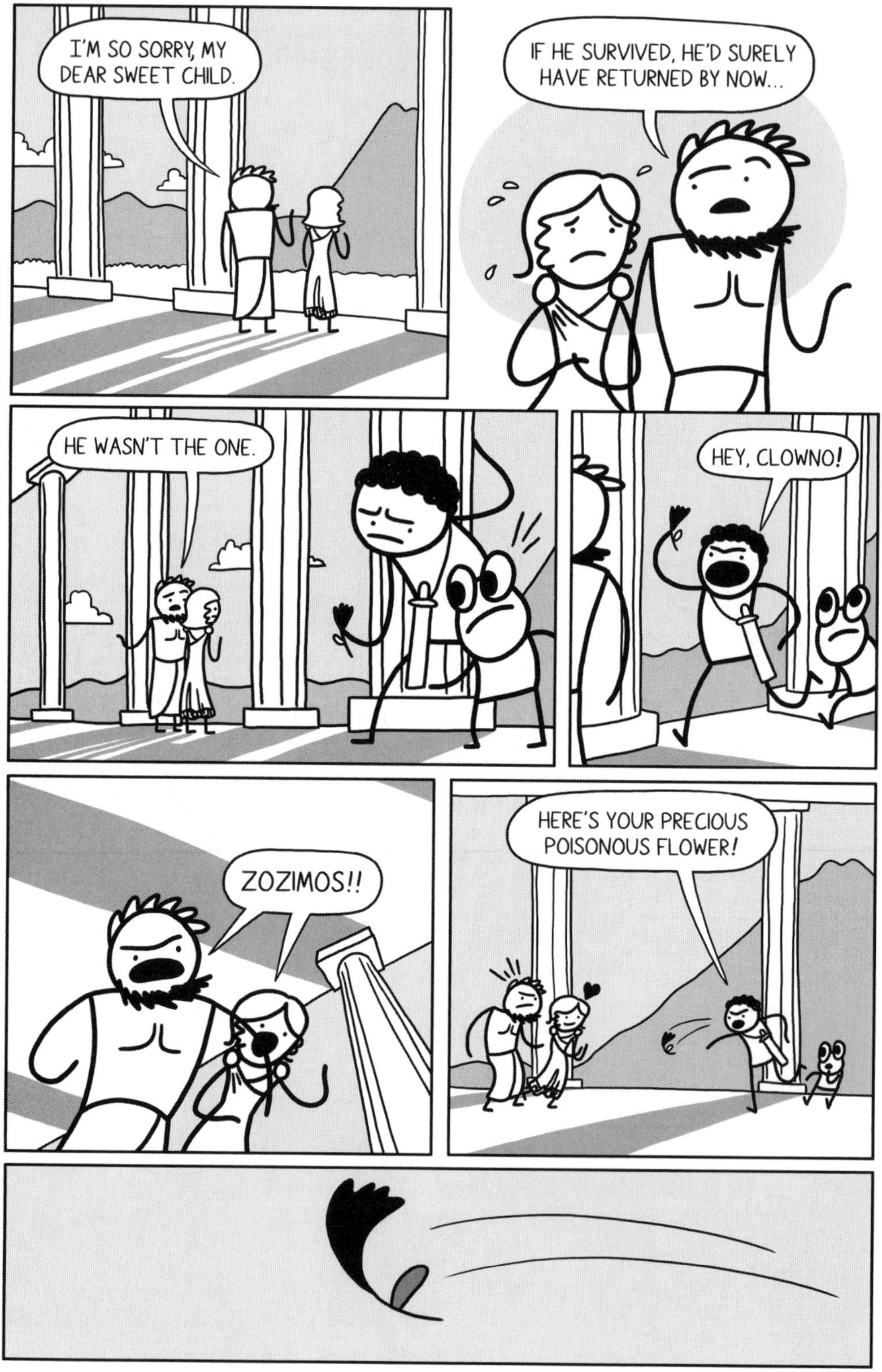
I'M SO SORRY, MY DEAR SWEET CHILD.
IF HE SURVIVED, HE'D SURELY HAVE RETURNED BY NOW...
HE WASN'T THE ONE.
HEY, CLOWNO!
ZOZIMOS!!
HERE'S YOUR PRECIOUS POISONOUS FLOWER!

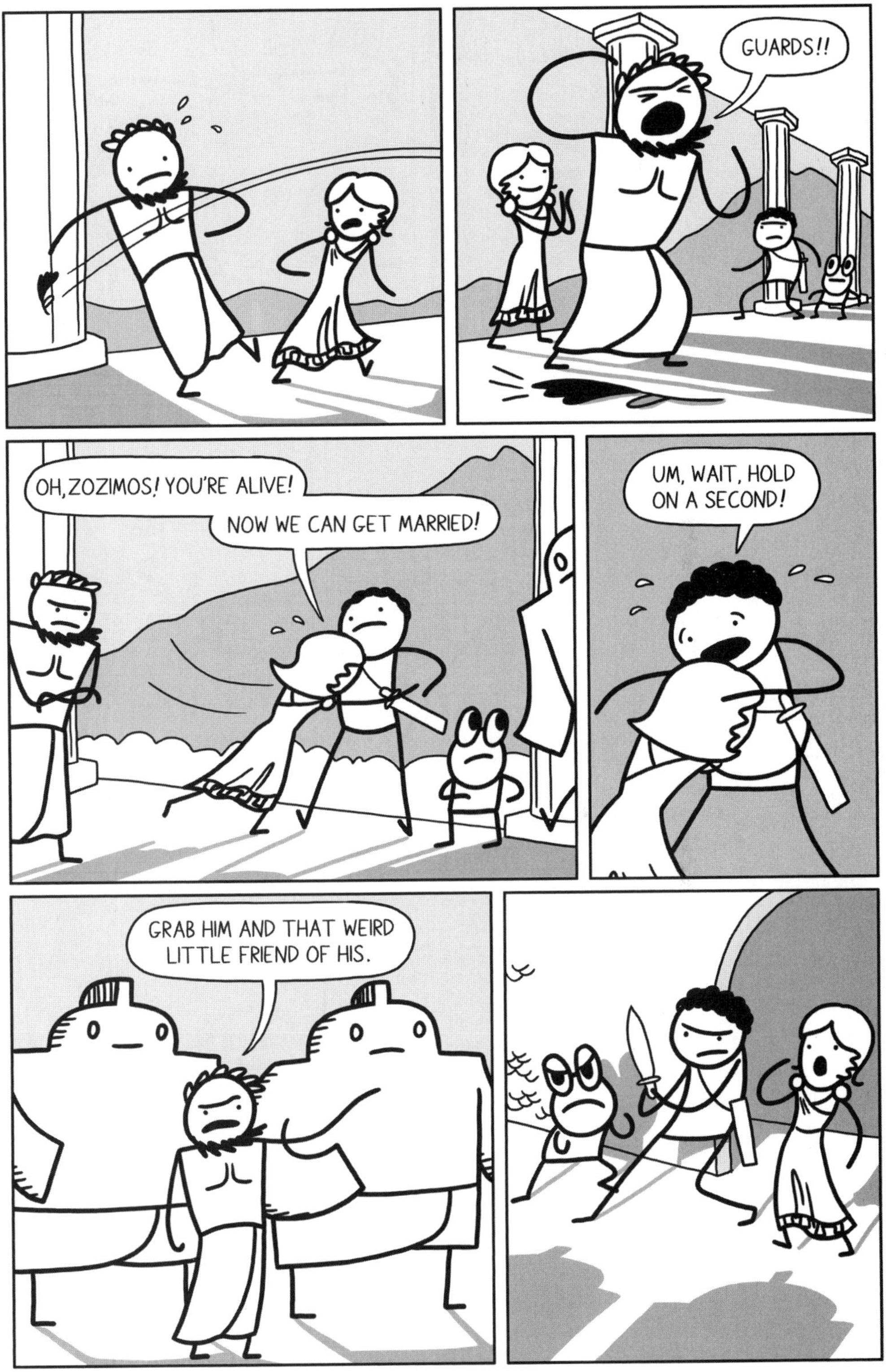
GUARDS!!
OH, ZOZIMOS! YOU'RE ALIVE!
NOW WE CAN GET MARRIED!
UM, WAIT, HOLD ON A SECOND!
GRAB HIM AND THAT WEIRD LITTLE FRIEND OF HIS.

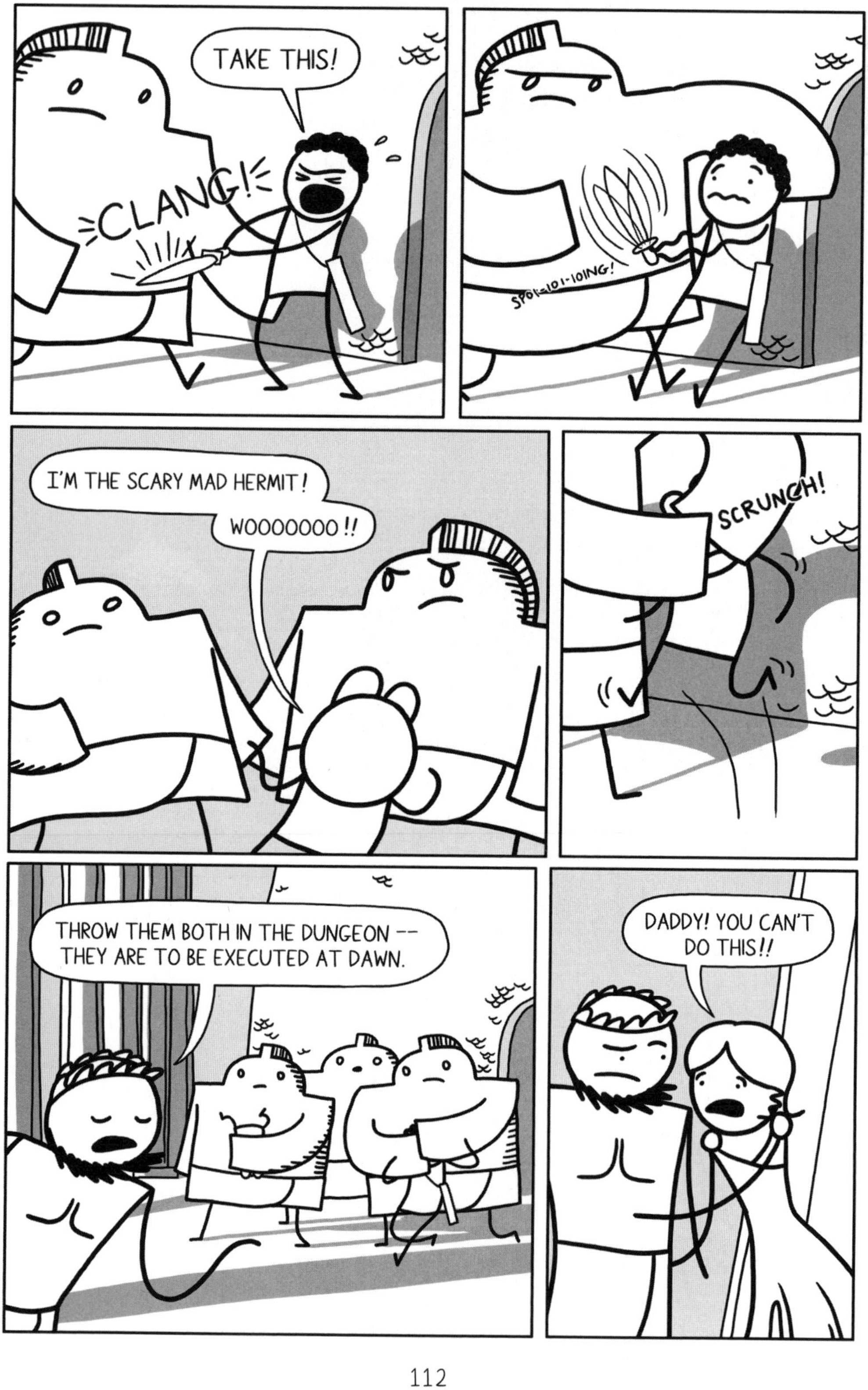
TAKE THIS!
CLANG!
SPOI-IOI-IOING!
I'M THE SCARY MAD HERMIT!
WOOOOOOO!!
SCRUNCH!
THROW THEM BOTH IN THE DUNGEON --
THEY ARE TO BE EXECUTED AT DAWN.
DADDY! YOU CAN'T DO THIS!!

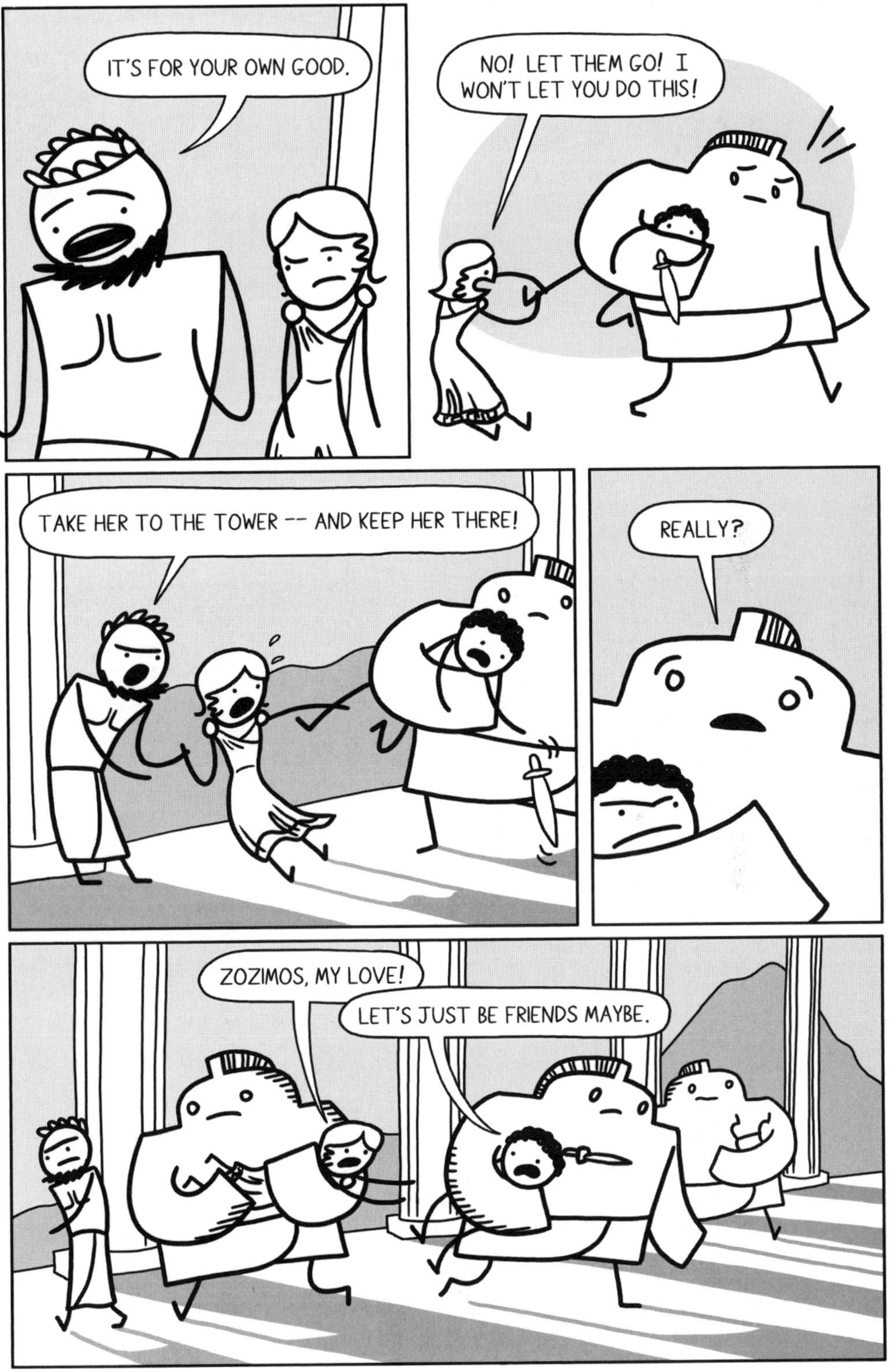

IT'S FOR YOUR OWN GOOD.
NO! LET THEM GO! I WON'T LET YOU DO THIS!
TAKE HER TO THE TOWER -- AND KEEP HER THERE!
REALLY?
ZOZIMOS, MY LOVE!
LET'S JUST BE FRIENDS MAYBE.

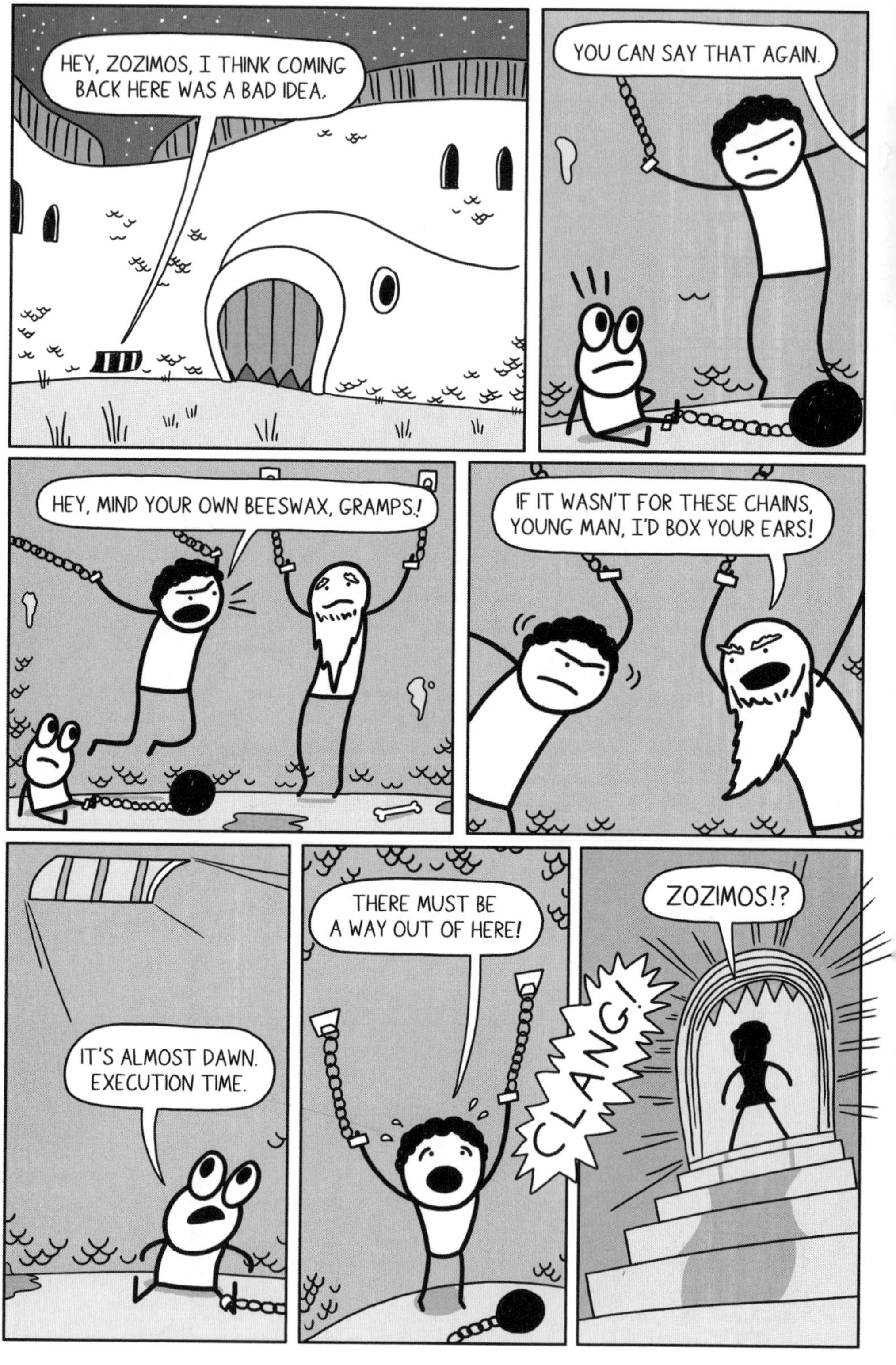
HEY, ZOZIMOS, I THINK COMING BACK HERE WAS A BAD IDEA.
YOU CAN SAY THAT AGAIN.
HEY, MIND YOUR OWN BEESWAX, GRAMPS!
IF IT WASN'T FOR THESE CHAINS, YOUNG MAN, I'D BOX YOUR EARS!
IT'S ALMOST DAWN. EXECUTION TIME.
THERE MUST BE A WAY OUT OF HERE!
CLANG!
ZOZIMOS!?

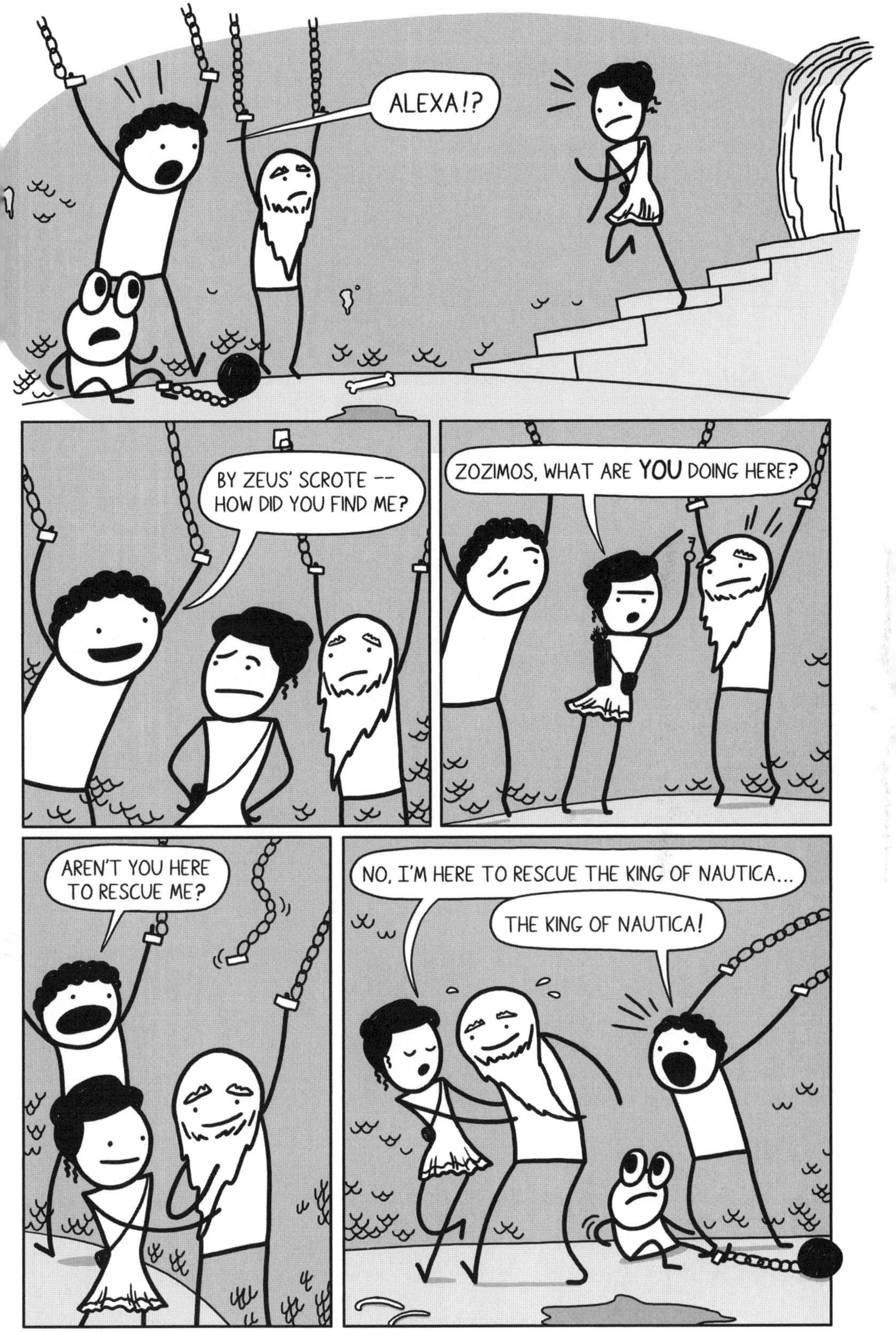
ALEXA!?
BY ZEUS' SCROTE -- HOW DID YOU FIND ME?
ZOZIMOS, WHAT ARE **YOU** DOING HERE?
AREN'T YOU HERE TO RESCUE ME?
NO, I'M HERE TO RESCUE THE KING OF NAUTICA...
THE KING OF NAUTICA!

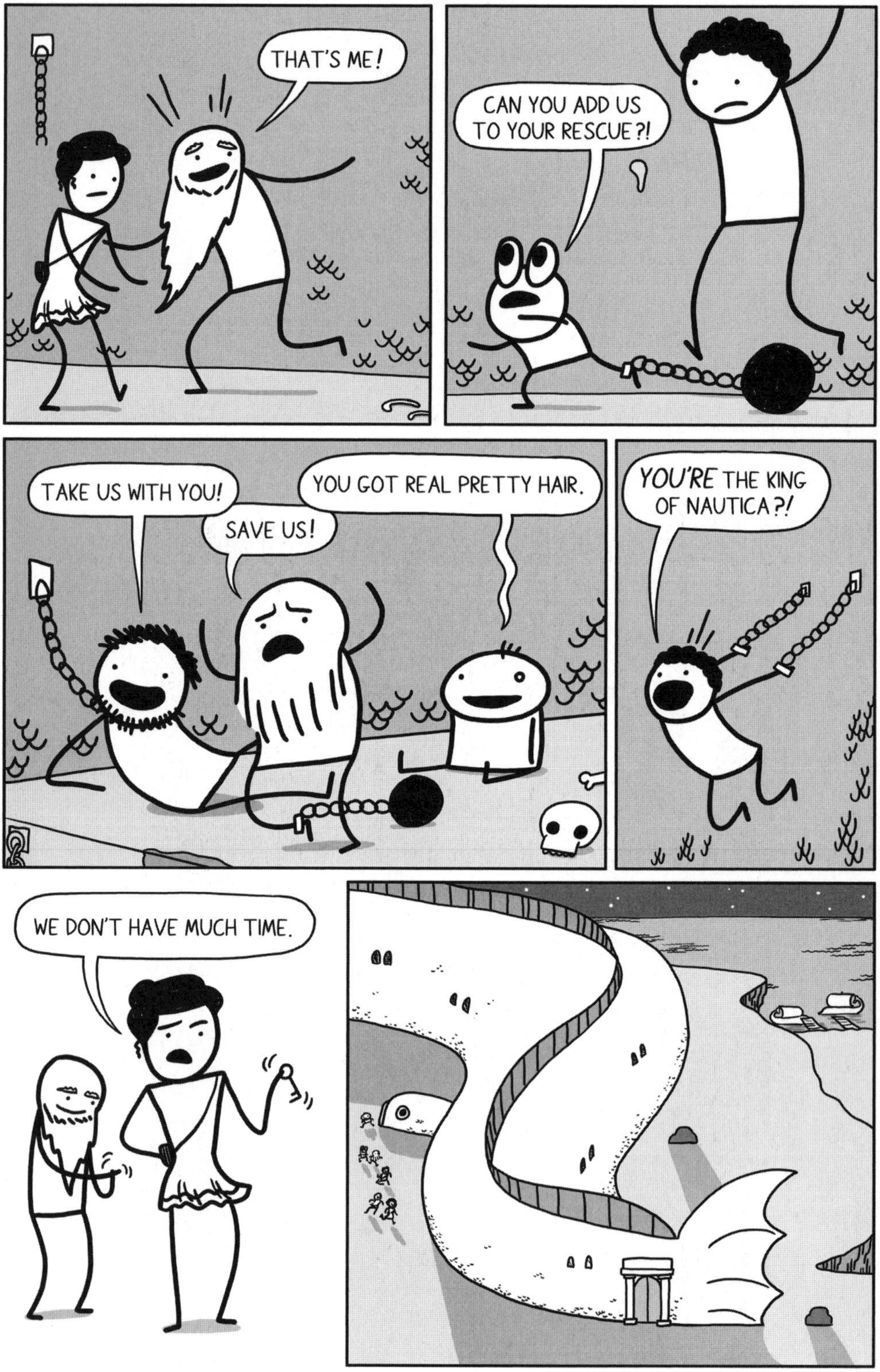
THAT'S ME!
CAN YOU ADD US TO YOUR RESCUE?!
TAKE US WITH YOU!
SAVE US!
YOU GOT REAL PRETTY HAIR.
YOU'RE THE KING OF NAUTICA?!
WE DON'T HAVE MUCH TIME.

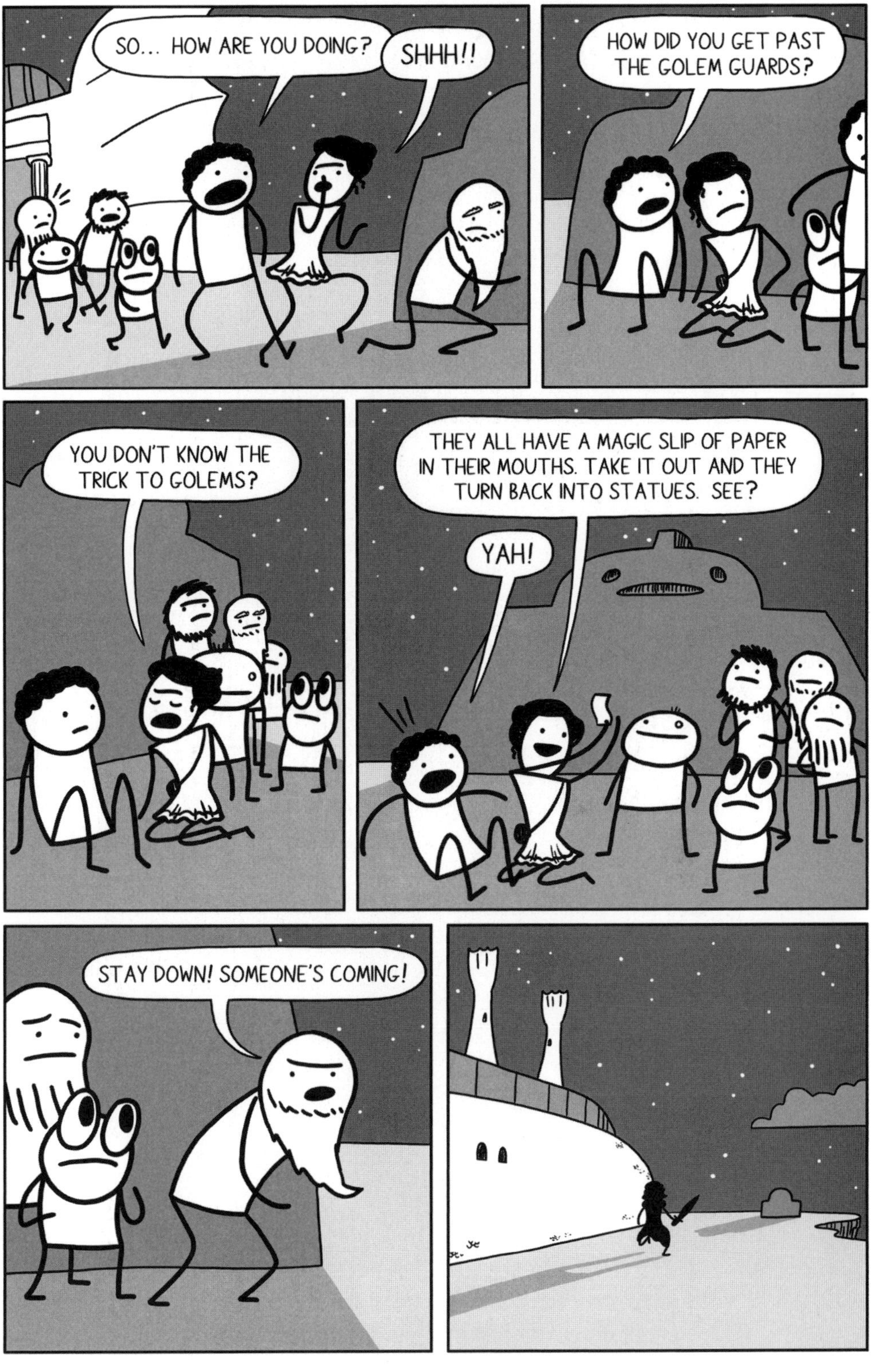
SO... HOW ARE YOU DOING?
SHHH!!
HOW DID YOU GET PAST THE GOLEM GUARDS?
YOU DON'T KNOW THE TRICK TO GOLEMS?
THEY ALL HAVE A MAGIC SLIP OF PAPER IN THEIR MOUTHS. TAKE IT OUT AND THEY TURN BACK INTO STATUES. SEE?
YAH!
STAY DOWN! SOMEONE'S COMING!

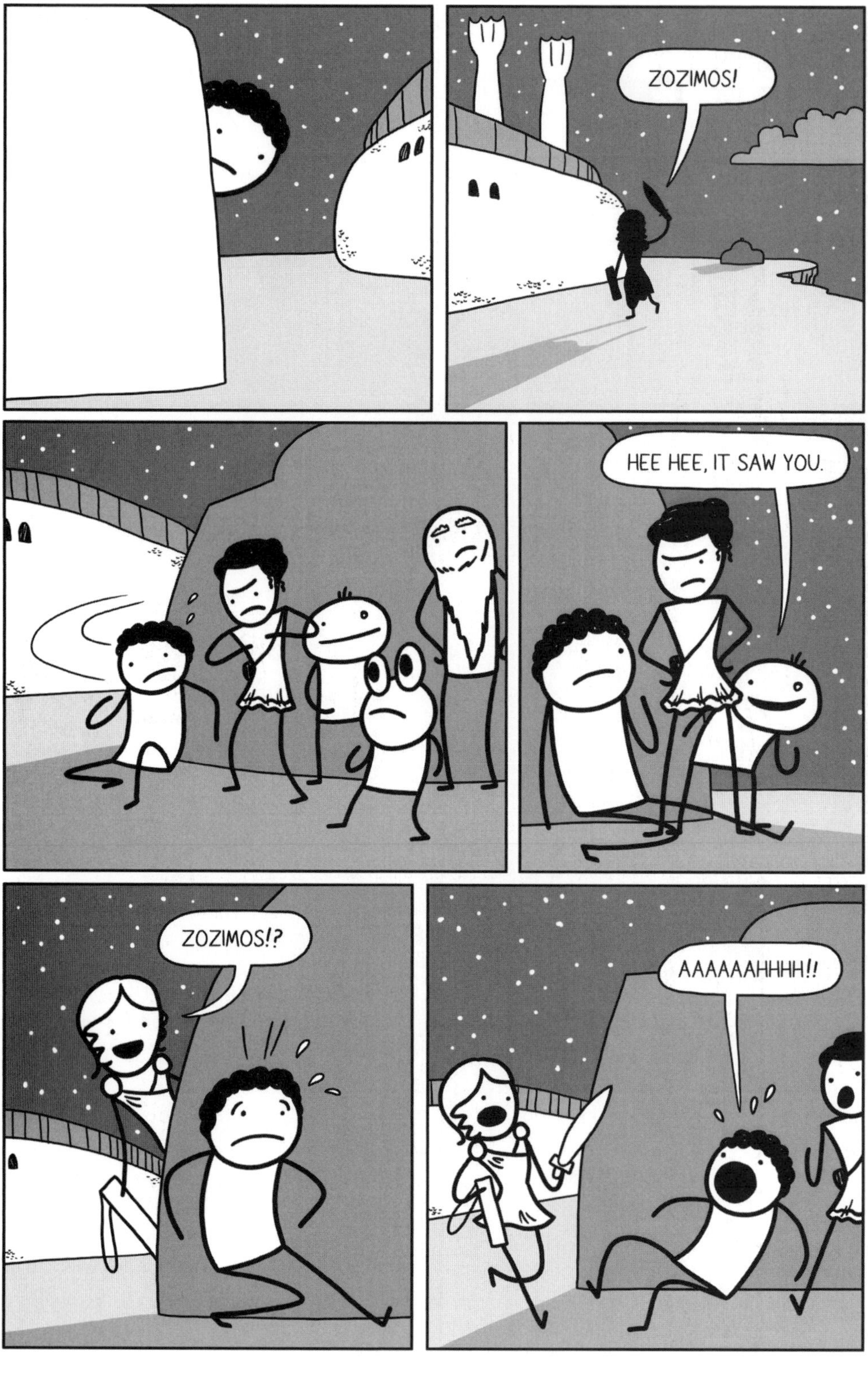
ZOZIMOS!
HEE HEE, IT SAW YOU.
ZOZIMOS!?
AAAAAAHHHH!!

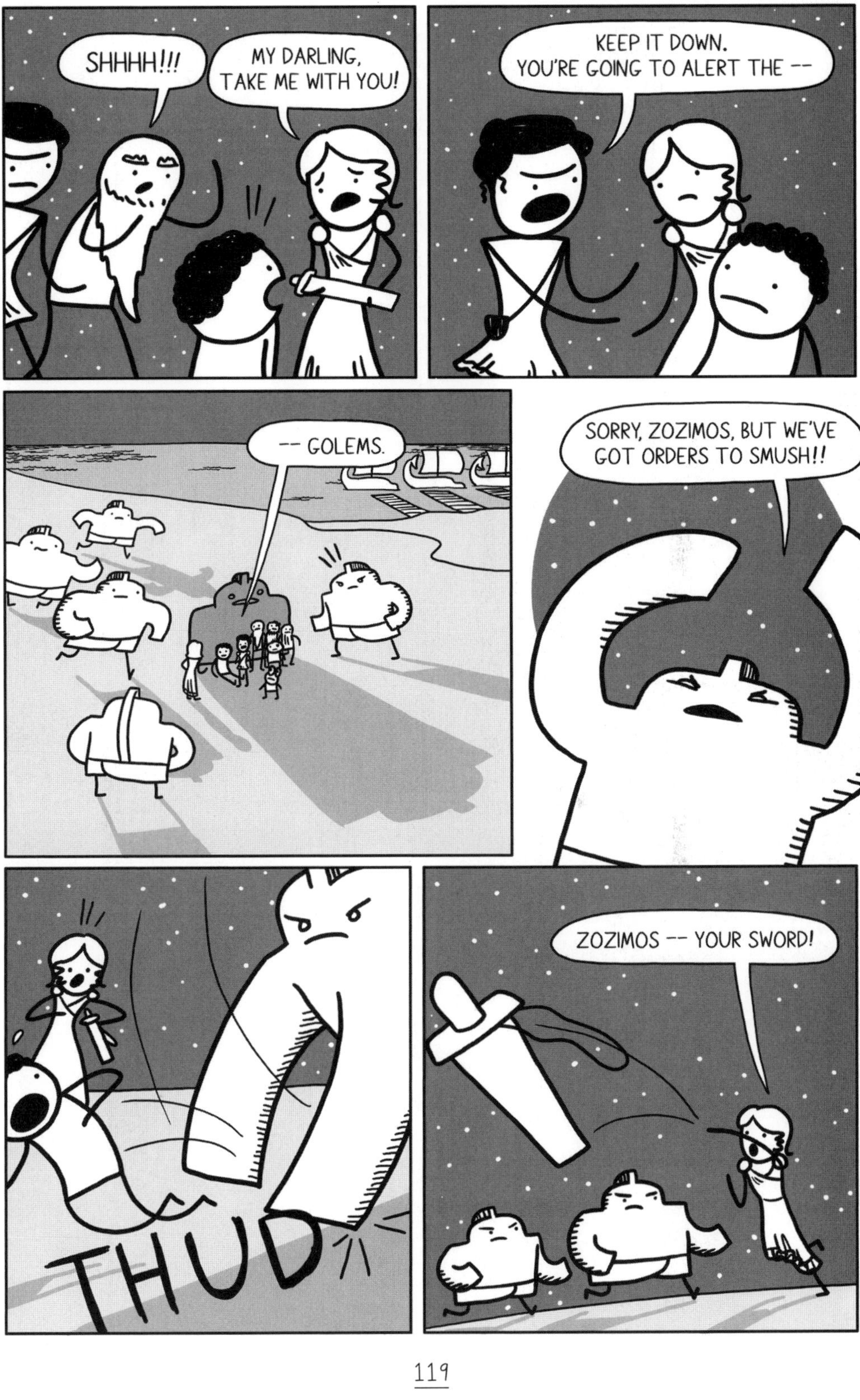
SHHHH!!!
MY DARLING, TAKE ME WITH YOU!
KEEP IT DOWN. YOU'RE GOING TO ALERT THE --
-- GOLEMS.
SORRY, ZOZIMOS, BUT WE'VE GOT ORDERS TO SMUSH!!
THUD
ZOZIMOS -- YOUR SWORD!

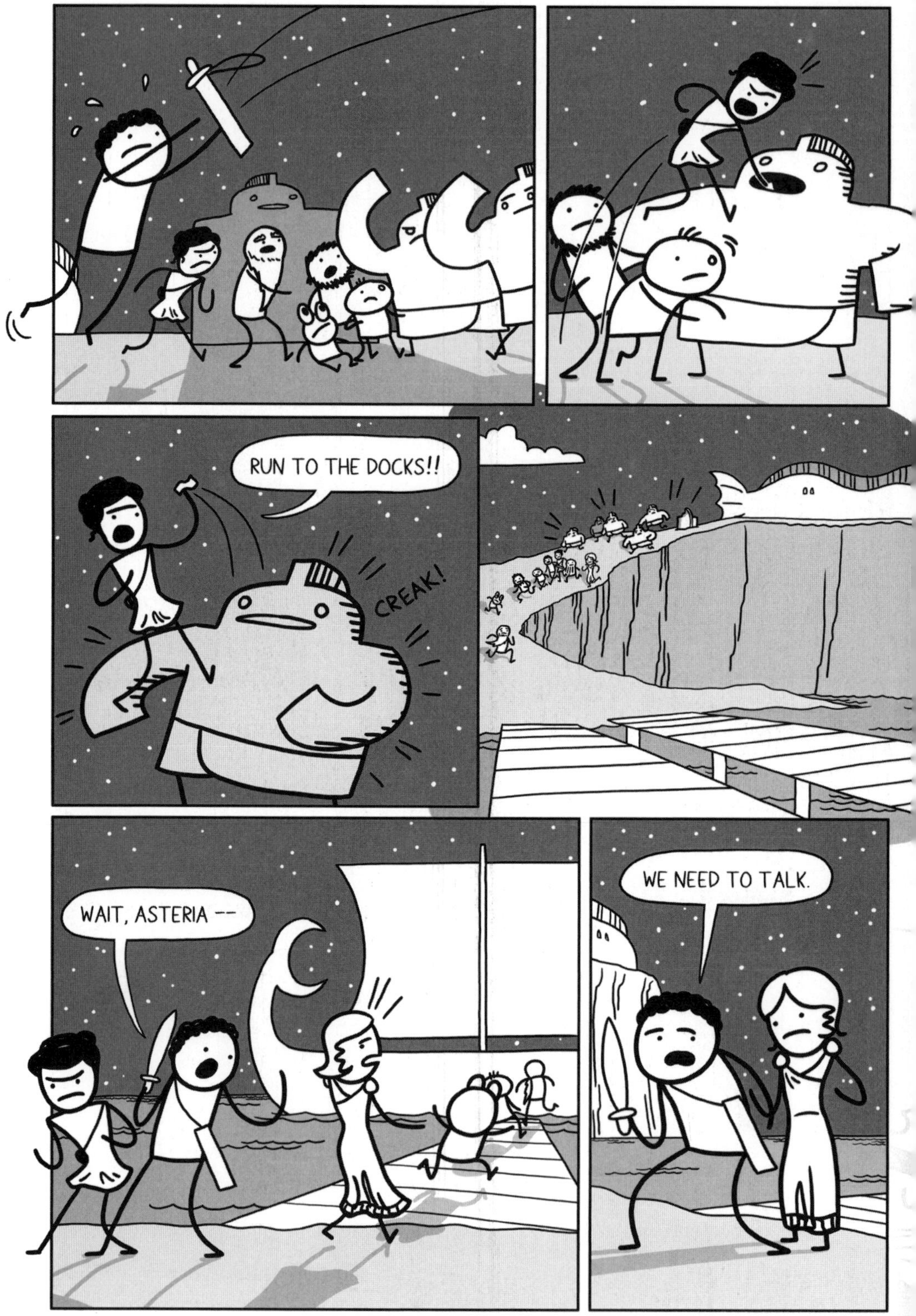
RUN TO THE DOCKS!!
CREAK!
WAIT, ASTERIA --
WE NEED TO TALK.

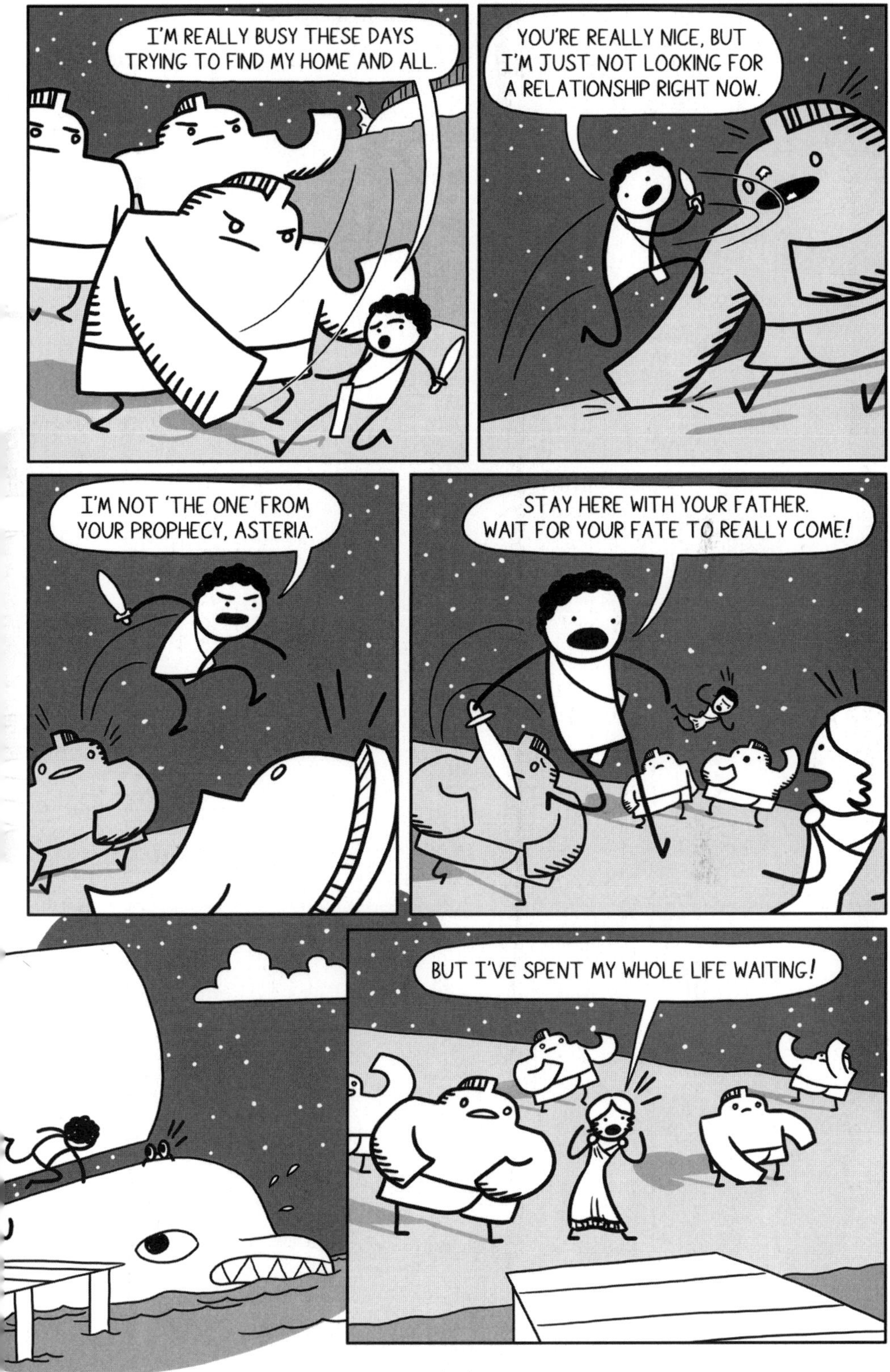

I'M REALLY BUSY THESE DAYS TRYING TO FIND MY HOME AND ALL.
YOU'RE REALLY NICE, BUT I'M JUST NOT LOOKING FOR A RELATIONSHIP RIGHT NOW.
I'M NOT 'THE ONE' FROM YOUR PROPHECY, ASTERIA.
STAY HERE WITH YOUR FATHER. WAIT FOR YOUR FATE TO REALLY COME!
BUT I'VE SPENT MY WHOLE LIFE WAITING!

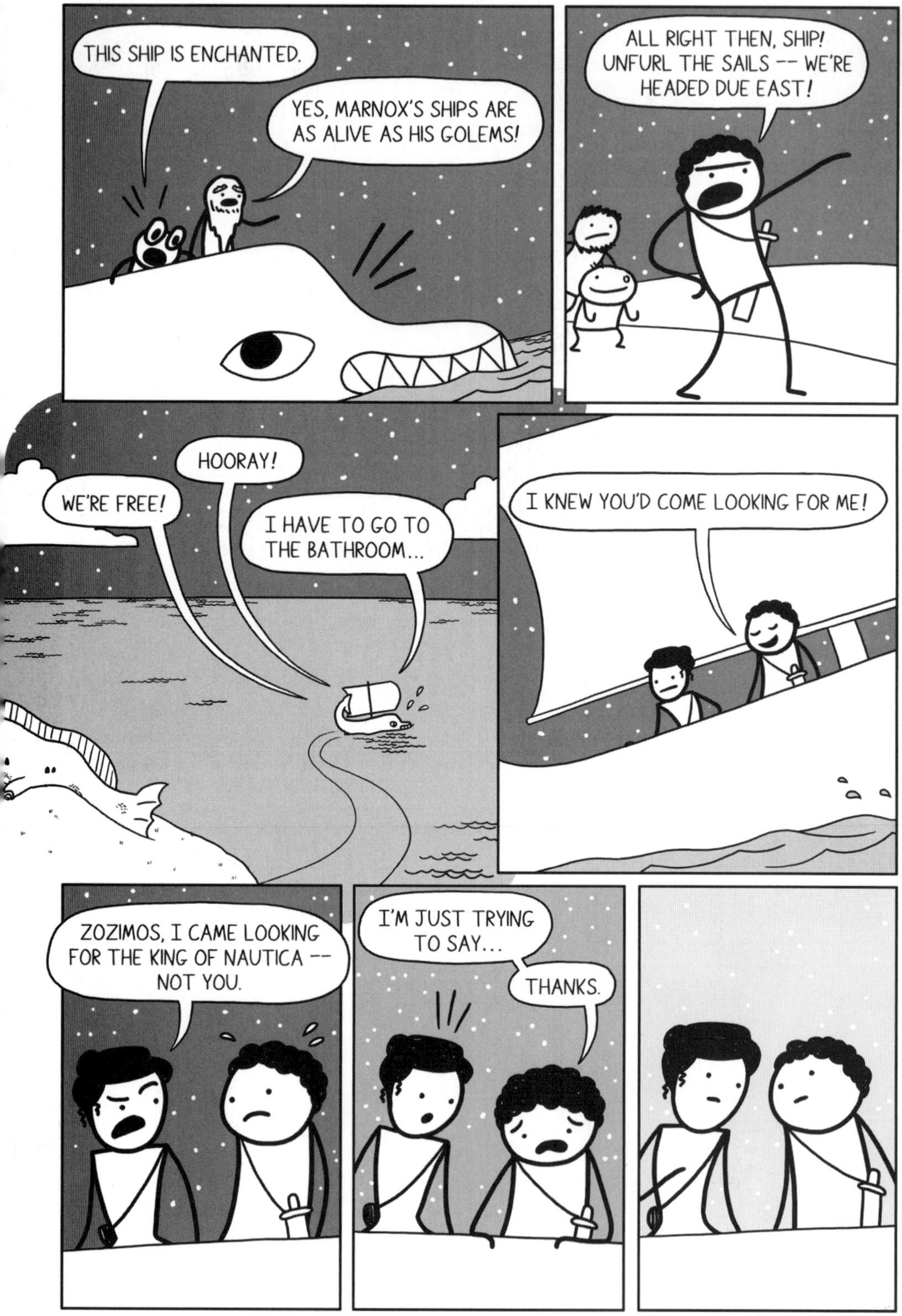
THIS SHIP IS ENCHANTED.
YES, MARNOX'S SHIPS ARE AS ALIVE AS HIS GOLEMS!
ALL RIGHT THEN, SHIP! UNFURL THE SAILS -- WE'RE HEADED DUE EAST!
WE'RE FREE!
HOORAY!
I HAVE TO GO TO THE BATHROOM...
I KNEW YOU'D COME LOOKING FOR ME!
ZOZIMOS, I CAME LOOKING FOR THE KING OF NAUTICA -- NOT YOU.
I'M JUST TRYING TO SAY...
THANKS.

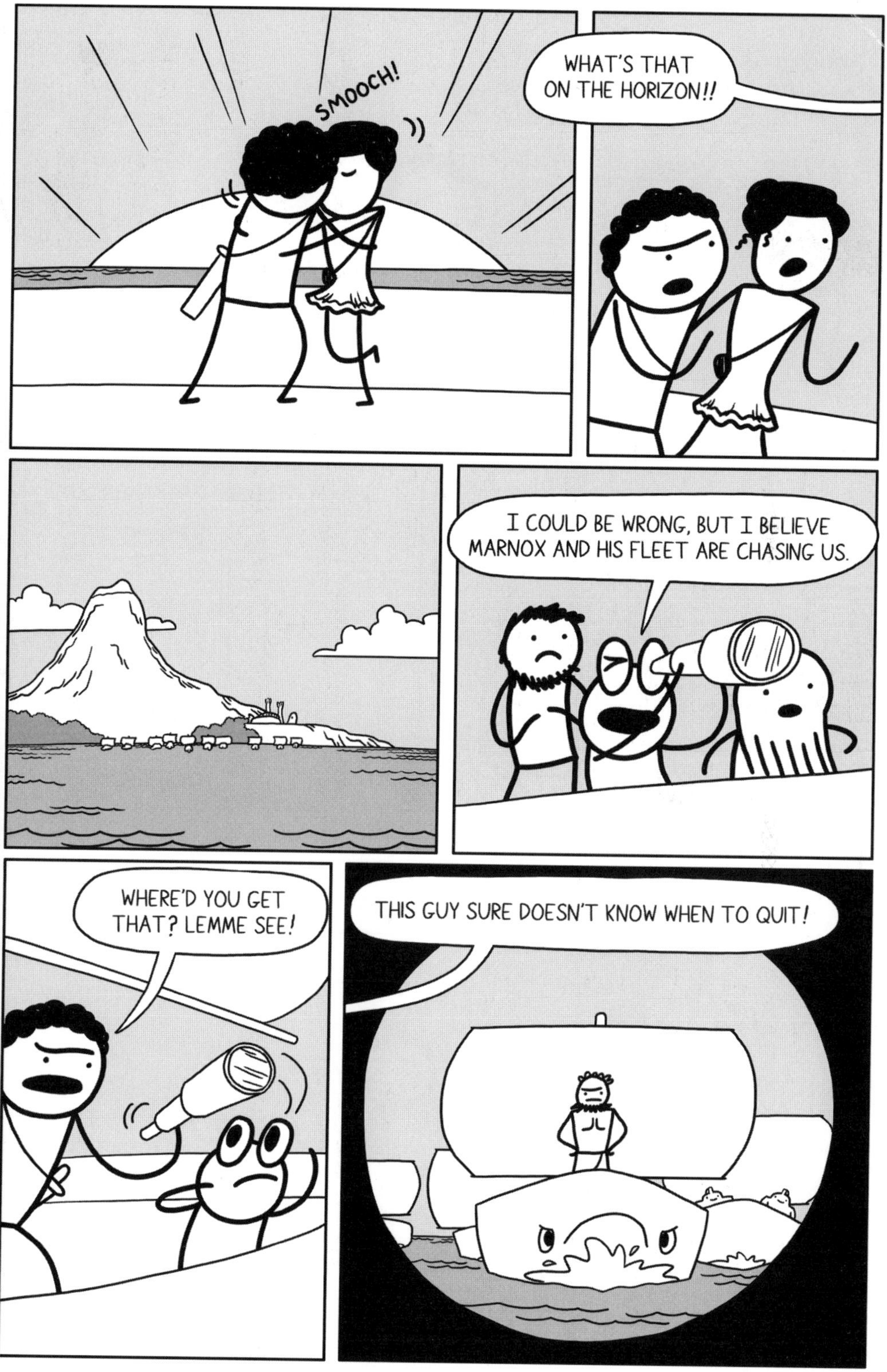
SMOOCH!
WHAT'S THAT ON THE HORIZON!!
I COULD BE WRONG, BUT I BELIEVE MARNOX AND HIS FLEET ARE CHASING US.
WHERE'D YOU GET THAT? LEMME SEE!
THIS GUY SURE DOESN'T KNOW WHEN TO QUIT!

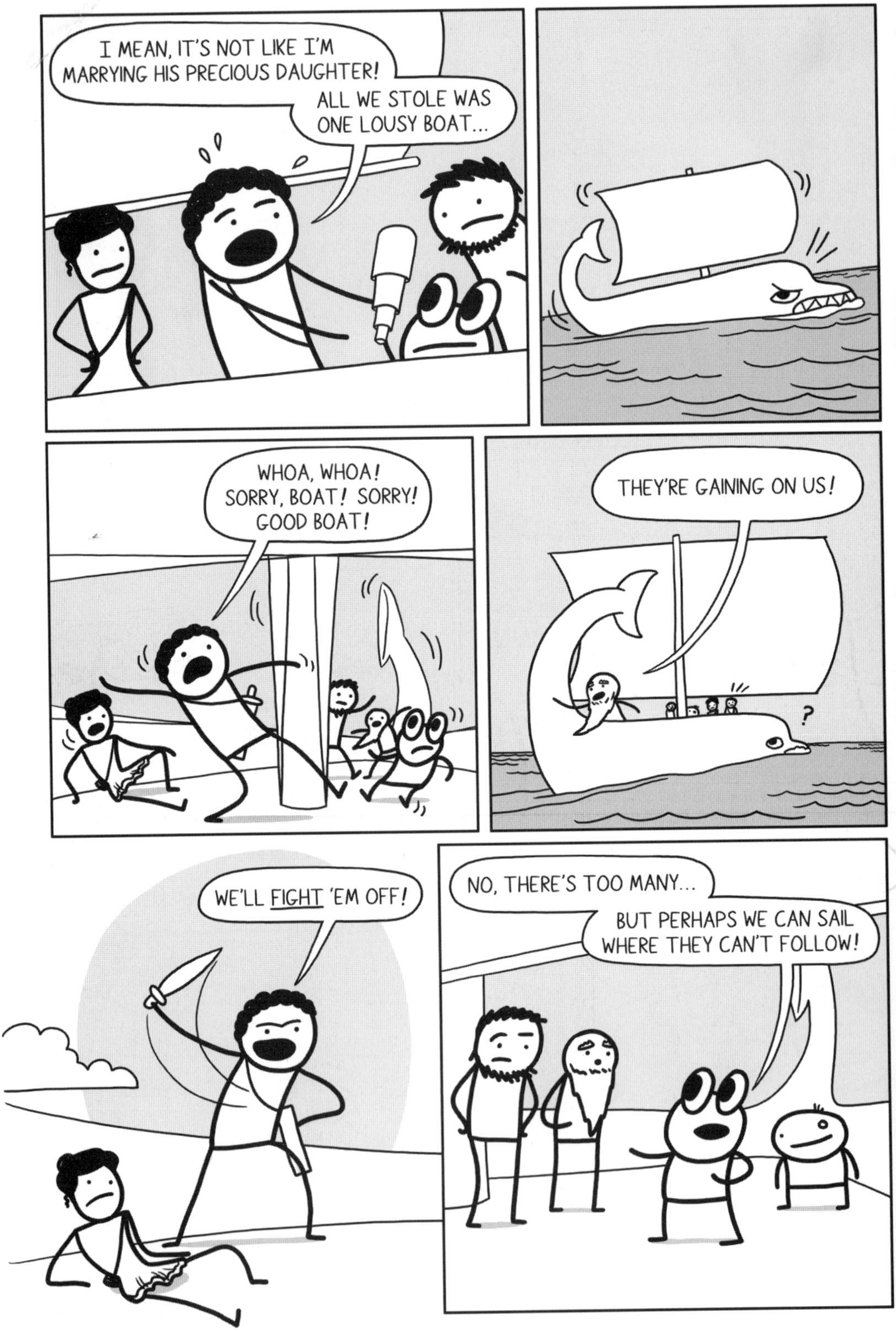
I MEAN, IT'S NOT LIKE I'M MARRYING HIS PRECIOUS DAUGHTER!
ALL WE STOLE WAS ONE LOUSY BOAT...
WHOA, WHOA! SORRY, BOAT! SORRY! GOOD BOAT!
THEY'RE GAINING ON US!
?
WE'LL FIGHT 'EM OFF!
NO, THERE'S TOO MANY...
BUT PERHAPS WE CAN SAIL WHERE THEY CAN'T FOLLOW!

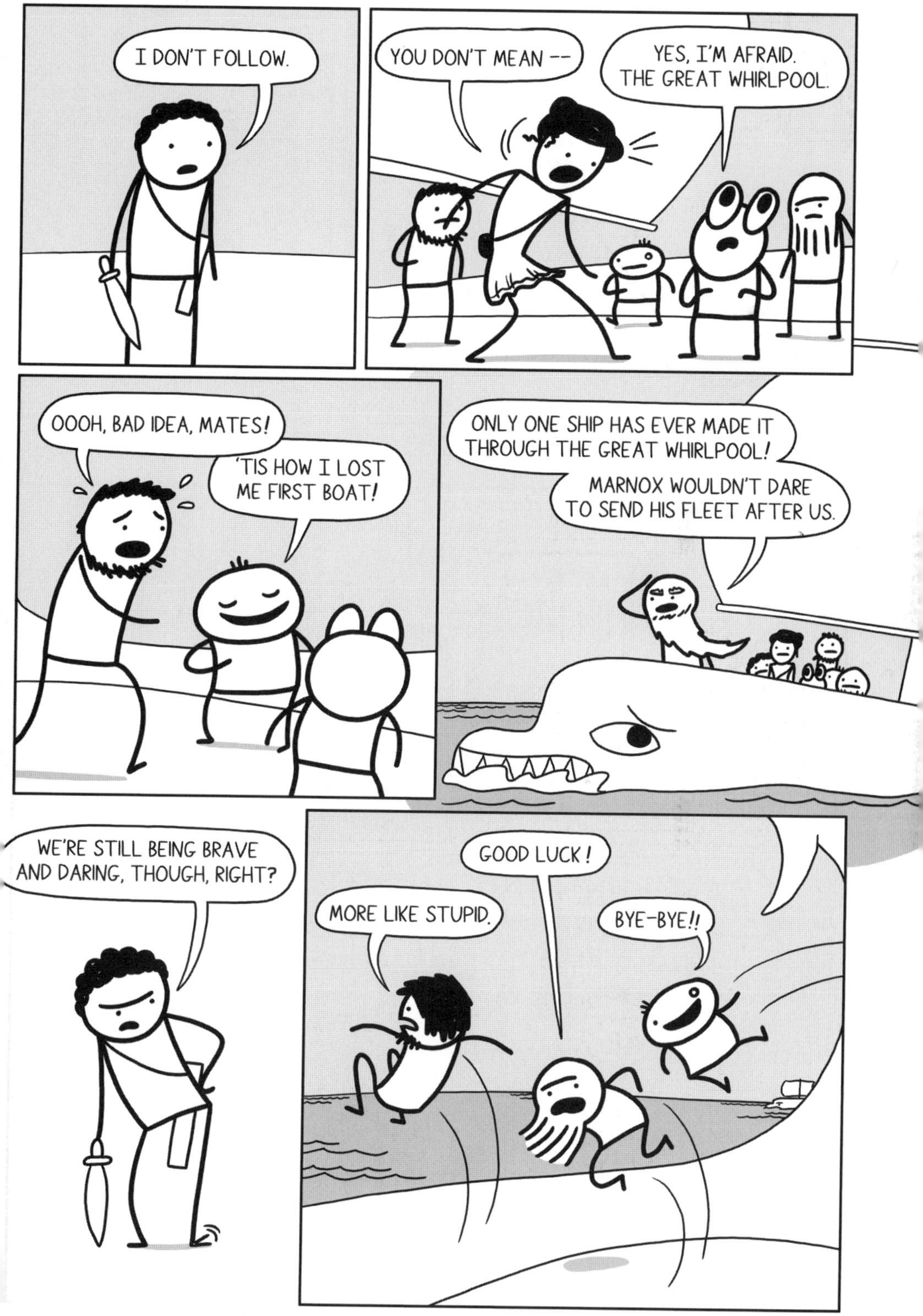
I DON'T FOLLOW.
YOU DON'T MEAN --
YES, I'M AFRAID. THE GREAT WHIRLPOOL.
OOOH, BAD IDEA, MATES!
'TIS HOW I LOST ME FIRST BOAT!
ONLY ONE SHIP HAS EVER MADE IT THROUGH THE GREAT WHIRLPOOL!
MARNOX WOULDN'T DARE TO SEND HIS FLEET AFTER US.
WE'RE STILL BEING BRAVE AND DARING, THOUGH, RIGHT?
GOOD LUCK!
MORE LIKE STUPID.
BYE-BYE!!

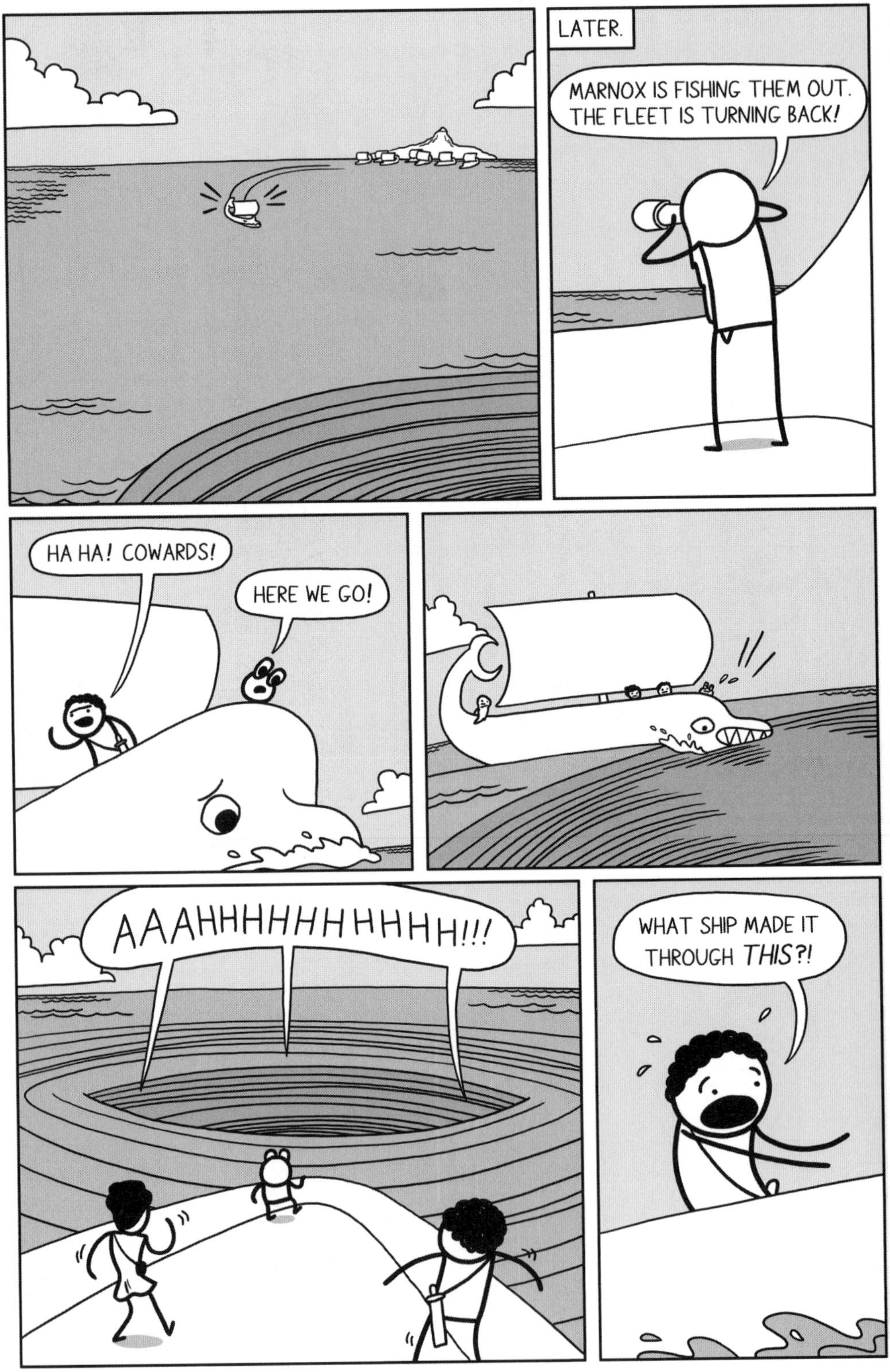
LATER.
MARNOX IS FISHING THEM OUT. THE FLEET IS TURNING BACK!
HA HA! COWARDS!
HERE WE GO!
AAAHHHHHHHHHHH!!!
WHAT SHIP MADE IT THROUGH THIS?!

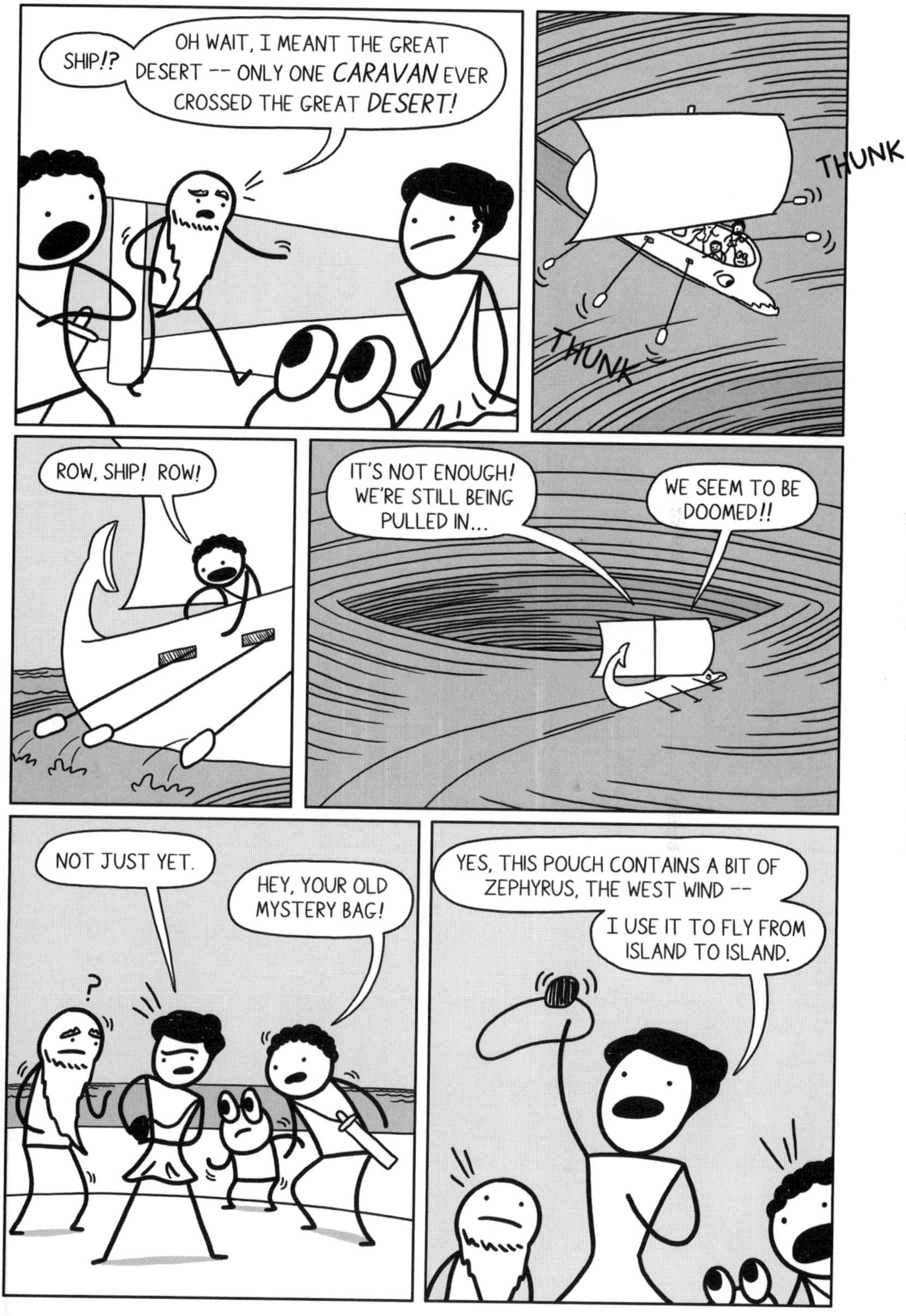
SHIP!?
OH WAIT, I MEANT THE GREAT DESERT -- ONLY ONE CARAVAN EVER CROSSED THE GREAT DESERT!
THUNK
THUNK
ROW, SHIP! ROW!
IT'S NOT ENOUGH! WE'RE STILL BEING PULLED IN...
WE SEEM TO BE DOOMED!!
NOT JUST YET.
HEY, YOUR OLD MYSTERY BAG!
?
YES, THIS POUCH CONTAINS A BIT OF ZEPHYRUS, THE WEST WIND --
I USE IT TO FLY FROM ISLAND TO ISLAND.

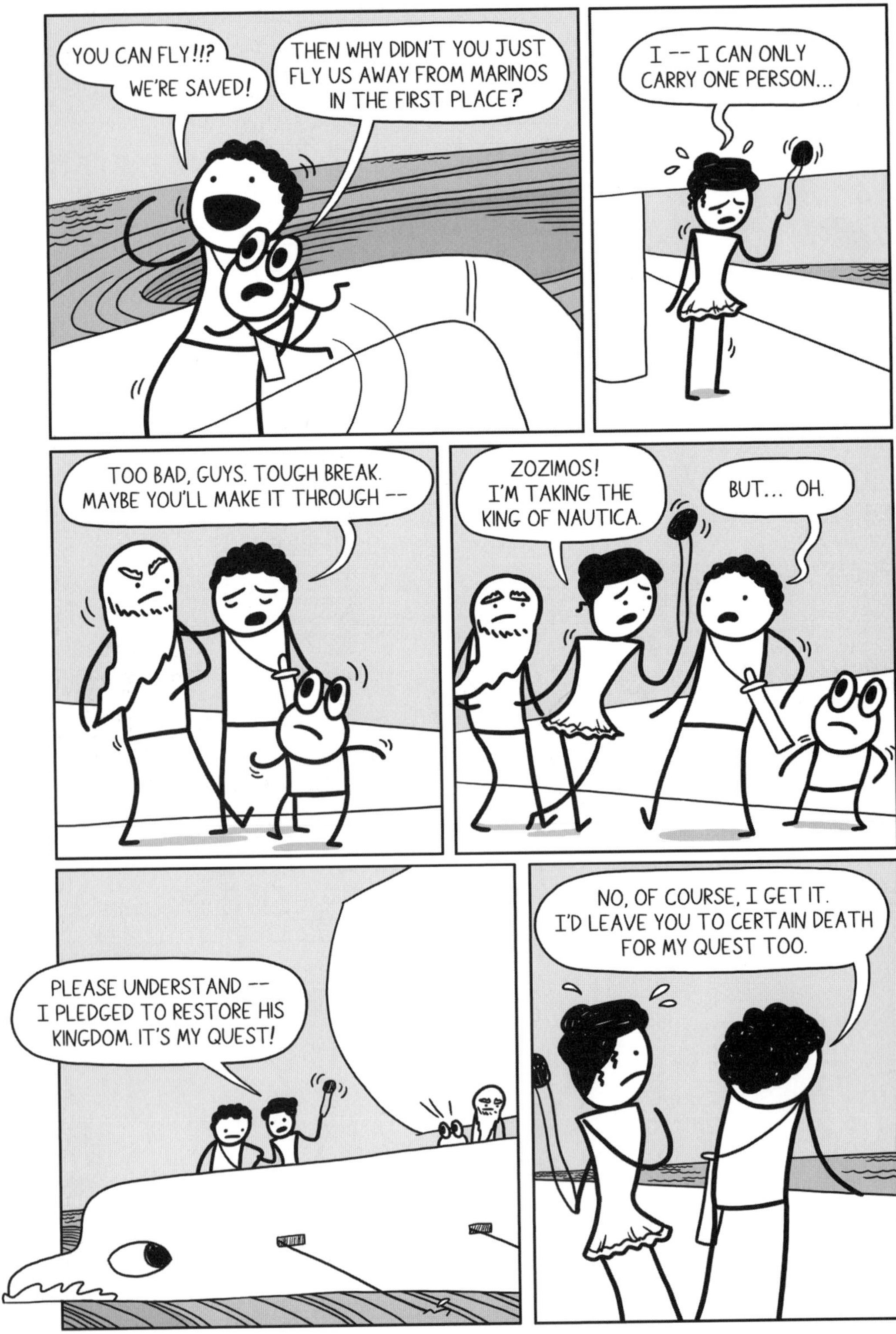
YOU CAN FLY!!? WE'RE SAVED!
THEN WHY DIDN'T YOU JUST FLY US AWAY FROM MARINOS IN THE FIRST PLACE?
I -- I CAN ONLY CARRY ONE PERSON...
TOO BAD, GUYS. TOUGH BREAK. MAYBE YOU'LL MAKE IT THROUGH --
ZOZIMOS! I'M TAKING THE KING OF NAUTICA.
BUT... OH.
PLEASE UNDERSTAND -- I PLEDGED TO RESTORE HIS KINGDOM. IT'S MY QUEST!
NO, OF COURSE, I GET IT. I'D LEAVE YOU TO CERTAIN DEATH FOR MY QUEST TOO.

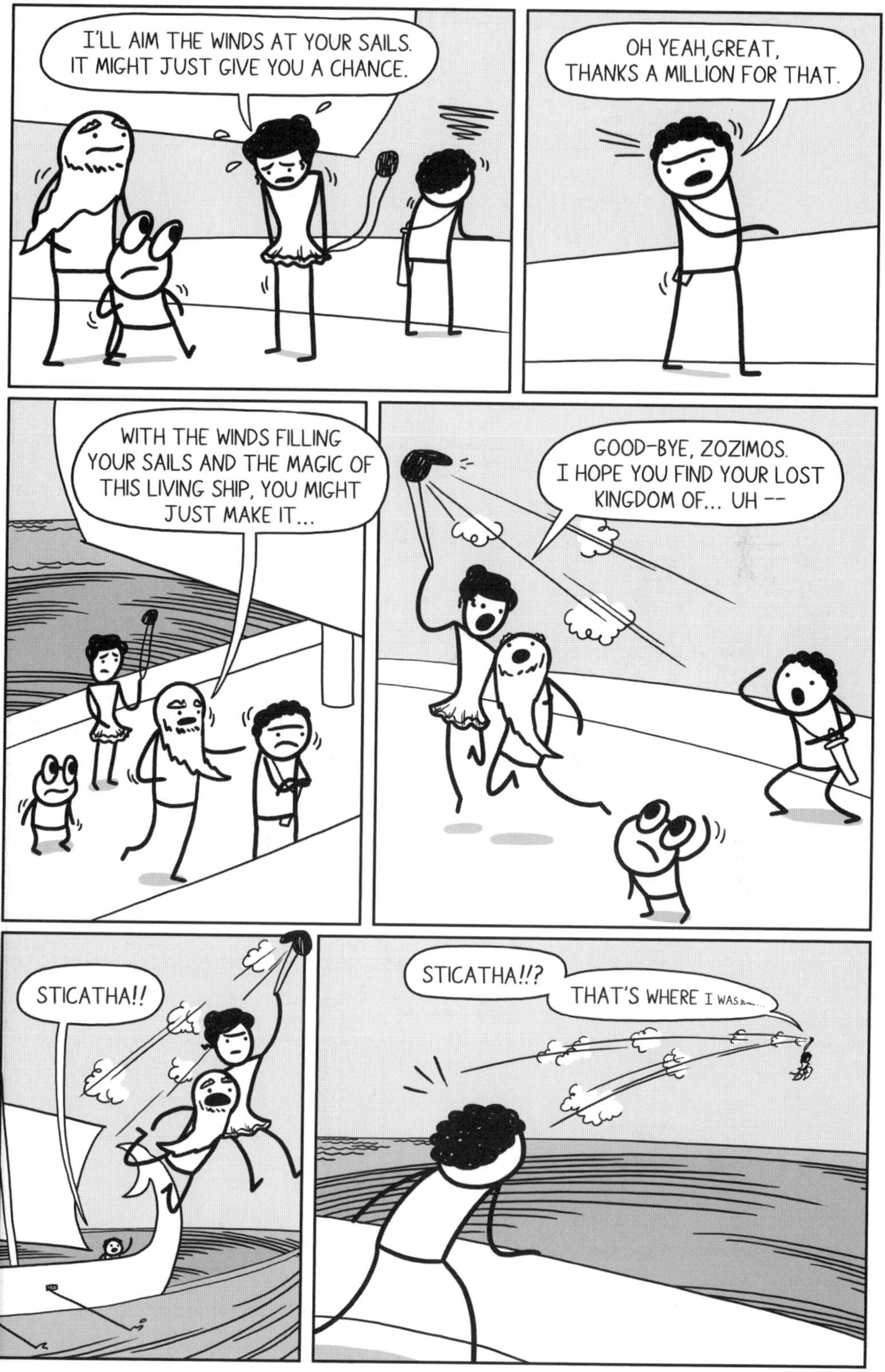
I'LL AIM THE WINDS AT YOUR SAILS. IT MIGHT JUST GIVE YOU A CHANCE.
OH YEAH, GREAT, THANKS A MILLION FOR THAT.
WITH THE WINDS FILLING YOUR SAILS AND THE MAGIC OF THIS LIVING SHIP, YOU MIGHT JUST MAKE IT...
GOOD-BYE, ZOZIMOS. I HOPE YOU FIND YOUR LOST KINGDOM OF... UH --
STICATHA!!
STICATHA!!?
THAT'S WHERE I WAS

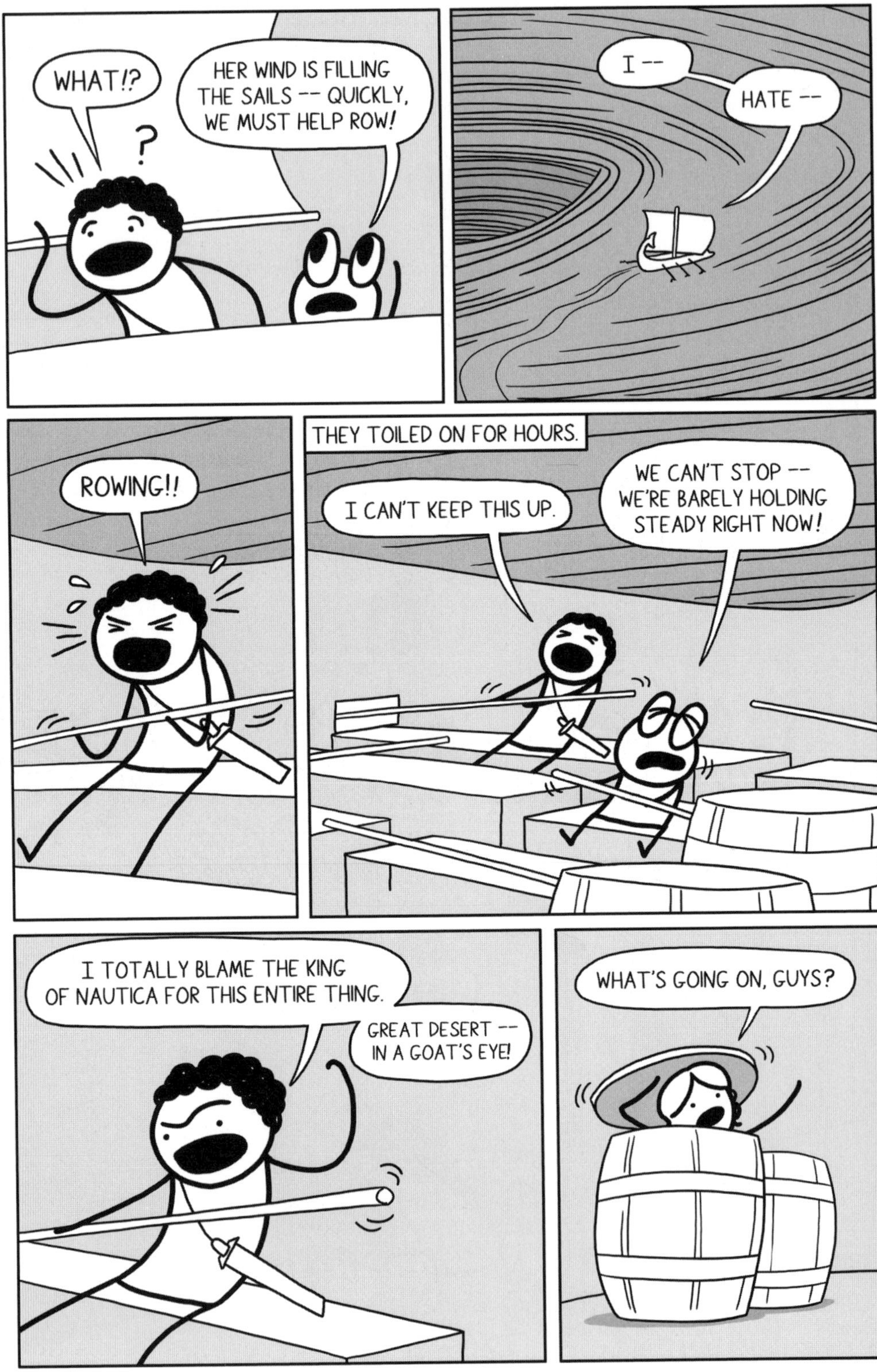
WHAT!?
HER WIND IS FILLING THE SAILS -- QUICKLY, WE MUST HELP ROW!
I --
HATE --
ROWING!!
THEY TOILED ON FOR HOURS.
I CAN'T KEEP THIS UP.
WE CAN'T STOP -- WE'RE BARELY HOLDING STEADY RIGHT NOW!
I TOTALLY BLAME THE KING OF NAUTICA FOR THIS ENTIRE THING.
GREAT DESERT -- IN A GOAT'S EYE!
WHAT'S GOING ON, GUYS?

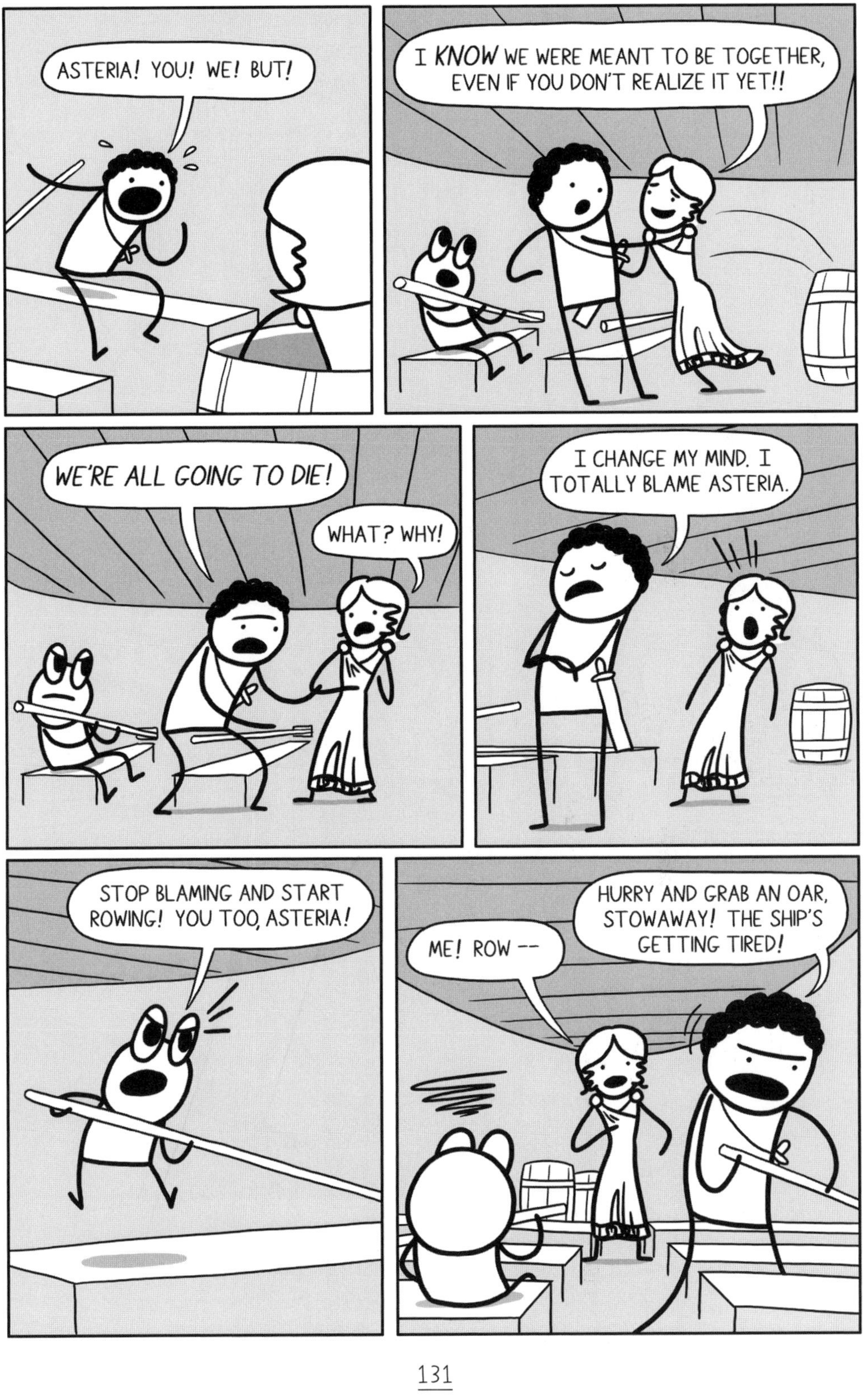
ASTERIA! YOU! WE! BUT!
I KNOW WE WERE MEANT TO BE TOGETHER, EVEN IF YOU DON'T REALIZE IT YET!!
WE'RE ALL GOING TO DIE!
WHAT? WHY!
I CHANGE MY MIND. I TOTALLY BLAME ASTERIA.
STOP BLAMING AND START ROWING! YOU TOO, ASTERIA!
ME! ROW --
HURRY AND GRAB AN OAR, STOWAWAY! THE SHIP'S GETTING TIRED!

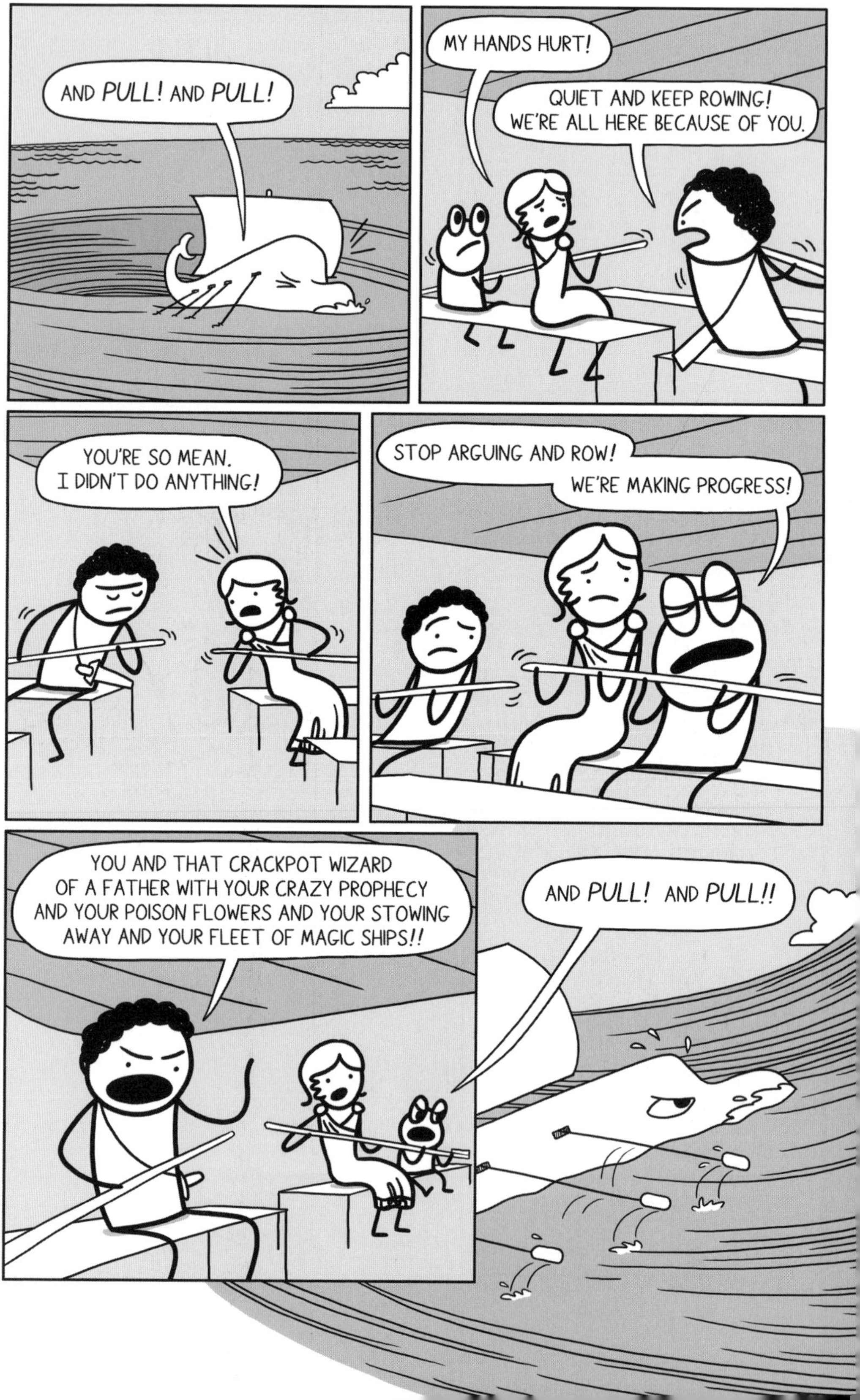
AND PULL! AND PULL!
MY HANDS HURT!
QUIET AND KEEP ROWING! WE'RE ALL HERE BECAUSE OF YOU.
YOU'RE SO MEAN. I DIDN'T DO ANYTHING!
STOP ARGUING AND ROW!
WE'RE MAKING PROGRESS!
YOU AND THAT CRACKPOT WIZARD OF A FATHER WITH YOUR CRAZY PROPHECY AND YOUR POISON FLOWERS AND YOUR STOWING AWAY AND YOUR FLEET OF MAGIC SHIPS!!
AND PULL! AND PULL!!

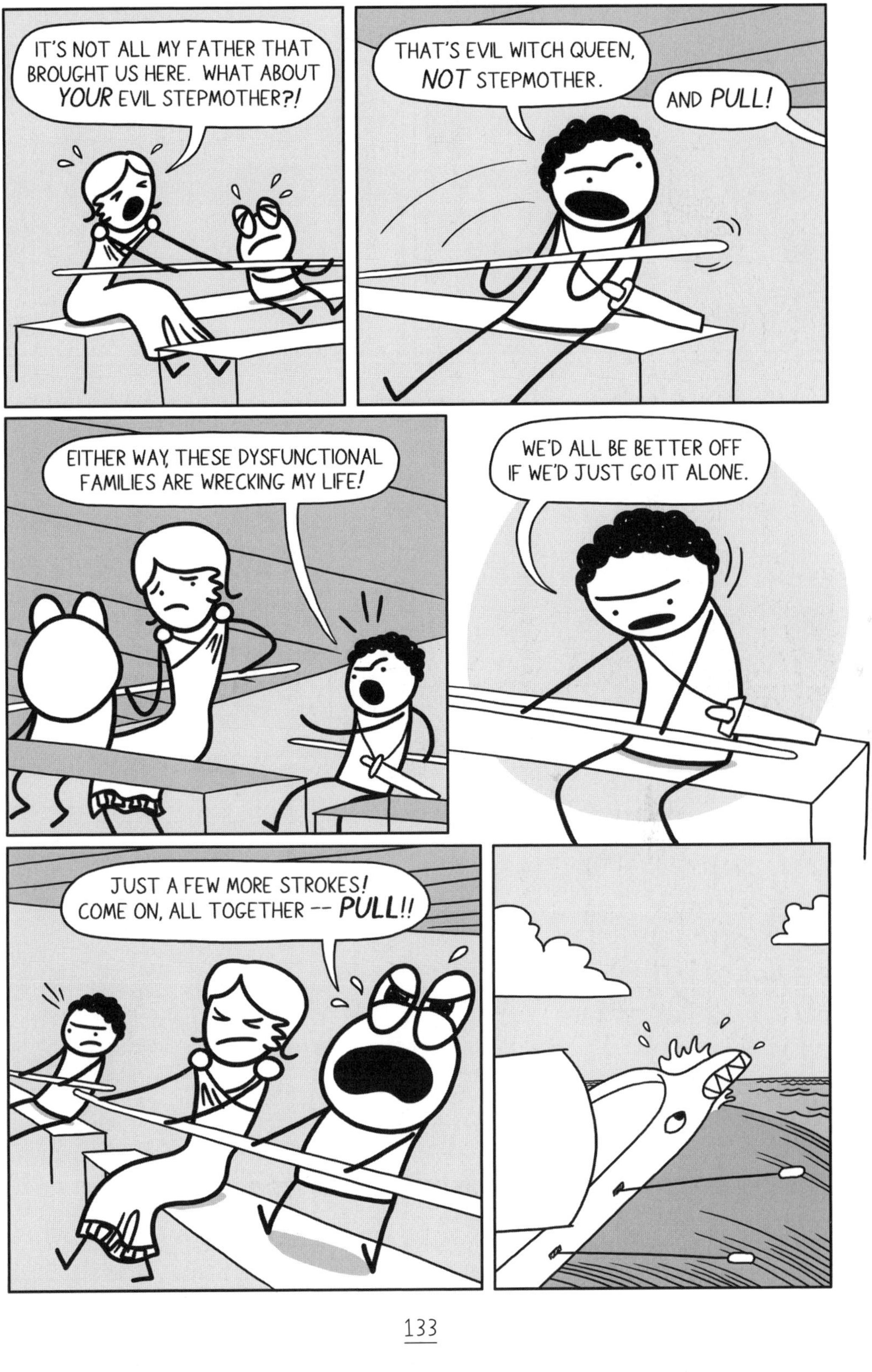
IT'S NOT ALL MY FATHER THAT BROUGHT US HERE. WHAT ABOUT *YOUR* EVIL STEPMOTHER?!
THAT'S EVIL WITCH QUEEN, *NOT* STEPMOTHER.
AND *PULL!*
EITHER WAY, THESE DYSFUNCTIONAL FAMILIES ARE WRECKING MY LIFE!
WE'D ALL BE BETTER OFF IF WE'D JUST GO IT ALONE.
JUST A FEW MORE STROKES! COME ON, ALL TOGETHER -- ***PULL!!***

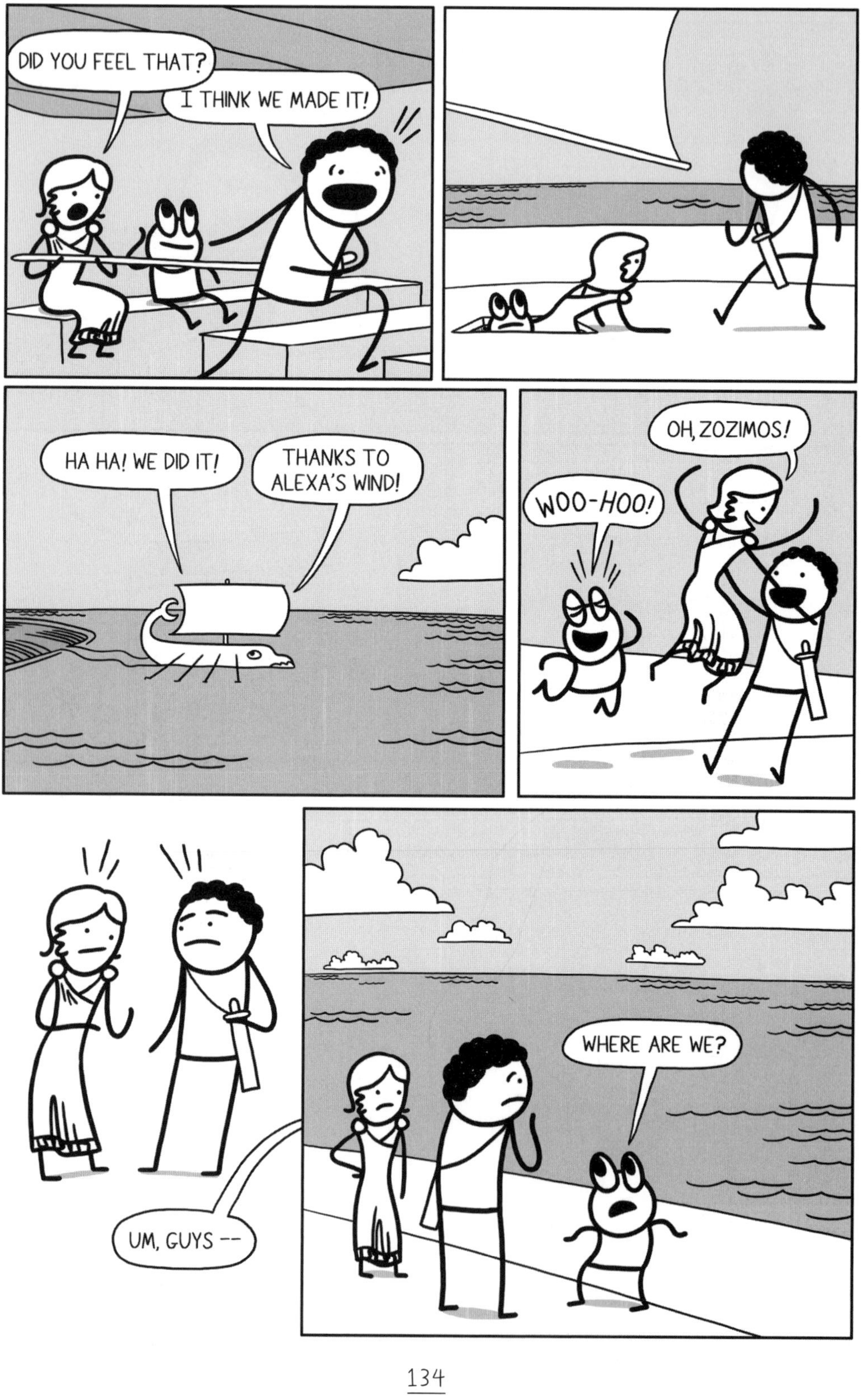
DID YOU FEEL THAT?
I THINK WE MADE IT!
HA HA! WE DID IT!
THANKS TO ALEXA'S WIND!
OH, ZOZIMOS!
WOO-HOO!
UM, GUYS --
WHERE ARE WE?

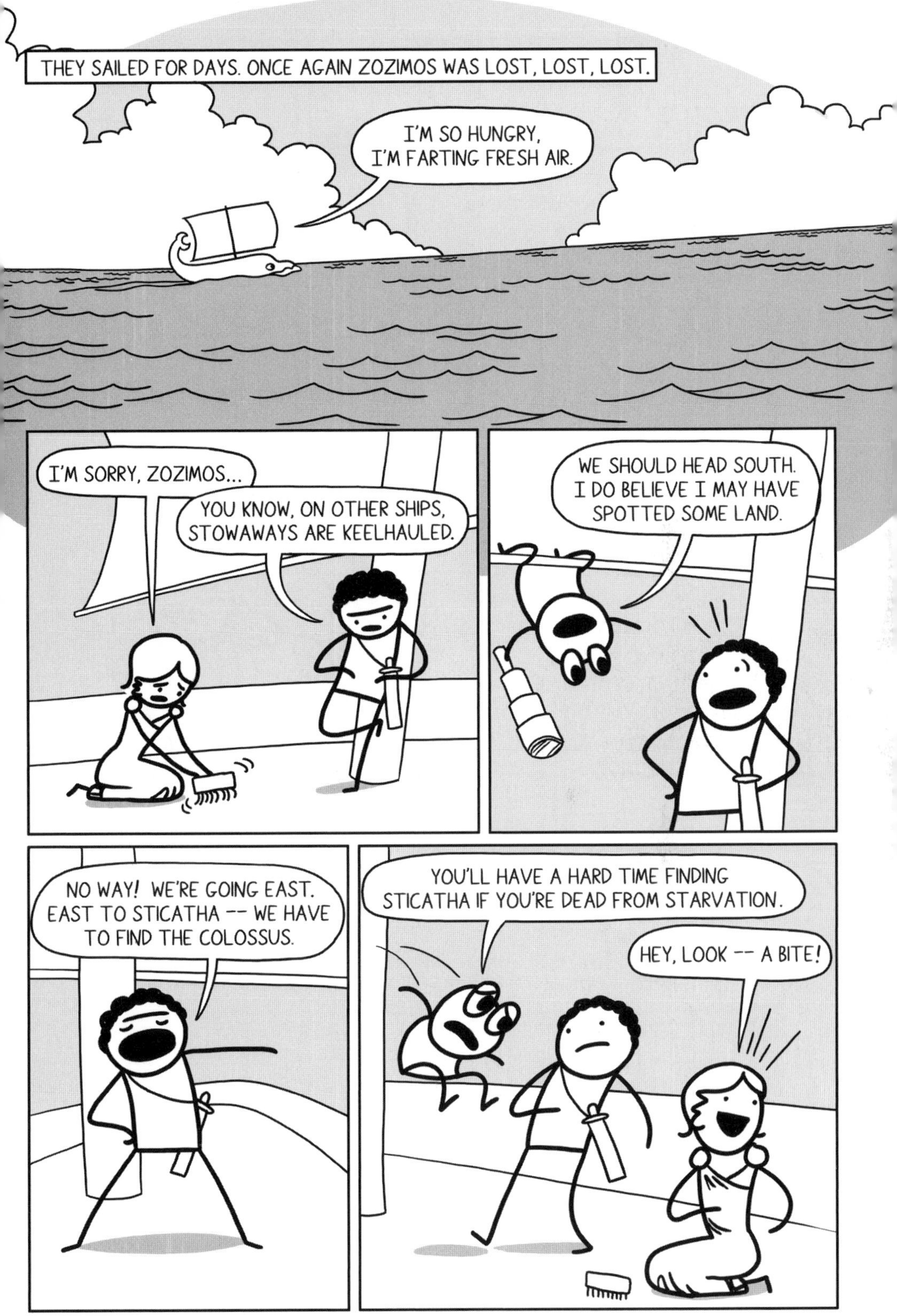
THEY SAILED FOR DAYS. ONCE AGAIN ZOZIMOS WAS LOST, LOST, LOST.
I'M SO HUNGRY, I'M FARTING FRESH AIR.
I'M SORRY, ZOZIMOS...
YOU KNOW, ON OTHER SHIPS, STOWAWAYS ARE KEELHAULED.
WE SHOULD HEAD SOUTH. I DO BELIEVE I MAY HAVE SPOTTED SOME LAND.
NO WAY! WE'RE GOING EAST. EAST TO STICATHA -- WE HAVE TO FIND THE COLOSSUS.
YOU'LL HAVE A HARD TIME FINDING STICATHA IF YOU'RE DEAD FROM STARVATION.
HEY, LOOK -- A BITE!

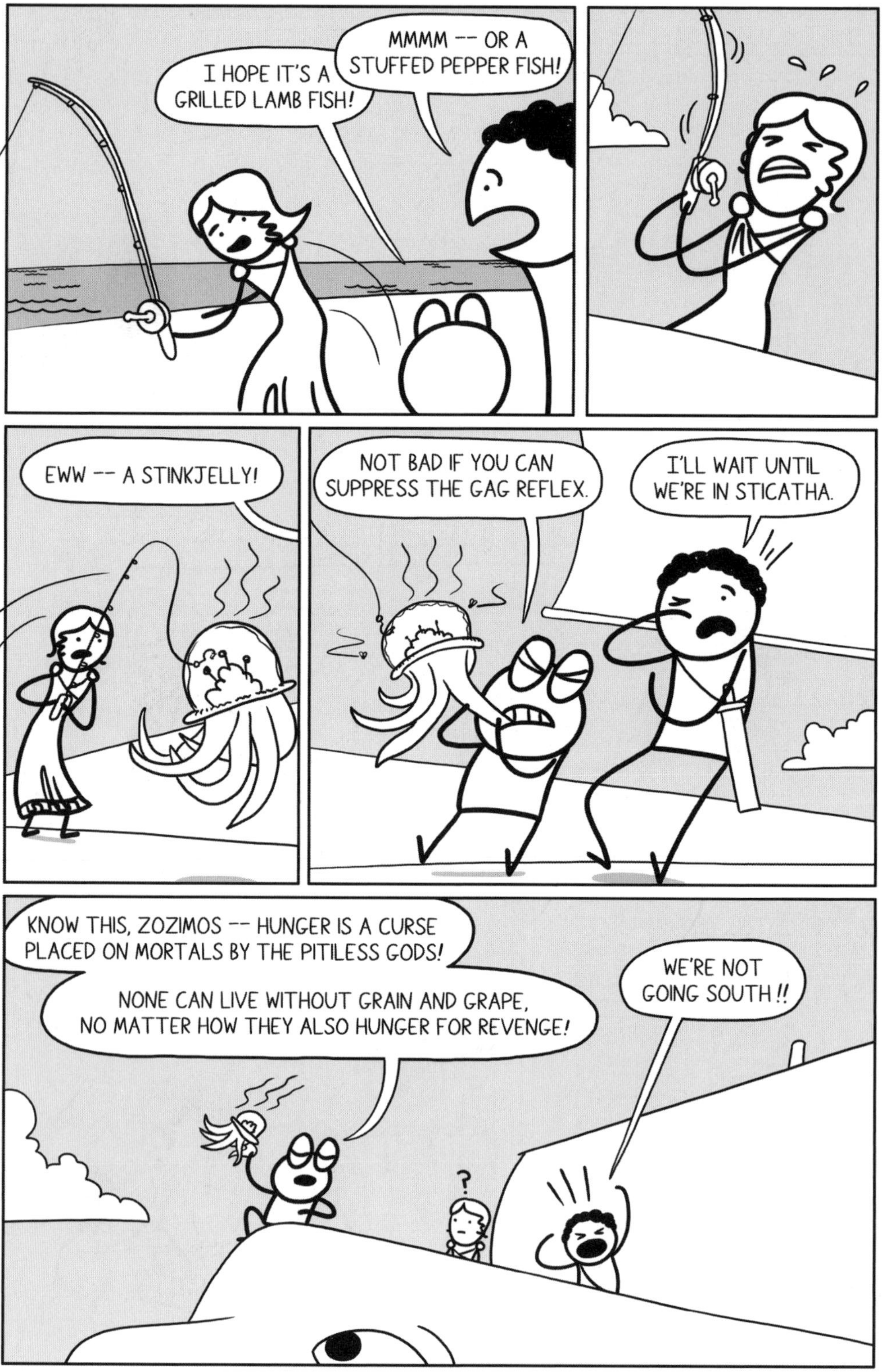
I HOPE IT'S A GRILLED LAMB FISH!
MMMM -- OR A STUFFED PEPPER FISH!
EWW -- A STINKJELLY!
NOT BAD IF YOU CAN SUPPRESS THE GAG REFLEX.
I'LL WAIT UNTIL WE'RE IN STICATHA.
KNOW THIS, ZOZIMOS -- HUNGER IS A CURSE PLACED ON MORTALS BY THE PITILESS GODS!
NONE CAN LIVE WITHOUT GRAIN AND GRAPE, NO MATTER HOW THEY ALSO HUNGER FOR REVENGE!
WE'RE NOT GOING SOUTH!!

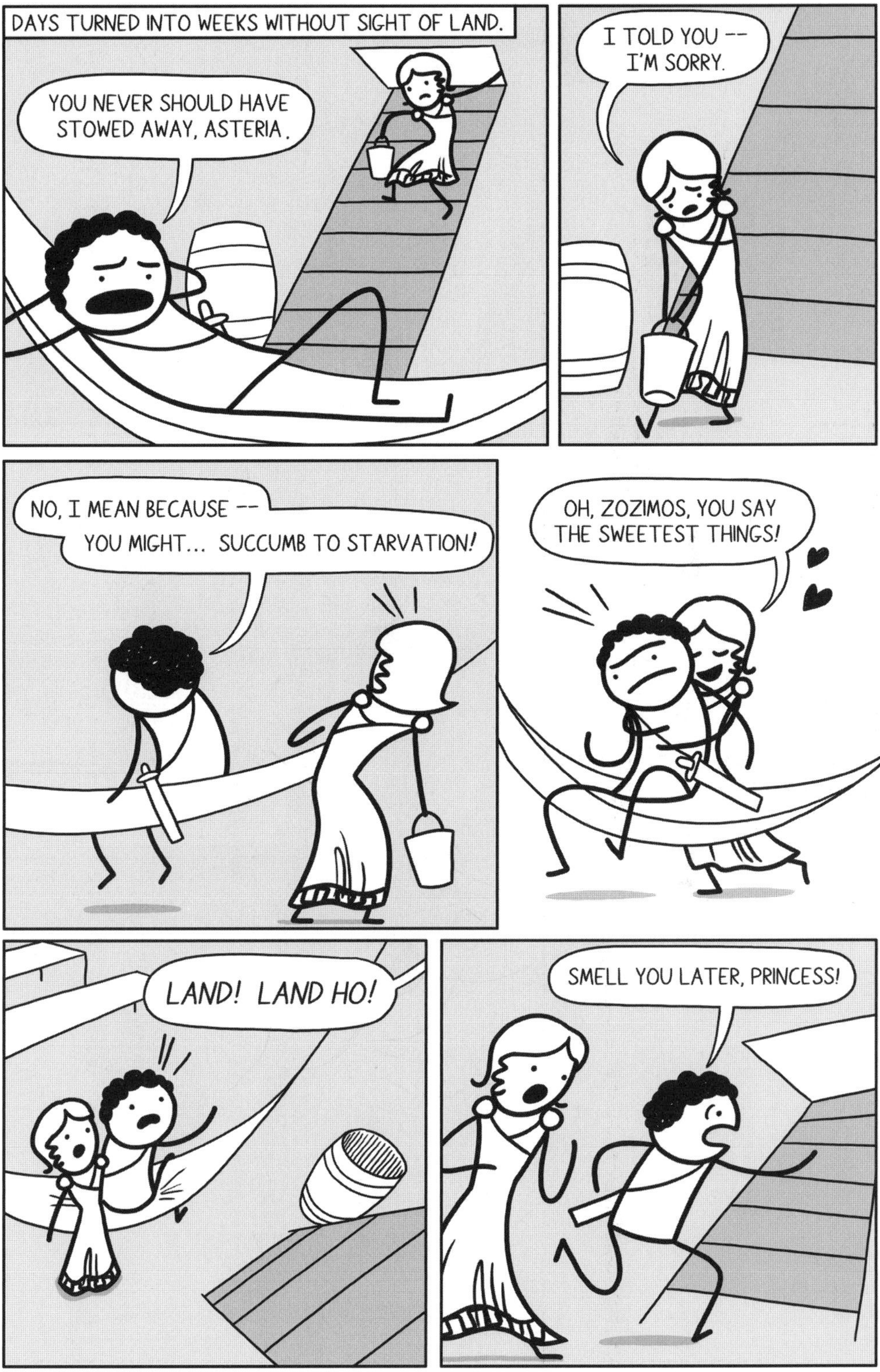
DAYS TURNED INTO WEEKS WITHOUT SIGHT OF LAND.
YOU NEVER SHOULD HAVE STOWED AWAY, ASTERIA.
I TOLD YOU -- I'M SORRY.
NO, I MEAN BECAUSE --
YOU MIGHT... SUCCUMB TO STARVATION!
OH, ZOZIMOS, YOU SAY THE SWEETEST THINGS!
LAND! LAND HO!
SMELL YOU LATER, PRINCESS!

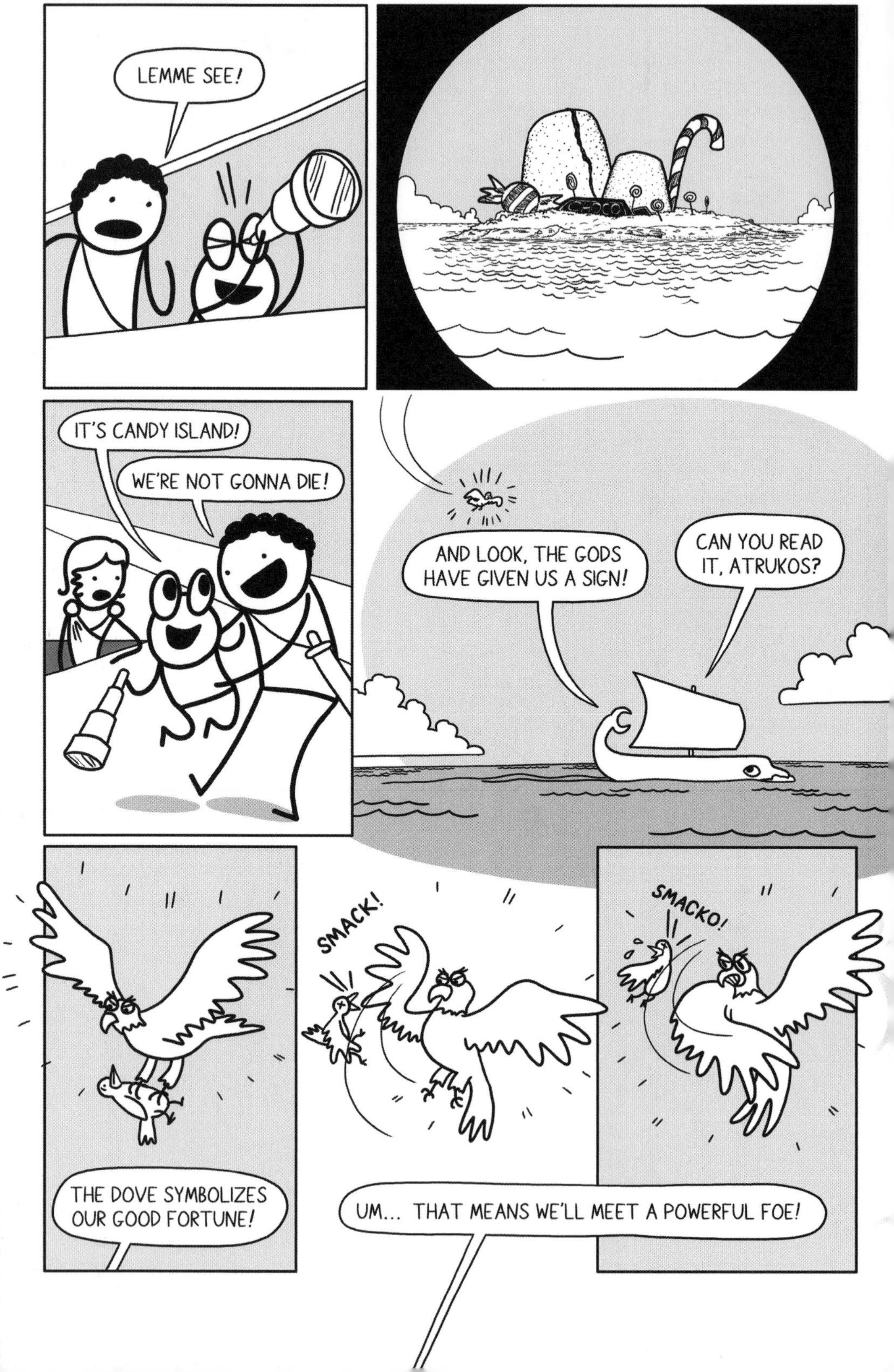
LEMME SEE!
IT'S CANDY ISLAND!
WE'RE NOT GONNA DIE!
AND LOOK, THE GODS HAVE GIVEN US A SIGN!
CAN YOU READ IT, ATRUKOS?
THE DOVE SYMBOLIZES OUR GOOD FORTUNE!
SMACK!
SMACKO!
UM... THAT MEANS WE'LL MEET A POWERFUL FOE!

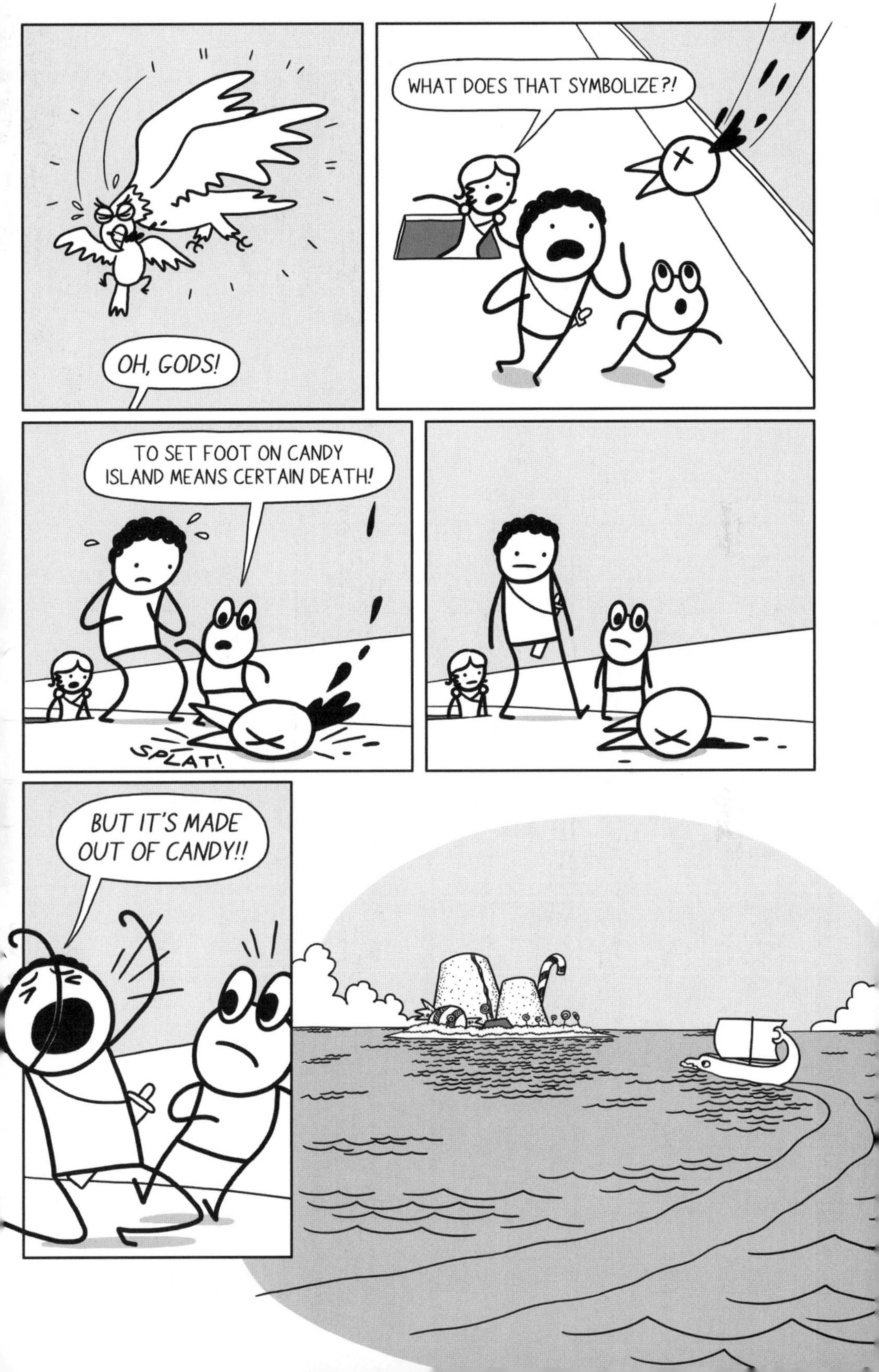
OH, GODS!
WHAT DOES THAT SYMBOLIZE?!
TO SET FOOT ON CANDY ISLAND MEANS CERTAIN DEATH!
SPLAT!
BUT IT'S MADE OUT OF CANDY!!

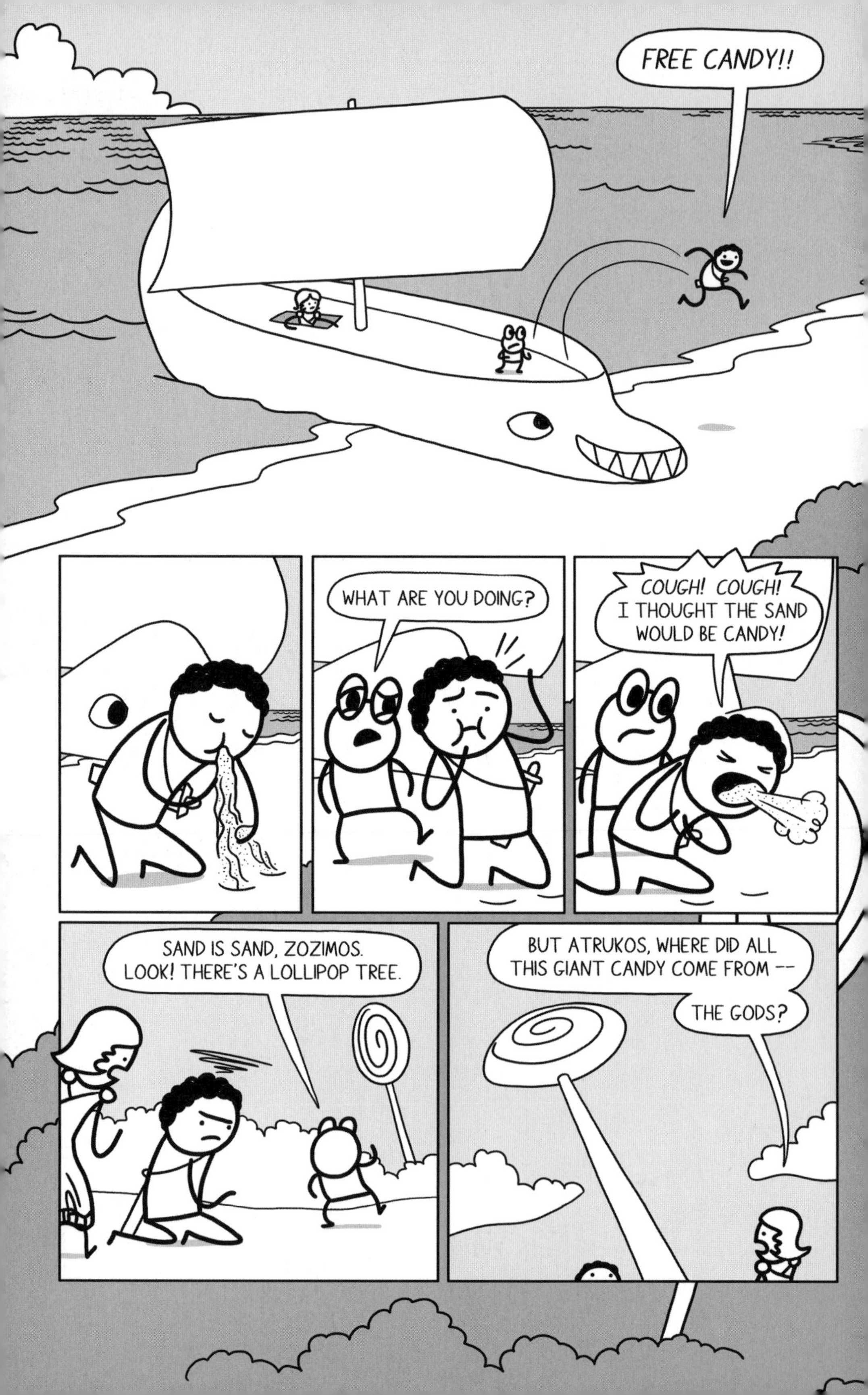
FREE CANDY!!
WHAT ARE YOU DOING?
COUGH! COUGH! I THOUGHT THE SAND WOULD BE CANDY!
SAND IS SAND, ZOZIMOS. LOOK! THERE'S A LOLLIPOP TREE.
BUT ATRUKOS, WHERE DID ALL THIS GIANT CANDY COME FROM --
THE GODS?

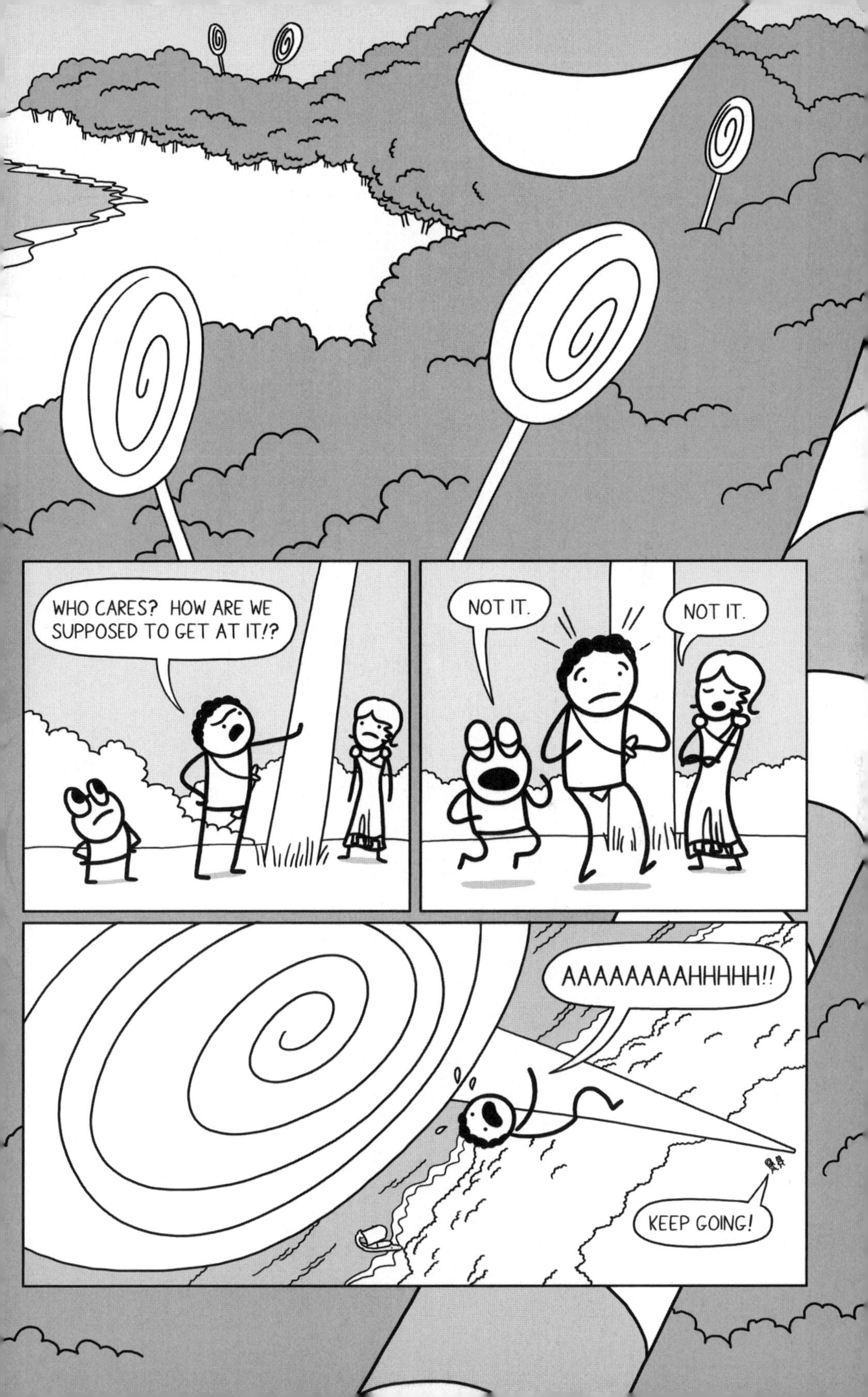
WHO CARES? HOW ARE WE SUPPOSED TO GET AT IT!?
NOT IT.
NOT IT.
AAAAAAAAHHHHH!!
KEEP GOING!

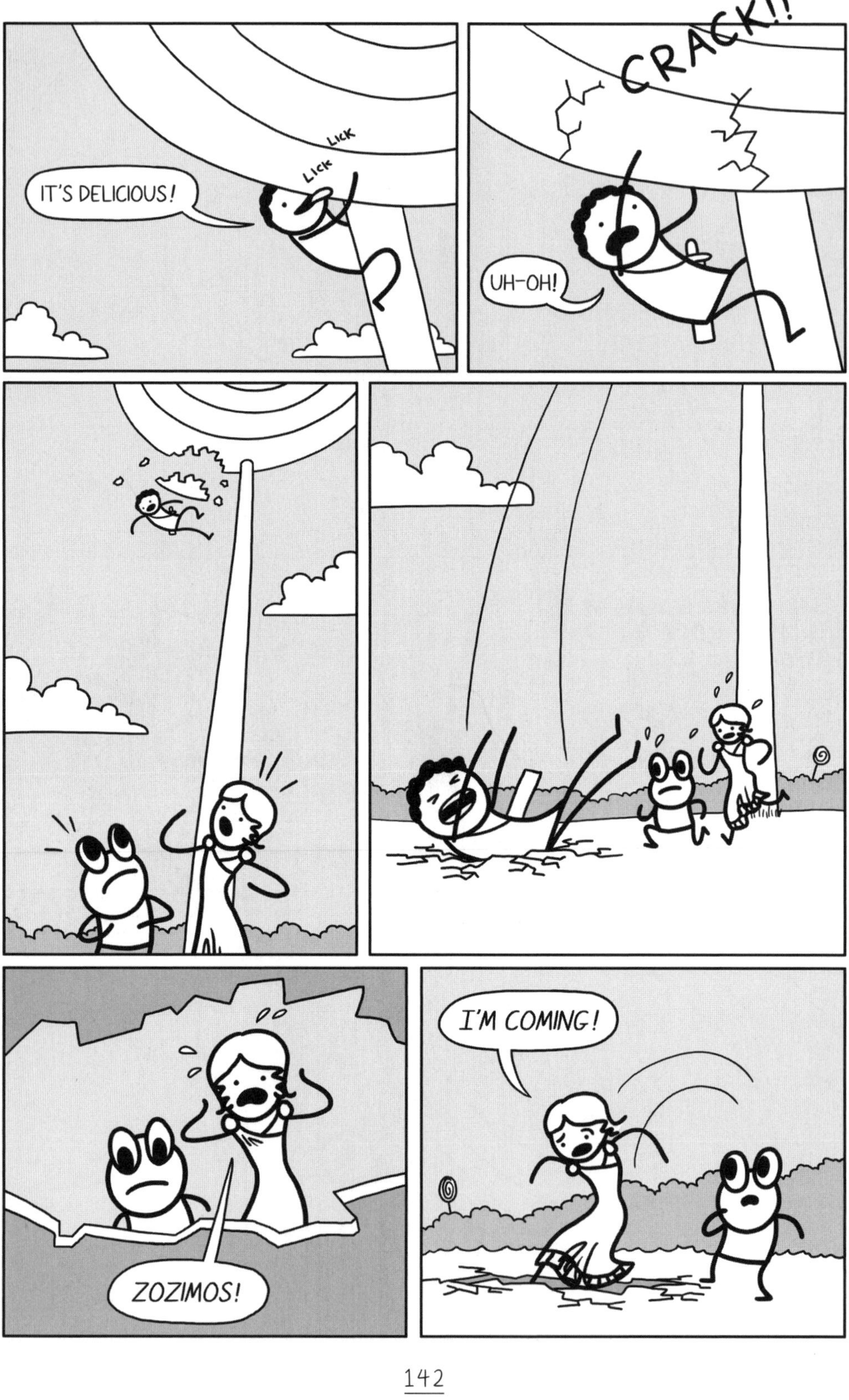
LICK
LICK
IT'S DELICIOUS!
CRACK!!
UH-OH!
ZOZIMOS!
I'M COMING!

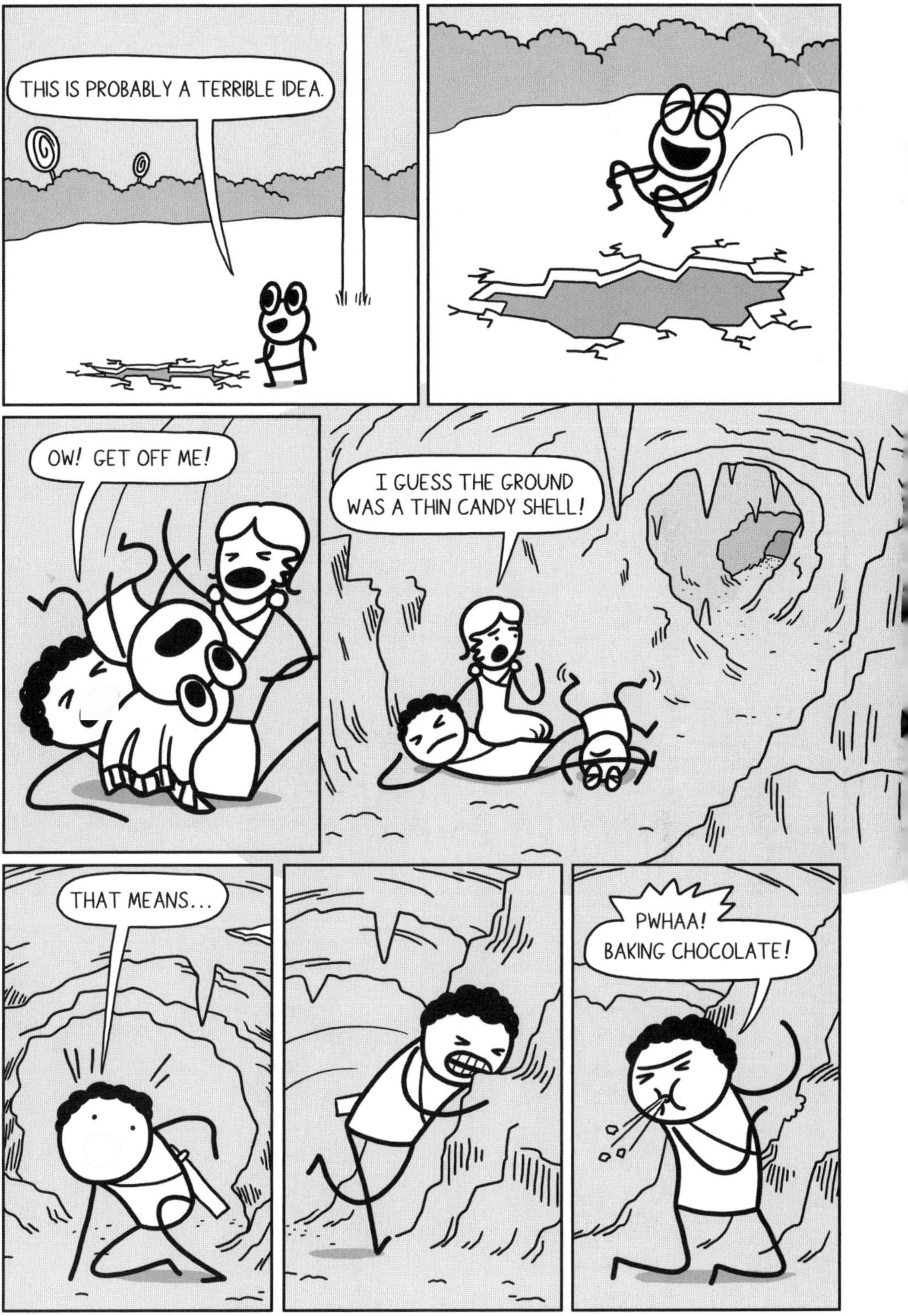
THIS IS PROBABLY A TERRIBLE IDEA.
OW! GET OFF ME!
I GUESS THE GROUND WAS A THIN CANDY SHELL!
THAT MEANS...
PWHAA! BAKING CHOCOLATE!

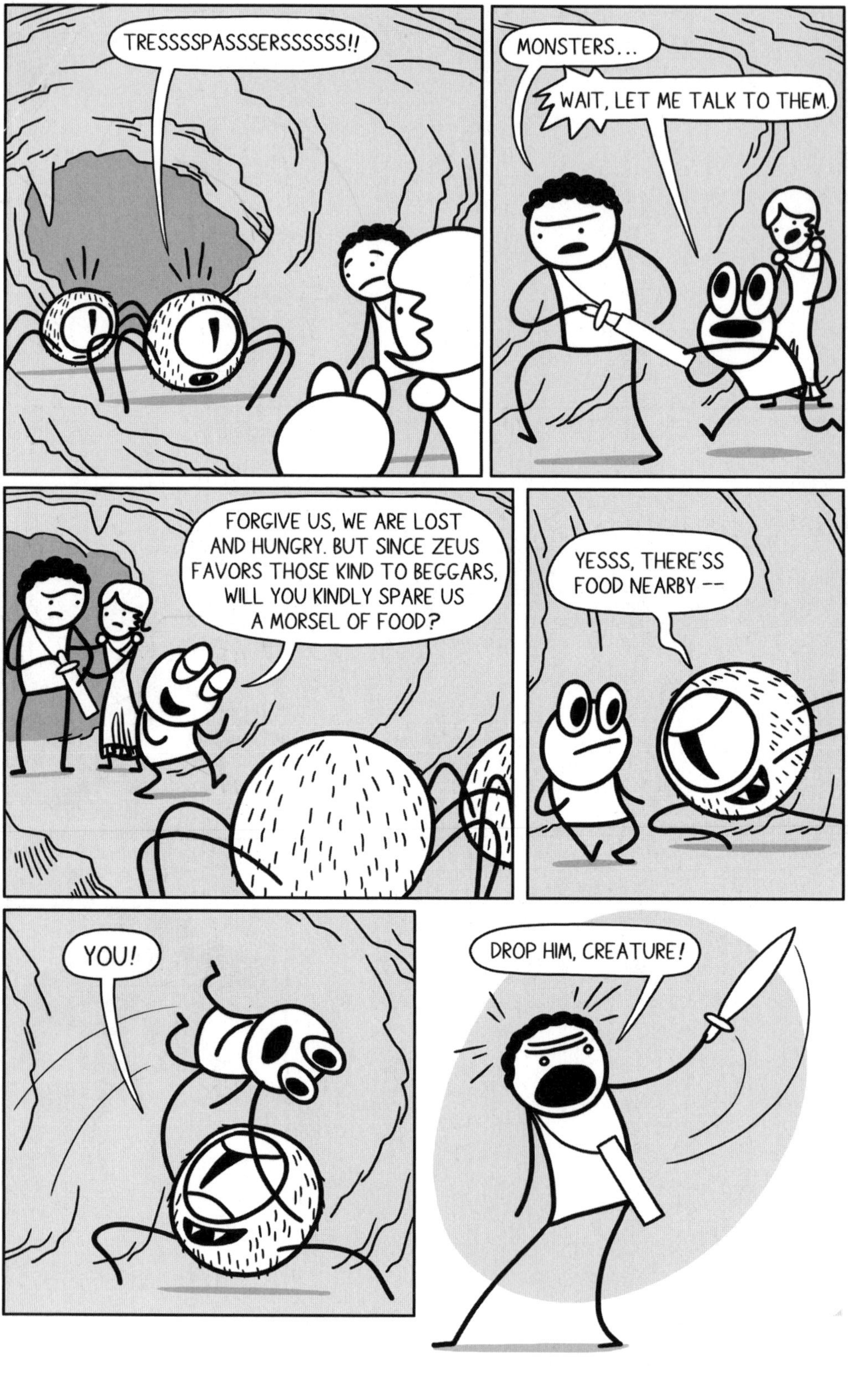
TRESSSSPASSSERSSSSSS!!
MONSTERS...
WAIT, LET ME TALK TO THEM.
FORGIVE US, WE ARE LOST AND HUNGRY. BUT SINCE ZEUS FAVORS THOSE KIND TO BEGGARS, WILL YOU KINDLY SPARE US A MORSEL OF FOOD?
YESSS, THERE'SS FOOD NEARBY --
YOU!
DROP HIM, CREATURE!

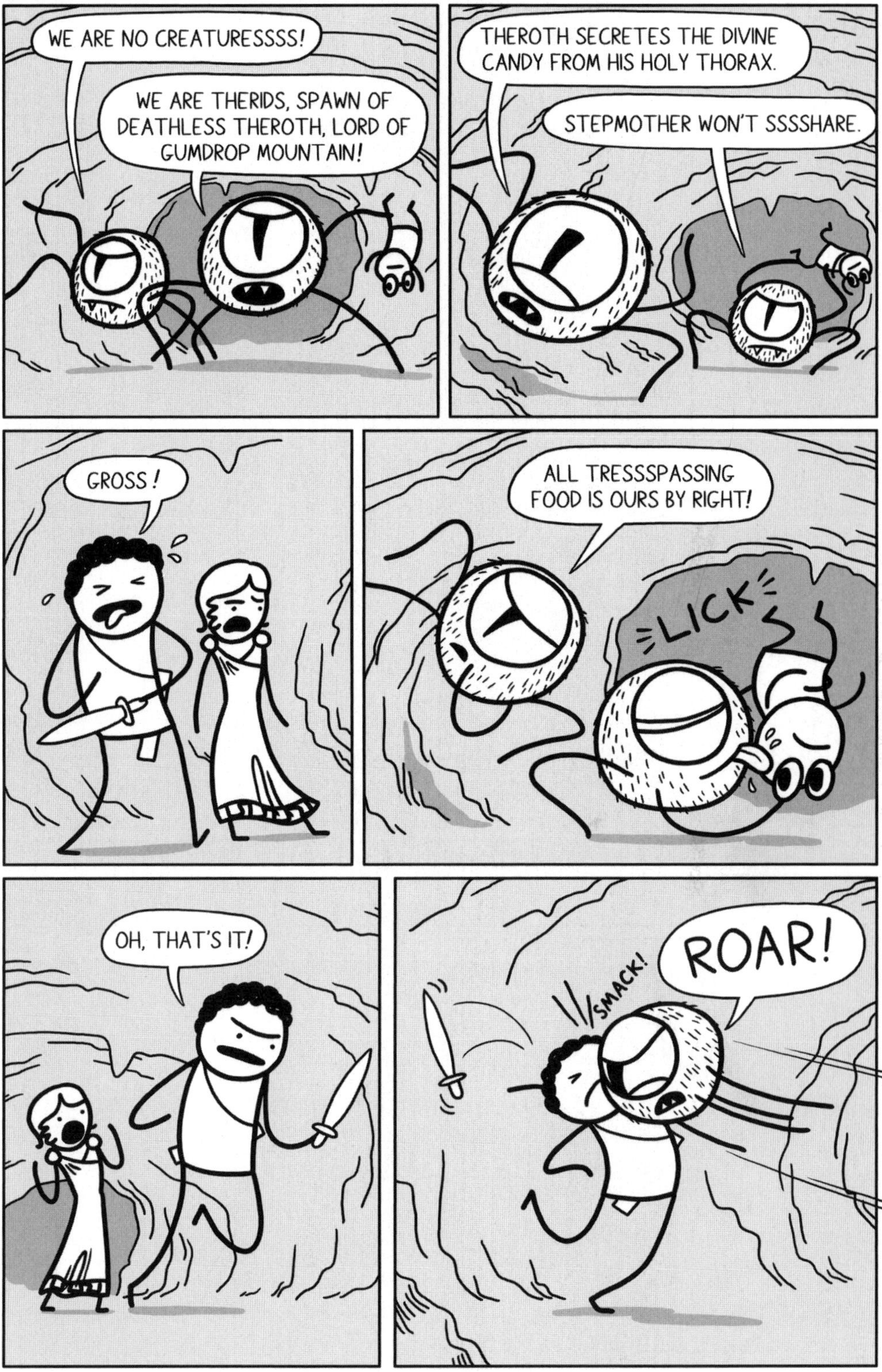
WE ARE NO CREATURESSSS!
WE ARE THERIDS, SPAWN OF DEATHLESS THEROTH, LORD OF GUMDROP MOUNTAIN!
THEROTH SECRETES THE DIVINE CANDY FROM HIS HOLY THORAX.
STEPMOTHER WON'T SSSSHARE.
GROSS!
ALL TRESSSPASSING FOOD IS OURS BY RIGHT!
LICK
OH, THAT'S IT!
SMACK!
ROAR!

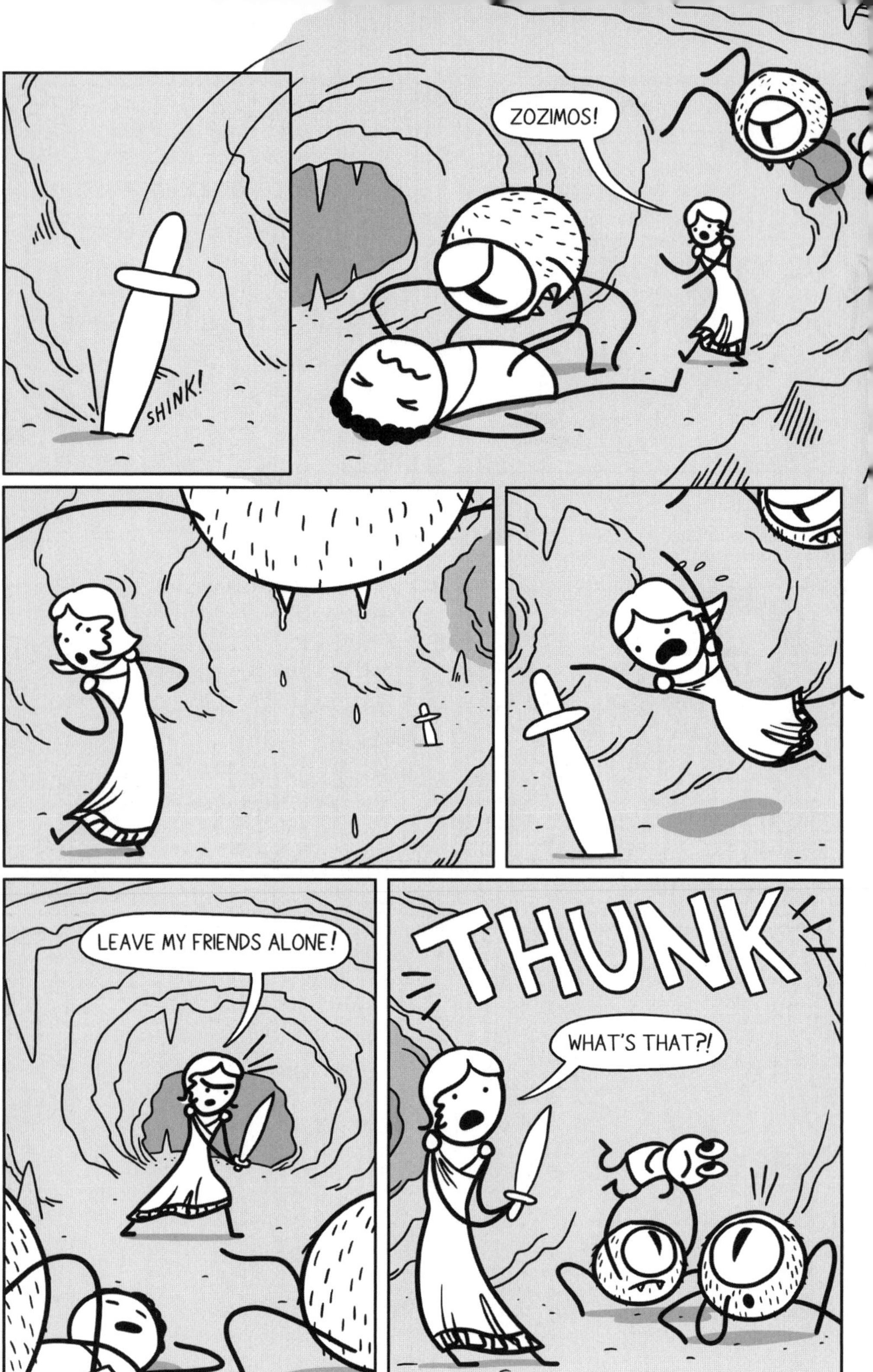
ZOZIMOS!
SHINK!
LEAVE MY FRIENDS ALONE!
THUNK
WHAT'S THAT?!

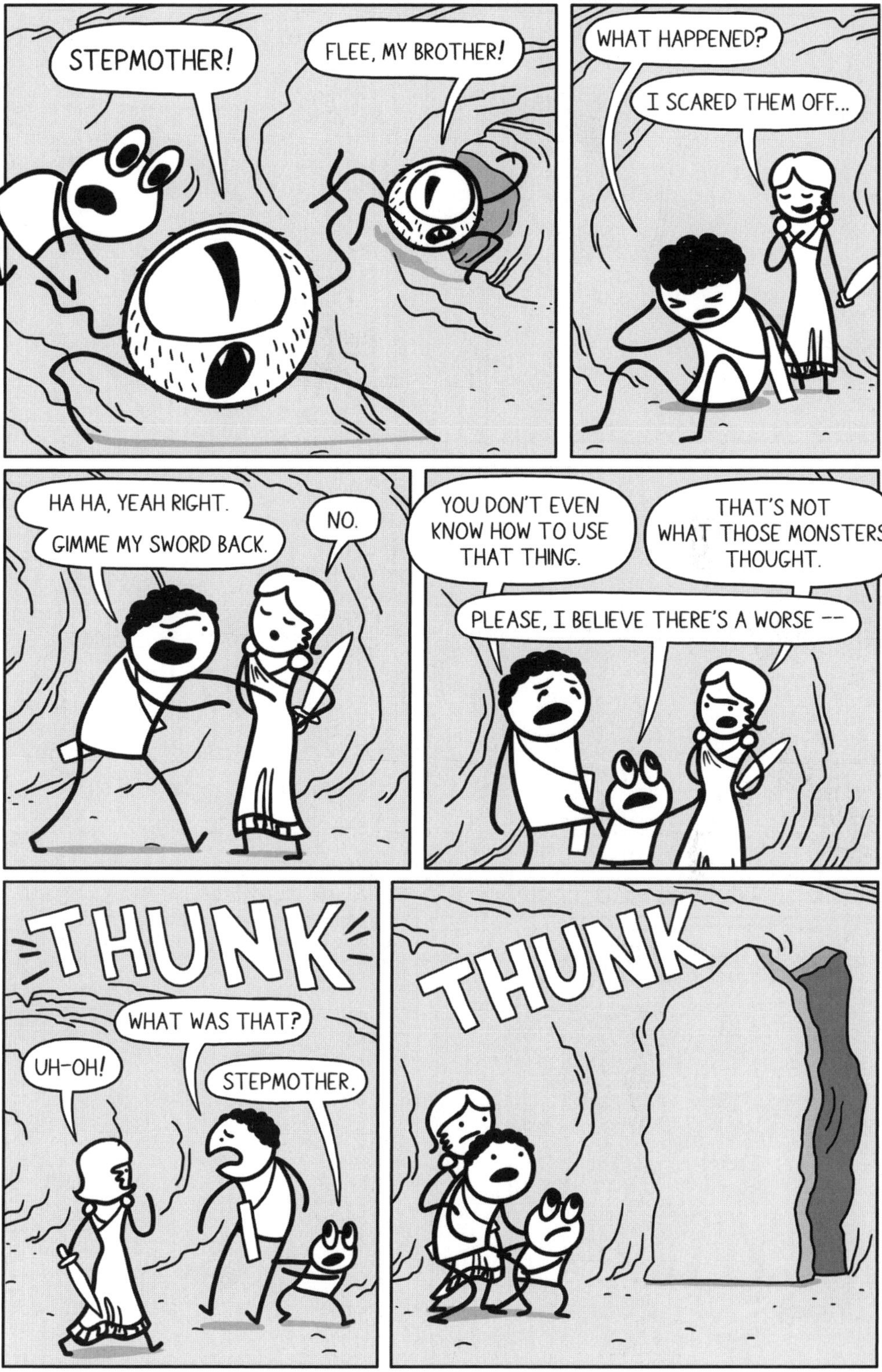

STEPMOTHER!
FLEE, MY BROTHER!
WHAT HAPPENED?
I SCARED THEM OFF...
HA HA, YEAH RIGHT.
GIMME MY SWORD BACK.
NO.
YOU DON'T EVEN KNOW HOW TO USE THAT THING.
THAT'S NOT WHAT THOSE MONSTERS THOUGHT.
PLEASE, I BELIEVE THERE'S A WORSE --
THUNK
WHAT WAS THAT?
UH-OH!
STEPMOTHER.
THUNK

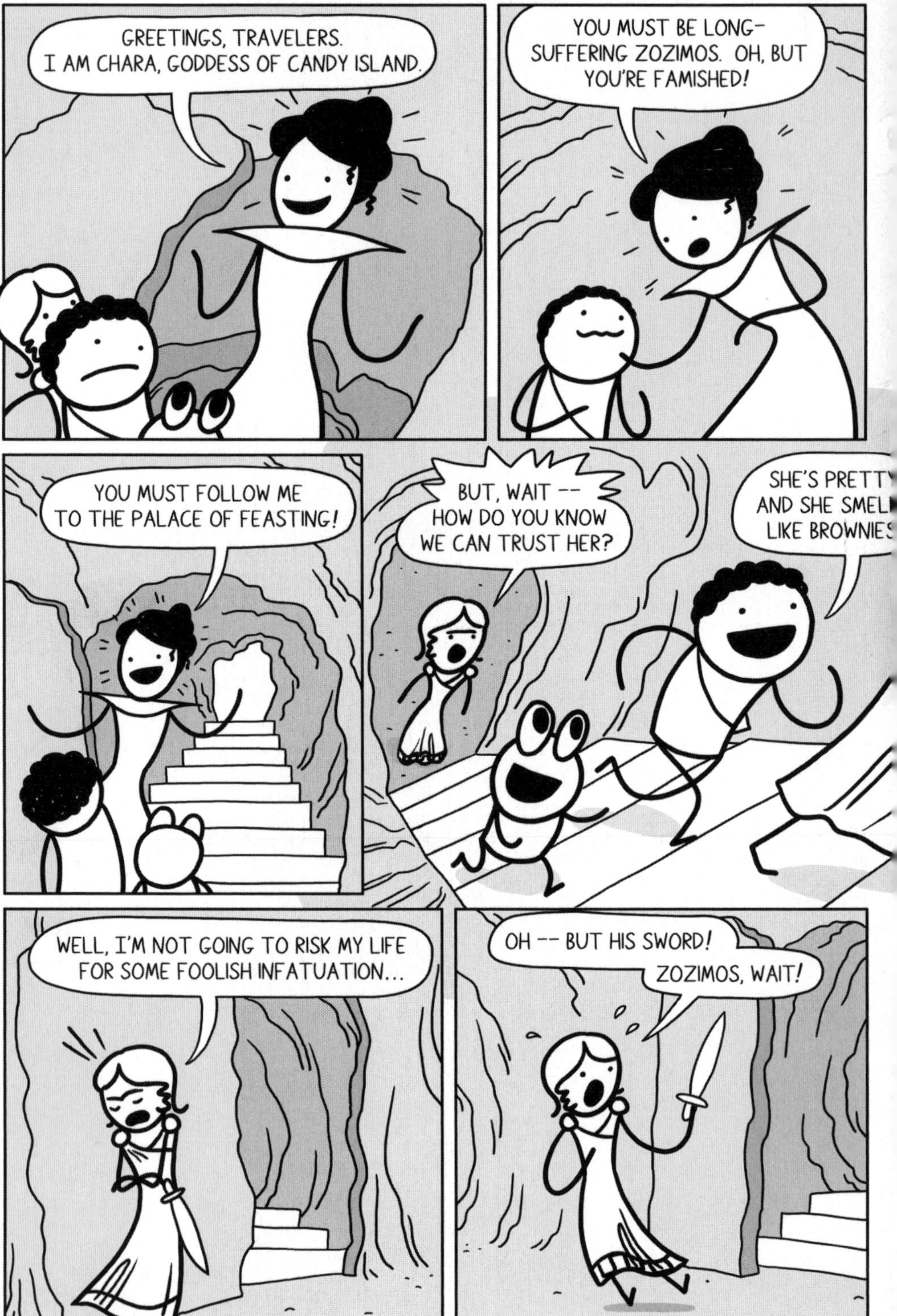
GREETINGS, TRAVELERS. I AM CHARA, GODDESS OF CANDY ISLAND.
YOU MUST BE LONG-SUFFERING ZOZIMOS. OH, BUT YOU'RE FAMISHED!
YOU MUST FOLLOW ME TO THE PALACE OF FEASTING!
BUT, WAIT -- HOW DO YOU KNOW WE CAN TRUST HER?
SHE'S PRETT
AND SHE SMEL
LIKE BROWNIES
WELL, I'M NOT GOING TO RISK MY LIFE FOR SOME FOOLISH INFATUATION...
OH -- BUT HIS SWORD!
ZOZIMOS, WAIT!

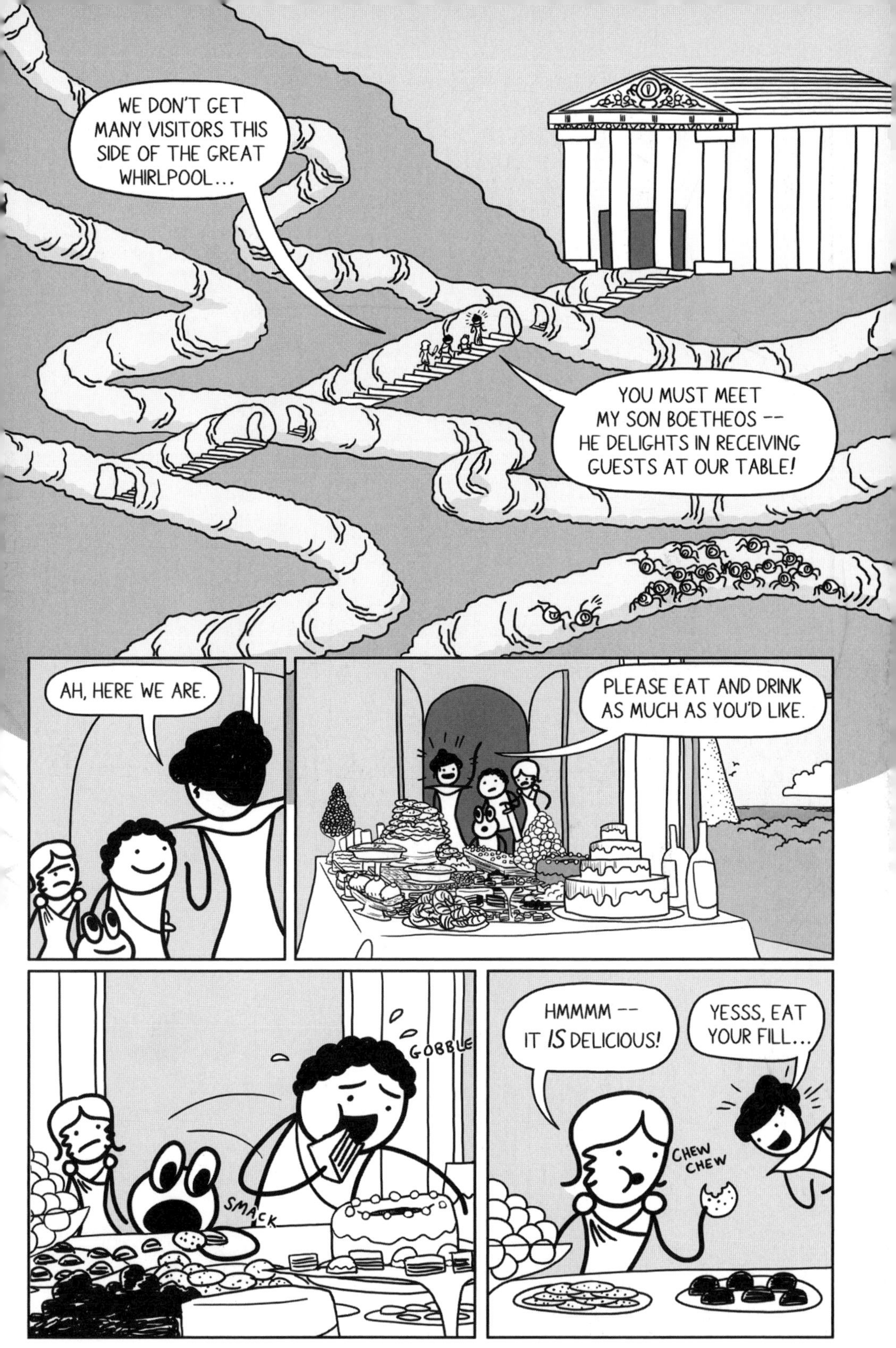
WE DON'T GET MANY VISITORS THIS SIDE OF THE GREAT WHIRLPOOL...
YOU MUST MEET MY SON BOETHEOS -- HE DELIGHTS IN RECEIVING GUESTS AT OUR TABLE!
AH, HERE WE ARE.
PLEASE EAT AND DRINK AS MUCH AS YOU'D LIKE.
GOBBLE
SMACK
HMMMM -- IT *IS* DELICIOUS!
CHEW CHEW
YESSS, EAT YOUR FILL...

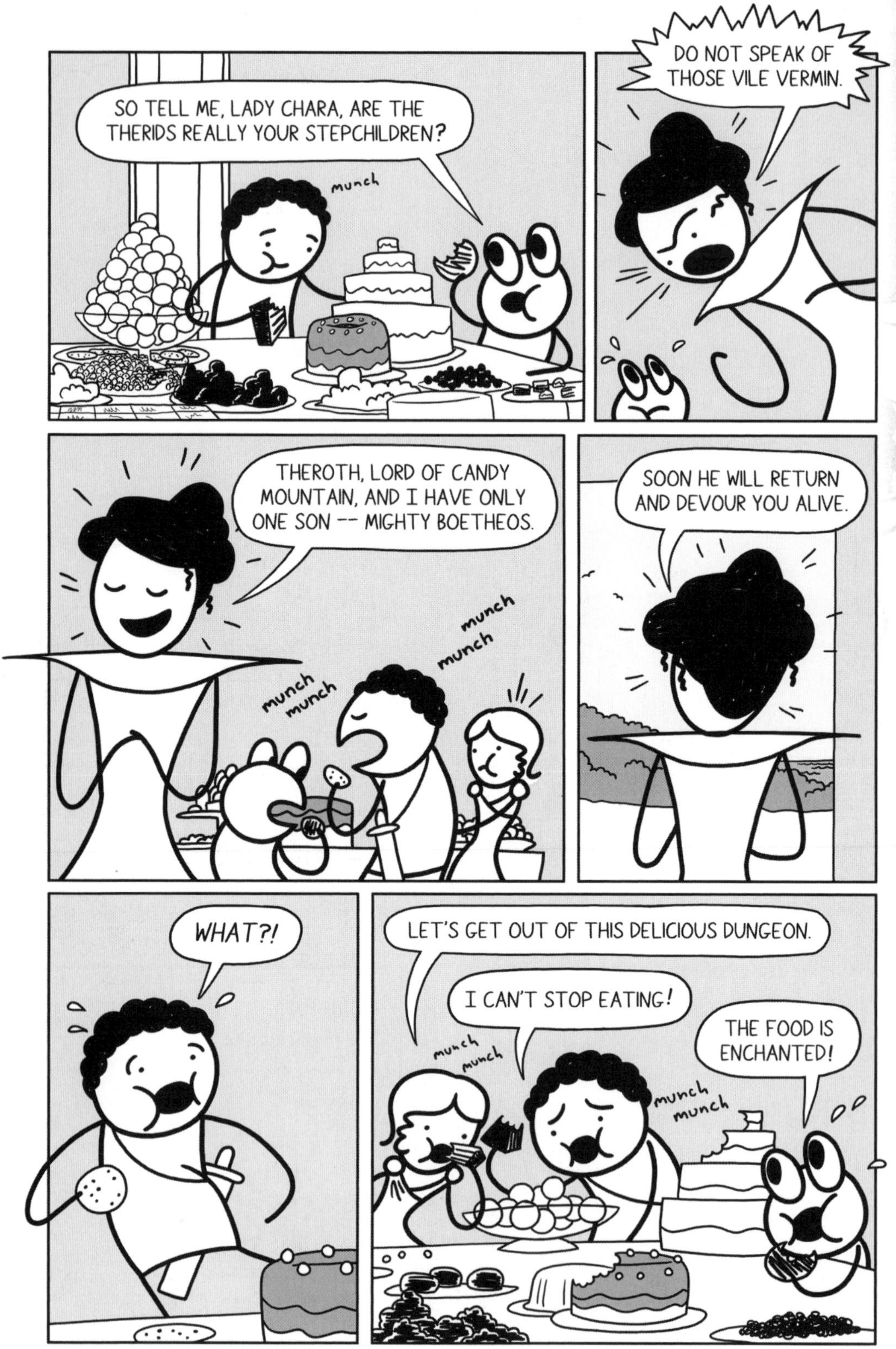
SO TELL ME, LADY CHARA, ARE THE THERIDS REALLY YOUR STEPCHILDREN?
munch
DO NOT SPEAK OF THOSE VILE VERMIN.
THEROTH, LORD OF CANDY MOUNTAIN, AND I HAVE ONLY ONE SON -- MIGHTY BOETHEOS.
munch munch
munch munch
SOON HE WILL RETURN AND DEVOUR YOU ALIVE.
WHAT?!
LET'S GET OUT OF THIS DELICIOUS DUNGEON.
I CAN'T STOP EATING!
THE FOOD IS ENCHANTED!
munch munch
munch munch

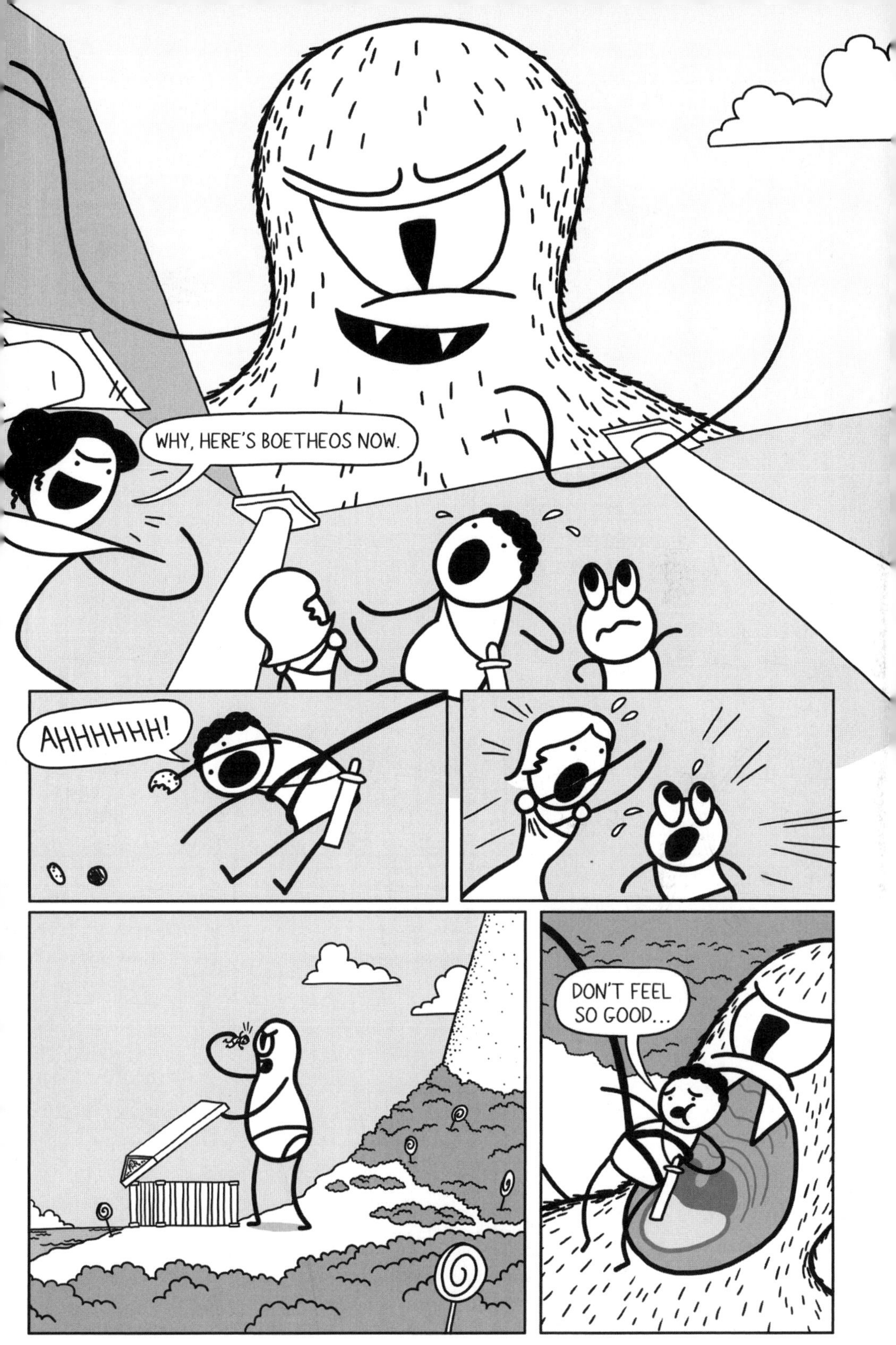
WHY, HERE'S BOETHEOS NOW.
AHHHHHH!
DON'T FEEL SO GOOD...

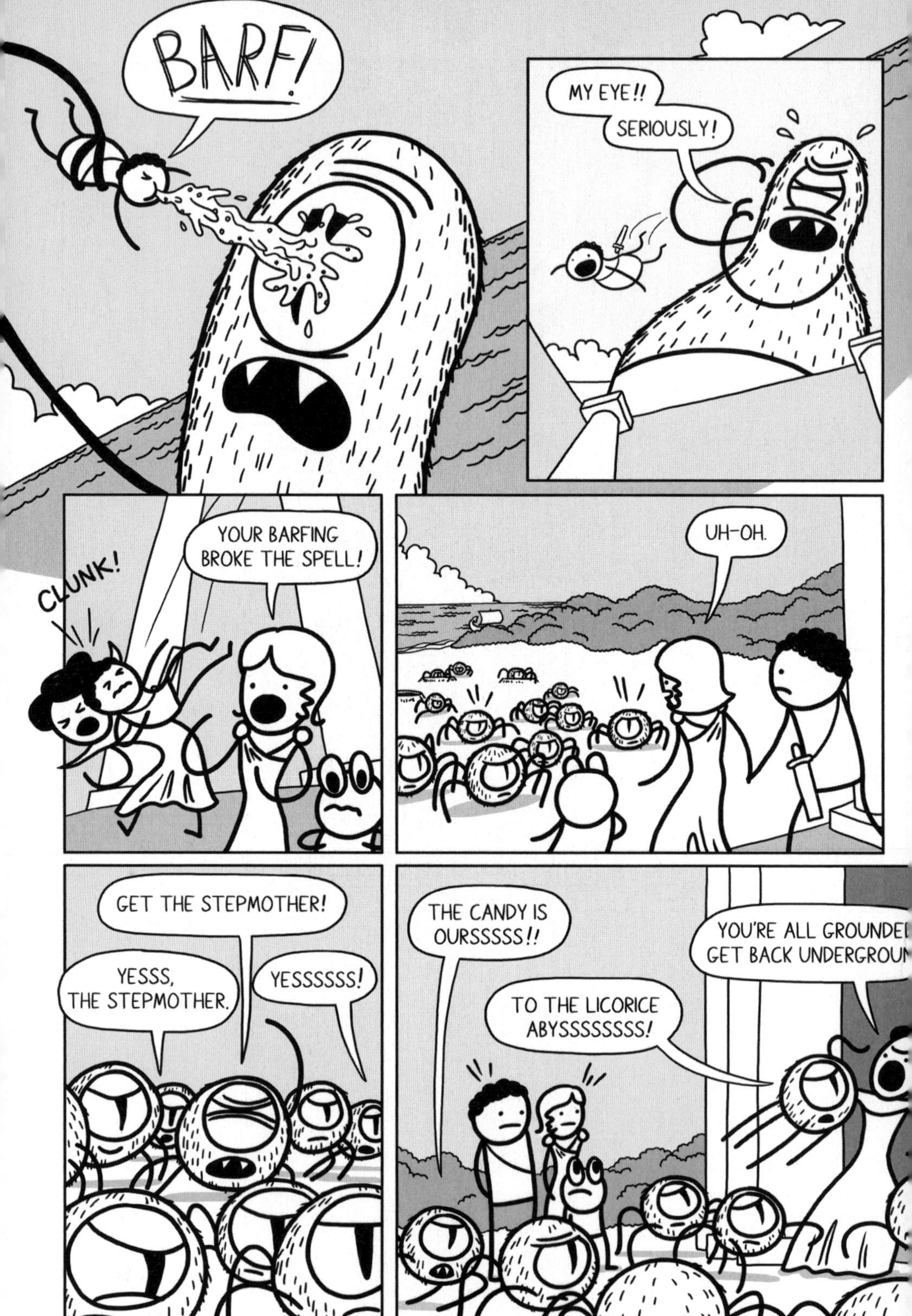
BARF!
MY EYE!!
SERIOUSLY!
CLUNK!
YOUR BARFING BROKE THE SPELL!
UH-OH.
GET THE STEPMOTHER!
YESSS, THE STEPMOTHER.
YESSSSSS!
THE CANDY IS OURSSSSS!!
TO THE LICORICE ABYSSSSSSSSS!
YOU'RE ALL GROUNDE
GET BACK UNDERGROU

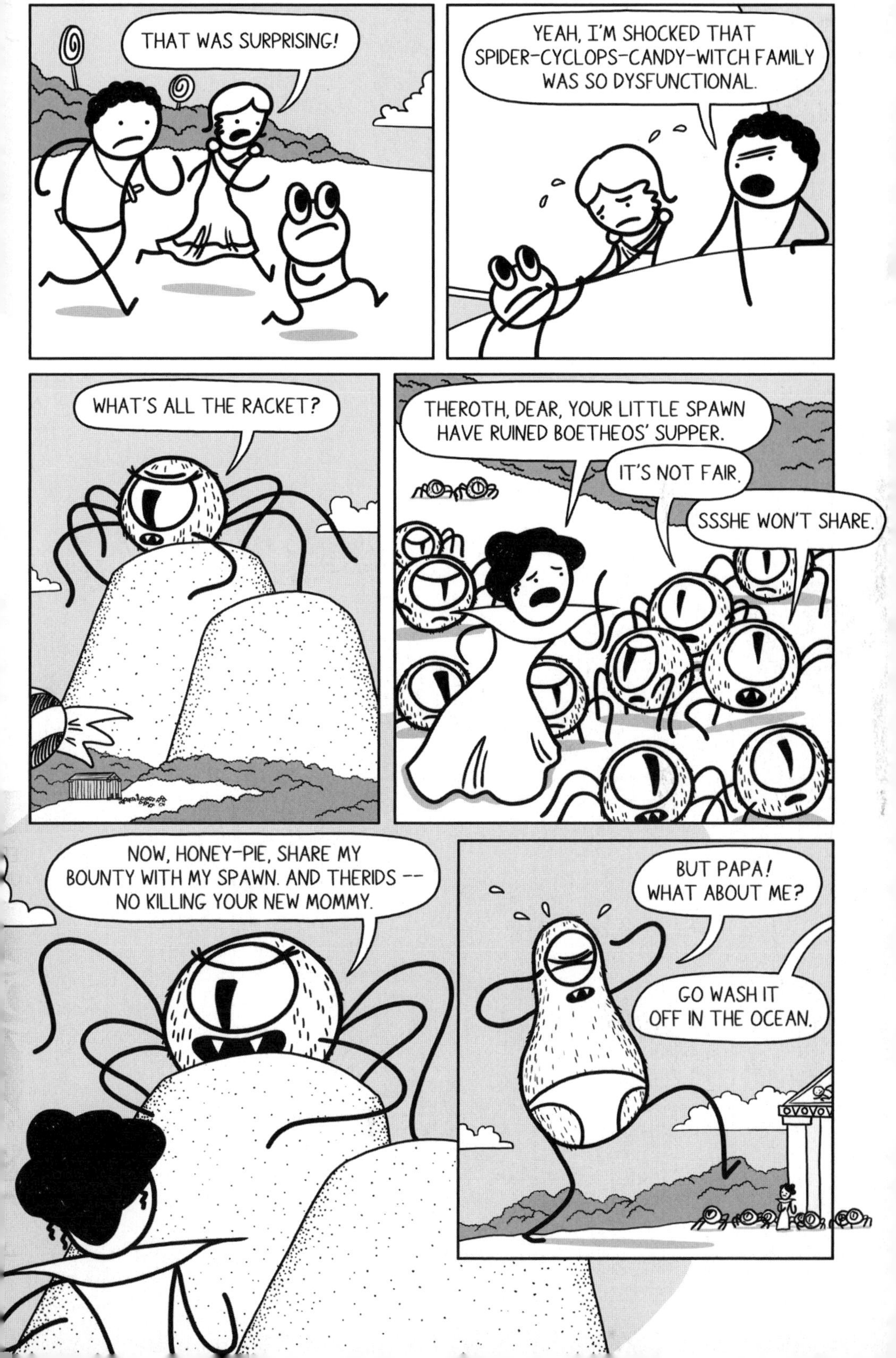
THAT WAS SURPRISING!
YEAH, I'M SHOCKED THAT SPIDER-CYCLOPS-CANDY-WITCH FAMILY WAS SO DYSFUNCTIONAL.
WHAT'S ALL THE RACKET?
THEROTH, DEAR, YOUR LITTLE SPAWN HAVE RUINED BOETHEOS' SUPPER.
IT'S NOT FAIR.
SSSHE WON'T SHARE.
NOW, HONEY-PIE, SHARE MY BOUNTY WITH MY SPAWN. AND THERIDS -- NO KILLING YOUR NEW MOMMY.
BUT PAPA! WHAT ABOUT ME?
GO WASH IT OFF IN THE OCEAN.

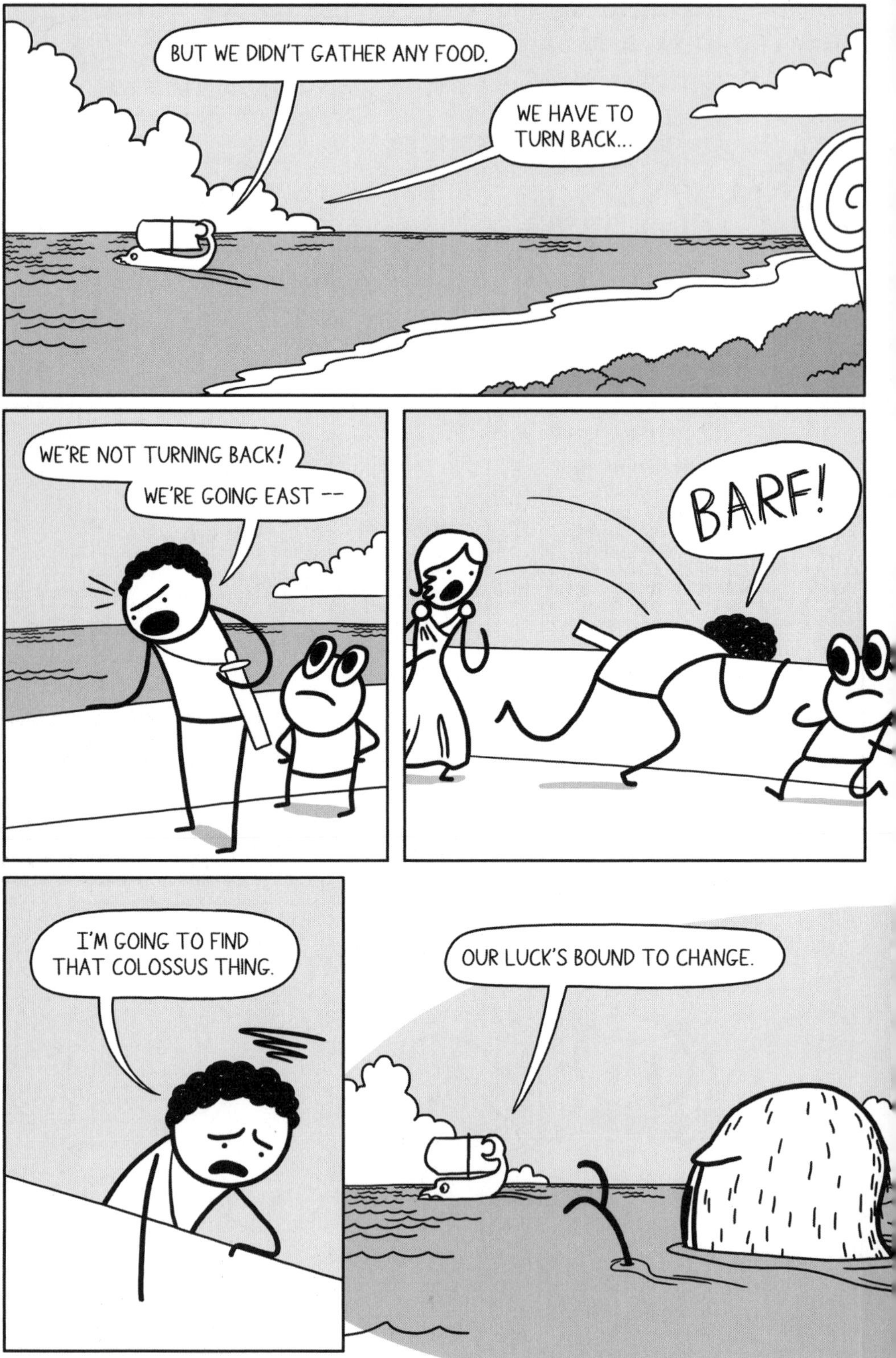
BUT WE DIDN'T GATHER ANY FOOD.
WE HAVE TO TURN BACK...
WE'RE NOT TURNING BACK!
WE'RE GOING EAST --
BARF!
I'M GOING TO FIND THAT COLOSSUS THING.
OUR LUCK'S BOUND TO CHANGE.

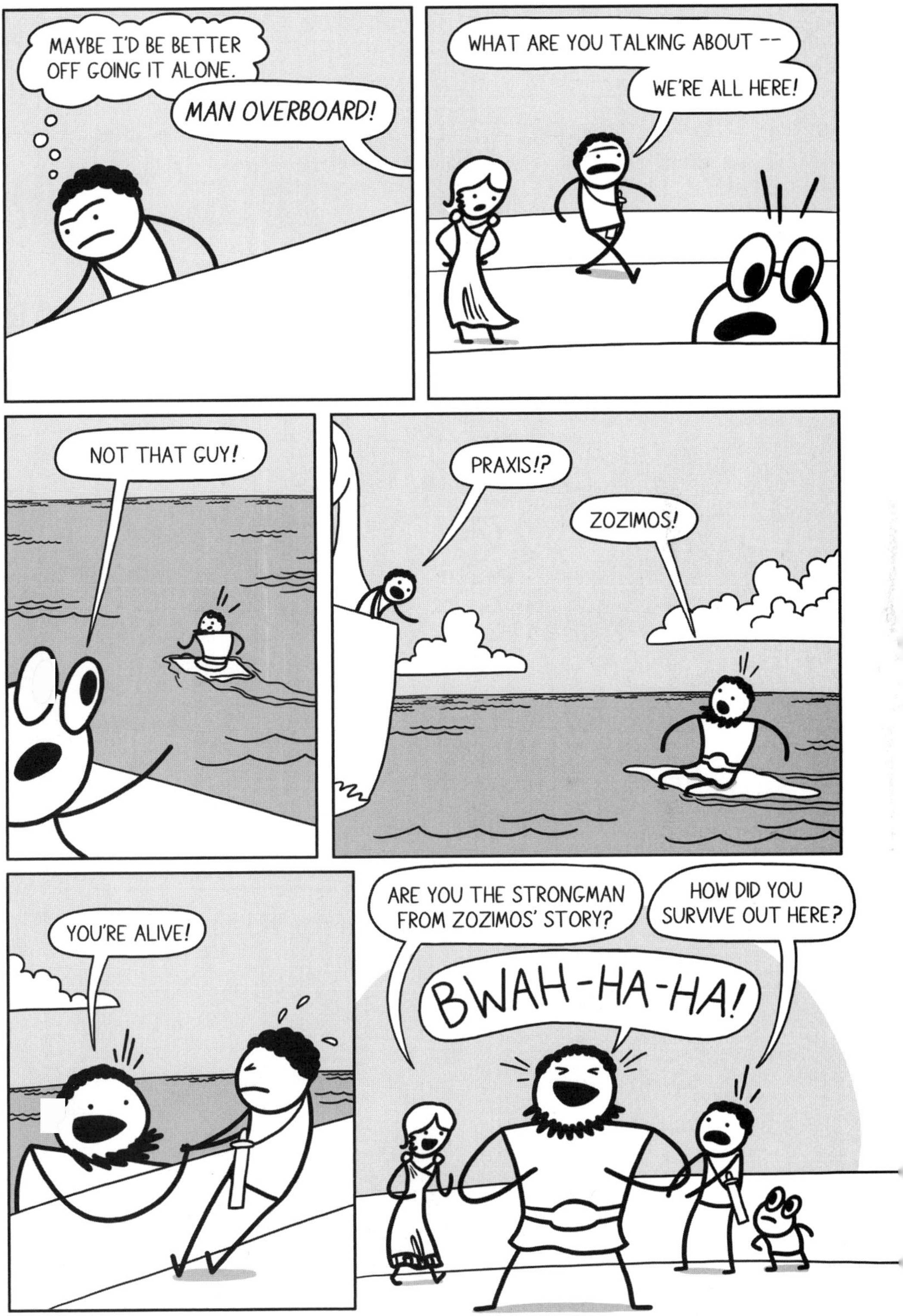
MAYBE I'D BE BETTER OFF GOING IT ALONE.
MAN OVERBOARD!
WHAT ARE YOU TALKING ABOUT --
WE'RE ALL HERE!
NOT THAT GUY!
PRAXIS!?
ZOZIMOS!
YOU'RE ALIVE!
ARE YOU THE STRONGMAN FROM ZOZIMOS' STORY?
HOW DID YOU SURVIVE OUT HERE?
BWAH-HA-HA!

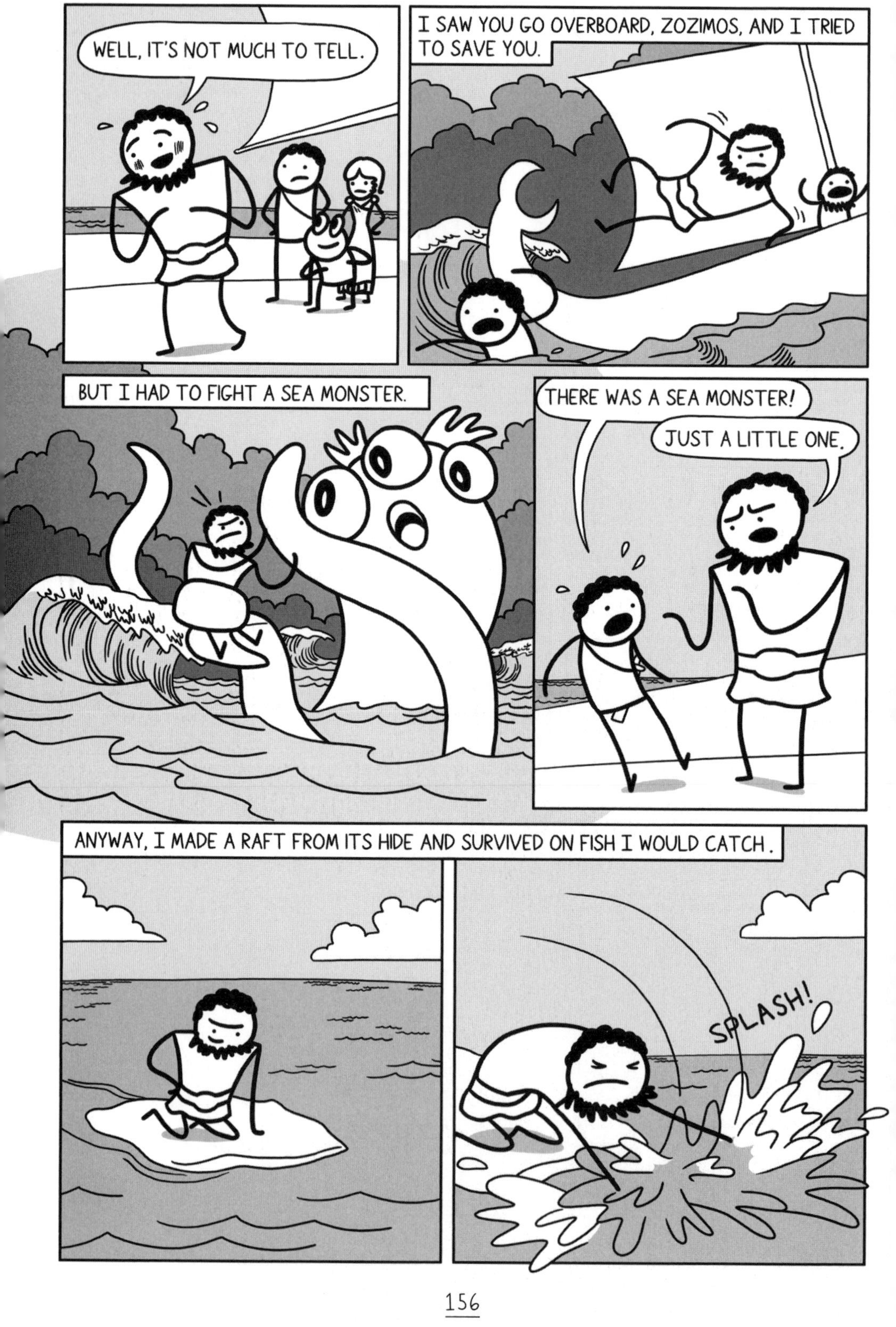
WELL, IT'S NOT MUCH TO TELL.
I SAW YOU GO OVERBOARD, ZOZIMOS, AND I TRIED TO SAVE YOU.
BUT I HAD TO FIGHT A SEA MONSTER.
THERE WAS A SEA MONSTER!
JUST A LITTLE ONE.
ANYWAY, I MADE A RAFT FROM ITS HIDE AND SURVIVED ON FISH I WOULD CATCH.
SPLASH!

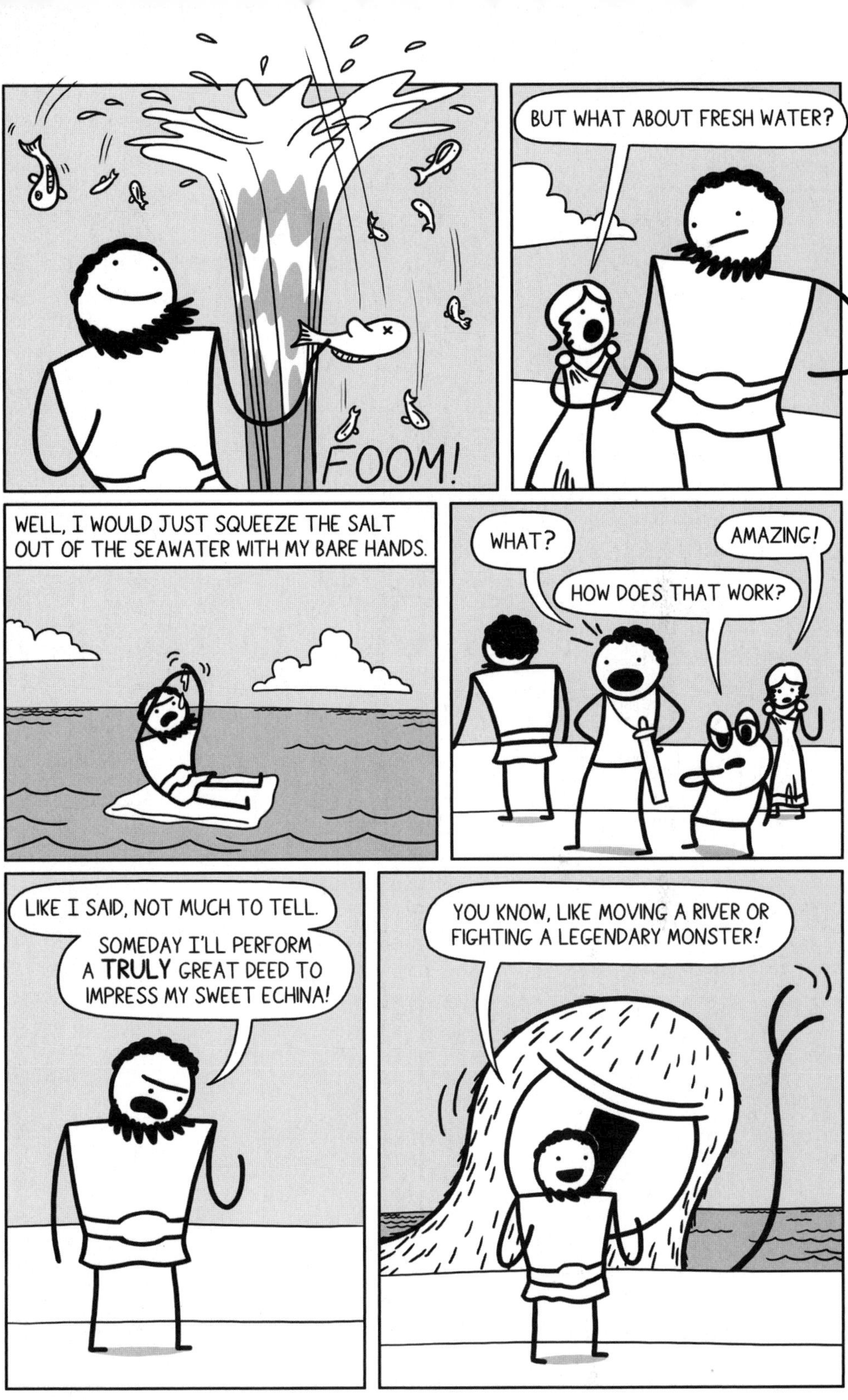
FOOM!
BUT WHAT ABOUT FRESH WATER?
WELL, I WOULD JUST SQUEEZE THE SALT OUT OF THE SEAWATER WITH MY BARE HANDS.
WHAT?
AMAZING!
HOW DOES THAT WORK?
LIKE I SAID, NOT MUCH TO TELL.
SOMEDAY I'LL PERFORM A **TRULY** GREAT DEED TO IMPRESS MY SWEET ECHINA!
YOU KNOW, LIKE MOVING A RIVER OR FIGHTING A LEGENDARY MONSTER!

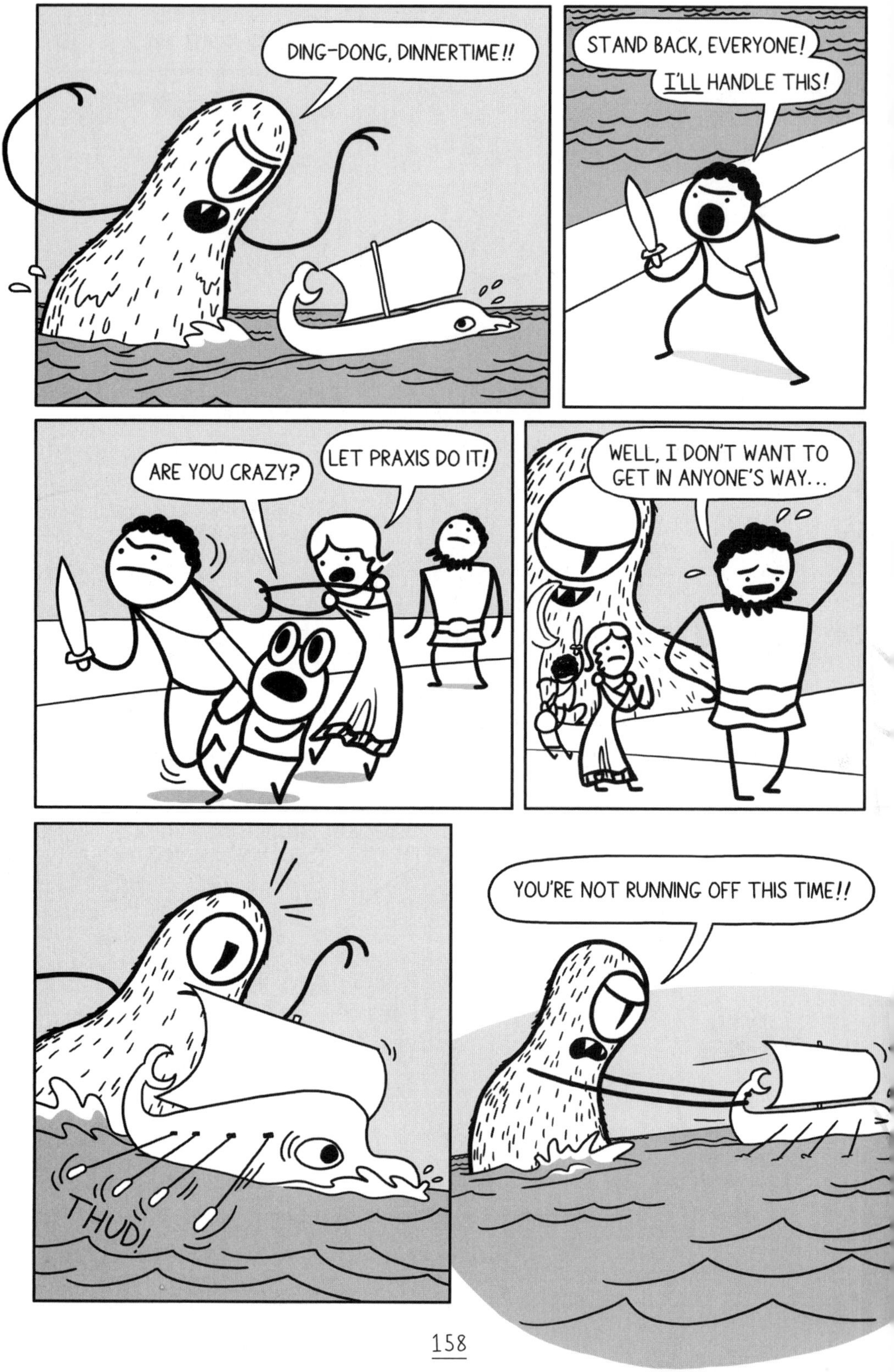
DING-DONG, DINNERTIME!!
STAND BACK, EVERYONE!
I'LL HANDLE THIS!
ARE YOU CRAZY?
LET PRAXIS DO IT!
WELL, I DON'T WANT TO GET IN ANYONE'S WAY...
THUD!
YOU'RE NOT RUNNING OFF THIS TIME!!

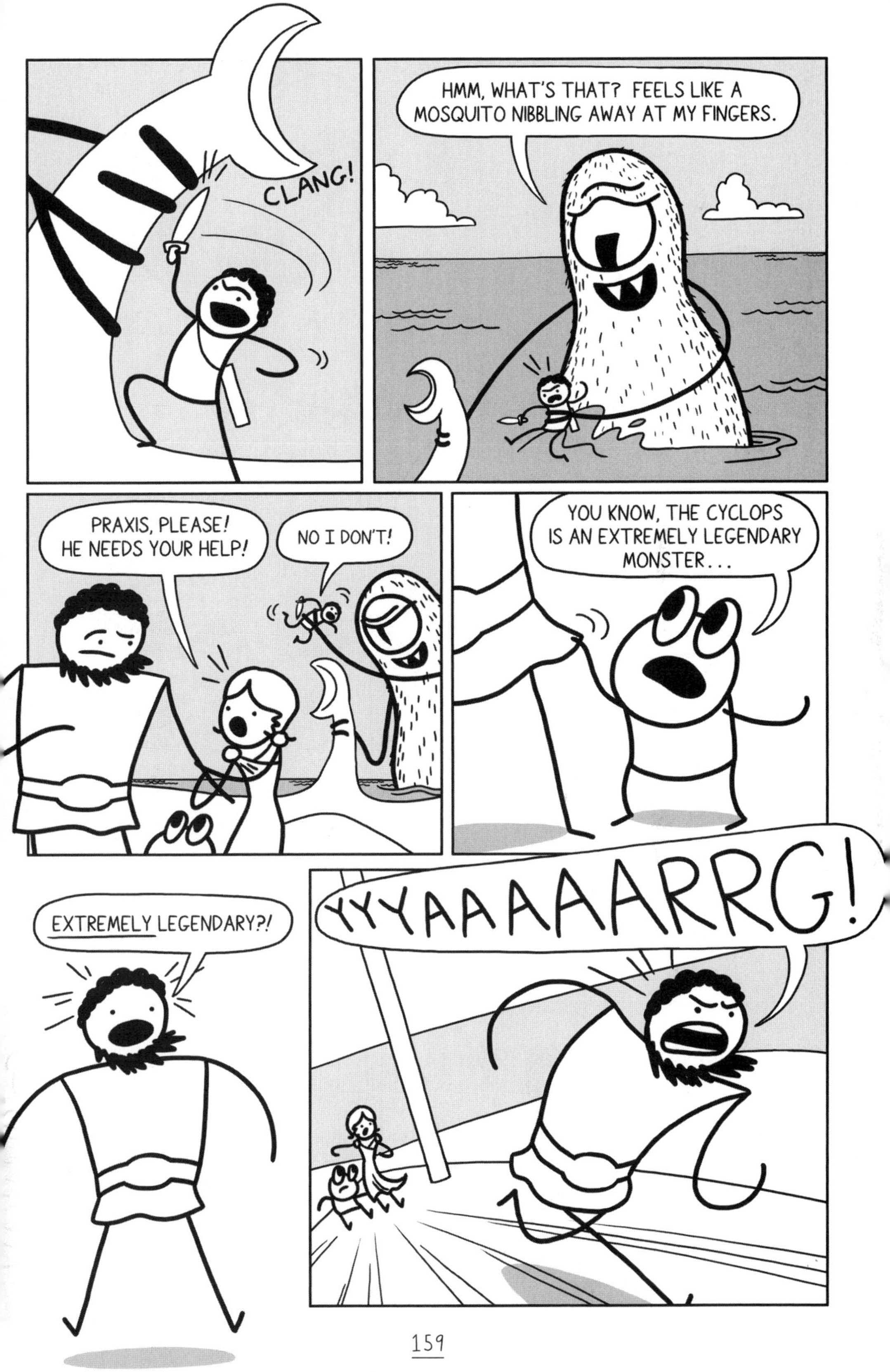

CLANG!
HMM, WHAT'S THAT? FEELS LIKE A MOSQUITO NIBBLING AWAY AT MY FINGERS.
PRAXIS, PLEASE! HE NEEDS YOUR HELP!
NO I DON'T!
YOU KNOW, THE CYCLOPS IS AN EXTREMELY LEGENDARY MONSTER...
EXTREMELY LEGENDARY?!
YYYAAAAAARRG!

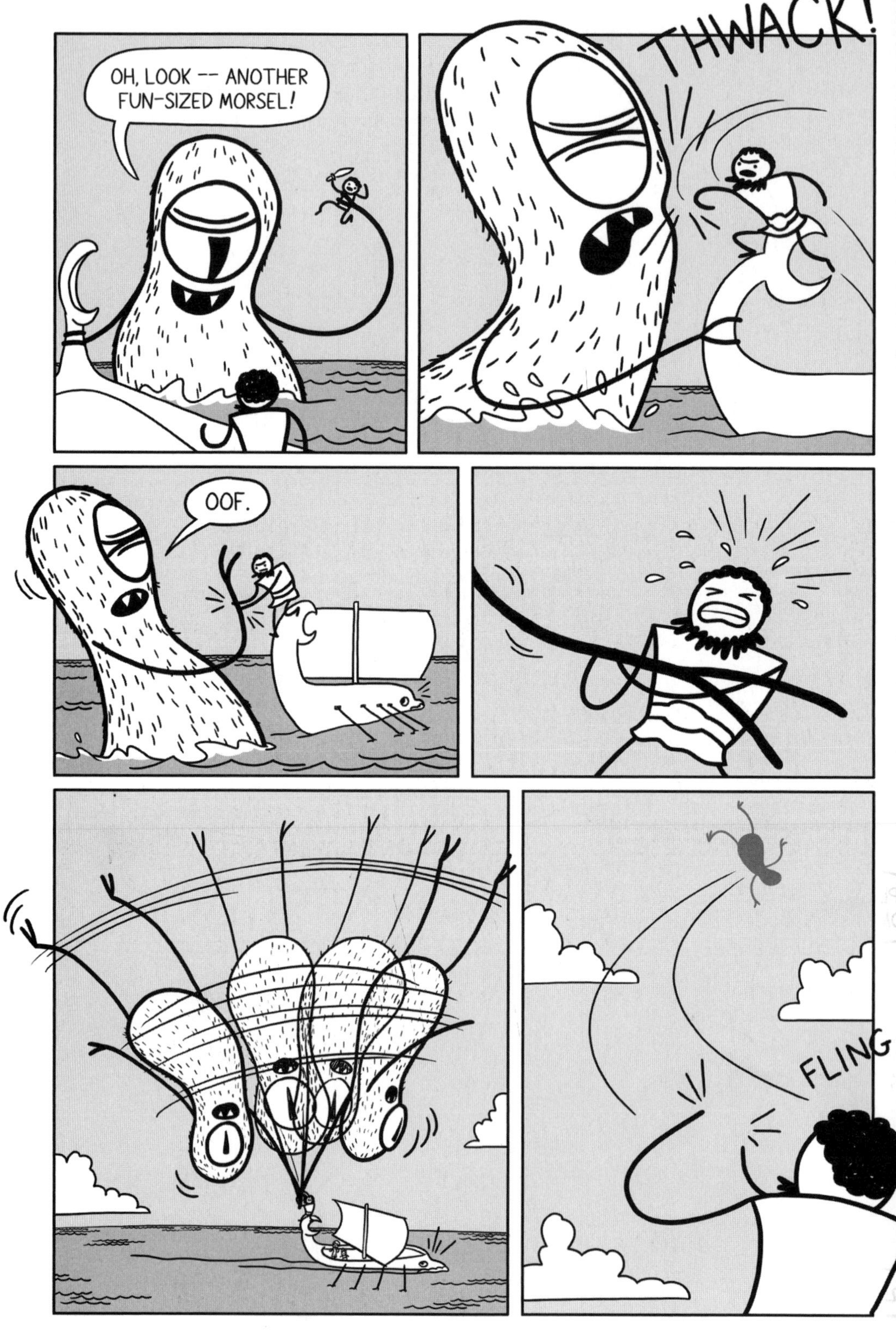
OH, LOOK -- ANOTHER FUN-SIZED MORSEL!
THWACK!
OOF.
FLING

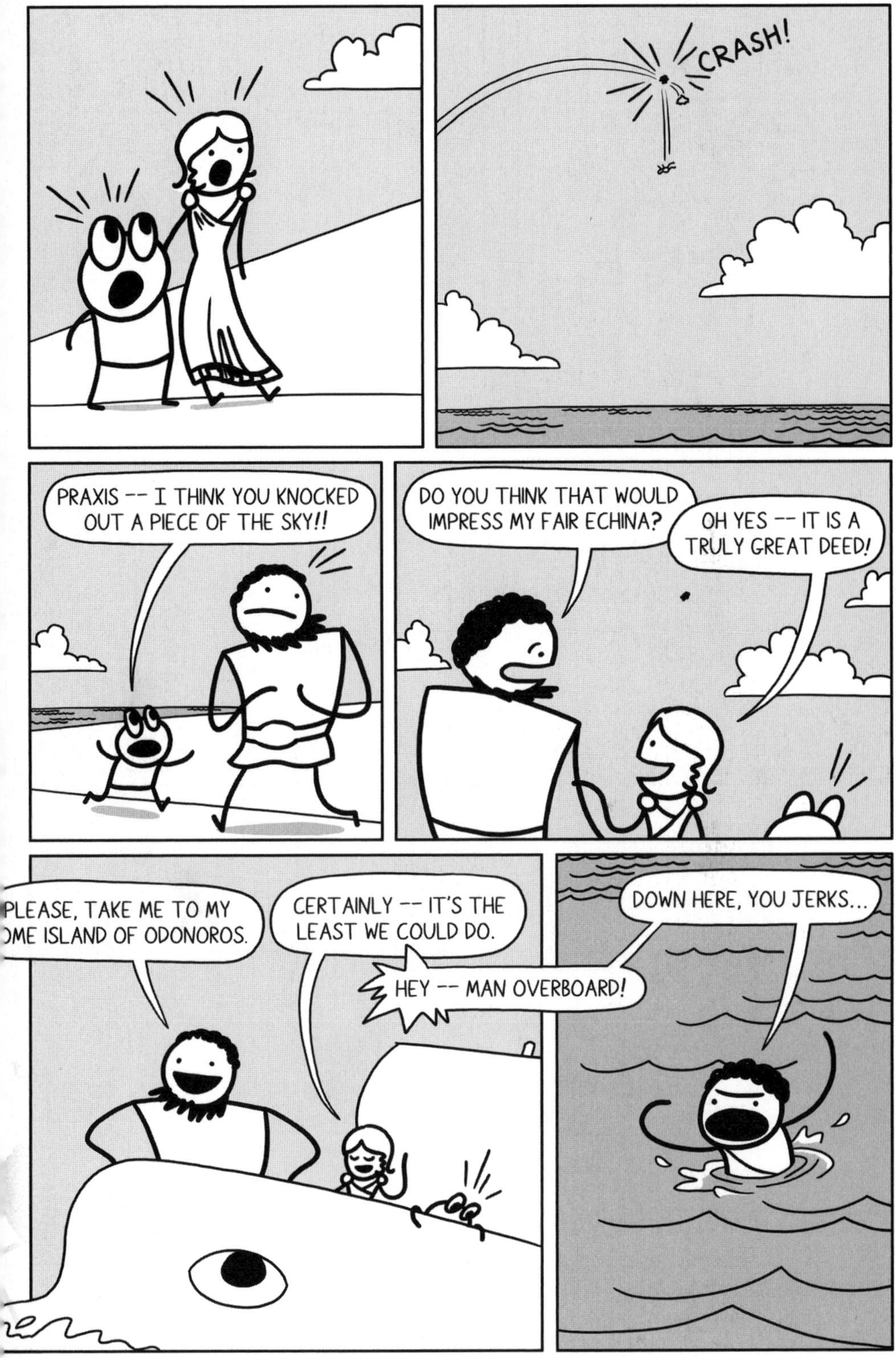
CRASH!
PRAXIS -- I THINK YOU KNOCKED OUT A PIECE OF THE SKY!!
DO YOU THINK THAT WOULD IMPRESS MY FAIR ECHINA?
OH YES -- IT IS A TRULY GREAT DEED!
PLEASE, TAKE ME TO MY OME ISLAND OF ODONOROS.
CERTAINLY -- IT'S THE LEAST WE COULD DO.
HEY -- MAN OVERBOARD!
DOWN HERE, YOU JERKS...

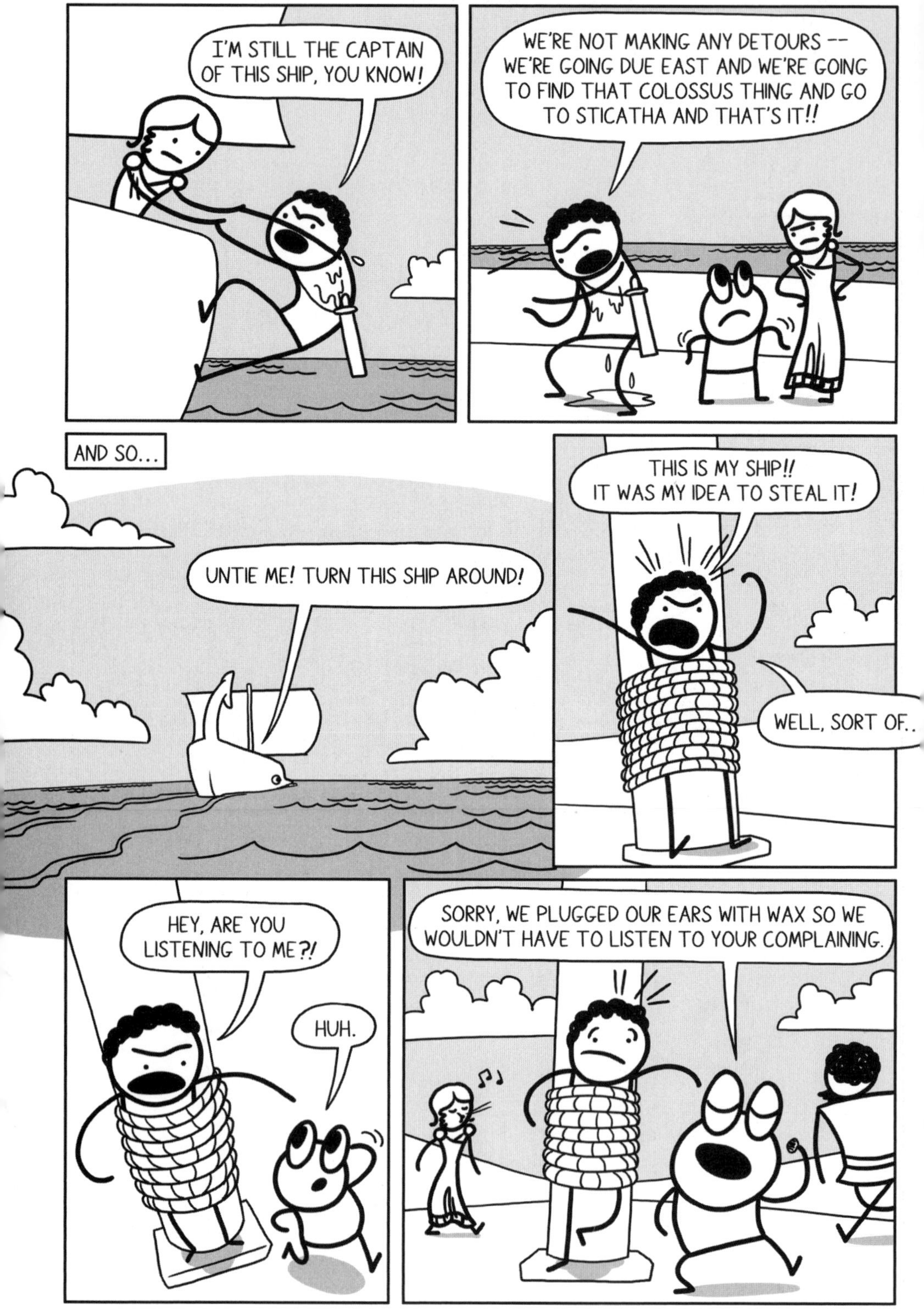
I'M STILL THE CAPTAIN OF THIS SHIP, YOU KNOW!
WE'RE NOT MAKING ANY DETOURS -- WE'RE GOING DUE EAST AND WE'RE GOING TO FIND THAT COLOSSUS THING AND GO TO STICATHA AND THAT'S IT!!
AND SO...
UNTIE ME! TURN THIS SHIP AROUND!
THIS IS MY SHIP!! IT WAS MY IDEA TO STEAL IT!
WELL, SORT OF..
HEY, ARE YOU LISTENING TO ME?!
HUH.
SORRY, WE PLUGGED OUR EARS WITH WAX SO WE WOULDN'T HAVE TO LISTEN TO YOUR COMPLAINING.

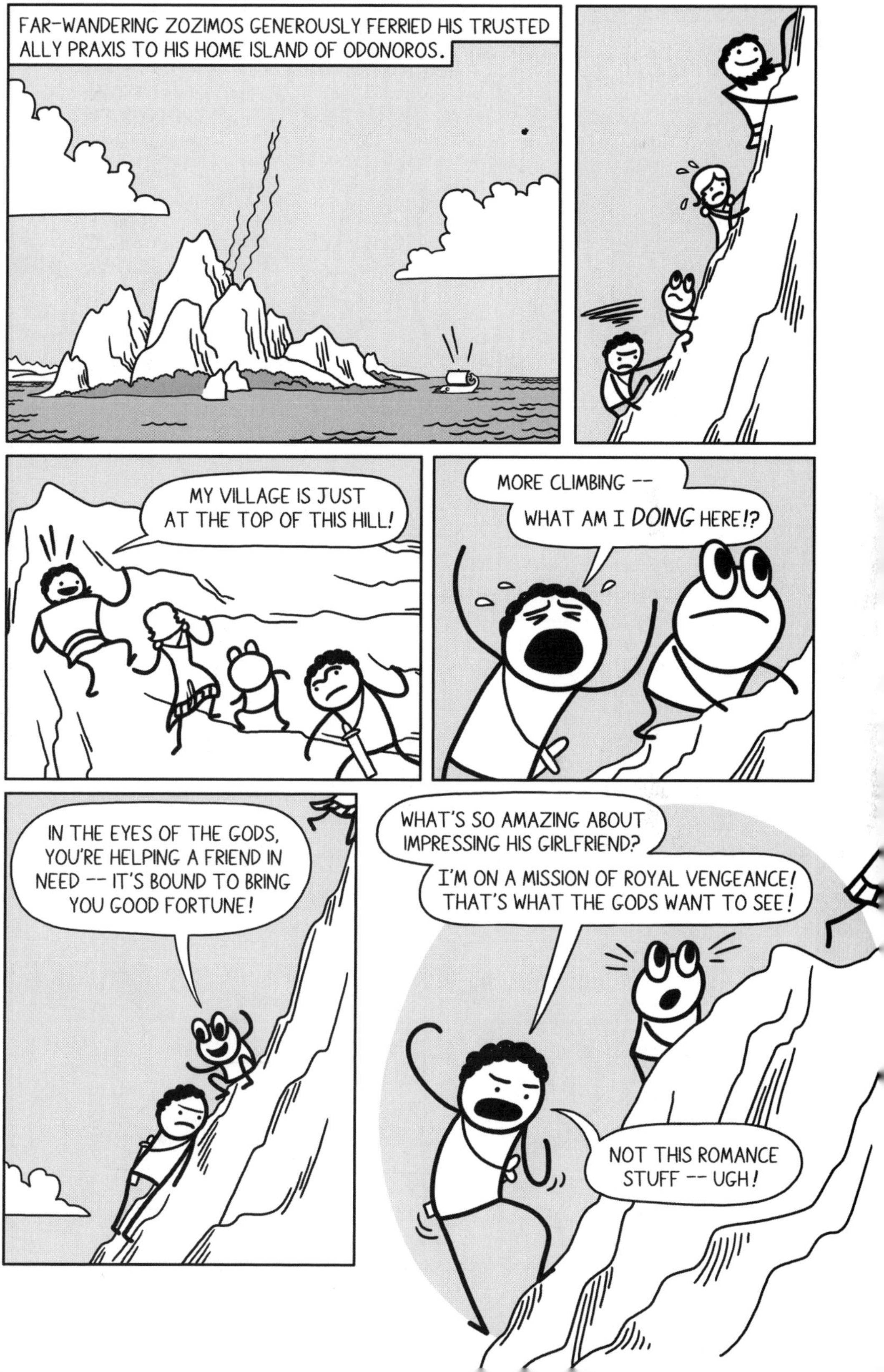
FAR-WANDERING ZOZIMOS GENEROUSLY FERRIED HIS TRUSTED ALLY PRAXIS TO HIS HOME ISLAND OF ODONOROS.
MY VILLAGE IS JUST AT THE TOP OF THIS HILL!
MORE CLIMBING -- WHAT AM I DOING HERE!?
IN THE EYES OF THE GODS, YOU'RE HELPING A FRIEND IN NEED -- IT'S BOUND TO BRING YOU GOOD FORTUNE!
WHAT'S SO AMAZING ABOUT IMPRESSING HIS GIRLFRIEND?
I'M ON A MISSION OF ROYAL VENGEANCE! THAT'S WHAT THE GODS WANT TO SEE!
NOT THIS ROMANCE STUFF -- UGH!

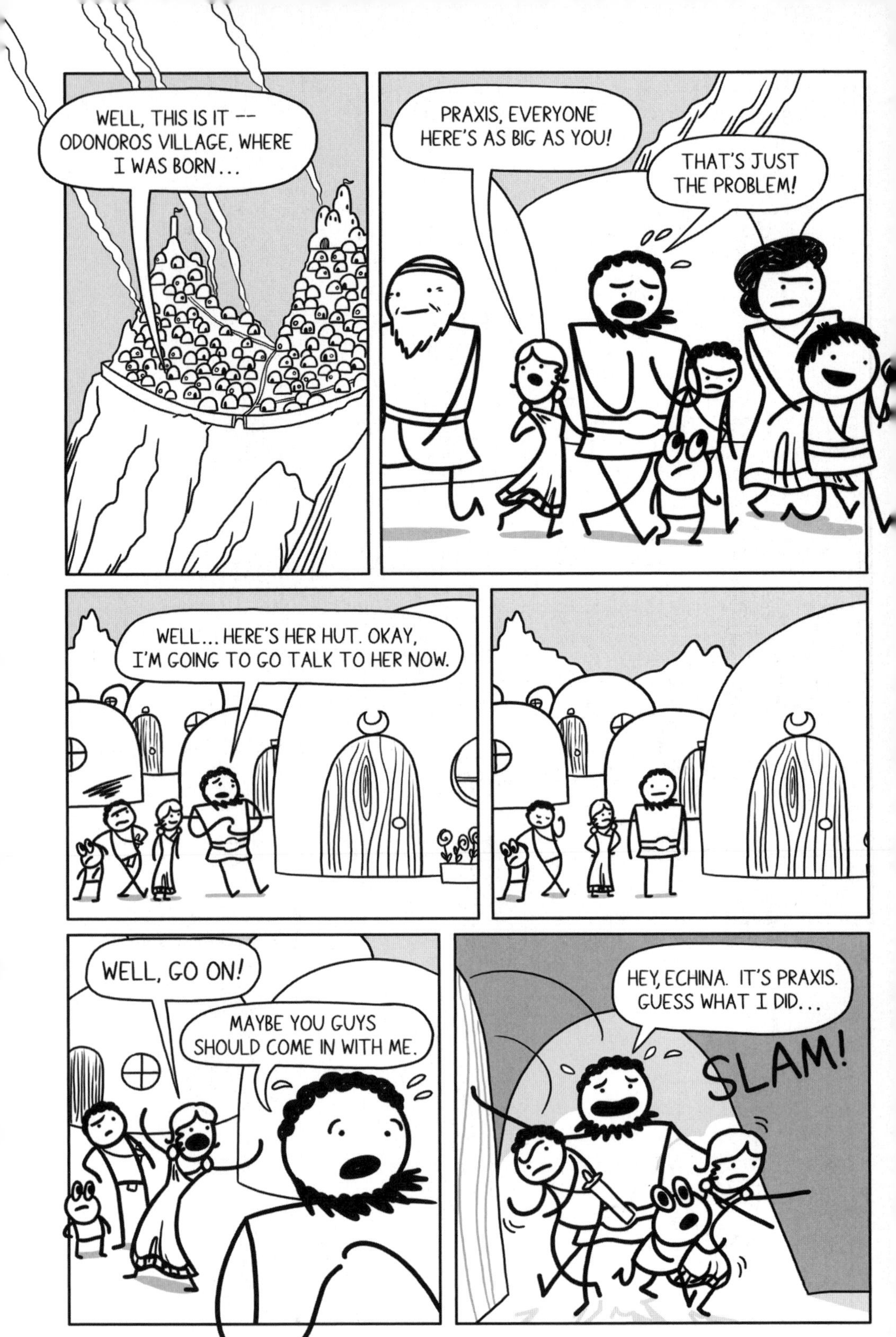
WELL, THIS IS IT -- ODONOROS VILLAGE, WHERE I WAS BORN...
PRAXIS, EVERYONE HERE'S AS BIG AS YOU!
THAT'S JUST THE PROBLEM!
WELL... HERE'S HER HUT. OKAY, I'M GOING TO GO TALK TO HER NOW.
WELL, GO ON!
MAYBE YOU GUYS SHOULD COME IN WITH ME.
HEY, ECHINA. IT'S PRAXIS. GUESS WHAT I DID...
SLAM!

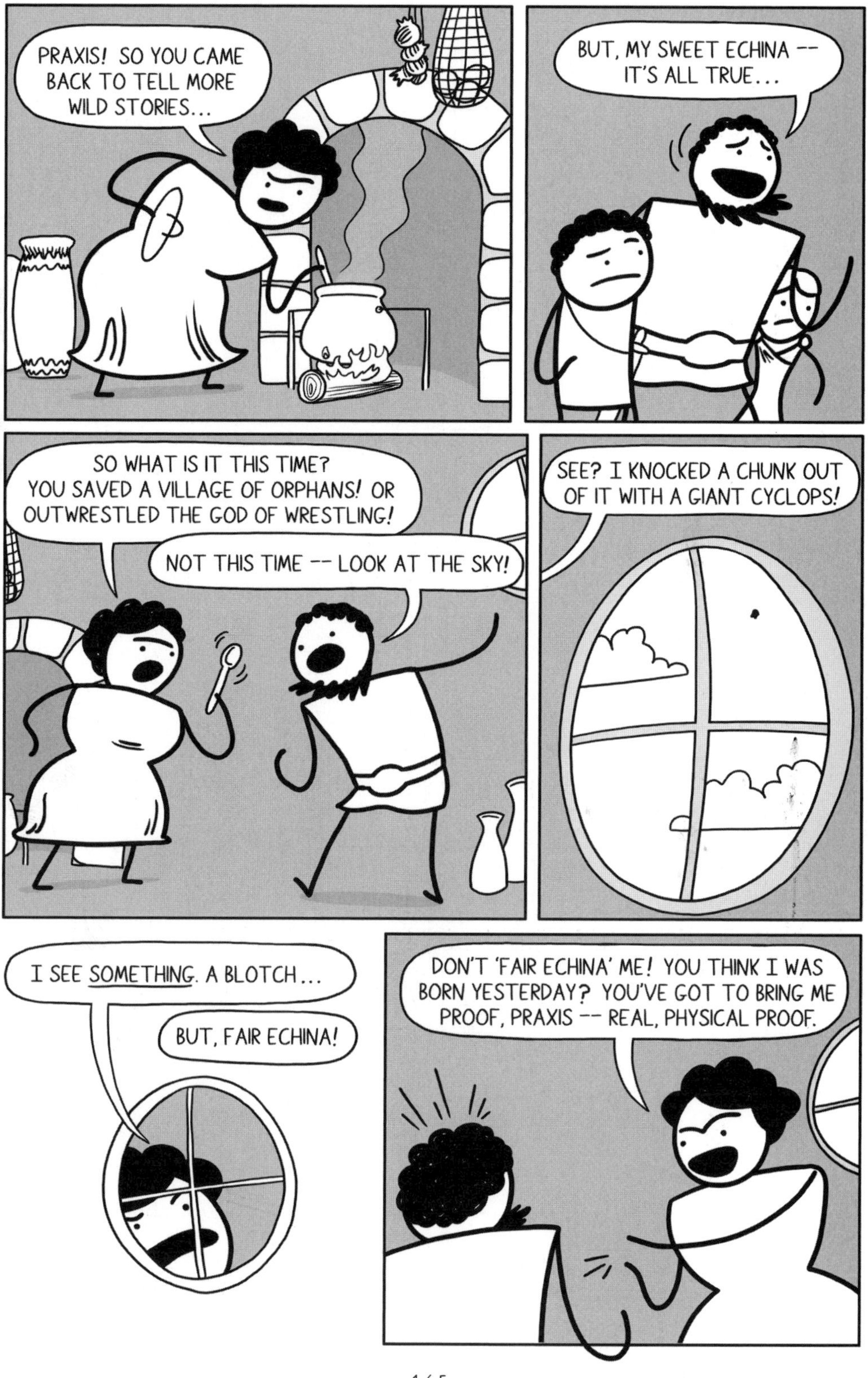
PRAXIS! SO YOU CAME BACK TO TELL MORE WILD STORIES...
BUT, MY SWEET ECHINA -- IT'S ALL TRUE...
SO WHAT IS IT THIS TIME? YOU SAVED A VILLAGE OF ORPHANS! OR OUTWRESTLED THE GOD OF WRESTLING!
NOT THIS TIME -- LOOK AT THE SKY!
SEE? I KNOCKED A CHUNK OUT OF IT WITH A GIANT CYCLOPS!
I SEE SOMETHING. A BLOTCH...
BUT, FAIR ECHINA!
DON'T 'FAIR ECHINA' ME! YOU THINK I WAS BORN YESTERDAY? YOU'VE GOT TO BRING ME PROOF, PRAXIS -- REAL, PHYSICAL PROOF.

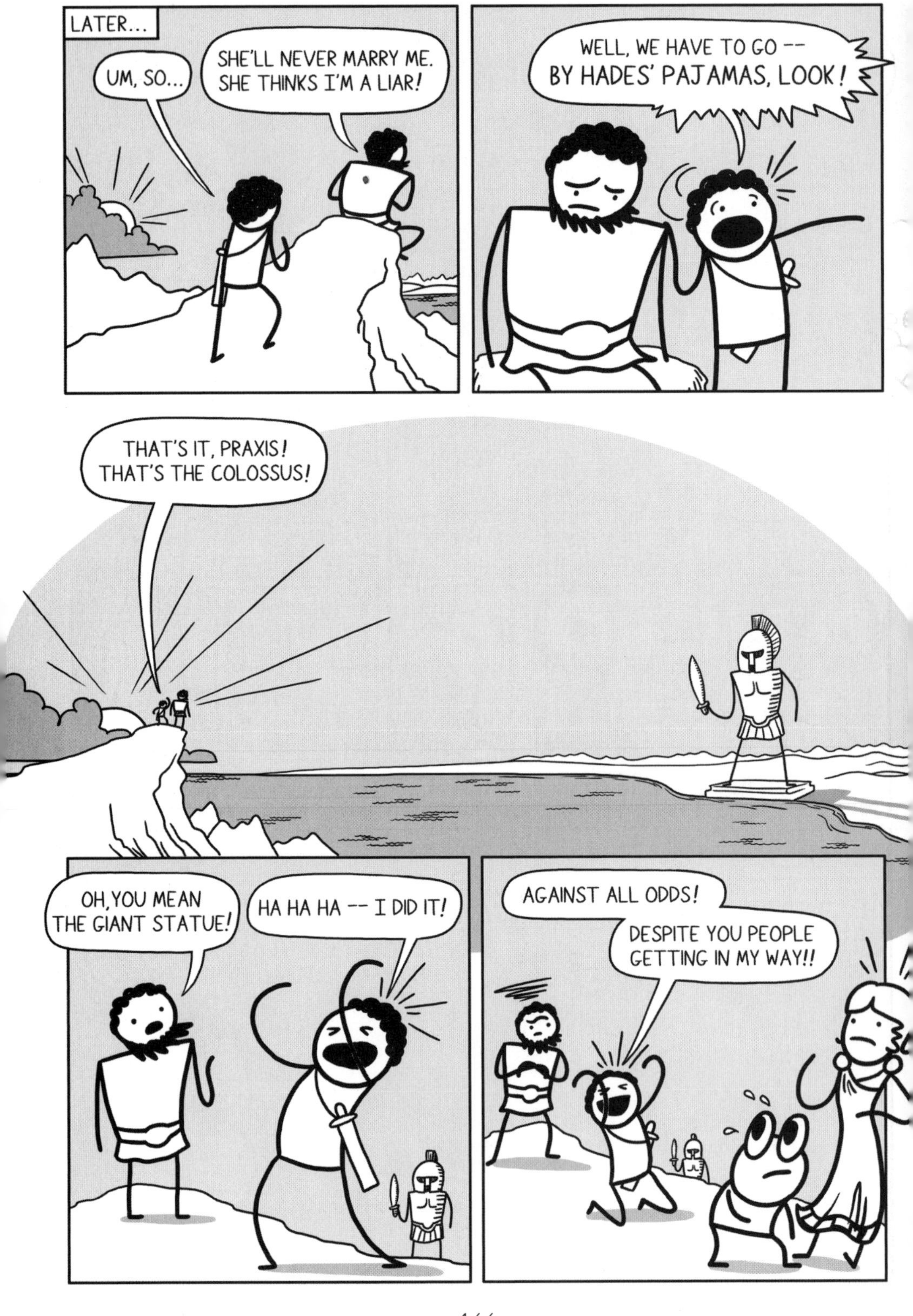
LATER...
UM, SO...
SHE'LL NEVER MARRY ME. SHE THINKS I'M A LIAR!
WELL, WE HAVE TO GO -- BY HADES' PAJAMAS, LOOK!
THAT'S IT, PRAXIS! THAT'S THE COLOSSUS!
OH, YOU MEAN THE GIANT STATUE!
HA HA HA -- I DID IT!
AGAINST ALL ODDS!
DESPITE YOU PEOPLE GETTING IN MY WAY!!

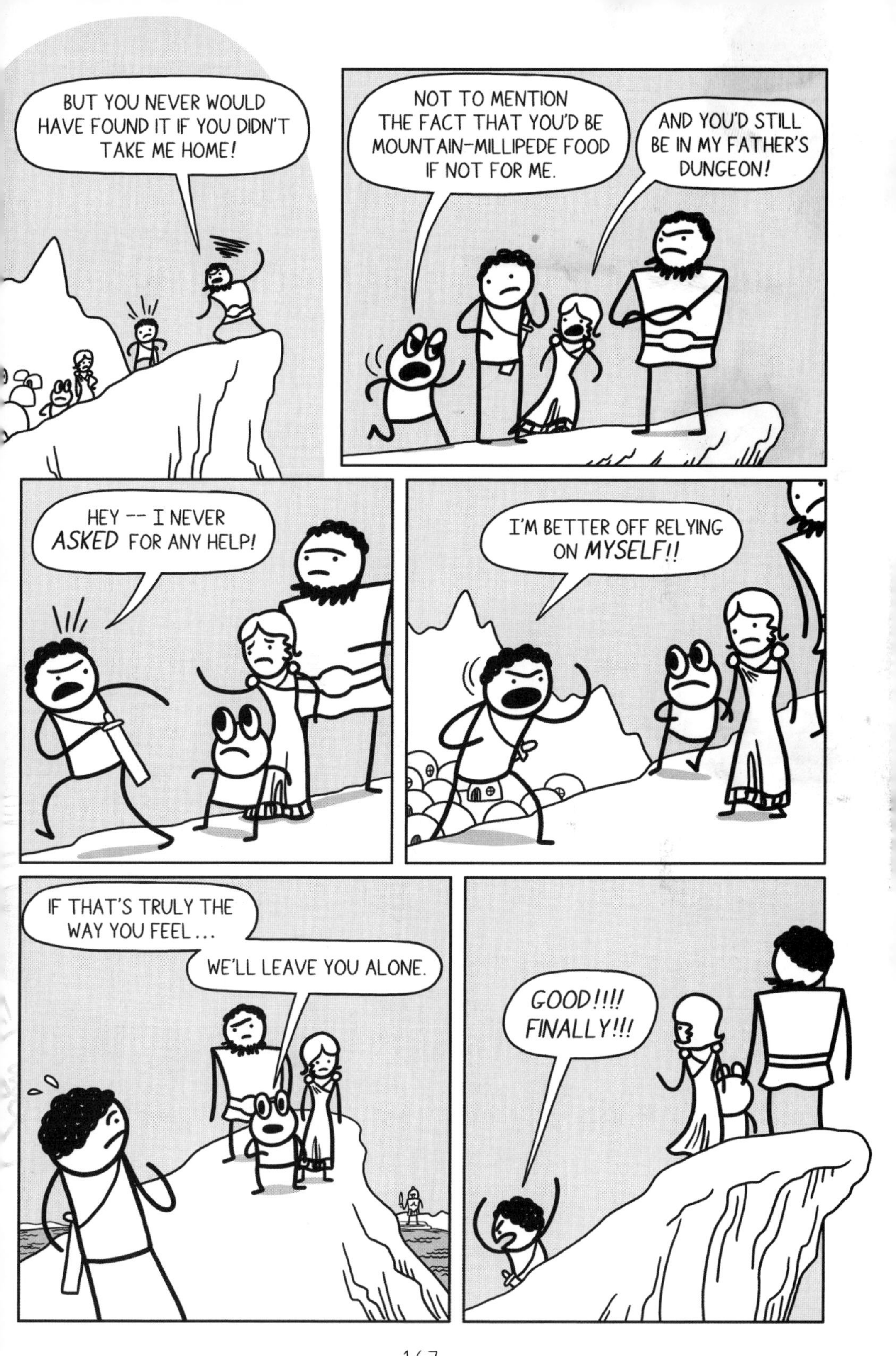
BUT YOU NEVER WOULD HAVE FOUND IT IF YOU DIDN'T TAKE ME HOME!
NOT TO MENTION THE FACT THAT YOU'D BE MOUNTAIN-MILLIPEDE FOOD IF NOT FOR ME.
AND YOU'D STILL BE IN MY FATHER'S DUNGEON!
HEY -- I NEVER ASKED FOR ANY HELP!
I'M BETTER OFF RELYING ON MYSELF!!
IF THAT'S TRULY THE WAY YOU FEEL...
WE'LL LEAVE YOU ALONE.
GOOD!!!! FINALLY!!!

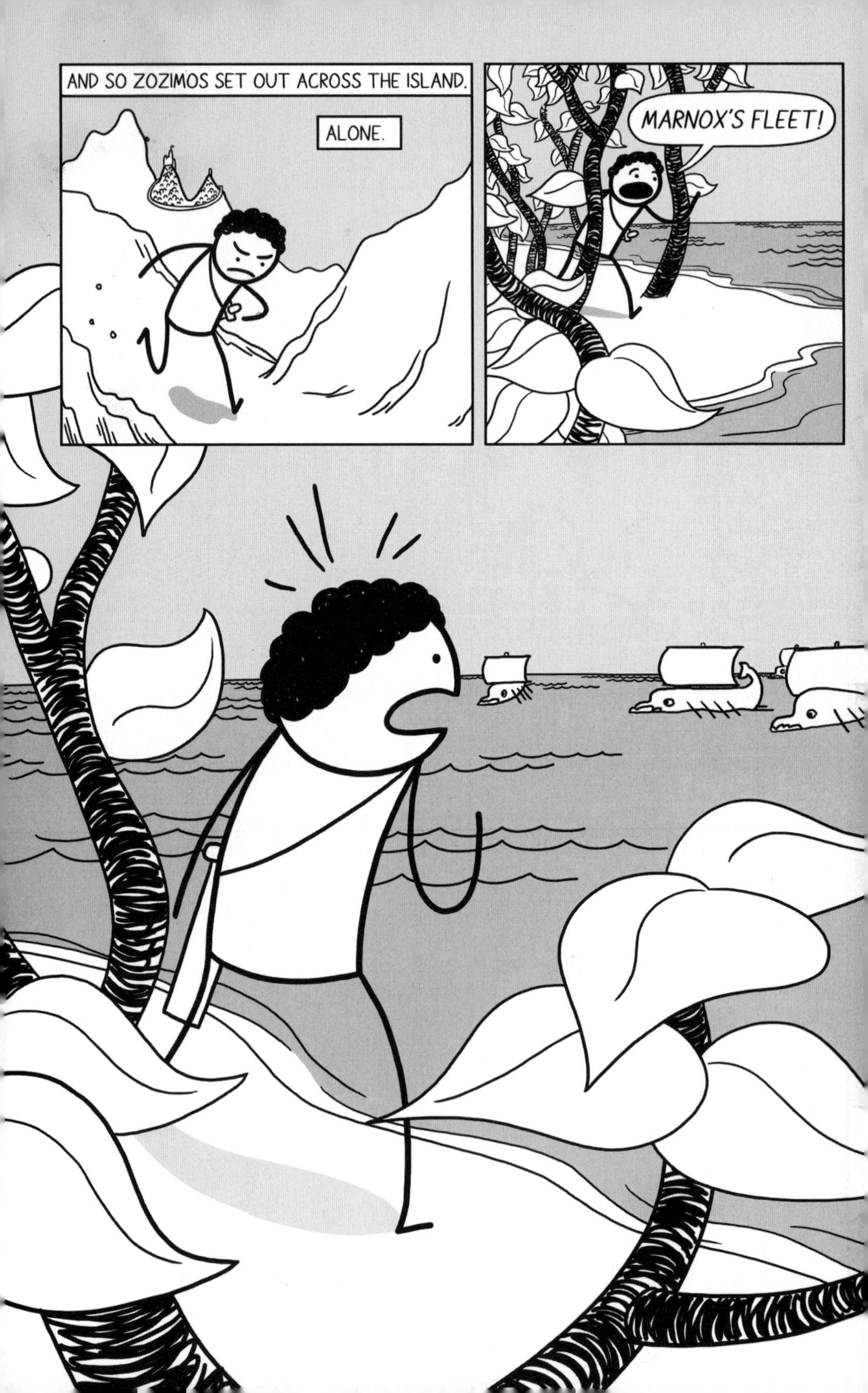
AND SO ZOZIMOS SET OUT ACROSS THE ISLAND.
ALONE.
MARNOX'S FLEET!

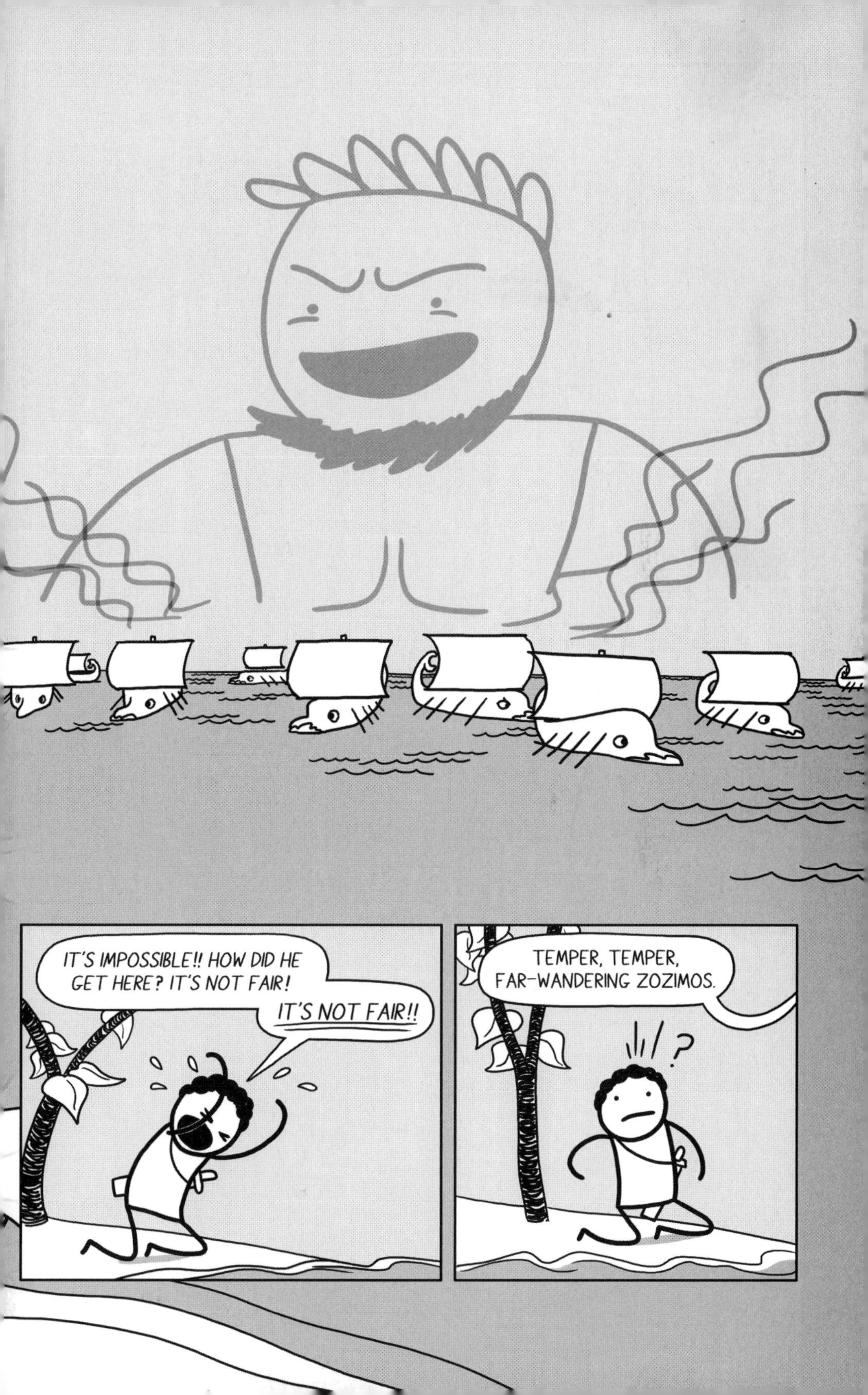
IT'S IMPOSSIBLE!! HOW DID HE GET HERE? IT'S NOT FAIR!
IT'S NOT FAIR!!
TEMPER, TEMPER, FAR-WANDERING ZOZIMOS.

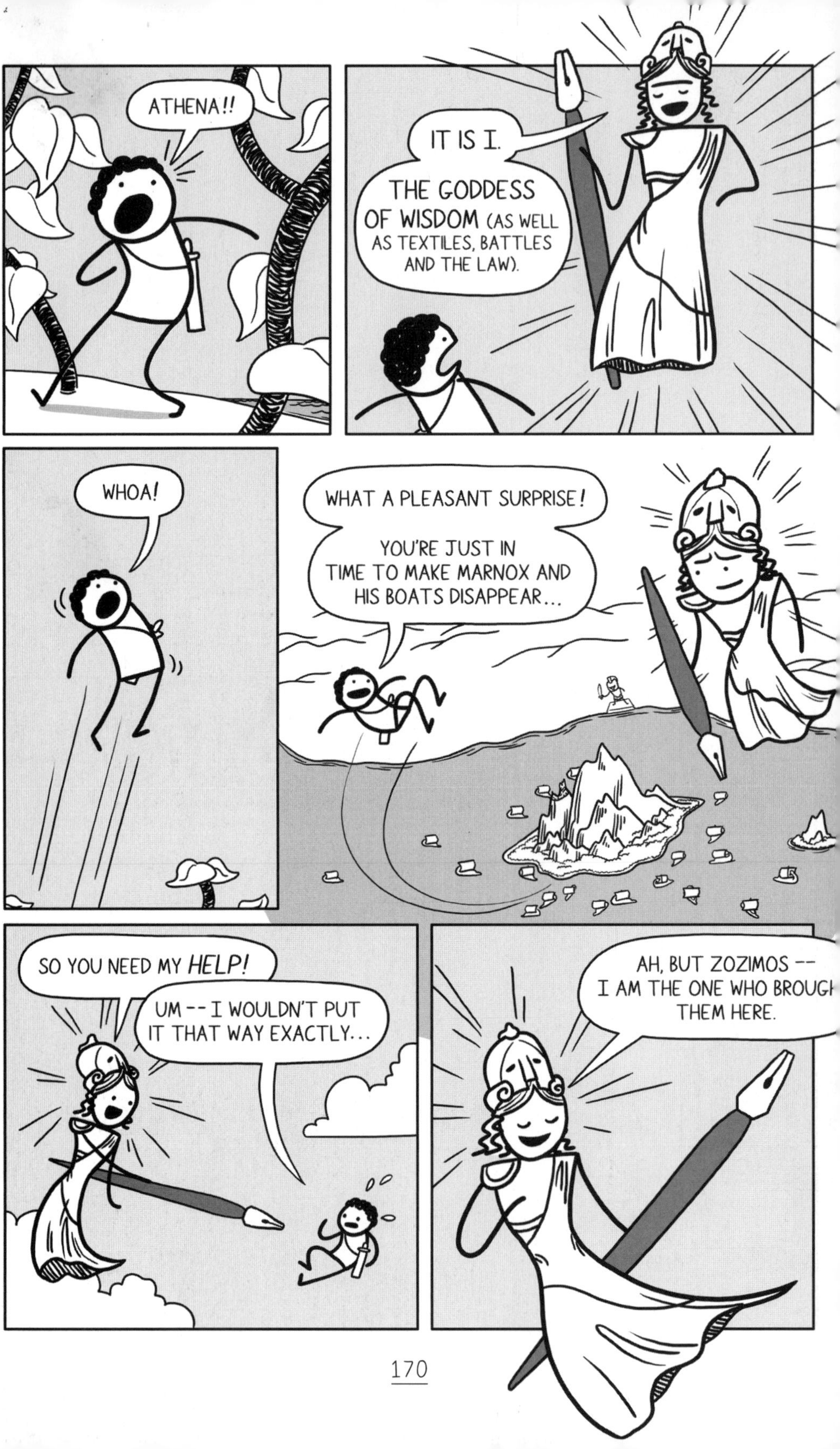
ATHENA!!
IT IS I.
THE GODDESS OF WISDOM (AS WELL AS TEXTILES, BATTLES AND THE LAW).
WHOA!
WHAT A PLEASANT SURPRISE!
YOU'RE JUST IN TIME TO MAKE MARNOX AND HIS BOATS DISAPPEAR...
SO YOU NEED MY *HELP!*
UM -- I WOULDN'T PUT IT THAT WAY EXACTLY...
AH, BUT ZOZIMOS -- I AM THE ONE WHO BROUGH
THEM HERE.

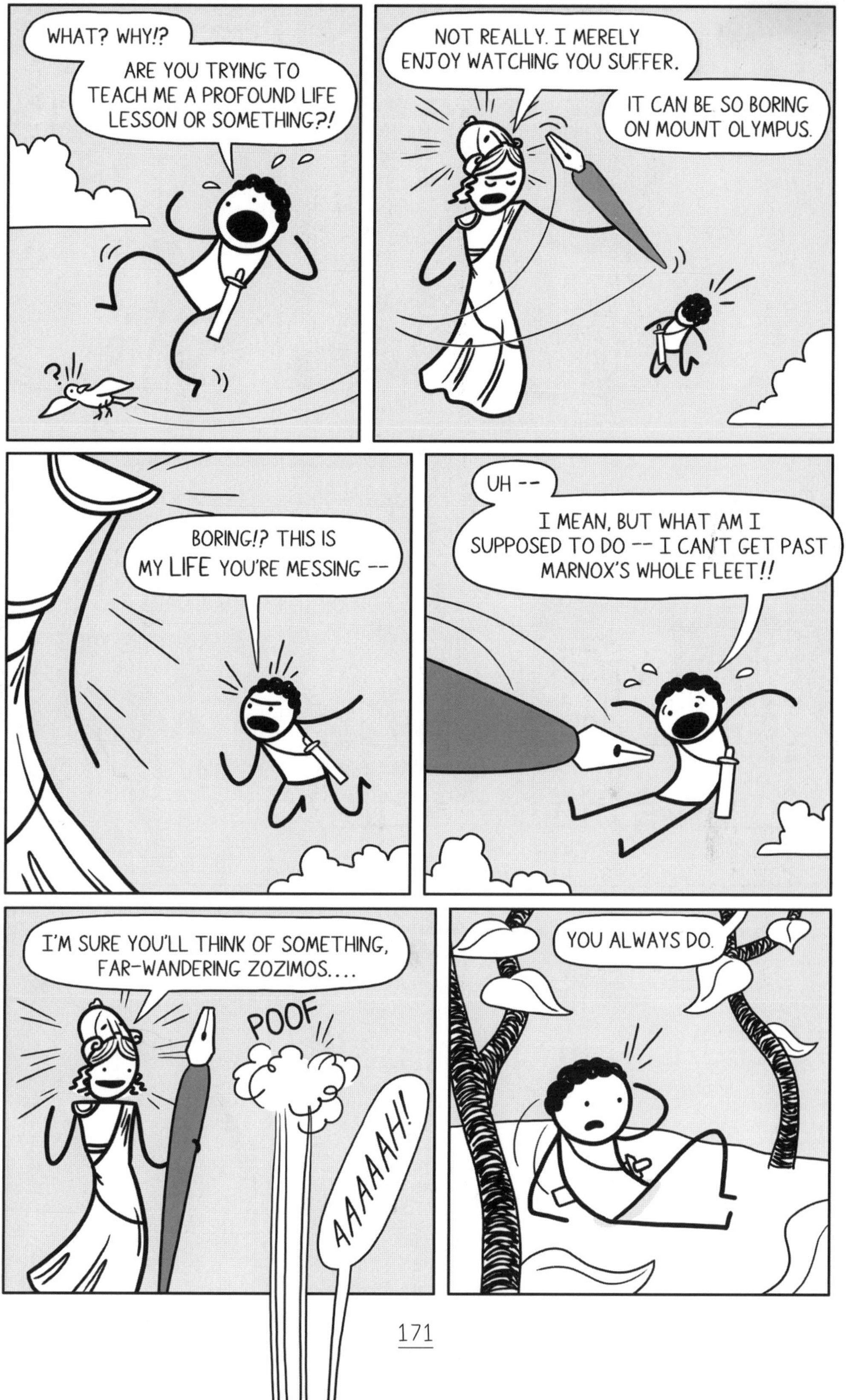
WHAT? WHY!?
ARE YOU TRYING TO TEACH ME A PROFOUND LIFE LESSON OR SOMETHING?!
?!
NOT REALLY. I MERELY ENJOY WATCHING YOU SUFFER.
IT CAN BE SO BORING ON MOUNT OLYMPUS.
BORING!? THIS IS MY LIFE YOU'RE MESSING --
UH --
I MEAN, BUT WHAT AM I SUPPOSED TO DO -- I CAN'T GET PAST MARNOX'S WHOLE FLEET!!
I'M SURE YOU'LL THINK OF SOMETHING, FAR-WANDERING ZOZIMOS....
POOF
AAAAAH!
YOU ALWAYS DO.

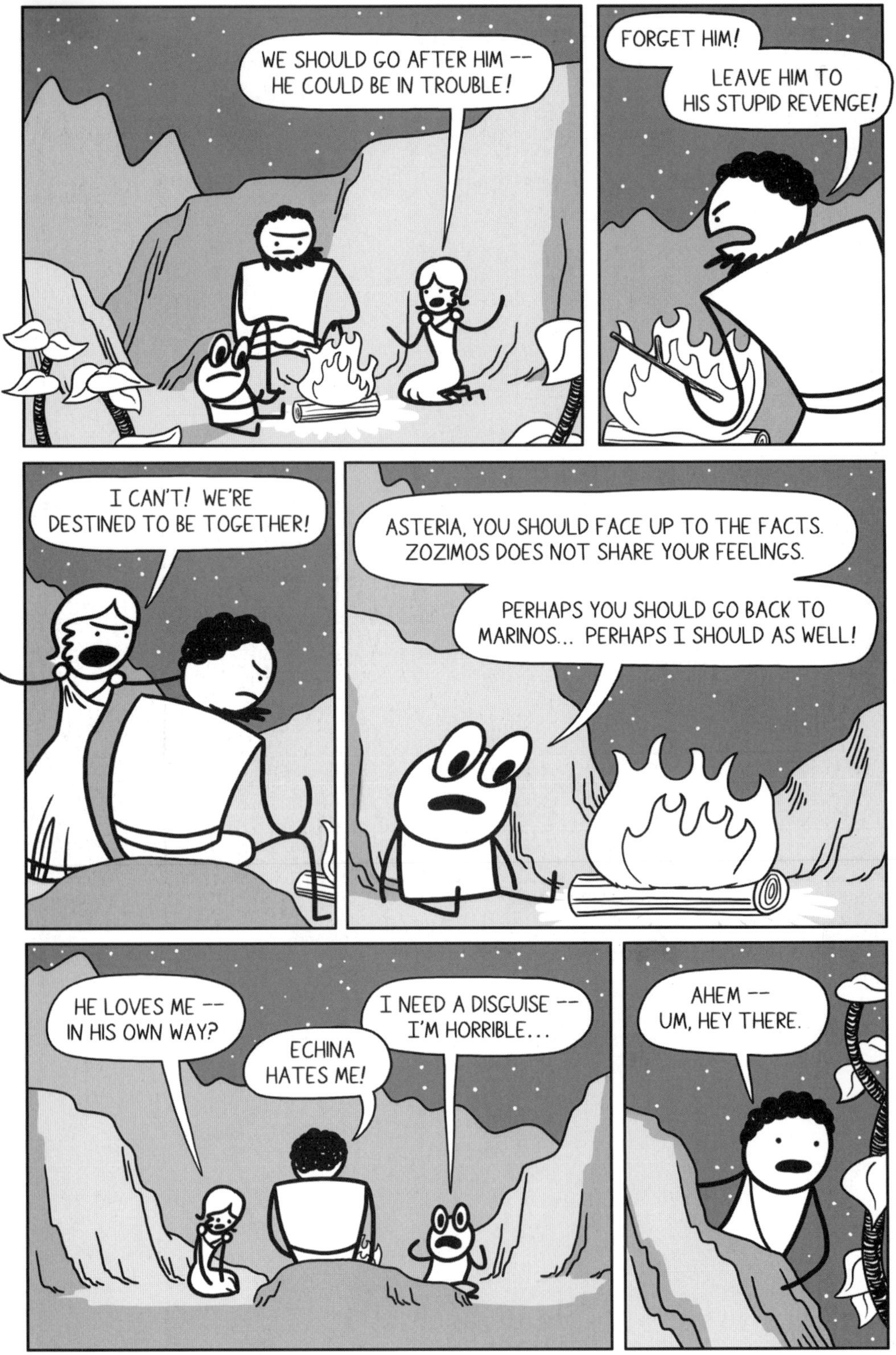
WE SHOULD GO AFTER HIM -- HE COULD BE IN TROUBLE!
FORGET HIM!
LEAVE HIM TO HIS STUPID REVENGE!
I CAN'T! WE'RE DESTINED TO BE TOGETHER!
ASTERIA, YOU SHOULD FACE UP TO THE FACTS. ZOZIMOS DOES NOT SHARE YOUR FEELINGS.
PERHAPS YOU SHOULD GO BACK TO MARINOS... PERHAPS I SHOULD AS WELL!
HE LOVES ME -- IN HIS OWN WAY?
ECHINA HATES ME!
I NEED A DISGUISE -- I'M HORRIBLE...
AHEM -- UM, HEY THERE.

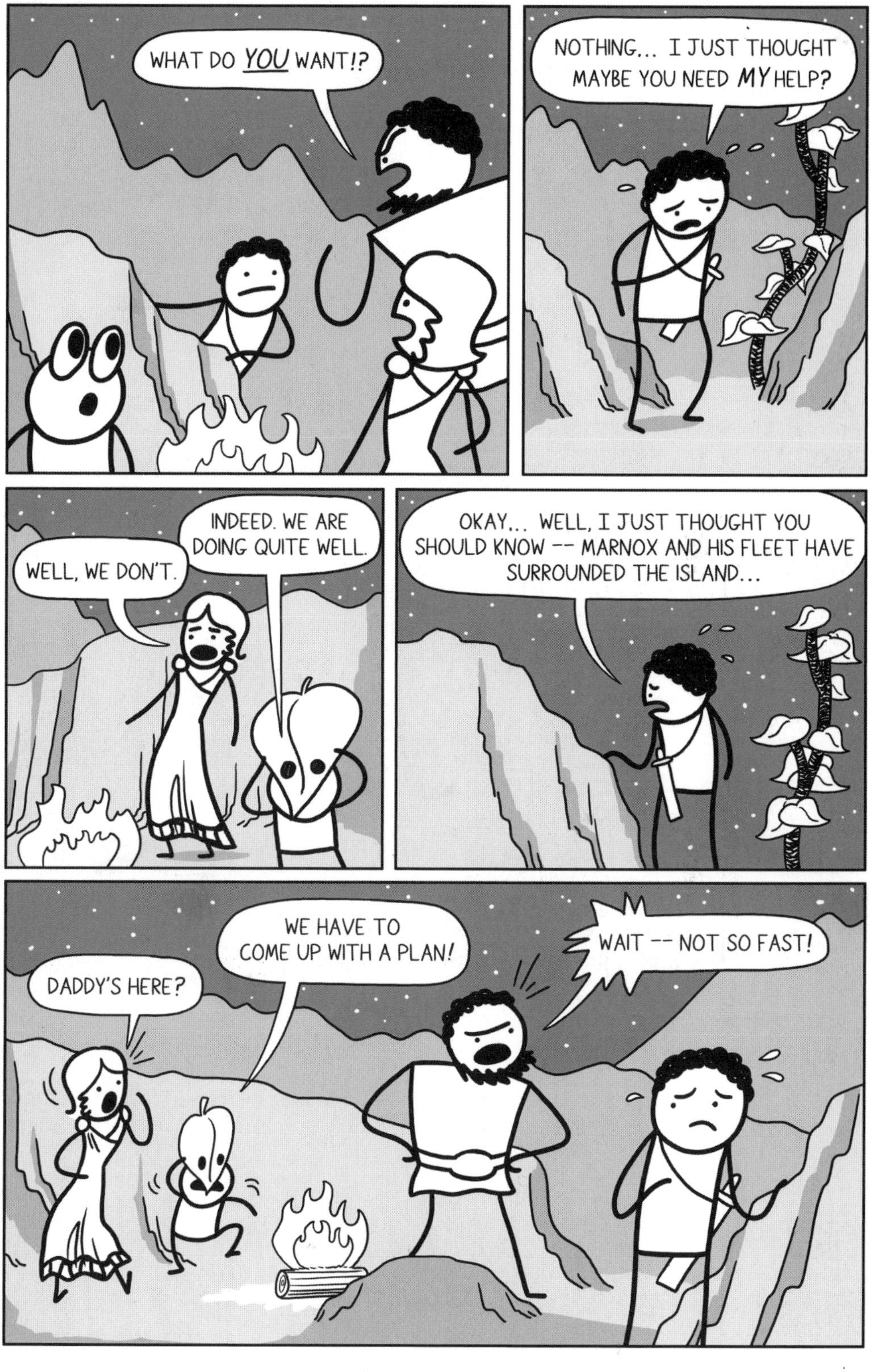
WHAT DO YOU WANT!?
NOTHING... I JUST THOUGHT MAYBE YOU NEED MY HELP?
WELL, WE DON'T.
INDEED. WE ARE DOING QUITE WELL.
OKAY... WELL, I JUST THOUGHT YOU SHOULD KNOW -- MARNOX AND HIS FLEET HAVE SURROUNDED THE ISLAND...
DADDY'S HERE?
WE HAVE TO COME UP WITH A PLAN!
WAIT -- NOT SO FAST!

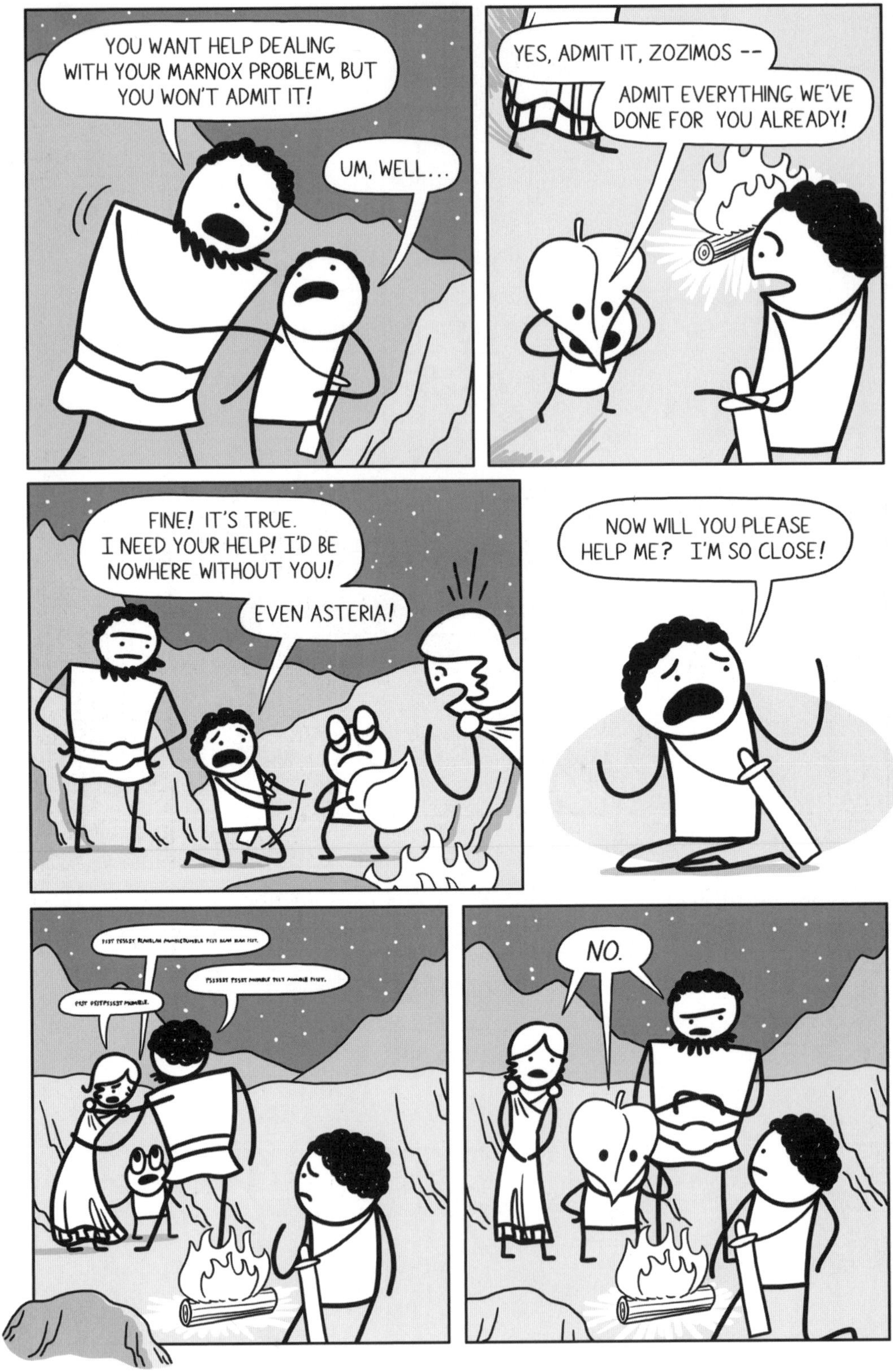

YOU WANT HELP DEALING WITH YOUR MARNOX PROBLEM, BUT YOU WON'T ADMIT IT!
UM, WELL...
YES, ADMIT IT, ZOZIMOS --
ADMIT EVERYTHING WE'VE DONE FOR YOU ALREADY!
FINE! IT'S TRUE. I NEED YOUR HELP! I'D BE NOWHERE WITHOUT YOU!
EVEN ASTERIA!
NOW WILL YOU PLEASE HELP ME? I'M SO CLOSE!
NO.

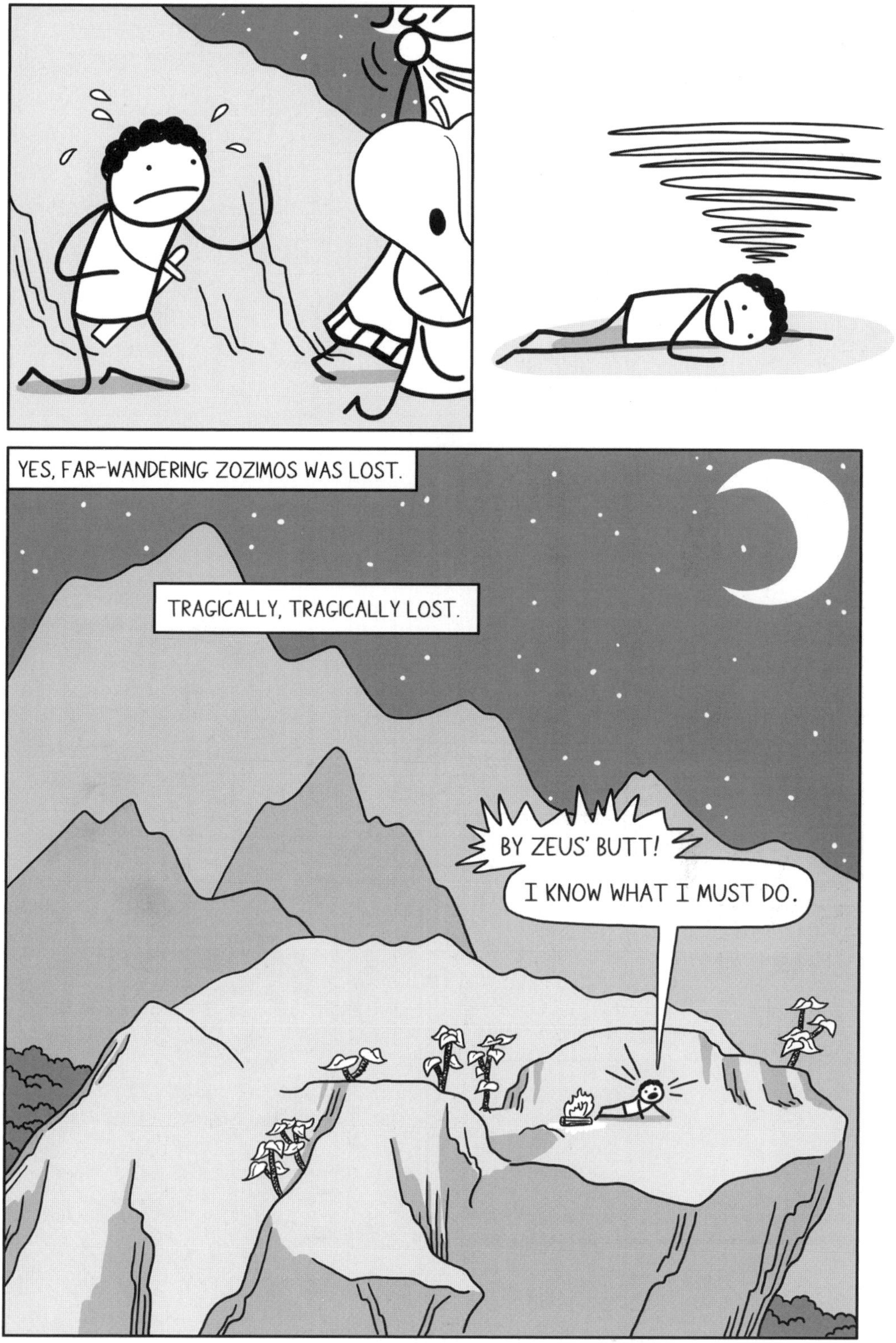
YES, FAR-WANDERING ZOZIMOS WAS LOST.
TRAGICALLY, TRAGICALLY LOST.
BY ZEUS' BUTT!
I KNOW WHAT I MUST DO.

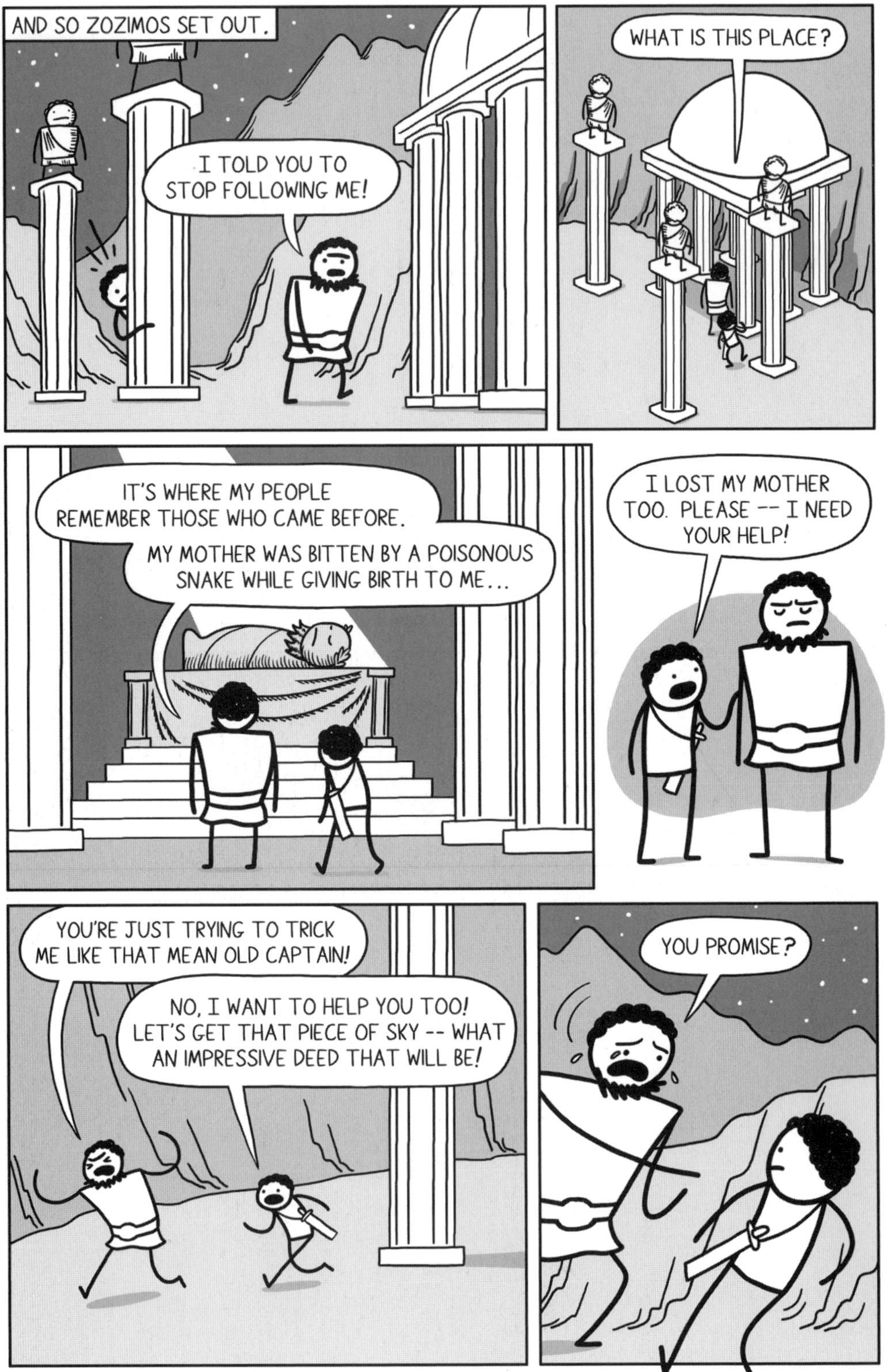
AND SO ZOZIMOS SET OUT.
I TOLD YOU TO STOP FOLLOWING ME!
WHAT IS THIS PLACE?
IT'S WHERE MY PEOPLE REMEMBER THOSE WHO CAME BEFORE.
MY MOTHER WAS BITTEN BY A POISONOUS SNAKE WHILE GIVING BIRTH TO ME...
I LOST MY MOTHER TOO. PLEASE -- I NEED YOUR HELP!
YOU'RE JUST TRYING TO TRICK ME LIKE THAT MEAN OLD CAPTAIN!
NO, I WANT TO HELP YOU TOO! LET'S GET THAT PIECE OF SKY -- WHAT AN IMPRESSIVE DEED THAT WILL BE!
YOU PROMISE?

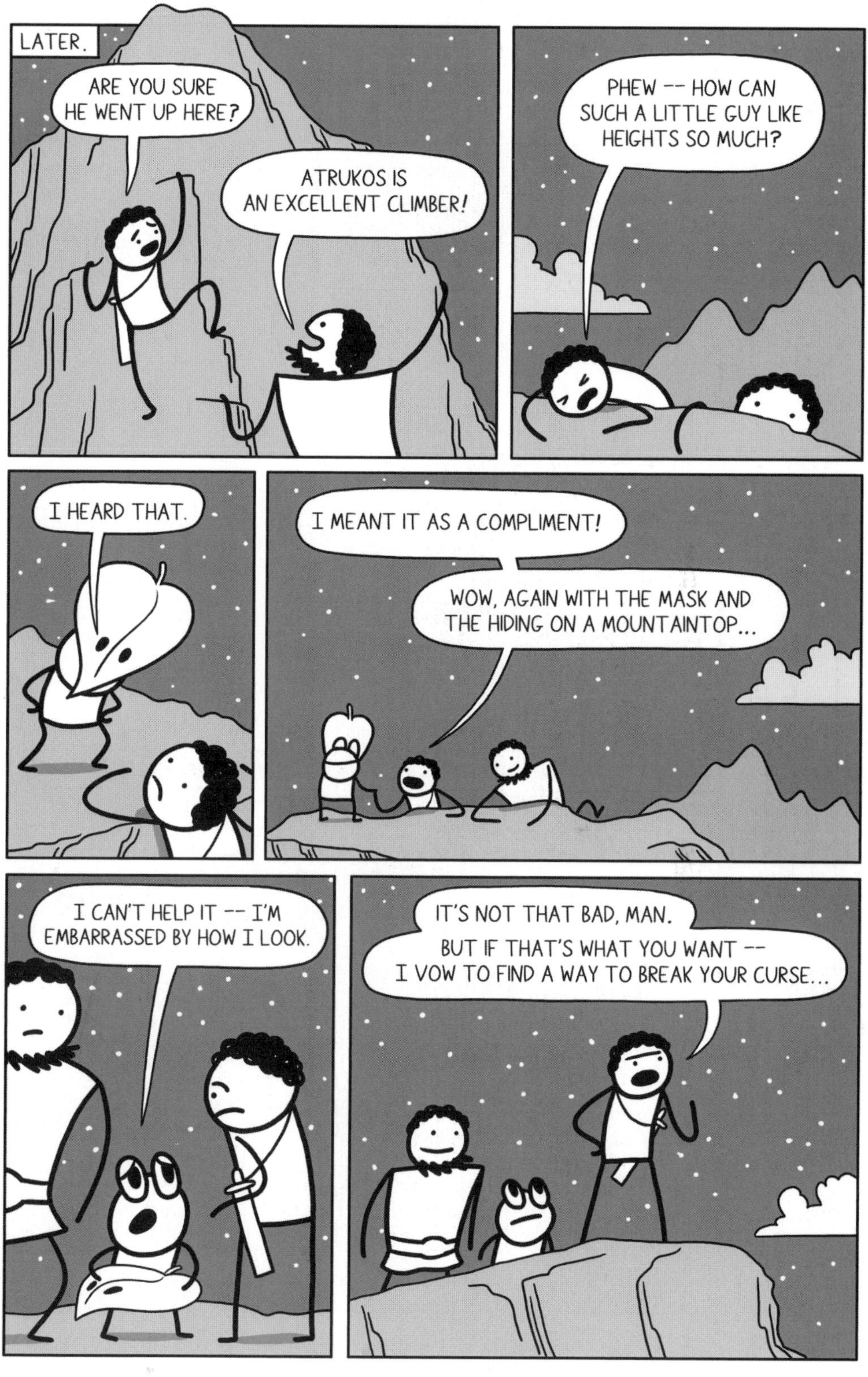
LATER.
ARE YOU SURE HE WENT UP HERE?
ATRUKOS IS AN EXCELLENT CLIMBER!
PHEW -- HOW CAN SUCH A LITTLE GUY LIKE HEIGHTS SO MUCH?
I HEARD THAT.
I MEANT IT AS A COMPLIMENT!
WOW, AGAIN WITH THE MASK AND THE HIDING ON A MOUNTAINTOP...
I CAN'T HELP IT -- I'M EMBARRASSED BY HOW I LOOK.
IT'S NOT THAT BAD, MAN.
BUT IF THAT'S WHAT YOU WANT -- I VOW TO FIND A WAY TO BREAK YOUR CURSE...

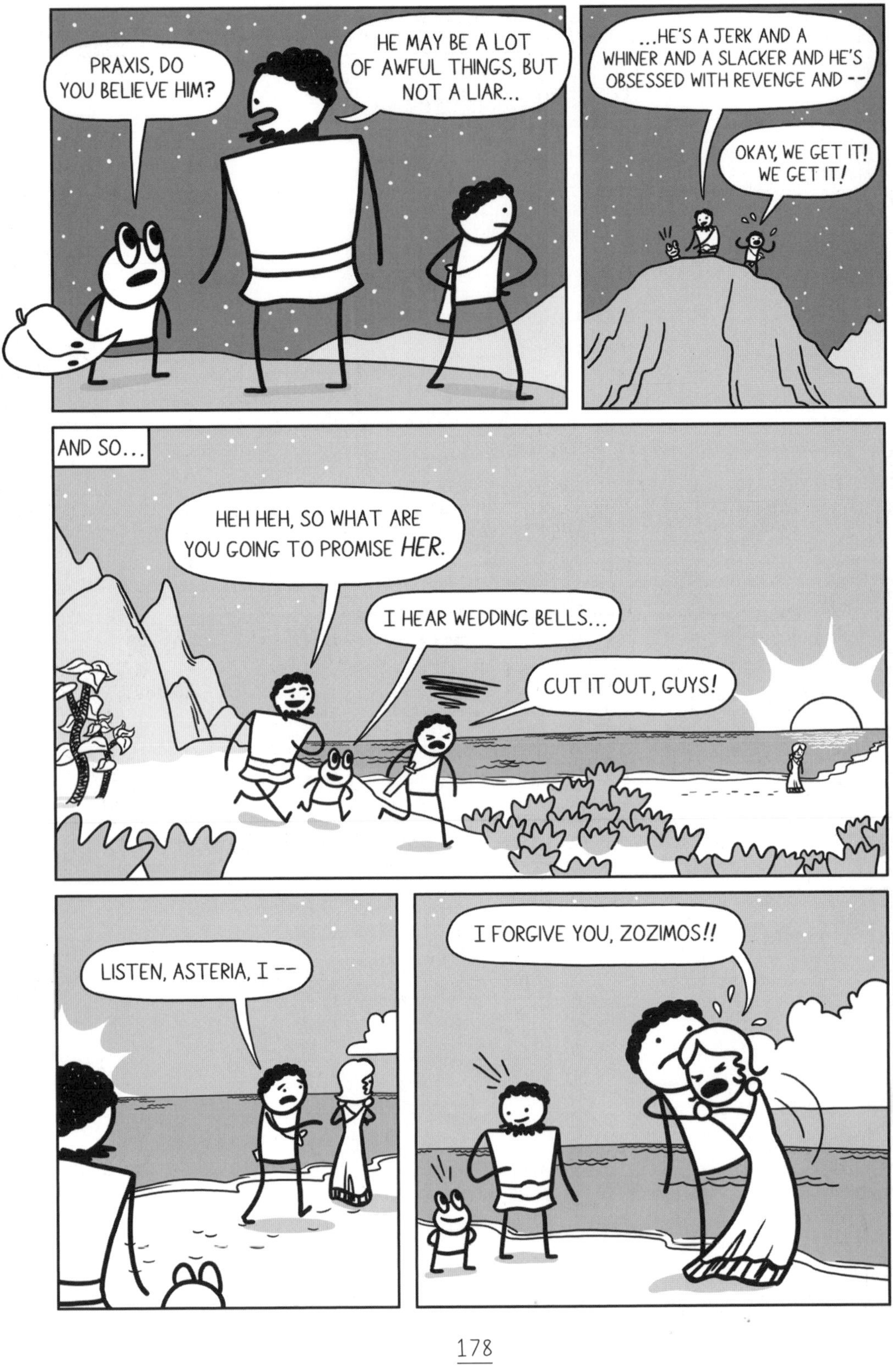
PRAXIS, DO YOU BELIEVE HIM?
HE MAY BE A LOT OF AWFUL THINGS, BUT NOT A LIAR...
...HE'S A JERK AND A WHINER AND A SLACKER AND HE'S OBSESSED WITH REVENGE AND --
OKAY, WE GET IT! WE GET IT!
AND SO...
HEH HEH, SO WHAT ARE YOU GOING TO PROMISE *HER*.
I HEAR WEDDING BELLS...
CUT IT OUT, GUYS!
LISTEN, ASTERIA, I --
I FORGIVE YOU, ZOZIMOS!!

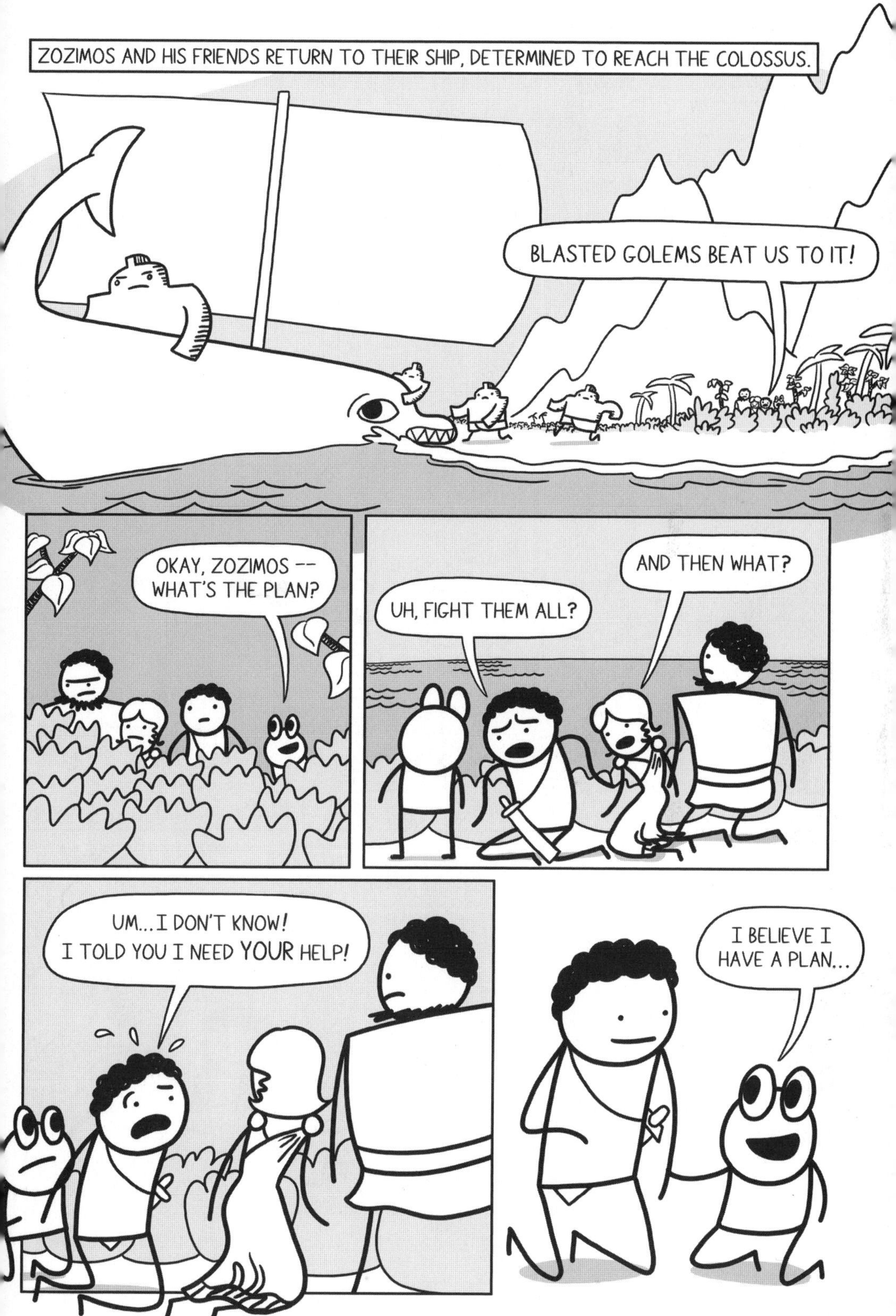
ZOZIMOS AND HIS FRIENDS RETURN TO THEIR SHIP, DETERMINED TO REACH THE COLOSSUS.
BLASTED GOLEMS BEAT US TO IT!
OKAY, ZOZIMOS -- WHAT'S THE PLAN?
UH, FIGHT THEM ALL?
AND THEN WHAT?
UM...I DON'T KNOW! I TOLD YOU I NEED YOUR HELP!
I BELIEVE I HAVE A PLAN...

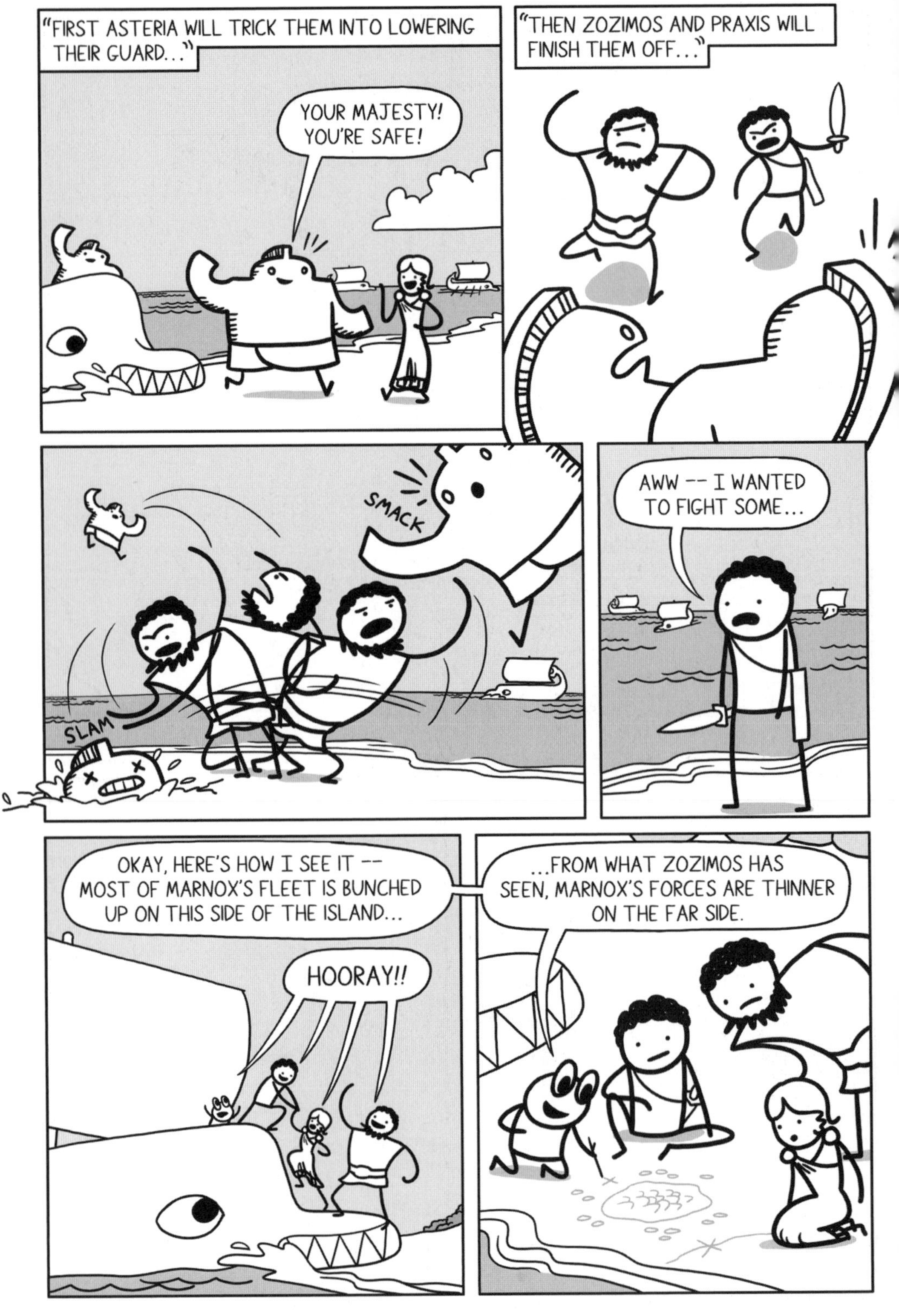
"FIRST ASTERIA WILL TRICK THEM INTO LOWERING THEIR GUARD..."
YOUR MAJESTY! YOU'RE SAFE!
"THEN ZOZIMOS AND PRAXIS WILL FINISH THEM OFF..."
SMACK
SLAM
AWW -- I WANTED TO FIGHT SOME...
OKAY, HERE'S HOW I SEE IT -- MOST OF MARNOX'S FLEET IS BUNCHED UP ON THIS SIDE OF THE ISLAND...
HOORAY!!
...FROM WHAT ZOZIMOS HAS SEEN, MARNOX'S FORCES ARE THINNER ON THE FAR SIDE.

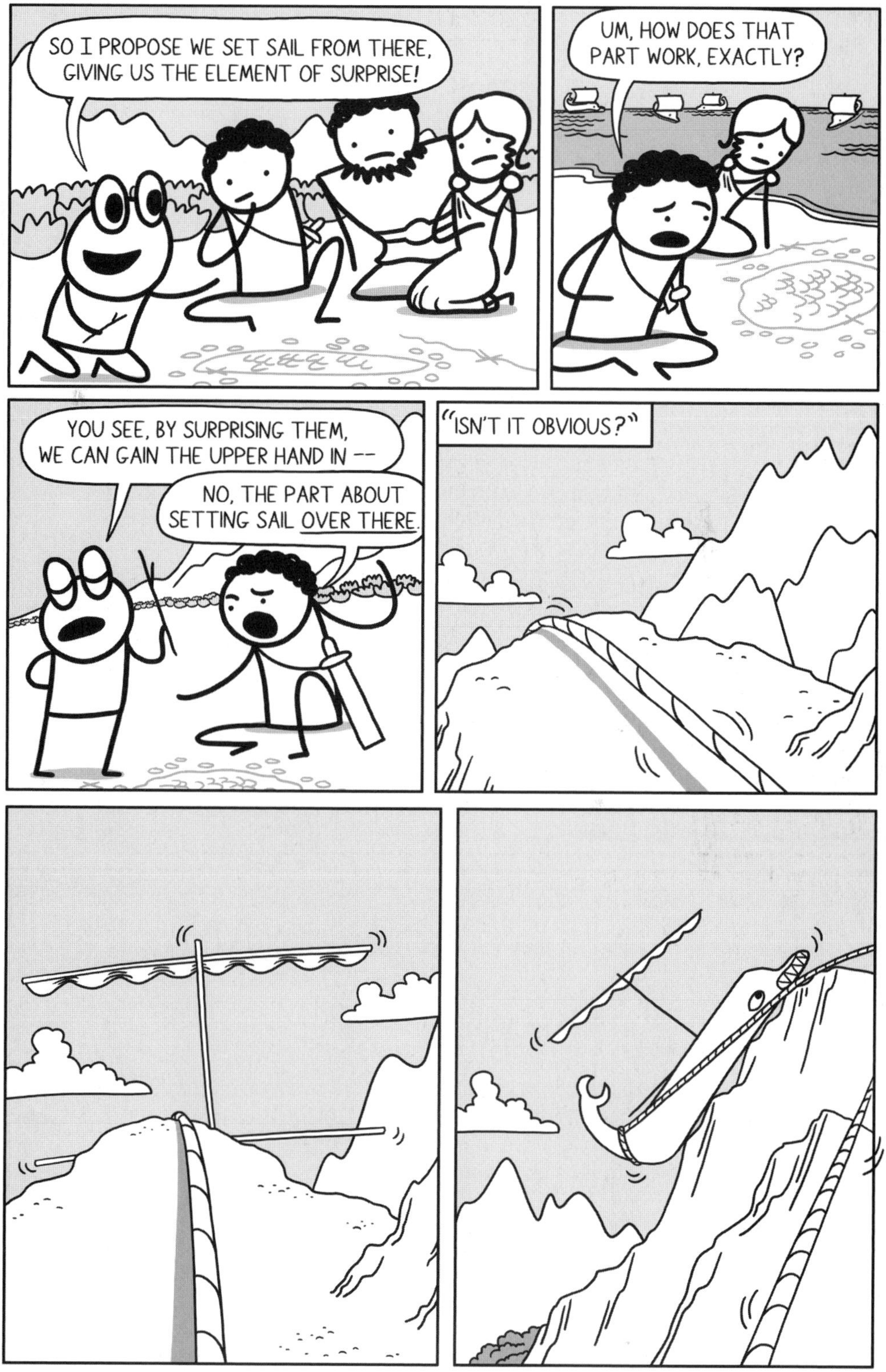
SO I PROPOSE WE SET SAIL FROM THERE, GIVING US THE ELEMENT OF SURPRISE!
UM, HOW DOES THAT PART WORK, EXACTLY?
YOU SEE, BY SURPRISING THEM, WE CAN GAIN THE UPPER HAND IN --
NO, THE PART ABOUT SETTING SAIL OVER THERE.
"ISN'T IT OBVIOUS?"

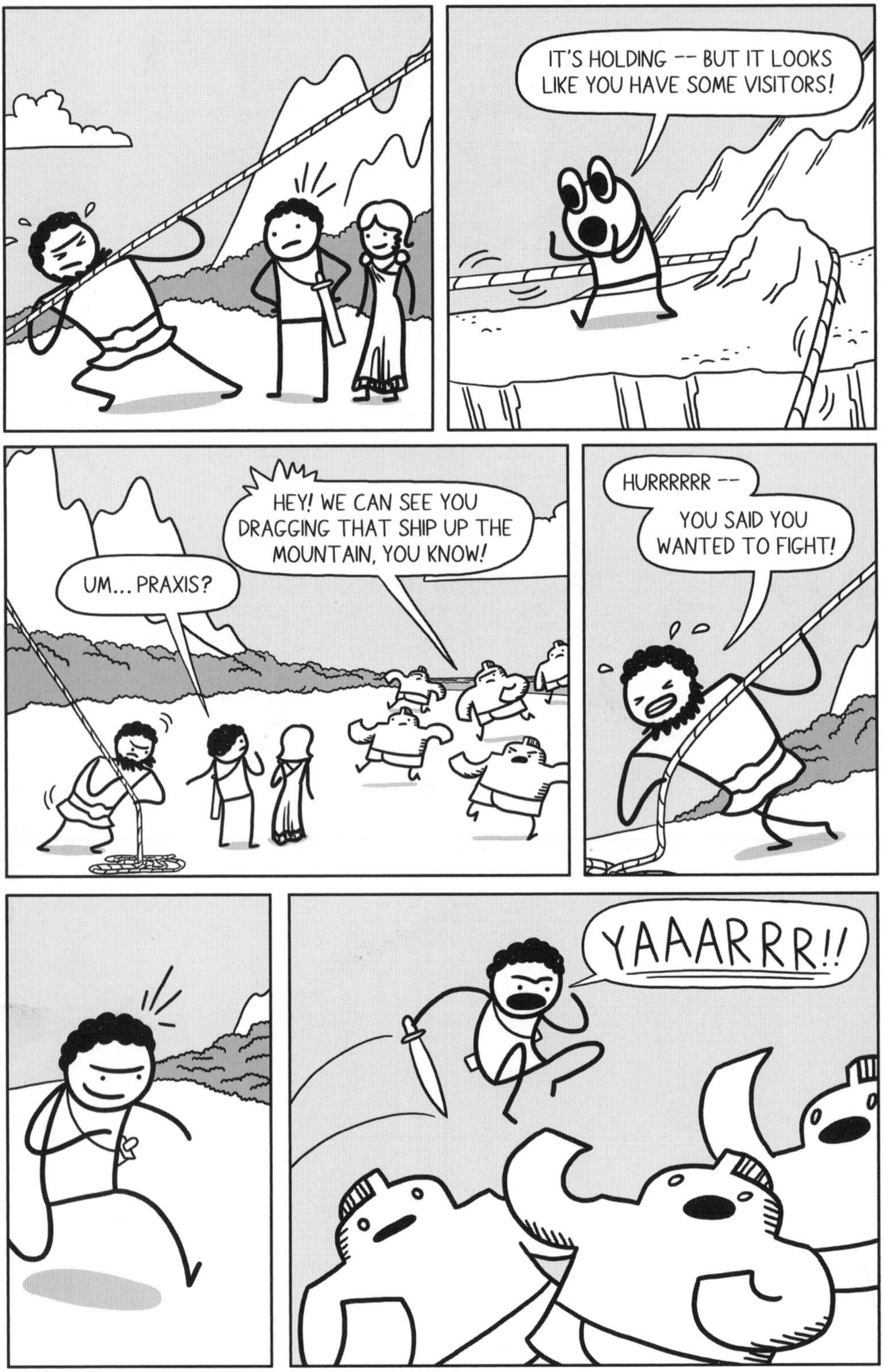
IT'S HOLDING -- BUT IT LOOKS LIKE YOU HAVE SOME VISITORS!
UM... PRAXIS?
HEY! WE CAN SEE YOU DRAGGING THAT SHIP UP THE MOUNTAIN, YOU KNOW!
HURRRRRR --
YOU SAID YOU WANTED TO FIGHT!
YAAARRR!!

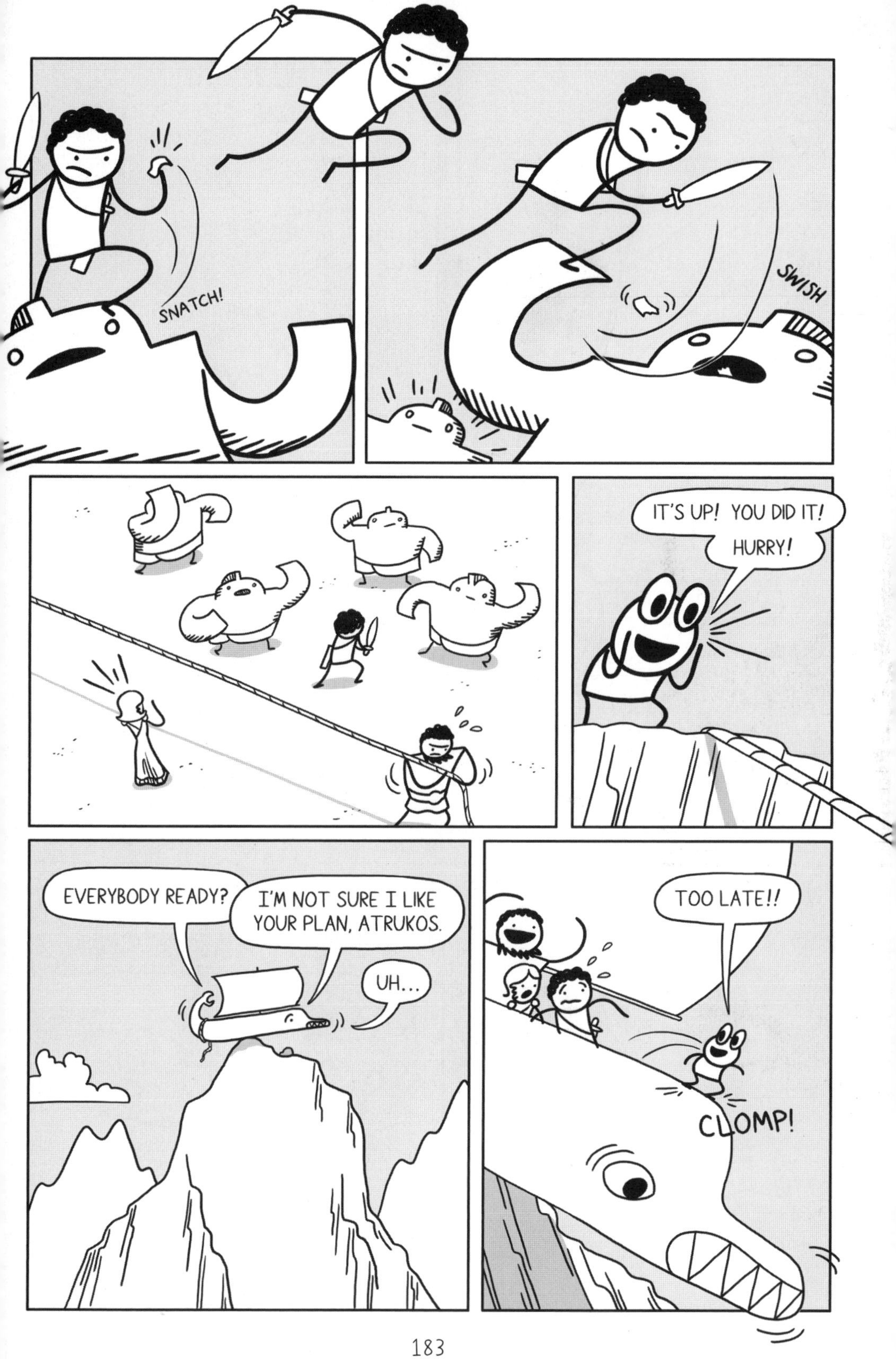
SNATCH!
SWISH
IT'S UP! YOU DID IT!
HURRY!
EVERYBODY READY?
I'M NOT SURE I LIKE YOUR PLAN, ATRUKOS.
UH...
TOO LATE!!
CLOMP!

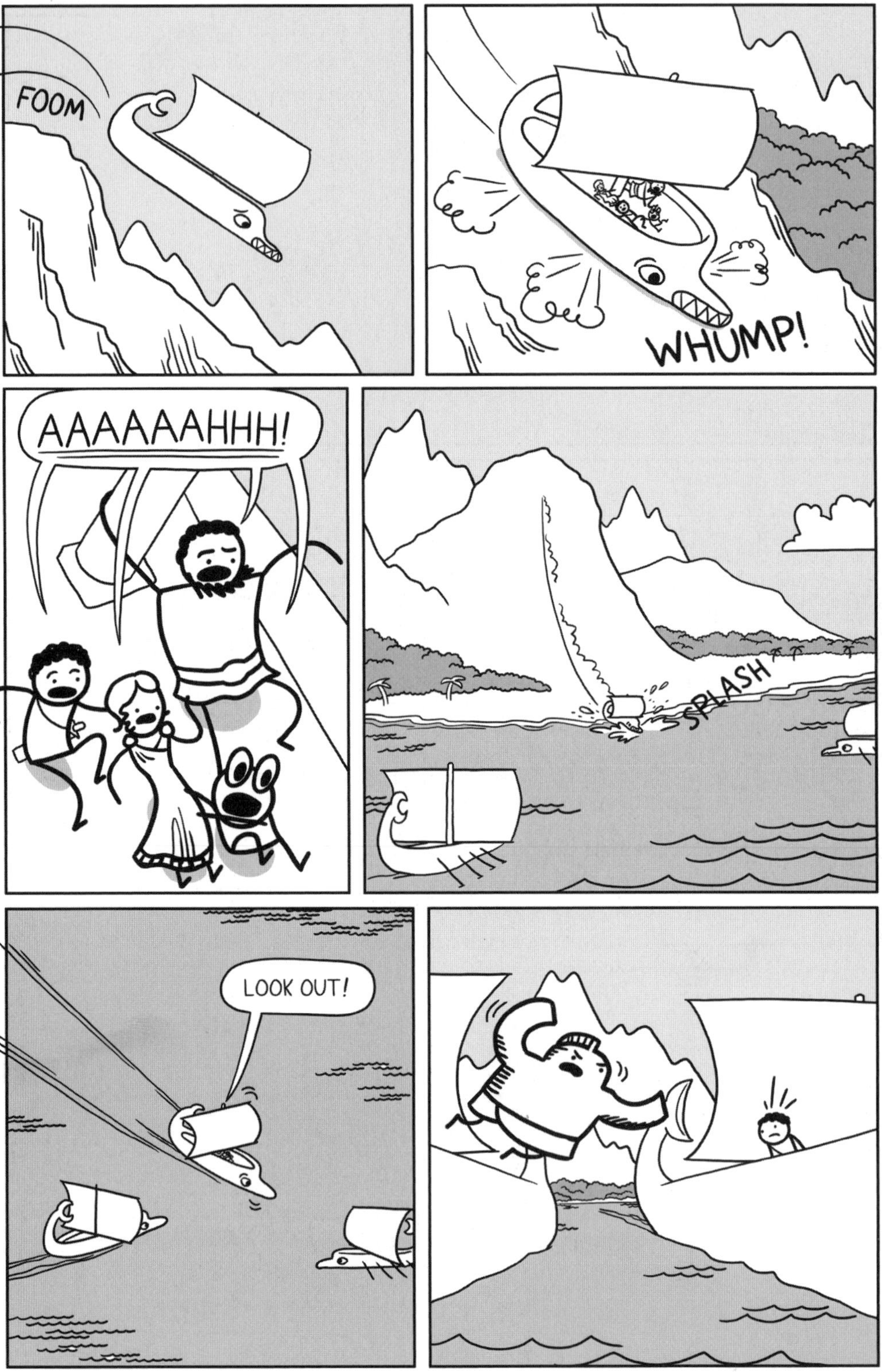
FOOM
WHUMP!
AAAAAAHHH!
SPLASH
LOOK OUT!

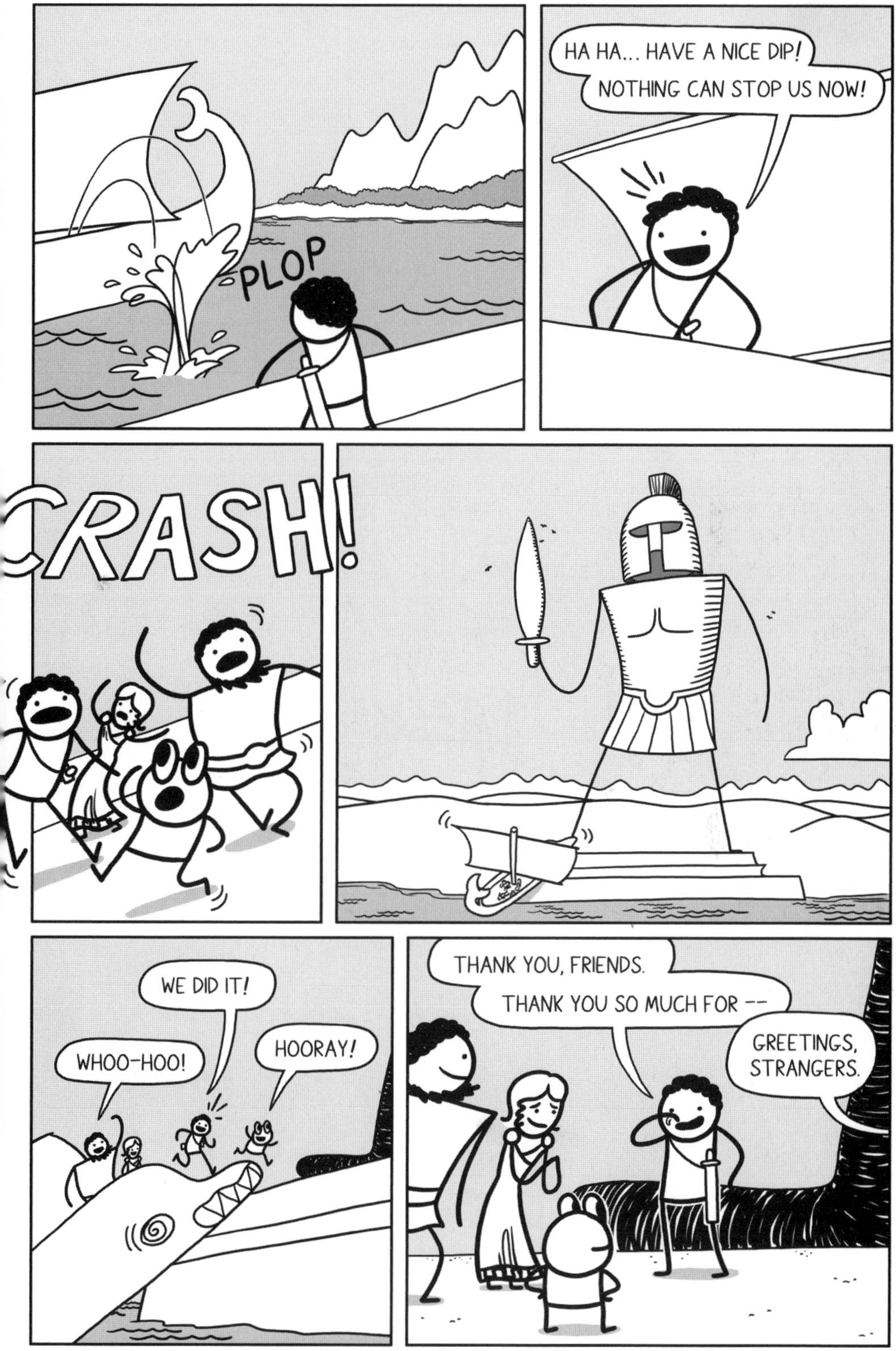
PLOP
HA HA... HAVE A NICE DIP!
NOTHING CAN STOP US NOW!
CRASH!
WHOO-HOO!
WE DID IT!
HOORAY!
THANK YOU, FRIENDS.
THANK YOU SO MUCH FOR --
GREETINGS, STRANGERS.

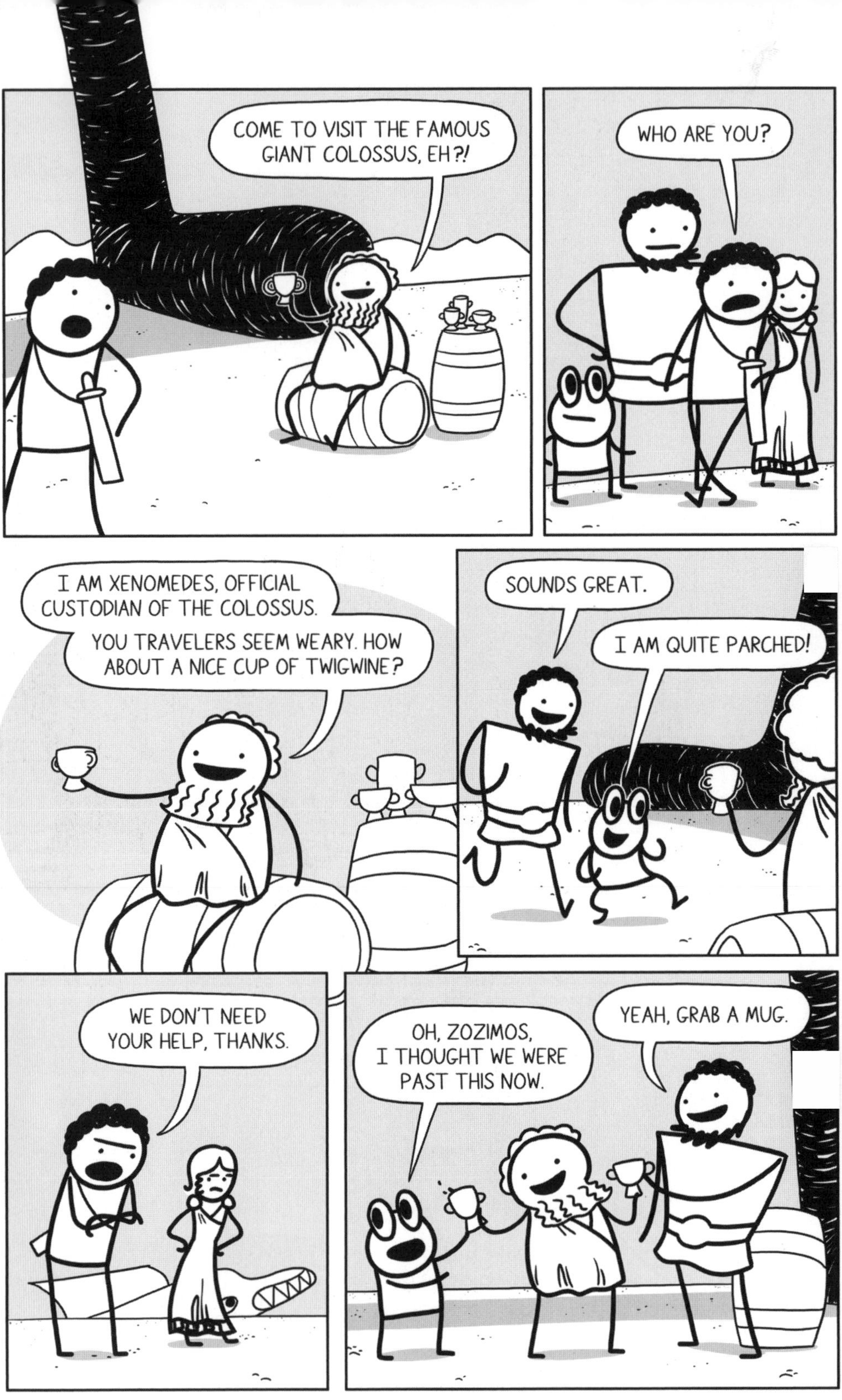
COME TO VISIT THE FAMOUS GIANT COLOSSUS, EH?!
WHO ARE YOU?
I AM XENOMEDES, OFFICIAL CUSTODIAN OF THE COLOSSUS.
YOU TRAVELERS SEEM WEARY. HOW ABOUT A NICE CUP OF TWIGWINE?
SOUNDS GREAT.
I AM QUITE PARCHED!
WE DON'T NEED YOUR HELP, THANKS.
OH, ZOZIMOS, I THOUGHT WE WERE PAST THIS NOW.
YEAH, GRAB A MUG.

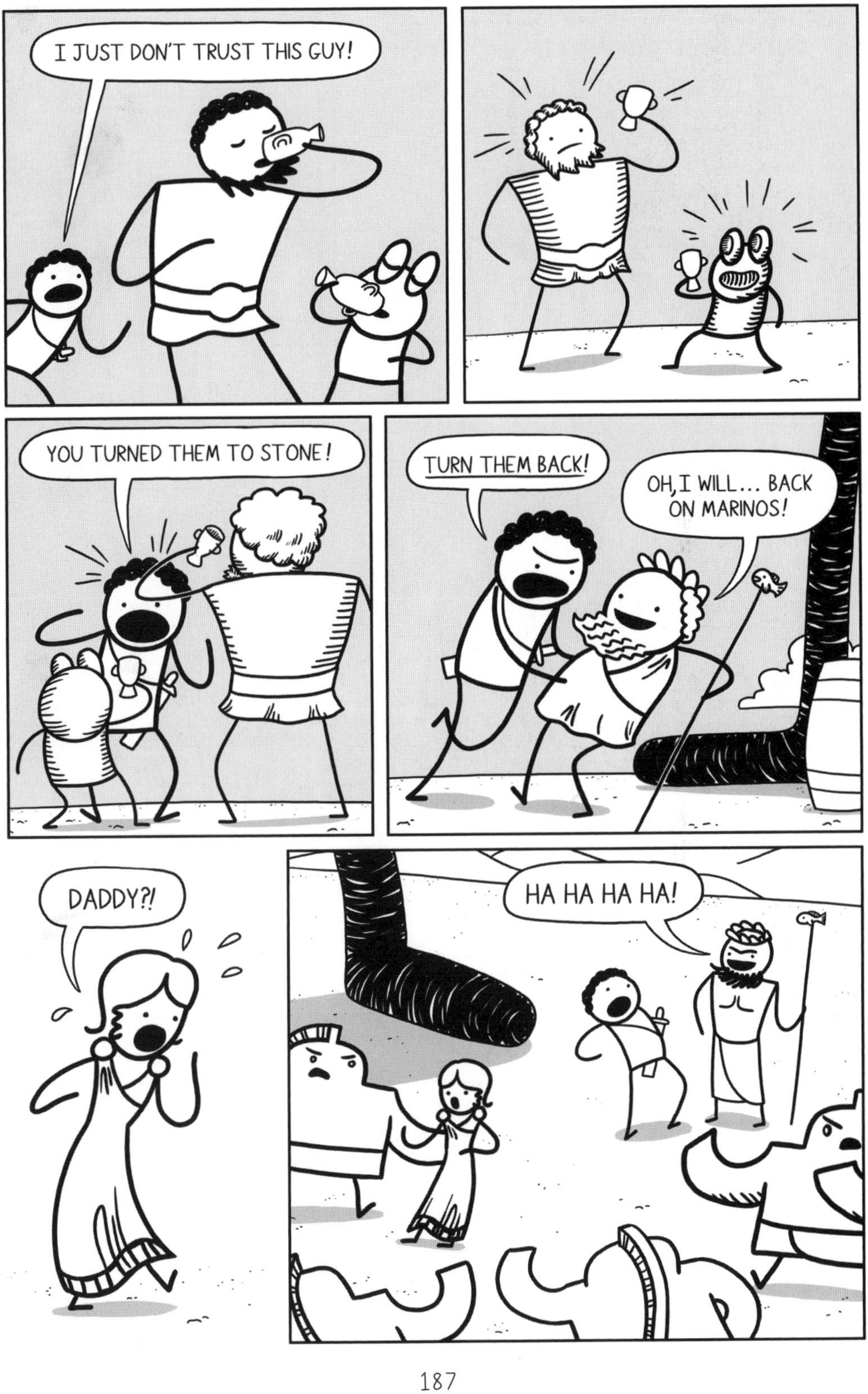
I JUST DON'T TRUST THIS GUY!
YOU TURNED THEM TO STONE!
TURN THEM BACK!
OH, I WILL... BACK ON MARINOS!
DADDY?!
HA HA HA HA!

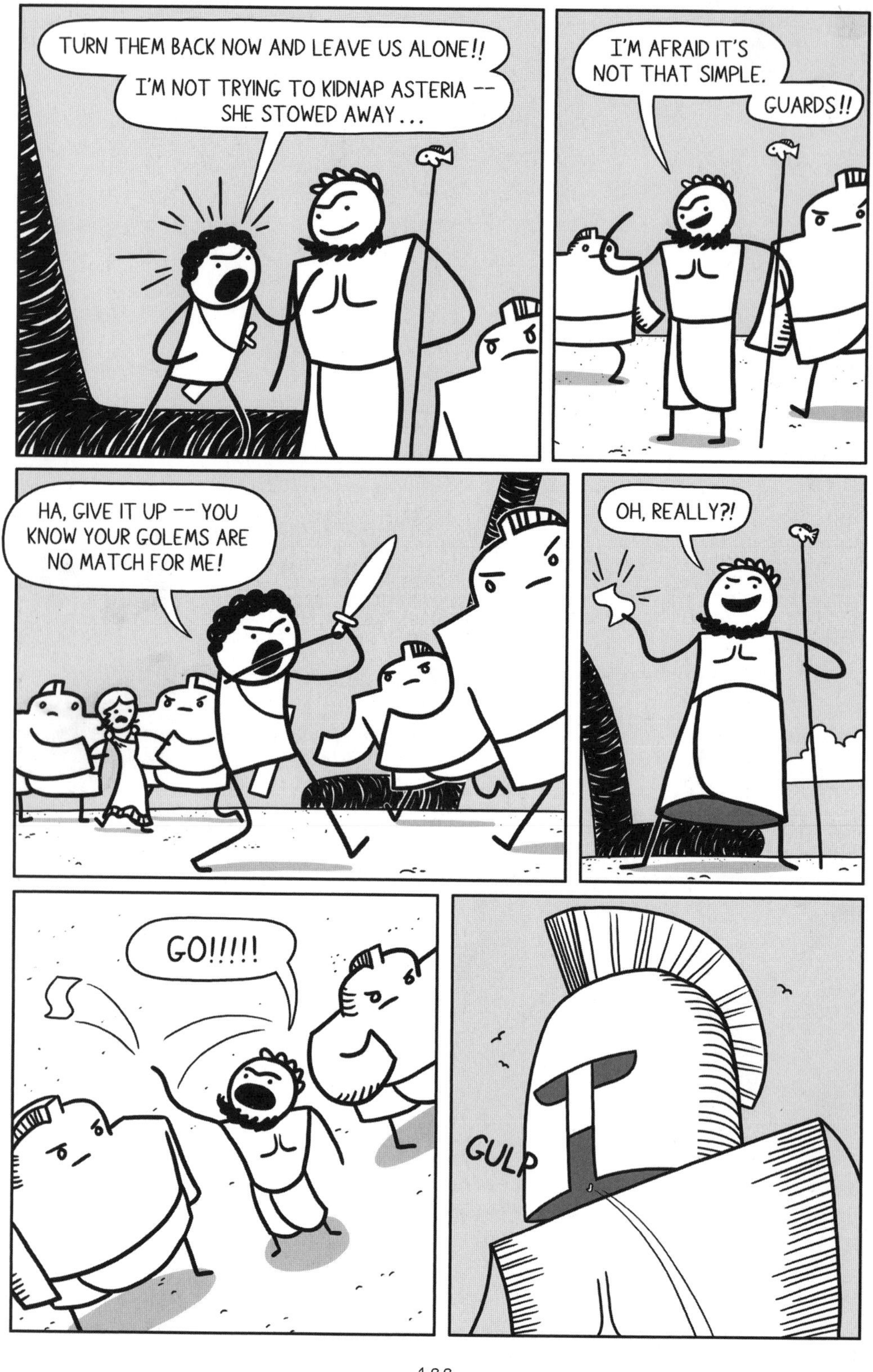
TURN THEM BACK NOW AND LEAVE US ALONE!!
I'M NOT TRYING TO KIDNAP ASTERIA -- SHE STOWED AWAY...
I'M AFRAID IT'S NOT THAT SIMPLE.
GUARDS!!
HA, GIVE IT UP -- YOU KNOW YOUR GOLEMS ARE NO MATCH FOR ME!
OH, REALLY?!
GO!!!!!
GULP

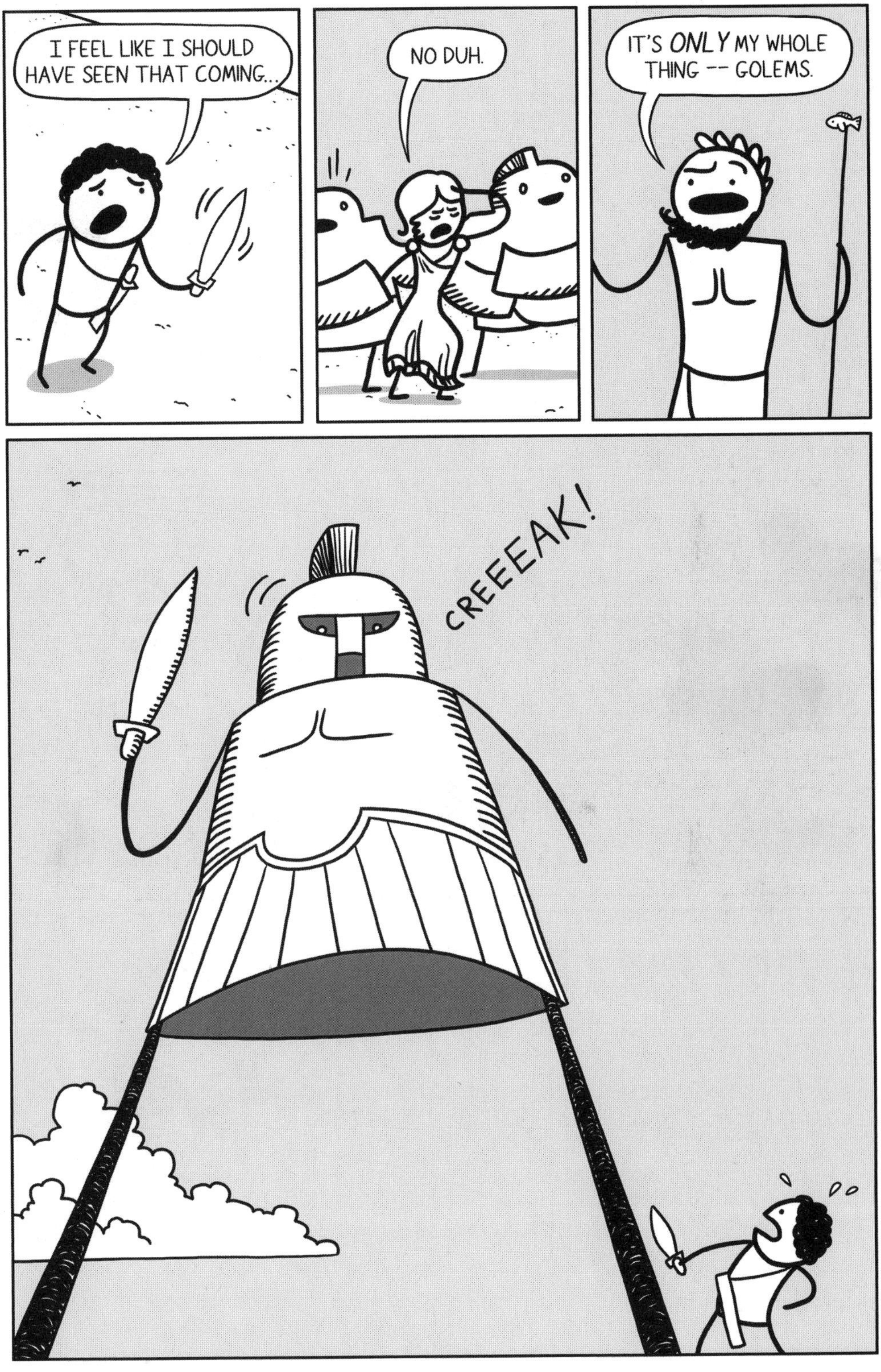
I FEEL LIKE I SHOULD HAVE SEEN THAT COMING...
NO DUH.
IT'S *ONLY* MY WHOLE THING -- GOLEMS.
CREEEAK!

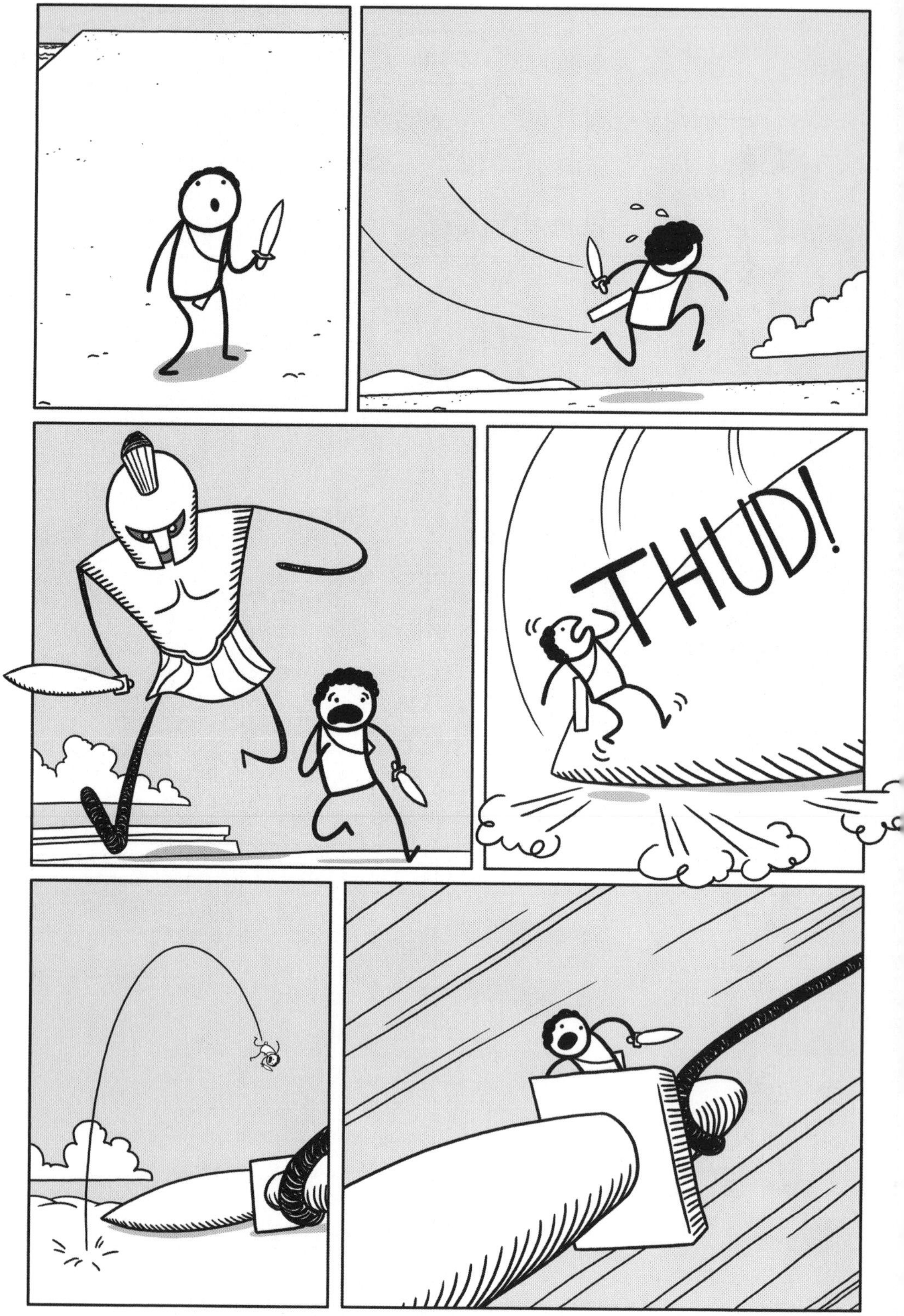
THUD!

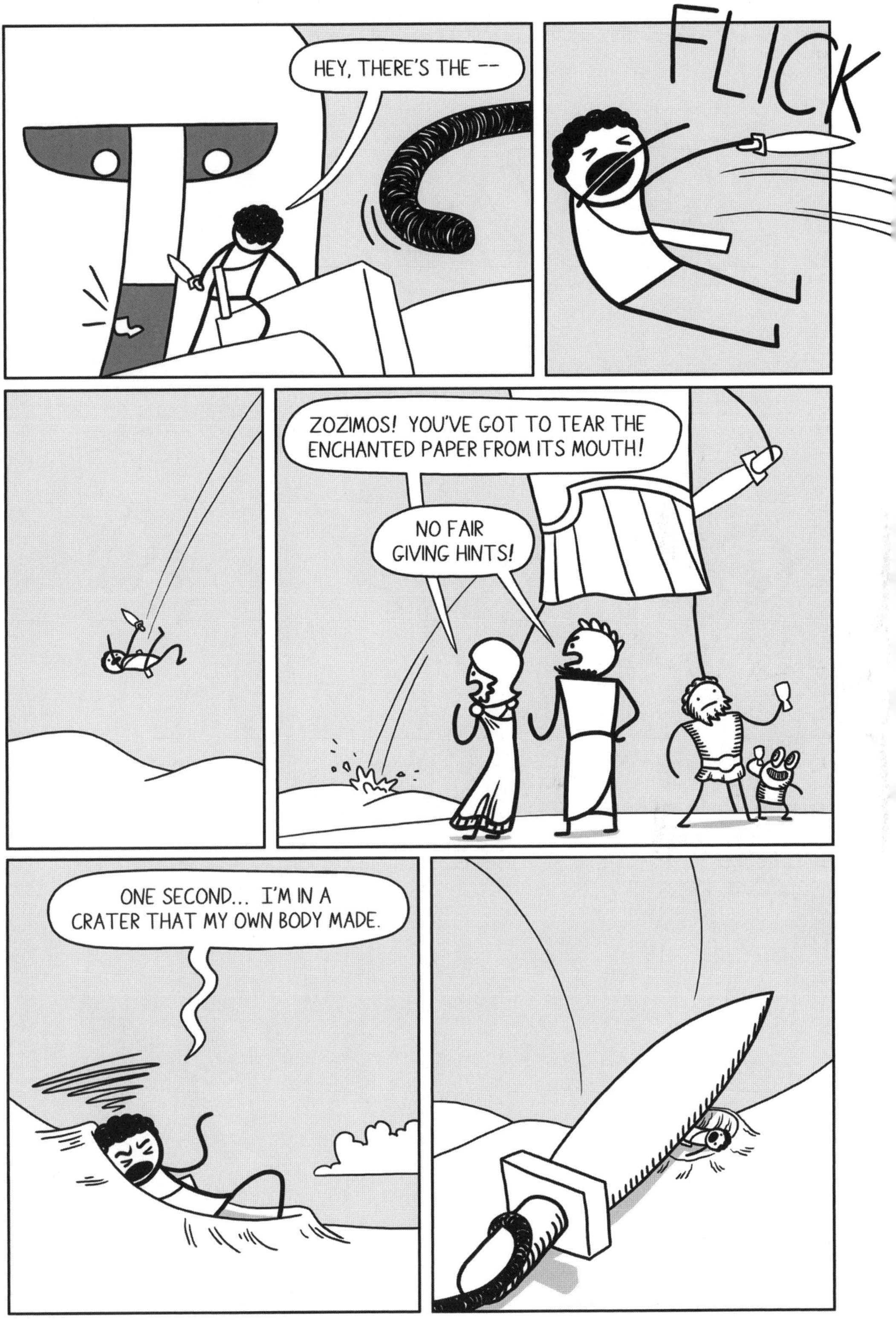
HEY, THERE'S THE --
FLICK
ZOZIMOS! YOU'VE GOT TO TEAR THE ENCHANTED PAPER FROM ITS MOUTH!
NO FAIR GIVING HINTS!
ONE SECOND... I'M IN A CRATER THAT MY OWN BODY MADE.

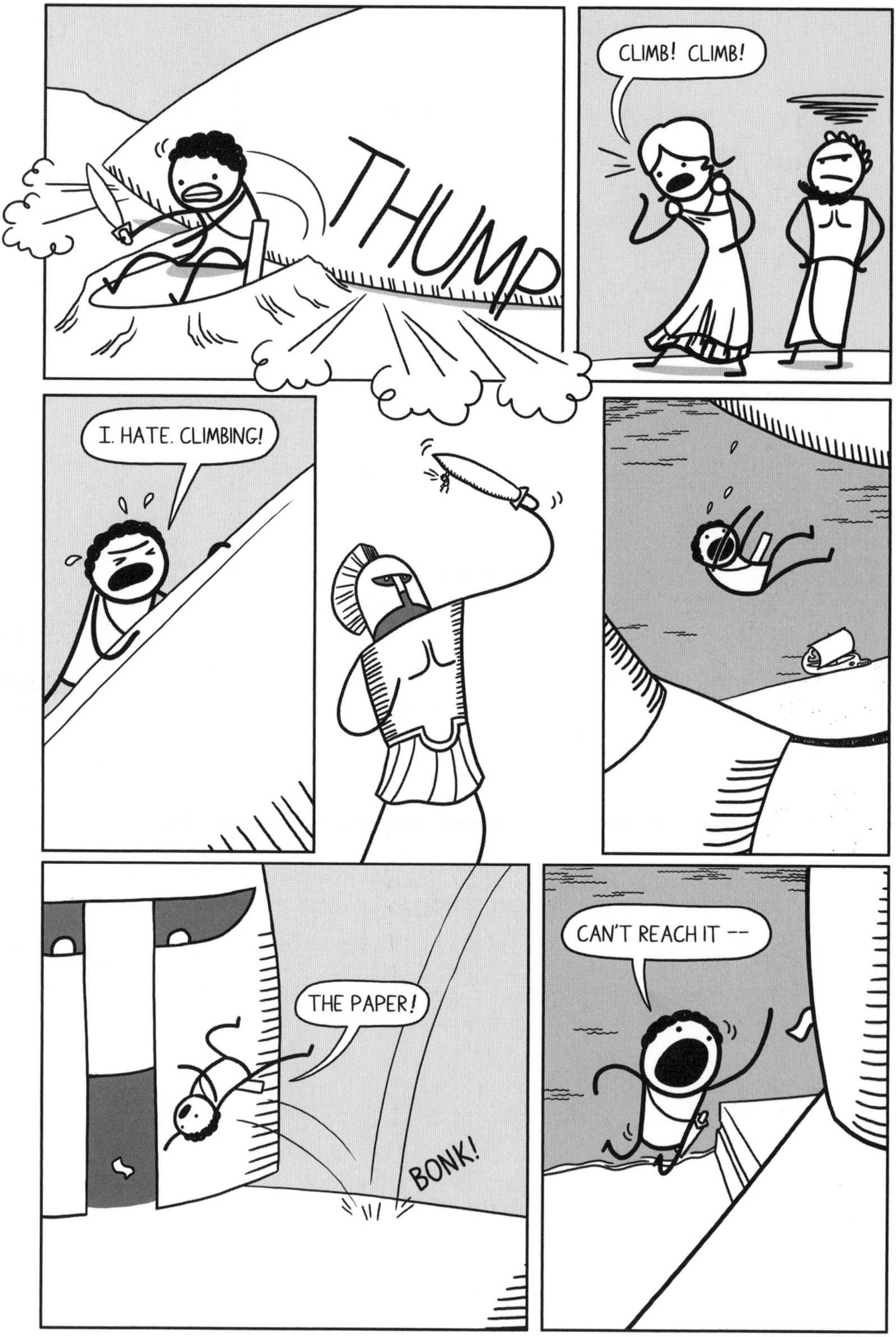
THUMP
CLIMB! CLIMB!
I. HATE. CLIMBING!
THE PAPER!
BONK!
CAN'T REACH IT --

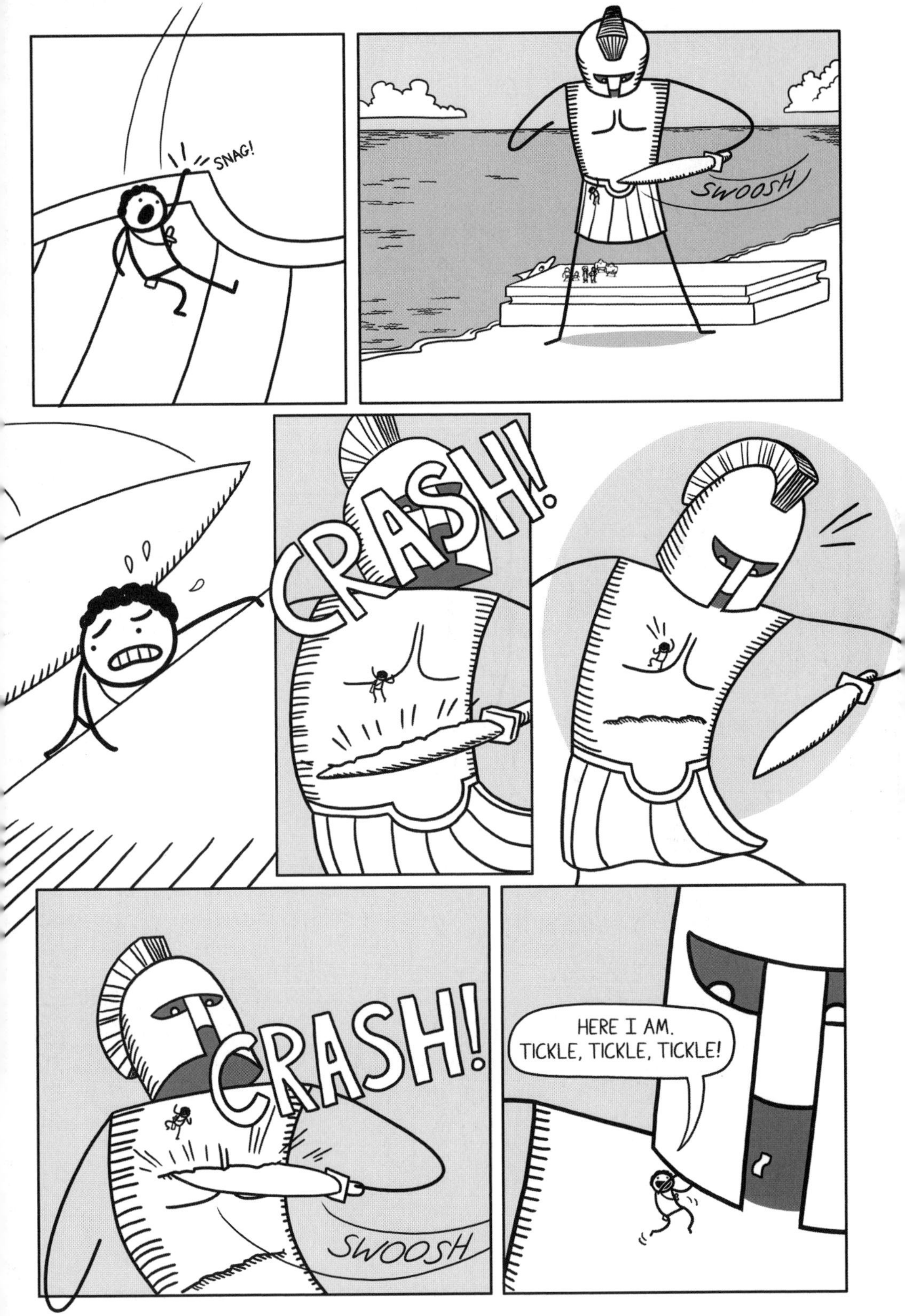
SNAG!
SWOOSH
CRASH!
CRASH!
SWOOSH
HERE I AM.
TICKLE, TICKLE, TICKLE!

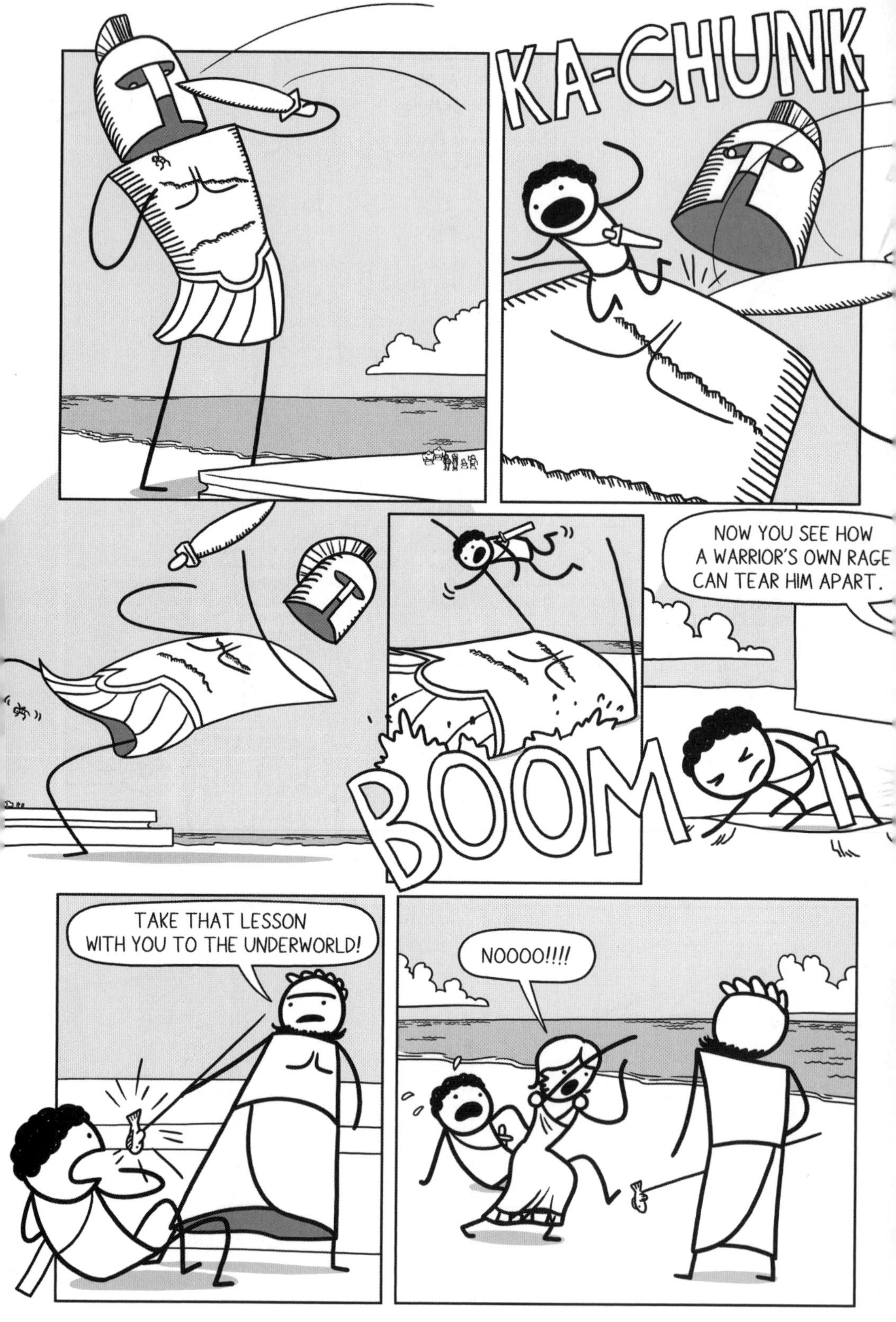
KA-CHUNK
NOW YOU SEE HOW A WARRIOR'S OWN RAGE CAN TEAR HIM APART.
BOOM
TAKE THAT LESSON WITH YOU TO THE UNDERWORLD!
NOOOO!!!!

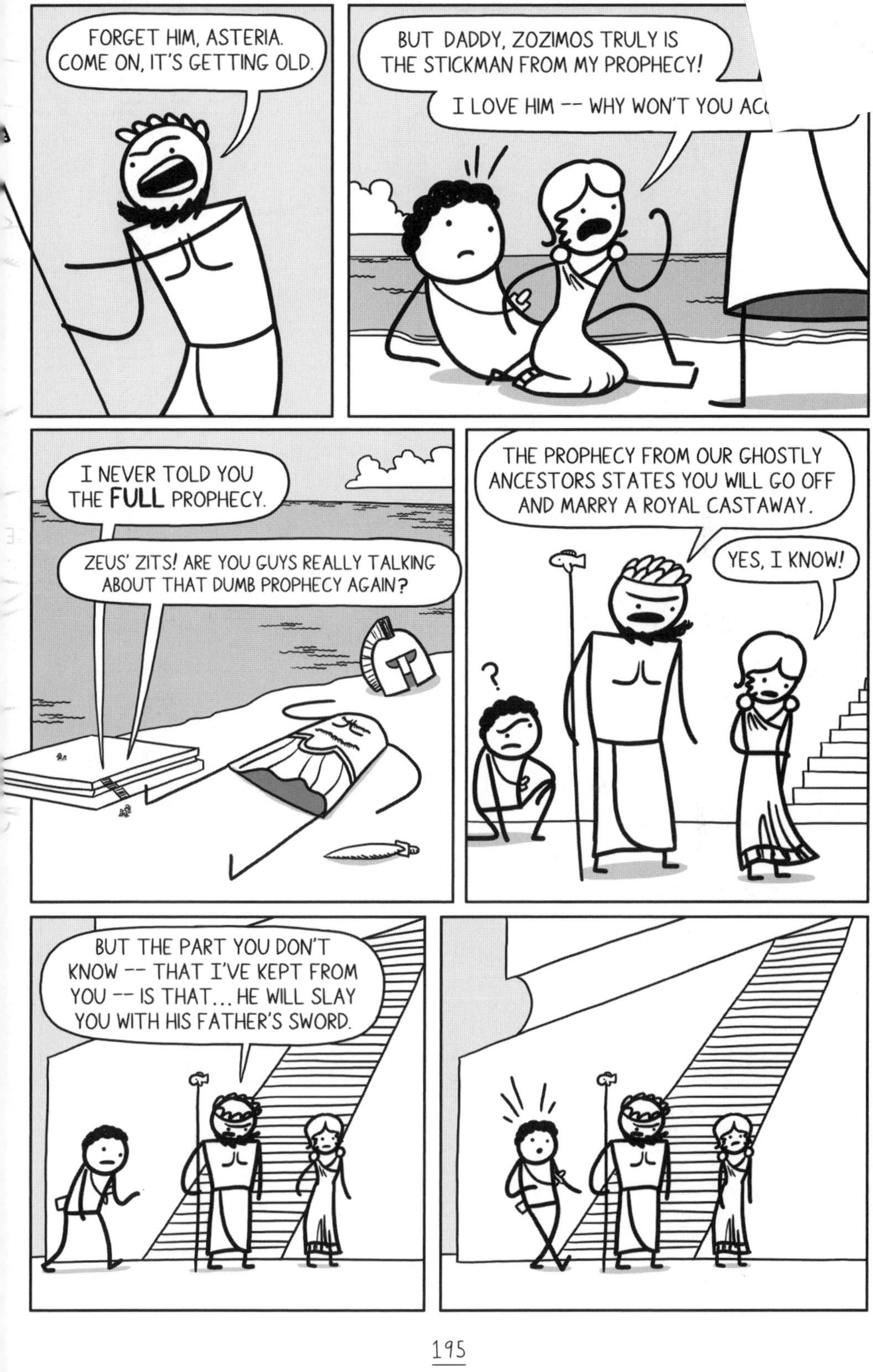
FORGET HIM, ASTERIA. COME ON, IT'S GETTING OLD.
BUT DADDY, ZOZIMOS TRULY IS THE STICKMAN FROM MY PROPHECY!
I LOVE HIM -- WHY WON'T YOU AC
I NEVER TOLD YOU THE **FULL** PROPHECY.
ZEUS' ZITS! ARE YOU GUYS REALLY TALKING ABOUT THAT DUMB PROPHECY AGAIN?
THE PROPHECY FROM OUR GHOSTLY ANCESTORS STATES YOU WILL GO OFF AND MARRY A ROYAL CASTAWAY.
YES, I KNOW!
?
BUT THE PART YOU DON'T KNOW -- THAT I'VE KEPT FROM YOU -- IS THAT... HE WILL SLAY YOU WITH HIS FATHER'S SWORD.

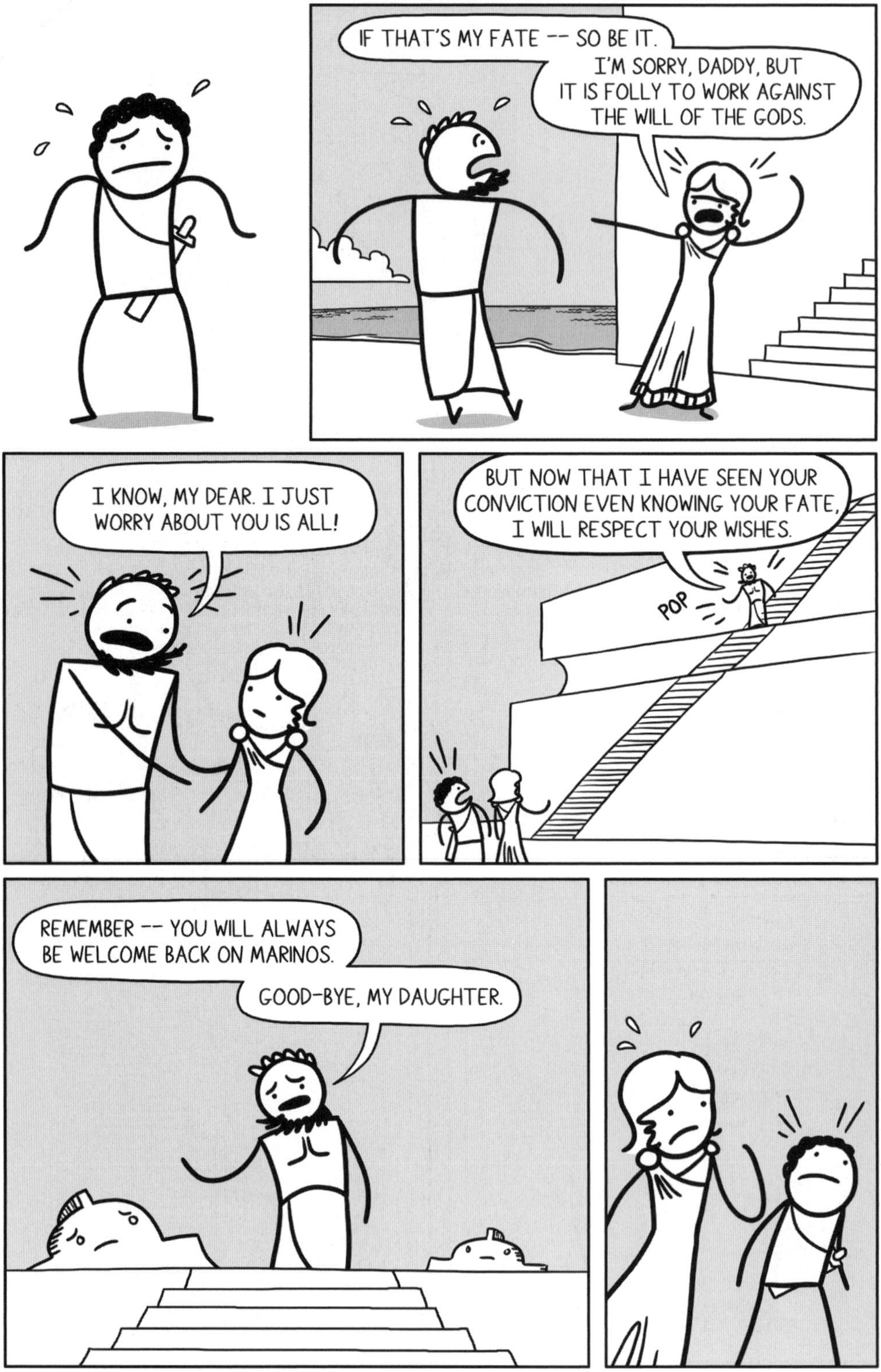
IF THAT'S MY FATE -- SO BE IT.
I'M SORRY, DADDY, BUT IT IS FOLLY TO WORK AGAINST THE WILL OF THE GODS.
I KNOW, MY DEAR. I JUST WORRY ABOUT YOU IS ALL!
BUT NOW THAT I HAVE SEEN YOUR CONVICTION EVEN KNOWING YOUR FATE, I WILL RESPECT YOUR WISHES.
POP
REMEMBER -- YOU WILL ALWAYS BE WELCOME BACK ON MARINOS.
GOOD-BYE, MY DAUGHTER.

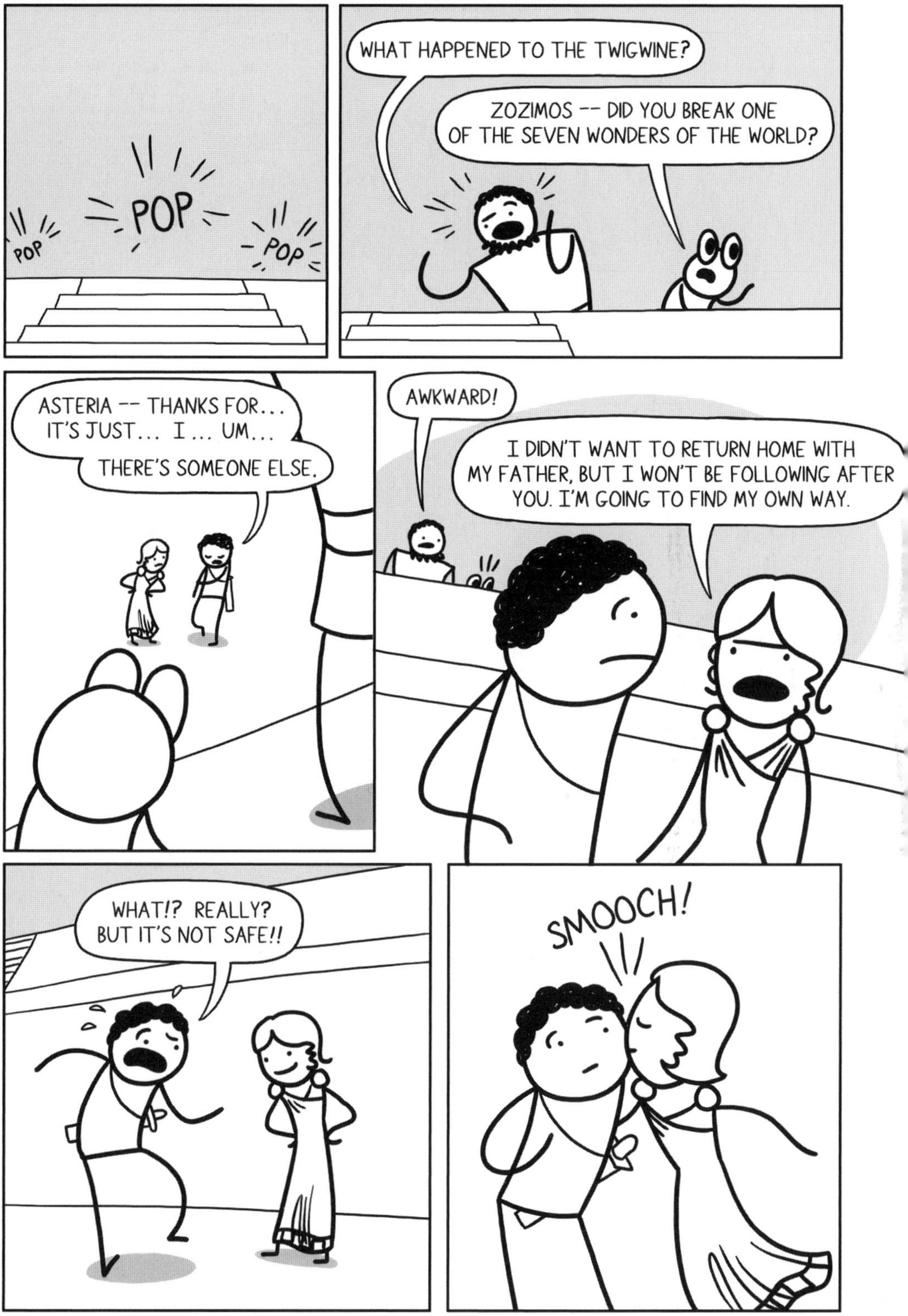
POP
POP
POP
WHAT HAPPENED TO THE TWIGWINE?
ZOZIMOS -- DID YOU BREAK ONE OF THE SEVEN WONDERS OF THE WORLD?
ASTERIA -- THANKS FOR... IT'S JUST... I... UM...
THERE'S SOMEONE ELSE.
AWKWARD!
I DIDN'T WANT TO RETURN HOME WITH MY FATHER, BUT I WON'T BE FOLLOWING AFTER YOU. I'M GOING TO FIND MY OWN WAY.
WHAT!? REALLY? BUT IT'S NOT SAFE!!
SMOOCH!

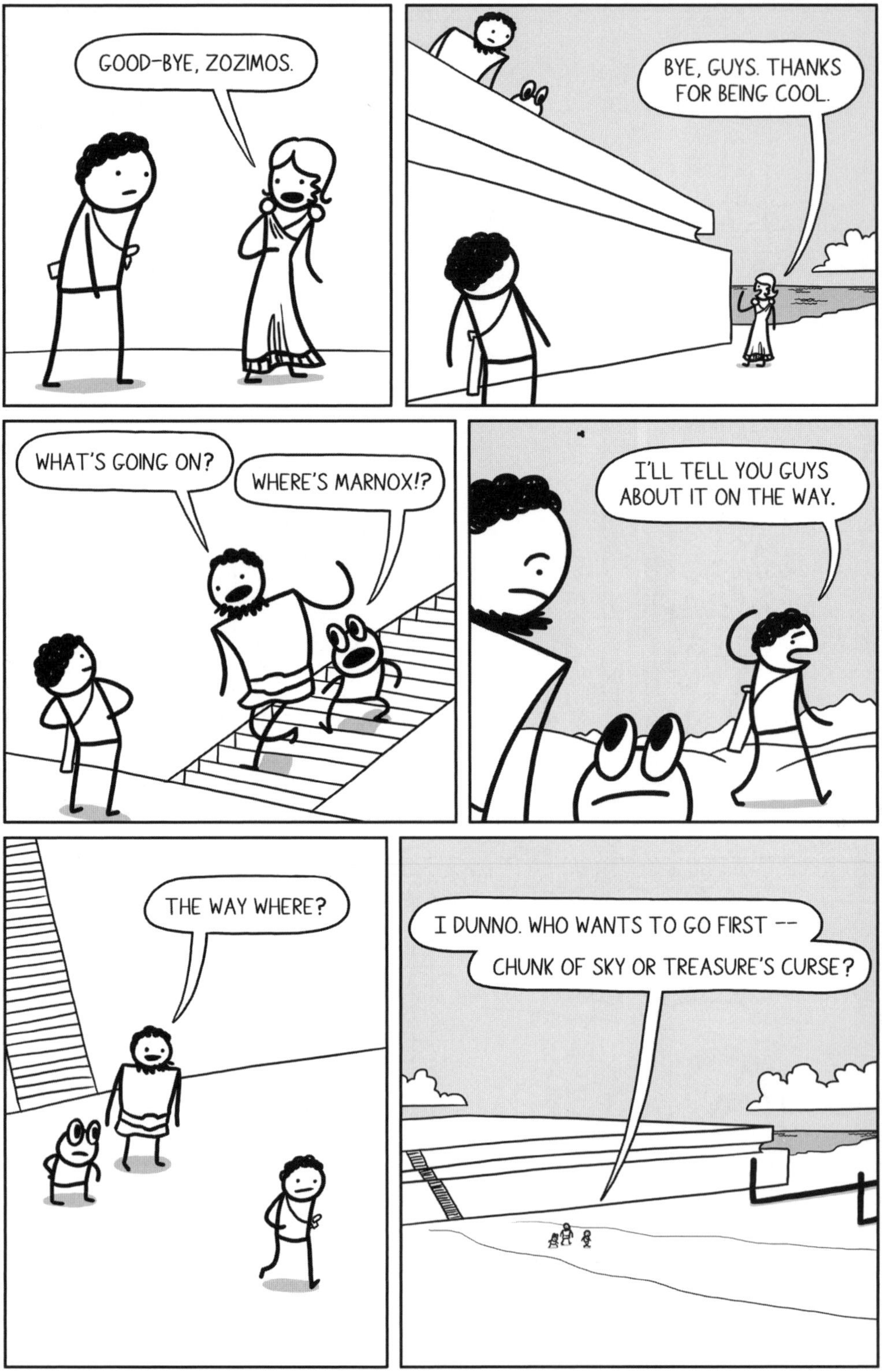
GOOD-BYE, ZOZIMOS.
BYE, GUYS. THANKS FOR BEING COOL.
WHAT'S GOING ON?
WHERE'S MARNOX!?
I'LL TELL YOU GUYS ABOUT IT ON THE WAY.
THE WAY WHERE?
I DUNNO. WHO WANTS TO GO FIRST --
CHUNK OF SKY OR TREASURE'S CURSE?

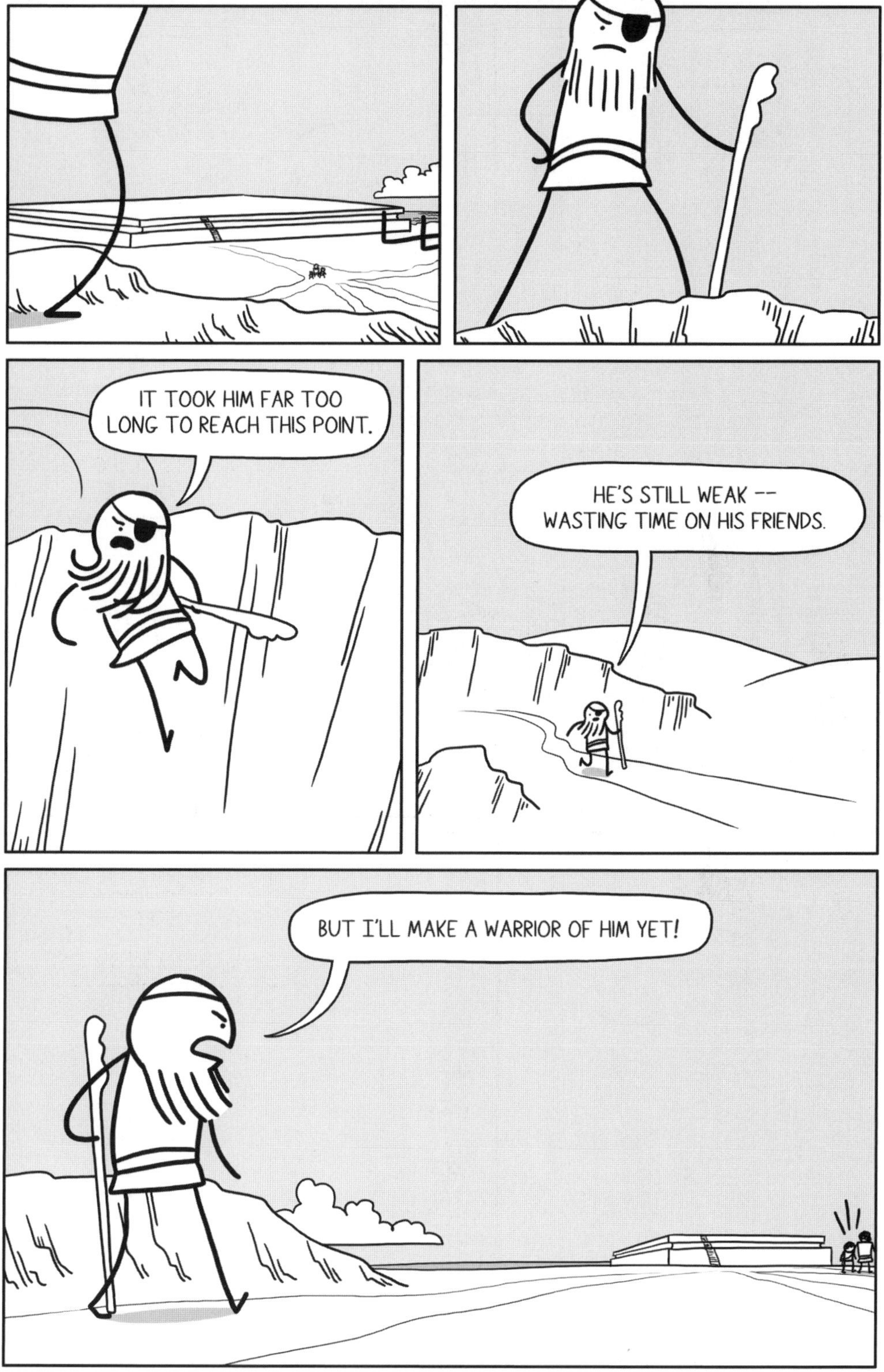
IT TOOK HIM FAR TOO LONG TO REACH THIS POINT.
HE'S STILL WEAK -- WASTING TIME ON HIS FRIENDS.
BUT I'LL MAKE A WARRIOR OF HIM YET!

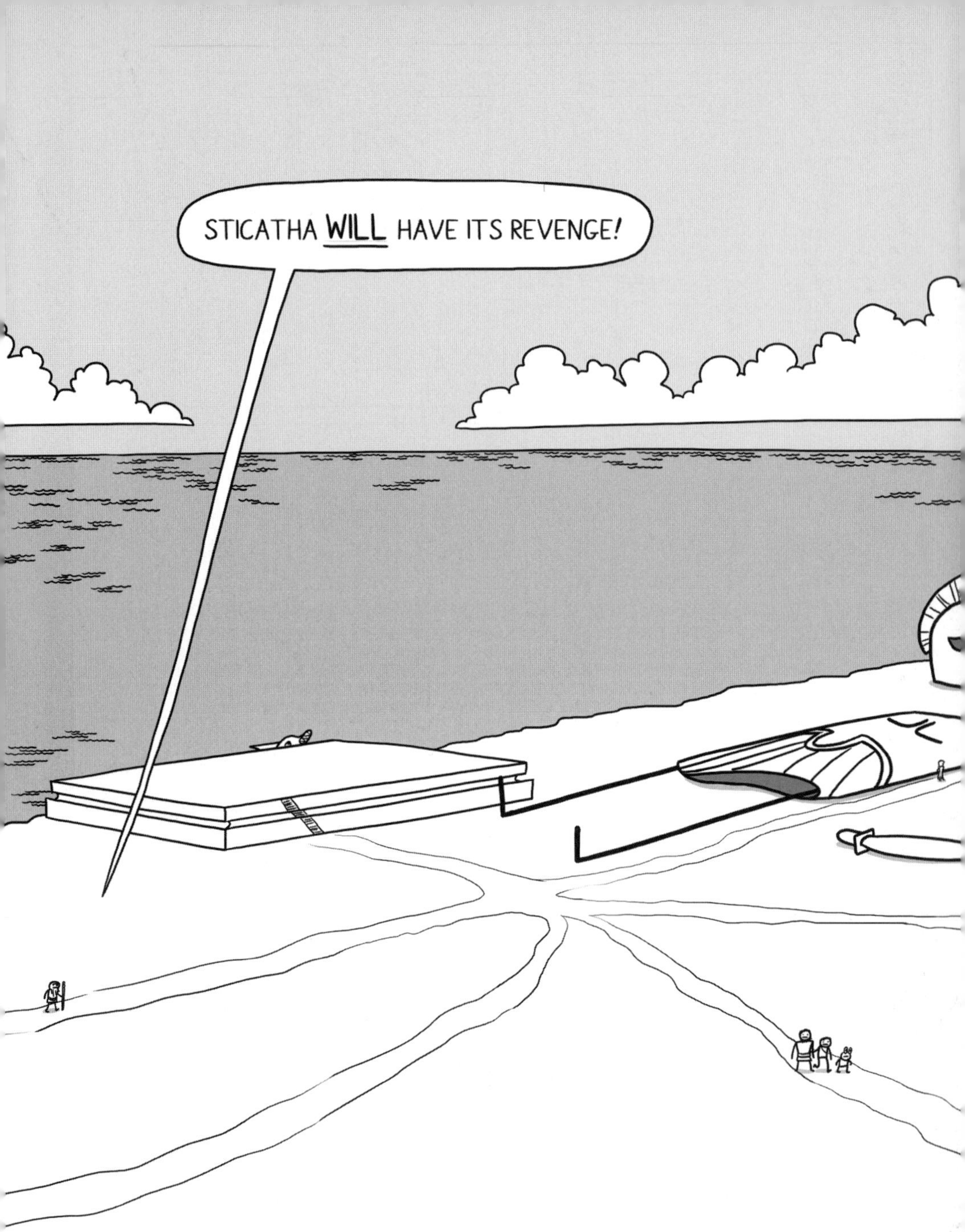
STICATHA WILL HAVE ITS REVENGE!

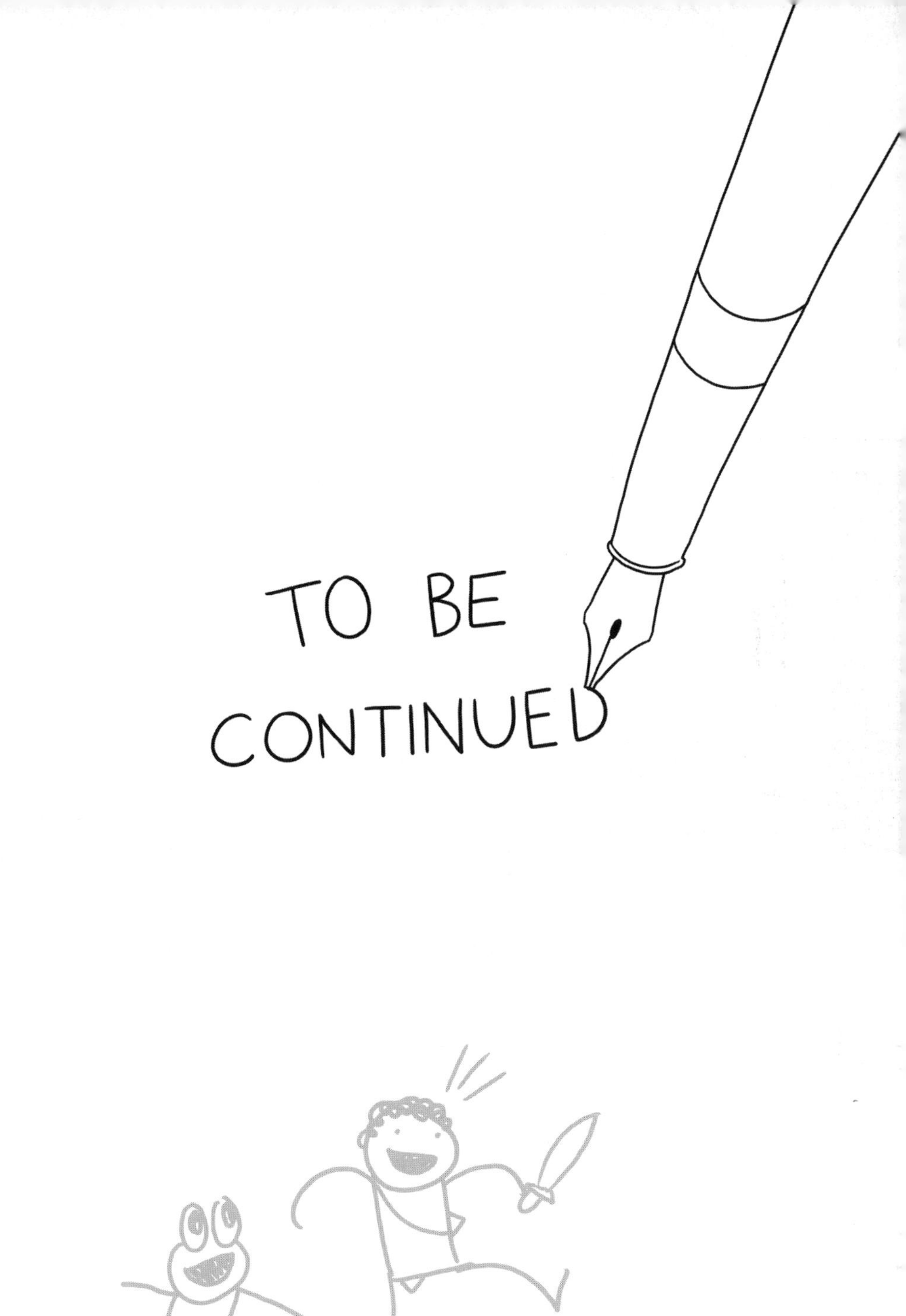
TO BE
CONTINUED

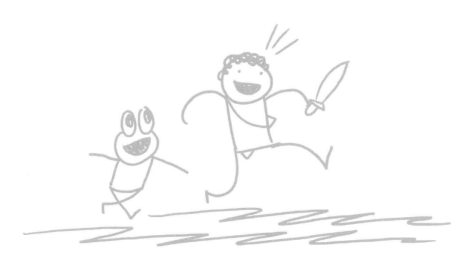

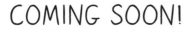

COMING SOON!

STICKMAN ODYSSEY

AN
EPIC
DOODLE

BOOK TWO